I0817835

BETTER BRITONS

Reproduction, National Identity, and the Afterlife of Empire

NADINE ATTEWELL

Better Britons

Reproduction, National Identity, and the Afterlife of Empire

UNIVERSITY OF TORONTO PRESS
Toronto Buffalo London

Toronto Buffalo London
www.utppublishing.com

ISBN 978-1-4426-4702-2 (cloth)

Library and Archives Canada Cataloguing in Publication

Attewell, Nadine, author
Better Britons : reproduction, national identity, and the afterlife of empire / Nadine Attewell.

Includes bibliographical references and index.
ISBN 978-1-4426-4702-2 (bound)

1. Human reproduction – Government policy – Great Britain – History – 20th century. 2. Human reproduction – Government policy – New Zealand – History – 20th century. 3. Human reproduction – Government policy – Australia – History – 20th century. 4. National characteristics, British – History – 20th century. 5. National characteristics, New Zealand – History – 20th century. 6. National characteristics, Australian – History – 20th century. 7. Decolonization – Great Britain – Colonies – History – 20th century. I. Title.

HQ766.5.G7A88 2014 304.6094109'04 C2013-903793-4

This book has been published with the help of a grant from the Canadian Federation for the Humanities and Social Sciences, through the Awards to Scholarly Publications Program, using funds provided by the Social Sciences and Humanities Research Council of Canada.

University of Toronto Press acknowledges the financial assistance to its publishing program of the Canada Council for the Arts and the Ontario Arts Council.

University of Toronto Press acknowledges the financial support of the Government of Canada through the Canada Book Fund for its publishing activities.

Contents

Illustrations

Acknowledgments

Any book that, like this one, has been a decade in the making, has accumulated innumerable debts. From Hong Kong and Britain, the island homelands from which my parents first ventured in the 1960s, to Richmond, British Columbia, where I grew up, histories of migration and settlement have shaped my own. The life of a junior scholar too can be a peripatetic one: *Better Britons* took me to Australia, the United Kingdom, and Aotearoa New Zealand, but was written in Ithaca, New York, part of the homeland of the Cayuga Nation; in St Paul, Minnesota, on traditional Dakota territory; on Paiute and Washoe land in Reno, Nevada; and in Hamilton, Ontario, part of the traditional territories of the Mississauga and Six Nations. I acknowledge the hospitality of all of these places, as well as the prior claims upon whose displacement and denial such hospitality too often sadly depends.

Working in state and other archives can be an expensive enterprise. I received generous funding from Cornell University, in the form of the Ta-Chung & Ya-Chao Liu Memorial Scholarship, research grants from the Graduate School, the Einaudi Center for International Studies, and Feminist Gender and Sexuality Studies, and a Dissertation Completion Fellowship; from the Social Sciences and Humanities Research Council of Canada; from the University of Nevada, Reno; and from McMaster University, in the form of an Arts Research Board Grant. Archival research can also be a lonely and dispiriting endeavour, from which it was always a pleasure to be recalled by family, friends, and interested colleagues: in Aotearoa New Zealand, the Te Punga whanau; in Australia, Ann McGrath, Robin Taylor, and the Hawes family; and in the United Kingdom, Derek and Jean Attewell, and the Cheung-Pauze family. A daunting task was further eased by the work of librarians, archivists, and technicians at the Alexander Turnbull Library (Wellington); the Auckland City Library; the

National Archives of Australia (Canberra); the National Library of Australia (Canberra); the library of the Australian Institute of Aboriginal and Torres Strait Islander Studies (Canberra); the State Library of New South Wales (Sydney); the British Library (London); the British Newspaper Archives (Colindale); the National Archives (Kew); and the Wellcome Library (London). Thanks, finally, to Derek Challis for allowing me to read the unpublished autobiographical writings of Robin Hyde, housed in the Auckland City Library.

I'm not sure I yet know how to "be" a scholar. I have learned, however, from listening to Deborah Achtenberg; Sara Ahmed; Chadwick Allen; Christina Baade; Sarah Brophy; Stacey Burton; Daniel Coleman; Elizabeth DeLoughrey; Marc Durand; Michelle Elleray; Daylanne English; Jen Hill; Molly Hite; Daniel Heath Justice; Rayna Kalas; Douglas Mao; Natalie Melas; Dorothy Mermin; Mary O'Connor; Magdalene Redekop; Peter Walmsley; and Lorraine York; from orientation sessions with fellow junior faculty, including Deborah Boehm; Devavani Chatterjea; Amber Dean; Justin Gifford; Faiza Hirji; Brett van Hoesen; Natasha Hurley; Albert Lacson; Kathryn Mattison; Rick Monture; Matthias Rudolf; Maura Tarnoff; Christopher Scott; and Eugenia Zuroski Jenkins; and from conversations with the next generation, including Jennifer Adese; Phanuel Antwi; Cassel Busse; Jessie Forsyth; Jocelyn Froese; Kasim Husain; Vinh Nguyen; Malissa Phung; Sarah Trimble; and Cameron Turner. But I have learned most of all from – and been sustained by – the laughter, good conversation, magnificent hospitality, and televisual and cinematic obsessions of friends with a variety of kinds of relationships with the academe: David Agruss; Asher Alkoby; Zubair Amir; Sarah Amato; Phanuel Antwi; Sze Wei Ang; Christina Baade, Alana Hudson, and Ernst Baade Hudson; Debbie Boehm, Patrick Jackson, and Ava Boehm Jackson; Wyatt Bonikowski; Nick Davis; Hilary Emmett; Jade Ferguson; Mike Garcia; Ed Goode; Susan Hall; Sarah Heidt; Janice Ho; Brett van Hoesen; Margaret Kaner; Hyowon Kim; Marlon Kuzmick; Bridgette Lord; Ramesh Mallipeddi; Kim Snyder Manganelli; Aya Miyagawa; Alyssa Mt. Pleasant; Angela Naimou; Lionel Nguyen Van The; Kevin O'Neill; Ryan Plumley; David Rando; Andrea Rehn; Shirleen Robinson; Matthias Rudolf; Nathalie Soini and Jeremy Heil; Sue Spearey; Helene Strauss; Alice Te Punga Somerville; Dorian Stuber; Katherine Terrell and Thomas Knauer; Sarah Trimble and Jen Twamley; Mimi Yiu; Kim Zarins; and Gena Zuroski Jenkins and Derek Jenkins. Out of these conversations has emerged what is best about *Better Britons*.

The process of bringing a manuscript to press is lengthy, arduous, and anxiety-inducing. Thanks to Sarah Amato, Daniel Coleman, and Michael Ross for both their willingness to read, at a very late date, the manuscript that became *Better Britons*, and their comments; thanks, as well, to the two anonymous colleagues who engaged with the manuscript in such thoughtful ways. I am grateful to Jessie Forsyth for her meticulous work in cleaning up my notes and citations, as to the University of Toronto Press personnel who have contributed to transforming a gaggle of Word documents into a beautiful object. My editor at UTP, Richard Ratzlaff, has superintended this process with acumen, care, and great humanity.

Better Britons is dedicated to my family.

BETTER BRITONS

Reproduction, National Identity, and the Afterlife of Empire

Introduction

In 2005, *and what remains*, a dystopian drama by the Māori/Cook Islands writer Miria George, opened to acclaim and controversy at the City Gallery in Wellington. In George's play, five New Zealanders gather in the international departures lounge at Wellington Airport: Ila, a jet-setting executive of South Asian descent; Pasifika graphic designer Solomon, bound on his first Overseas Experience; Anna, a Malaysian-born airport cleaner; a Māori woman named Mary; and Peter, her Pākehā (that is to say, white) partner.[1] The year is 2010. Citing high rates of teenage pregnancy and child abuse, the state is threatening to sterilize all Māori women. As a consequence, Māori have decided to leave Aotearoa New Zealand – permanently. Mary is the "last" Māori to depart.[2]

Many reviewers found the play's premise a stretch. John Smythe titled his review "Inconceivable," writing, "to leap from contemporary problems to mass deportations, ethnic cleansing, the Liberal Government of 2010 … forcibly sterilising all Maori women, … is to stretch credibility to the breaking point."[3] Laurie Atkinson claimed that "the play's futuristic setting (2010) and the ethnically cleansed New Zealand is impossible to swallow."[4] For Smythe and Atkinson, that the New Zealand government should seek to restrict the reproduction of an entire class of citizens is "inconceivable." History suggests otherwise: in 1924, inspired by multiple North American exemplars, a New Zealand parliamentary committee counselled sterilizing "all mental defectives and sexual offenders."[5] Although the state declined to pursue this recommendation, where such policies were implemented – in Canada and the United States, for example – they targeted an array of (perceived) disabilities, including Indigeneity.[6] Aboriginals account for a disproportionate number of the men and women approved for sterilization by the Alberta Board of Eugenics between 1928 and 1972.[7] Given the histories of reproductive violence that George's play, although science fiction, yet invokes, Smythe and Atkinson's professions of incredulity are both curious and telling. Histories of reproductive violence shock us, perhaps because we are not accustomed to conceiving of the reproductive body as a locus of national imagining and state action. *and what remains* dispels any notion that the private sphere, to which reproductive acts and behaviours are often understood as belonging, persists untouched by the obligations of political life and the machinations of the state, confirming Homi Bhabha's insight that "the recesses of domestic space [are] sites for history's invasions."[8] At the same time, it is shocking how shocking we find histories of reproductive violence, even those regimes with which we ourselves are contemporary. Why do we always seem to be in the process of forgetting such institutions as the Oregon Board of Eugenics, which conducted its last compulsory sterilization in 1981? According to the nineteenth-century French philosopher Ernest Renan, forgetting, even "historical error, are essential factors in the making of a nation."[9] At the end of George's play, Ila confronts her compatriots with the truth about the government's covert program of sterilization. A chorus of denials rings out: "I didn't know," says Peter; "I know nothing of it," says Anna; "I didn't know that," says Solomon (71). It is as if the sterilization of Indigenous bodies portended the sterilization of colonial histories, their expulsion from the national history of New Zealand. Read symptomatically, then, John Smythe's punning headline, which dismisses George's concern with sterilization as aesthetically and politically sterile, proves unexpectedly revealing. By "bring[ing] to light [the forgotten] deeds of violence" that sustain colonizing nation states like New Zealand, discussions of the play's aesthetic viability make visible the gaps in national memory.[10] The inconceivability of *and what remains* emerges as an effect of the kind of violence, inflicted in the name of settler national becoming, that the play itself recalls, describes, and indicts. What is more, it clears the way for further instantiations of such violence: some viewers may have found George's vision of an "ethnically cleansed" New Zealand difficult to swallow, but in the last two years, two Pākehā commentators have publicly called for Māori to be sterilized in the name of "protecting" their children.[11]

Better Britons reflects on the centrality of reproduction to settler and British projects of nation building, charting those histories of reproductive interventionism that render George's euphemistically named "Birth Control Programme" only too plausible (69). Through readings of literature and policy from Britain, Australia, and New Zealand, *Better Britons* considers how an array of reproductive acts, imperatives, and experiments helped to constitute British and settler identity in the twentieth century. Common to the texts that I discuss is the sense that reproductive behaviours bear upon not only gender and sexual identities, as we often assume, but civic, national, and racial ones as well. The compulsion to consecrate the reproductive body as a locus of national definition can be traced at least as far back as the eighteenth century, if not earlier. Still, the early-twentieth-century ascendancy of eugenics suggests the unprecedented degree to which, by the turn of the twentieth century, national fortunes were taken to depend upon the reproductive behaviours of citizen-subjects.

The early decades of the twentieth century also, of course, mark the beginning of the end of the British empire. It is true that Britain continued to pursue an active imperial agenda into the 1930s and beyond. Between 1900 and 1920, meanwhile, Australia and New Zealand took over the administration of several territories in the Pacific, including Papua (Australia, 1906), New Guinea (Australia, 1920), Niue (New Zealand, 1901), the Cook Islands (New Zealand, 1901), and Samoa (New Zealand, 1918). But a series of challenges to British military supremacy, and the increasing purchase of anti-colonial critiques not just in the colonies but in Britain itself, took their toll. As Eric Hobsbawm puts it, drawing attention to the sense of crisis that drove and permeated processes of political reform in Britain and its empire, "never had a larger area of the globe been under the formal or informal control of Britain than between the two world wars, but never before had the rulers of Britain felt less confident about maintaining their old imperial superiority."[12] At the Imperial Conference of 1926, leaders recognized not only the five dominions – Australia, Canada, New Zealand, South Africa, and the Irish Free State – but (in principle) India as "equal in status" with and in no way subordinate to Britain.[13] Formalized as the 1931 Statute of Westminster, the Balfour Declaration may have been intended less to dissolve the imperial bond than transform it, but in retrospect, it can be seen to have laid the groundwork for the more overt decolonization programs of the post–Second World War era. Forty years later, much of Britain's erstwhile empire had passed out of its control. Bringing work that foregrounds the colonial logics and imperial inflections of British and settler narratives of identity into conversation with feminist, queer, and Indigenous studies work on the reproductive grammar of belonging and citizenship,[14] *Better Britons* tracks projects of post-imperial nation-(re)formation as they remake and are remade in the intimate domain of bodily, sexual, and reproductive life.[15] Framing decolonization as a crisis of inheritance, in which the search for new identities and institutions is dogged by the need to come to terms with the legacies of empire, I show twentieth-century states and subjects turning to reproduction to articulate and resolve post-imperial predicaments of identity. Even as I investigate how particular reproductive projects – from the large-scale experiments in controlled breeding described by Aldous Huxley in *Brave New World* (1932) to the practice of abortion – theorize reproduction, define race, organize space, and tell time in pursuit of a more perfect nation, I trace changing conceptions of settler and British identity in the era of decolonization. Throughout *Better*

Britons, reproductive acts and processes emerge as meaning-rich sites wherein states and subjects alike can be observed registering, working out, and contesting the direction of national life. In addition, I ask what follows when the question of whether one (truly) belongs to a political community at once determines and is determined by whether and what one can reproduce. What do we learn about the post-imperial forms of Australianness, Britishness, and New Zealandness when their embodiedness and reproducibility are understood to be defining?

Better Britons is, then, about the afterlife of empire insofar as the projects of nation building with which it is concerned identify sexual reproduction as key to, and a potent figure for, the (re)constitution of the national body after the "end" of empire. As will be clear from my discussion of *and what remains*, however, I am also interested in empire's ongoing afterlife, that is, the multiple and varied ways in which empire lives on, notwithstanding – or even thanks to – the reports of its demise. The different dimensions of this afterlife have been thoroughly mapped by critics of the term postcolonial, as well as of the field of intellectual and political activity it delineates. Thus, for example, Anne McClintock and Ella Shohat have (separately) questioned the postcoloniality of settler nations, suggesting that the term postcolonial "masks the white settlers' colonialist-racist policies toward indigenous people not only before independence but also after the official break from the imperial center."[16] Indeed, many Indigenous thinkers and activists deny the relevance of the postcolonial frame to contemporary Indigenous peoples, for whom the "post" in postcolonial remains an aspiration. Nor is settler colonialism the only sign that we live in a "colonial present": think of the relationships of dominance that New Zealand currently maintains with Niue and the Cook Islands, or the neo-colonial enterprise that has embroiled Britain in Iraq and Afghanistan.[17] In addition, although it is important, as Robert Young reminds us, to pay tribute to "the great historical achievements of resistance against colonial power," it must be acknowledged that the project of decolonization remains everywhere incomplete, not just in those locales and for those subjects most bitterly affected by imperial rule, but in those locales and for those subjects whom it largely benefited.[18] Paul Gilroy has been an especially vigorous critic of what he sees as an unwillingness on the part of ordinary Britons to confront the nation's imperial past. Writing in 2005, he laments Britons' seeming determination to diminish, deny, and, if possible, actively forget an imperial history that has become "a source of discomfort, shame, and perplexity," a forgetting that, he notes, has given rise to an "additional catastrophe: the error of imagining that postcolonial peoples are only unwanted alien intruders without any substantive historical, political, or cultural connections to the collective life of their fellow subjects."[19] Racial discourses developed for imperial use linger in the attitudes towards incomers that condition British debates about immigration, asylum, security, and welfare even in the twenty-first century, decades after Britain relinquished control of the vast majority of its overseas possessions. But as I show in chapter 5, these attitudes are also shaped (somewhat paradoxically) by what Sara Ahmed might call the "overing" of empire, that is, the refusal to recognize empire's influence in the present, or even that it has touched the lived experience of any subjects at all, with the consequence that Britons today find it difficult to "disentangle the disruptive effects supposedly produced by an immigrant presence from the residual but potent effects of lingering but usually unspoken colonial relationships and imperial fantasies."[20] Empire is among the "tendential ... forces that have defined the *givenness* of the historical terrain" for metropolitan, settler, and colonized peoples alike, a fact which declarations of its end do nothing to unsettle, only (strategically) occlude.[21] Thus, anti-racist and anti-colonial activists must, as Daniel Coleman puts it, "carry out the historical work that traces [the] genealogy [of white supremacy], or 'the ideological lineage of this belief system,'" not just because we have forgotten "the brutal elements of our racial history," but because an amnesia about the brutal elements of our racial history and their continued life in the present enables the reproduction of white supremacy transgenerationally.[22]

It may seem peculiar that I have chosen to contest the notion that we are somehow "after" empire by describing the persistence of what has been declared over, done with, done *for*, as a kind of afterlife. However, doing so calls attention to the uncanniness of this persistence as an anachronism that unhinges the present by the force with which it returns us, in Gilroy's words, to "ground we feel we should have left long ago."[23] (The post in postcolonial is productive for similar reasons.) And no wonder, since, as Jacques Derrida points out in *Specters of Marx*, the dead must above all be prevented from coming back: "Quick, do whatever is needed to keep the cadaver localized, in a safe place, decomposing right where it was inhumed."[24] Read in conjunction with *Specters of Marx*, Avery Gordon's work in *Ghostly Matters* suggests that attending to the operations of those "tendential lines of forces" which constitute the "givenness of the historical terrain" as a form of haunting can materialize – and does not trivialize – the extent to which the inheritances with which we are willy nilly burdened actually impinge upon, while seeming removed from, everyday life.[25] In contrast, as I show throughout *Better Britons*, British and settler subjects have repeatedly turned to projects of reproductive management to imagine themselves as post-imperial, secured against the haunting force of such histories of violence as are their inheritance. Ultimately, I argue, the convergence of projects of reproductive management and governance is not just one of the *things* the inhabitants of colonizing nation states like Britain, Australia, and New Zealand have forgotten about the colonial past; it is one of the *ways* in which they have worked, and continue to work, to disown "the burdens of their colonial inheritance."[26]

In the remainder of the introduction, I elaborate on the connections sketched above. I draw on work in history, anthropology, literary and cultural studies, queer studies, critical race studies, and Indigenous and postcolonial studies to flesh out Miria George's insight that the reproductive body functions as a critical site of national imagining. Bringing the scholarship on reproduction together with work on the imperial history of Britishness, I outline the case for a comparative approach to British and settler projects of reproductive reform. What emerges when settler and British texts are read together as raising questions about the post-imperial fate of Britishness? I then turn to the methodological issues raised by *and what remains*'s status as a speculative fiction, highlighting the importance of utopian thinking to early-twentieth-century reproductive discourses and practices of governance, and hence this book. Indeed, the introduction concludes in a speculative mode: if, as I show throughout *Better Britons*, the reproductive turn has tended to throw up configurations of British and settler identity anchored in a willed amnesia about the nation's colonial past and present, what does this tell us about what is required for their decolonization?

Crises

In the first decades of the twentieth century, Stuart Hall and Bill Schwarz argue, the British state suffered a set of crises fuelled by anxieties about the feasibility and righteousness of the imperial mission and working-class and feminist demands for inclusion in the political life of the nation.[27] According to Hall and Schwarz, such "crises occur when the social formation can no longer be reproduced on the basis of the pre-existing system of social relations."[28] But although crises are in this sense always crises of reproduction, nowhere do Hall and Schwarz mention the crisis of *sexual* reproduction that historians have identified as taking shape around the turn of the twentieth century, when British fertility rates dropped from an average of six live births per woman to two, and reproductive discourses of racial and national renewal acquired the force of common sense.[29] The omission is unexceptional. As Alys Eve Weinbaum observes, reproduction has often been "associated all but exclusively with women's bodies and the domestic realm – with private issues of fertility, childbearing, and motherhood, rather than with politically charged issues of racism, nation building, and imperial expansion."[30]

As part of the ongoing struggle to secure women's reproductive rights, feminists have done much to clarify the state's interest in regulating reproductive, sexual, and family life. More recently, a different light has been shed on the politics of sexuality and reproduction by queer theorists like Lauren Berlant, Lee Edelman, and Jasbir Puar, who contest the heteronormativity of forms of association, governance, and even politics itself.[31] The modern nation, scholars now recognize, is experienced not only "'out there' in the state, in formal political discourse, or in citizens' transactions with the state, but also very deeply within, as it colours and shades human beings' most intimate moments" and relationships.[32] This interpenetration of the intimate and the political takes forms at once mundane and outrageous. Like most people, I was born into (a) citizenship. To quote Jacqueline Stevens, "One is a member of a political society (and hence a state) either because one's parents are [jus sanguinis] or because one is born there [jus solis]."[33] It is of course possible to acquire citizenship, but this process is known as naturalization, which indicates that the paradigmatic citizen is one who is not made but born. I am a Canadian citizen by virtue of where I was born (Richmond, British Columbia). I am also a citizen of the United Kingdom of Great Britain and Northern Ireland, this by virtue of the fact that my father is a citizen of the United Kingdom, and was legally married to my Hong Kong–born mother at the time of my birth. National communities are thus constituted through the institutions of marriage and reproduction. At the same time, the forms of kinship are regulated by the nation state, so that birthright citizens are no more born, ultimately, than are naturalized citizens. In order to claim my rights of citizenship, I must certify to the satisfaction of the Canadian state that I was indeed born in Canada. Similarly, the United Kingdom will not acknowledge me as a citizen if it cannot recognize my parents' marriage as legal. In this way, legislation such as the United States's 1996 Defense of Marriage Act (DOMA) affects determinations of citizenship. Since DOMA defines marriage as "a legal union between one man and one woman as husband and wife," "it is not marriage *per se* but a marriage that fits the definition of United States law that may constitute United States citizens."[34] Engaging in forms of intimacy, sex, and marriage that do not comply with either the official prescriptions of the state or the unofficial prescriptions of liberal ideology can prove disenfranchising, effectively if not actually. In the late nineteenth and early twentieth centuries, argues Patricia E. Chu, "immigrant groups whose marriage practices resembled arranged marriages in any way were characterized as unfit to be Americans because they lacked a fundamental understanding of the free consent that grounded American democratic government and civic participation."[35] It is not then surprising that many gays and lesbians experience the abrogation of their right to be, let alone marry, as an assault on their citizenship. Jacqui Alexander laments, "I am an outlaw in the country of my birth: a national; but not a citizen."[36] My parents met, married, and live in Canada, which recently legalized same-sex marriage, and has never explicitly prohibited interracial marriage. However, in 1939, an eighteen-year-old white Ontario woman named Velma Demerson was labelled an "incorrigible" and imprisoned for the crime of cohabiting with a man of Chinese descent, Harry Yip. She gave birth to their son in the Andrew Mercer Ontario Reformatory for Females.[37] Stories like Velma Demerson and Harry Yip's make it difficult for me, a woman of mixed racial descent, to ignore the role that the state has played – and continues to play – in the bedrooms of the nation.[38]

All political societies develop mechanisms to guarantee their reproduction. In *The Laws*, Plato suggests that "the correct policy for every [nascent] state will probably be to pass marriage laws first" so as to ensure a new generation of citizens.[39] Even advocates of radical social or political transformation tend to assume the survival of the polity, Lee Edelman notes, via forms of reproduction that include the biological.[40] This is not to say that all post-Athenian polities conceive of and manage reproduction and sexuality in the same way; what Michael Warner calls "repro-culture" changes over time.[41] Scholars have found in the contemporary United States a rich archive with which to think the politics of reproduction. However, many of the boldest attempts to yoke reproductive to national health date from the late nineteenth and early twentieth centuries, flowerings of that quintessentially modern form of governance Michel Foucault calls biopolitics, and whose emergence he dates to the eighteenth century. According to Foucault, "one of the great innovations in the techniques of power in the eighteenth century" was the emergence of population control as a form of governance: as individuals were remade into populations with "specific phenomena and ... peculiar variables" – "birth and death rates, life expectancy, fertility, state of health, frequency of illnesses, patterns of diet and habitation" – so they were rendered governable.[42] As a result of this new focus on "the characteristic movements of life," he says, Euro-American societies came to consider their futures "tied not only to the number and uprightness of their citizens, to their marriage rules and family organization, but to the manner in which each individual made use of his sex."[43] More specifically, the bourgeoisie "placed its hopes for the future in sex by imagining it to have ineluctable effects on generations to come."[44] Sex is linked with the future through reproduction: although its effects are not confinable to the production of children, that sex can have a future, can indeed be the future, derives from its role in procreation. It is the capacity for generation that is thought to be fortified or irreparably damaged by the manner in which we use our sex.

With the rise of eugenics in the late nineteenth century, such a biopolitical model of citizenship, in which meaningful citizenship is reserved for those deemed able to contribute to the nation's future through sex, achieved unprecedented explicitness and ubiquity.[45] In a 1912 address to the British medical profession, the biometrician, sexologist, and eugenicist Karl Pearson expressed his conviction that the "progress of medical and sanitary science" had largely suspended "the automatic action [that is, natural selection] whereby a race progressed mentally and physically."[46] Although Pearson could not deny the ethical imperative to improve housing stock, to care for premature babies, to educate the poor, he urged his audience to consider implementing a program of what he termed artificial selection. Being born, he asserted, everyone "has the right to live, but the right to live does not in itself convey the right to everyone to reproduce their kind."[47] In the estimation of Francis Galton, who coined the term eugenics in 1883, "the more suitable races or strains of blood" should be given "a better chance of prevailing speedily over the less suitable," the former encouraged to breed with one another, the latter discouraged from breeding altogether.[48] The early twentieth century also saw the development of powerful infant and maternal welfare movements dedicated to placing maternity and childrearing on a scientific basis. Not all those committed to improving infant and maternal welfare deployed eugenicist means or invoked eugenicist ends; some positioned themselves in explicit opposition to eugenics. Reformers mobilized just that commitment to social amelioration lamented (half-seriously) by mainline eugenicists like Pearson, disseminating information about childrearing via childcare manuals and newly established infant welfare clinics.[49] Like eugenicists, however, maternalists concerned themselves with the reproductive health of the nation, believing official interference in the reproductive lives of citizen-subjects to be justified and necessary, and upholding maternity as the highest form of female citizenship.

It is this turn to reproduction as a framework for explanation and action rather than eugenics or maternalism per se that interests me in *Better Britons*. What accounts for its appeal? Scholars have usually viewed British reproductive discourse as shaped by a deep-rooted preoccupation with class. Like many of their contemporaries, British eugenicists were deeply worried, as one scholar writes, by the "lack of synchrony between the rhetoric of progress … and the facts on the ground, the evidence in front of people's eyes, of poverty and degradation at the heart of ever richer empires."[50] The populace appeared to be degenerating, reverting atavistically to an earlier stage of human evolution.[51] How could such degenerates be admitted to the franchise? An "evil inheritance," Galton warned, results in unworthy successors, "weakly children who are constitutionally incapable of growing up into serviceable citizens."[52] Pearson bemoaned the economic considerations that obliged middle- and upper-class families to practise contraception even as government "legislation, municipal hygiene, state support, medical progress and unlimited charity" fostered high birth and low mortality rates among the poor.[53] Such differential rates of reproduction among the classes could lead only, he thought, to the downfall of the race.

Settler thinkers also expressed disquiet about the degeneracy of the poor and working classes, which they associated with mental deficiency, or feeble-mindedness. But if settler eugenicists prioritized white racial health, they did not therefore not concern themselves with the fertility of Indigenous and non-white immigrant others. Founded in 1907, the Plunket Society, which revolutionized infant care in New Zealand and overseas, used the slogan "Our Best Immigrants Are the Babies" to promote the virtues of a national population composed of New Zealand–born "native" rather than British-born immigrant citizens.[54] Twenty years later, an article in the Wellington-based newspaper *The Dominion* echoed Plunket in urging New Zealand to a more robust natalism: "We talk long and earnestly about immigration, and undoubtedly all concerned would be happier if the white population were spread more in keeping with the natural resources of the British Empire; but the baby is the best of all immigrants."[55] Although *The Dominion* nowhere mentions Māori, the emphasis it lays on birthing rather than importing white New Zealanders, that is, on stocking the country with "indigenous" rather than immigrant citizens, betrays anxiety about the threat Māori pose settler claims to New Zealand. In Australia, meanwhile, the most intrusive of the state's interventions in this period targeted the reproductive choices and child-rearing practices of Indigenous people as a means, precisely, of shoring up the whiteness of White Australia (see chapter 2). This is not to mention immigration restriction, which Stephen Garton claims as "the conspicuous success story of eugenic public policy in Australia and New Zealand."[56]

It is likewise misleading to portray British reproductive discourse as focused exclusively on class threats to the body politic. In the first place, British eugenicists *did* concern themselves with the problem of a racially diverse national body. Neither immigration nor immigration restriction are post–Second World War phenomena in Britain.[57] Galton begins his discussion of eugenics by applauding Britons' willingness to exclude Chinese and Jewish immigrants in "the name of keeping out bad blood."[58] The organization he helped found, the Eugenics Society, later sponsored a study that devoted special attention to the growing population of mixed-race children in Britain's port cities.[59] In the 1930s, Kenyan eugenicists conducted studies of African intellectual capacity that aroused the interest of the British scientific community.[60] In the second place, distinguishing between race- and class-focused variants of reproductive and national discourse can obscure the ways in which race and class function not only as symmetrical discourses, analogically linked (class is like race, race is like class), but also as "overlapping and interchangeable ones," articulated through the discourse of sexuality.[61] Definitions of responsible citizenship and bourgeois civility are gendered, sexualized, and therefore racialized. In nineteenth-century Europe, for example, black women and (white) prostitutes came to be identified with one another as embodiments of abnormality, sexual perversion, and disease.[62] Within this context, the Contagious Diseases Acts of 1864, 1866, and 1869, which targeted British women who failed to adhere to the prevailing sexual mores of the time, can be read as attempts to secure whiteness against the threat of racial and national difference coded as sexual deviance.[63] In fact, the measures instituted by the British government to manage outbreaks of venereal disease, including the use of lock hospitals to confine symptomatic women, had already been introduced in India to protect the British troops stationed there.[64] Service overseas wreaked havoc on British minds and bodies, but it also exposed British humanity as degenerated to start with.[65] The Second Boer War boosted British interest in infant and maternal health by exposing the poor physical condition of army-age men, many of whom suffered from poverty-related diseases such as rickets.[66] Appalled by the failure of so many British men to meet the army's minimum health standards, the 1904 Inter-Departmental Committee on Physical Deterioration recommended prioritizing child health as a means of improving national physical efficiency. In this instance, poverty mattered insofar as it unfit men to perform British dominance overseas. Contemporaries committed to programs of reproductive reform were not blind to their importance for Britain's imperial mission: in 1920, the judge presiding over the London trial of three alleged abortionists warned, "Those who have as many enemies as the British Empire must for their own safety have plenty of children to meet those enemies in the gate. We have many gates to defend."[67] In Australia, Lynette Finch has suggested, fear of the rising "Asiatic and Negroid races" helped integrate the working classes into the population, "making them sufficiently familiar and 'like' the middle class" that their (reproductive) health could be seen as key to preserving the nation against the threat of "those enemies in the gate."[68] Justice Darling's comments hint at a similar incorporation of even impoverished Britons.

The discourse of reproduction is bound to sound and function differently in different contexts. Although all eugenicists conceived of the national body as imperilled, under threat from within and without by others whose difference was understood to be biologically derived and hence inheritable, eugenicists developed distinct brands of the well-born science that reflected local intellectual traditions and political and socio-economic pressures.[69] It would be irresponsible to ignore the relative success of eugenic legislative agendas in settler nations like Australia, Brazil, and the United States. In their comparative study of eugenicist legislative campaigns in Britain and the United States, Randall Hansen and Desmond King identify the protests of organized labour as a key reason why eugenics failed to gain legislative traction in Britain.[70] Granted such differences, still, it is critical not to overlook those aspects of early-twentieth-century reproductive discourse that are shared across national borders, including the sense of racial threat which needs to be read in relation to anxieties about the role of empire in reproducing national life.

Writing in 2003, the historian Marilyn Lake wondered whether the "imperial relationship" was too much with us: "For historians interested in placing Australia in the world," she observes, "the relationship between metropole and colony – between *British Imperialism and Australian Nationalism* – has remained the focus of most studies," arguably reinforcing "the old imperial hegemony, subsuming all history within the boundaries of the imperial relationship, creating not so much a series of parallels, but a series of studies of *Empire and Others*."[71] Lake is right to urge settler historians to consider relationships other than the imperial. Still, juxtaposing settler with British texts reveals more than the entanglement of British with settler colonial history. It is my wager that a comparative approach can yet be productive insofar as it sheds light on post-imperial nation formation at both the centre and the (settler colonial) periphery, revealing a family likeness in the reformist projects through which settler and metropolitan states strove to (re)constitute themselves during and after the "event" of decolonization.

In both cases, I want to suggest, decolonization made visible, even as it was also in part a response to, the spatial confusion attendant upon living in empire, which oriented subjects to an array of (overlapping) geopolitical terrains and scales, including the local, the national, the metropolitan, and the imperial. As well as referencing metropolitan fantasies of creating better Britons in (a consequently better) Britain, the title of this book, *Better Britons*, bespeaks the once commonplace troping of New Zealand and Australia as Better Britains (a subject I explore in greater detail in chapter 1). What James Belich terms "Dominion Britonism" persisted well into the twentieth century, fed by metropolitan discourses of attachment that found concrete expression in, for example, the sponsored emigration schemes of the immediate post–Second World War period.[72] At the same time, it has often seem impossible, even undesirable, for Britons to go on being British in the Antipodes, a region whose very name announces its difference from Britain. The twentieth-century story of settler identity is dominated by the struggle to repatriate Britishness, that is, to develop viable local, viable *because* local(ized), nationalisms.[73] Neither Australia nor New Zealand ratified the 1931 Statute of Westminster until the 1940s. Some historians therefore question whether these nations welcomed the independence to which they acceded following the First World War. Belich insists that early-twentieth-century Antipodean expressions of allegiance to Britain are explicable only if the development of a truly New Zealand or Australian nationalism is dated to the second half of the century.[74] But this doesn't explain why the search for alternatives to Britishness figures as prominently as it does in interwar Antipodean cultural and political discourse. Stuart Murray helps us to see the New Zealand Centennial celebrations of 1940 – and by extension the Australian Sesquicentennial celebrations of 1938 – as both an expression of, and spur to, national pride, "play[ing] to the concept of the national 'people' at home, and portray[ing] a unit of capable nationality to those abroad."[75] It seems moreover significant that some of the earliest New Zealand- and Australian-focused collections of poetry and criticism, including Eric McCormick's *Letters and Art in New Zealand* (1940) and Allen Curnow's influential anthology *A Book of New Zealand Verse* (1945), date from the 1940s, heralding the establishment of a national literary canon. Michelle Elleray proposes that we understand the ambivalence audible in interwar Antipodean discourses of identity as a feature rather than a bug, signalling "the settler subject's contingent relation to his or her geospatial locality."[76] After all, no matter how close the colony's relationship with Britain, the settler inhabits a space "designated alien, foreign or exotic by English-centered views of the Empire."[77] In a 1936 address to the Fourteenth Congress of the Chambers of Commerce of the British Empire, W.E. Parry, then New Zealand's minister for internal affairs, mourned settler efforts to make a home of New Zealand by turning it into Britain. "In our efforts to be another Britain in the Southern Hemisphere," Parry said, "we have recklessly imported plants and animals which, amenable to control in their natural environment, have run away as cancerous growths here."[78] He then called for a reorientation to the local. However, the space of the colony is not easily rearticulated as home, no matter how domesticated it may appear. For settlers, as Terry Goldie writes in the Canadian context, "the Indian is Other and therefore alien. But the Indian is indigenous and therefore cannot be alien. So the Canadian must be alien. But how can the Canadian be alien within Canada?"[79] In this way, settler national identity is structured, as Goldie puts it, by the "impossible necessity of becoming indigenous."[80]

Unlike settlers, Britons have had neither to prove themselves capable of self-rule, nor to assert their rights of sovereignty against the claim of Indigenous priority, what Elizabeth Povinelli calls "the governance of the prior."[81] I want nevertheless to posit a degree of isomorphism between metropolitan and settler predicaments of identity in the twentieth century, especially as decolonization begins to rewrite Britain's relationship with its empire. If home is a "mythic place of desire" for diasporic subjects, including white settlers, it is no less difficult an object for those individuals who stay behind.[82] Recent scholarship has drawn attention to the ways in which Britishness was made, remade, and unmade through the circulation of British bodies, texts, and institutions overseas, imperial rule shaping metropolitan as well as (settler) colonial cultures, economies, and identities. Robert Young goes so far as to propose that "Englishness in the nineteenth century was … created for the diaspora," taking the form of a translatable identity "that could be adopted or appropriated anywhere by anyone who cultivated the right language, looks, and culture."[83] Indeed, until after the Second World War, persons born or naturalized in any of a certain class of British territories, including Britain itself, shared the common status of British subject; all such persons could settle in Britain without having to pass through immigration controls. It is important to acknowledge the *formal* egalitarianism of imperial frameworks of identity and belonging, especially in view of the explicitly discriminatory framework with which they were replaced beginning in the 1950s. At the same time, Young passes too quickly over the transformative power of translation, giving short shrift to the anxiety which the travels (and travails) of Britishness engendered in Britons both at home and overseas. Highlighting the instability of an identity thus pressed into global circulation, Ian Baucom describes empire as "less a place where England exerts control than the place where England loses command of its own narrative of identity."[84] Even where it is possible to distinguish between Britishness and Englishness, or between kinds of Englishness or Britishness, as products developed primarily for export overseas, it is not clear that this difference has operated with any degree of consistency, reflecting the confusion attendant upon an identity pressed into service across the highly differentiated landscape of Britain itself, not to mention the wider empire.[85] As early as 1902, J.A. Hobson was worrying that imperial expansion weakened the bonds between Britain and its settler colonies by incorporating into the political community of Britishness people "destitute of real power of self-government."[86] The dominions soon after demanded the right to determine the porosity of their own borders by discriminating against British subjects in matters such as immigration.[87] But the imperial state continued to mine the contradictions of Britishness until after the Second World War, when the numbers of (non-white) overseas British subjects migrating to Britain rose dramatically, raising questions about whether Britishness could or should continue to coincide "with the territory of the nation *and* the [former] empire."[88]

The reproductive turn intervenes in such predicaments of identity in numerous complex and entangled ways. It is often asserted that conceiving of the nation as made and marred by reproductive acts racializes citizenship, transforming national belonging into something that is embodied as, for example, whiteness. Assuming the reproducibility of citizenship, of those physical, psychological, moral, gender, racial, class, and sexual competencies that are the property of the ideal citizen, turns citizenship into something that can only be transmitted biologically, like race, and therefore as race. As a consequence, the ideal citizen possesses not just the competencies necessary for citizenship, but the capacity to transmit those competencies biologically, that is, via (sexual) reproduction. Of course, as Foucault observes, so that the body politic may live, some subjects must die. By engaging in forms of non-reproductive sex, subjects demonstrate their unfitness for citizenship, both insofar as they deviate from the moral line and insofar as they fail to reproduce. In this way, the abjection of kin and family networks not organized around reproductive heterosexuality locates many subjects beyond the pale of meaningful citizenship, effectively "straightening" citizenship.[89] Reproductive discourses of citizenship differentiate among reproductive bodies as well as between reproductive and non-reproductive bodies, with judgments about who should be part of the body politic doubling as judgments about who should be permitted to reproduce the body politic. As Cathy J. Cohen notes, many subjects who might otherwise "fit into the category of heterosexual" are construed as lacking in ways that open their sexual and reproductive choices to suspicion.[90] In chapters 3 and 4, I consider the plight of women who, mothering at the margins, are positioned not so much on the side of heteronormativity as outside it.

That the reproductive turn racializes belonging by figuring the survival of the nation in biological terms as a matter of life and (some people's) death is among its most important effects. Individuals are marked for death by reason of their incorrect or incomplete embodiment of citizenship. But attempts to harness reproduction to the project of nation building do not only identify the kinds of bodies – white, healthy, heterosexual, middle-class – that properly belong to the nation. Or rather, identifying the kinds of bodies that properly belong to the nation is not all such efforts are designed to accomplish. Scholars working in the field of Indigenous studies have cautioned us against overlooking the specifically *colonial* dimensions of reproductive futurism.[91] How does imperialism manifest, as Mark Rifkin suggests, in projects of making straight?[92] Taking to heart Kanaka Maoli scholar J. Kēhaulani Kauanui's injunction to consider "land and indigeneity … in relation to the study of racial formations," I ask how the straightening and racializing projects of reproductive discourses of citizenship function in concert with, and even as, colonial projects of de- and re-territorialization.[93] Through identifying Indigenous people as racial threats to the body politic, the state denies that any territorial challenge remains to be resolved. In *and what remains*, only Māori are targeted for intervention, suggesting that the state is less concerned about the presence of Māori qua people of colour within the borders of the nation than it is about the survivance of Māori qua Indigenous people.[94] To paraphrase Patrick Wolfe, who Indigenous people are is where they are.[95] Although the texts I discuss hinge nation building on the embodiedness of the reproductive process, they also do a kind of spatial work, striving to resolve the contradictions in British and settler identity by suturing identity to the space of the local. For George's New Zealanders, it's to the extent that Māori, as prior occupants of the land, at once necessitate and interfere with this process that their removal becomes imperative.

In a sense, however, who Indigenous people are is also what they have been, or perhaps, *that* they have been (here): the priority that so disturbs settler nationalisms remains, as Elizabeth Povinelli puts it, "factually, phenomenologically present in the modality of *descendants*."[96] This is not to say that Indigenous people are of the past, atavistic. Instead, I am asking what happens when history gets rendered as embodied and therefore reproducible. The texts gathered here meditate uneasily on colonial histories of violence, which, archived in an array of marked bodies, disturb the smooth reproduction of the nation. A preoccupation with the proliferating presence of racialized bodies within the boundaries of the nation should thus be read not (or not only) as paranoia about the possibility of contamination but as fear of "a cultural archive" in which the illegitimacy of the state has been "comprehensively inscribed."[97] Indigenous people appear, that is, both as errors settlers should strive to write out of their utopian blueprints for the nation, and as reminders of that history of dislocation that renders the territorial legitimacy of the nation contingent at best. Attempts to do something about the presence of such bodies by denying their capacity and even right to reproduce are also, as I show in chapter 2, attempts to consolidate hegemonic projects of homemaking by rewriting history. In a similar way, Paul Gilroy argues, British overseas subject-incomers have seemed to some Britons to bring forward "all the discomforting ambiguities of the empire's painful and shameful but apparently nonetheless exhilarating history," as if they were "unwitting bearers of the imperial and colonial past."[98] If legislation such as the 1971 Immigration Act, which denies such subjects the right to settle in Britain on the grounds that their connection to the space of Britain lacks genealogical warrant, works to racialize citizenship, it also serves, as I argue in chapter 5, to delegitimate those powerful alternative claims to the property of Britain and Britishness to which the nation's history as an imperial power has given rise.

Certainly, conceiving of the nation as made and marred by reproductive acts works to racialize citizenship. Certainly, the reproducibility of race lends racial discourse its invidious efficacy. The force of what Weinbaum calls the "race/reproduction bind" cannot be denied.[99] But the neatness of this formulation leaves other dimensions of the politics of reproduction unaccounted for. As I track the complex ways in which reproductive acts and imperatives motor national narratives, I make clear the extent to which claims about the kinds of bodies that are proper to the community of the nation encode claims about the kinds of spaces and histories that are proper to the community of the nation, *and vice versa.* Keyed to reproduction, the post-imperial forms of British and settler national identity are therefore defined not, or not only, by their racial character. Rather, they develop narratives of racialization and emplacement that converge in the making of national bodies, linking particular bodies to particular spaces through a willed amnesia about the colonial past.

Projects

Rather than attempt an exhaustive account of reproductive discourse and policy in Britain and its settler colonies, *Better Britons* develops close readings of five reproductive projects. Thus, for example, chapter 1 investigates the politics of early-twentieth-century reproductive utopianism through scrutinizing fictional representations of utopian experiments in reproductive reform, while chapter 2 is devoted to a reading of "breeding out the colour," an interwar program of uplift sanctioned by the Australian state that turned on the procurement of white husbands for women of mixed Indigenous and white descent.

Assembling a diverse reading archive that includes science fictions like *Brave New World*, modernist novels like Jean Rhys's *Voyage in the Dark* (1934), film, government memoranda, and political speeches, the book is marked by the revisionist projects of what has come to be known as the new modernist studies. However, it also departs from them. Over the past two decades, the field of modernist studies has undergone "expansion" (to use Douglas Mao and Rebecca Walkowitz's term) according to an array of imperatives.[100] The provocations of postcolonial theory have helped to shift the spatial and temporal coordinates of modernism, inspiring scholars to attend not just to early-twentieth-century writing by Asians and Africans (among others), but to "complex intellectual and economic transactions among, for example, Europe, Africa, the United States, and the Caribbean" throughout the long twentieth century as well. Critics now also regularly read across the great divides that were once thought to separate the high literary from the popular, the avant-garde from the middlebrow, and the minor from the mainstream.[101] Far from the elitist, apolitical literary movement of caricature, the modernisms to which the new modernist studies have introduced us are exciting to teach and think about. Still, the revisionist projects characteristic of the new modernist studies can be critiqued for their tendency to expand and add to rather than transform our definitions, narratives, and archives of modernism.[102] As Patricia Chu observes, either the "critical commonplaces of modernism" remain intact, elevating "the same group of artists as the ones whose strategies define the movement," or they are so evacuated as to become useless, as when all works "written within a particular span of years" or possessing "a particular cultural content, such as eugenics," are declared modernist.[103] In response, Chu calls for a theory of modernism that can accommodate a realist writer like Sara Jeannette Duncan and a pre–Hayes Code horror film like *White Zombie* (1932) alongside a Jean Toomer or T.S. Eliot without losing sight of their very different, but equally meaningful, aesthetic commitments. In *Better Britons*, I have pursued a different approach.

Like Kristin Bluemel, I think that modernism is probably "best thought of as a kind of writing, discourse, or orientation rather than a period that competes with others for particular years or texts or personalities," or that threatens to scant the inevitable diversity of cultural production at any one moment or place.[104] But where does such a definition of modernism leave those texts – memoranda, for example – that cannot be accommodated by the kinds of theories of modernism Chu would have us develop? Is it clear, moreover, that modernism is the only or best way to frame those texts that can thus be accommodated? It can seem as though the object of modernist studies is to know more about modernism, to which the new modernist studies has contributed by proliferating modernist objects. This is not a fair description of what the field has achieved: we have learned important things, in particular, about the relationship between art, aesthetics, and politics, that enduring but also characteristically modernist preoccupation. But what if modernism did not always frame – and was not always in the frame of – our analyses? I am attempting to sight two lines of departure for (or perhaps from) the field here. The first requires that critics be more explicit about what attending to the "modernism" of a given text or cultural formation allows us to do or see. Might we re-describe the "modernist" in modernist studies as the heuristic rather than the object of analysis? I am not proposing something along the lines of the turn towards "subjectless critique" that has permitted queer theorists to participate substantively in conversations about texts and issues which might not read as queer, yet invite a queer reading as sites of violence with a role to play in the reproduction of normativity (although it would be worth considering whether, in reading modernism, we are also training ourselves to read like modernists, as well as what this entails).[105] Rather, I am suggesting that we more often inquire into the ways in which we are oriented such that some analytical objects come into view while others do not. In a recent essay, Stephen Ross asks why the new modernist studies have taken "the hard way out" of "seeking to integrate traditionally non-modernist texts into modernist studies," rather than the "easier" solution of eschewing "the label *modernist* for something more general, like *twentieth-century literature*": "what drives the cathexis of *modernism* so deep that we would rather tie ourselves in knots to sustain its integrity rather than simply moving on to another term"?[106] I too find this perplexing, but suspect that modernism's persistence isn't so much the result of a dogged commitment to difficulty as a sign of just how hard it in fact is to decentre such disciplinary devices (I am not suggesting we abandon them altogether), which orient us in ways that an exercise in rebranding alone cannot undo. According to Sara Ahmed,

> Orientations are about the direction we take that puts some things and not others in our reach. So the object … can be apprehended only insofar as it has come to be available to me: its reachability is not simply a matter of its place or location (the white paper on the table, for instance), but instead is shaped by the orientations I have taken that mean I face some ways more than others (toward this kind of table, which marks out the space I tend to inhabit).[107]

Recognizing what our existing orientations do (not) enable us to apprehend might, in turn, open the door to other orientations, to modernism, certainly, but to those objects, *in addition*, that both do and do not come into view when our orientation is to modernism (or when we are oriented by modernism). How else might we orient ourselves to the historical period(s) that are currently claimed for modernism?[108] How other than according to the various chronologies of modernism might we organize our cultural histories of the twentieth century? In what other conversations will we find ourselves (to have been) participating?

The textual juxtapositions pursued in *Better Britons* are underwritten by historical propinquity combined with a certain continuity of preoccupation (incidentally, the same one Chu references, i.e., eugenics). In a sense, however, it is through being brought together, through being thus aligned, that the texts under consideration here manifest a "family" likeness: as Ahmed writes, "the desire for connection generates likeness, at the same time that likeness is read as the sign of connection."[109] If the texts I discuss do not share aesthetic strategies – what aesthetic strategies could the (formally) modernist fictions of Rhys and Eleanor Dark possibly share with the science fictions of Huxley and H.G. Wells *and* the memoranda of an Australian bureaucrat? – or even an attention to literary form as a site where the exigencies of modernity may be negotiated, they do share a set of preoccupations that might nonetheless be described as modernist, insofar as they display, or are about, that investment in standardization, streamlining, rational planning, and active management that historians of design, architecture, and planning in particular often identify as high modernist. This is the modernism of the interventionist state as James Scott defines it, which aspires to "the administrative ordering of nature and society … a sweeping, rational engineering of all aspects of social life in order to improve the human condition."[110] It is the modernism associated with the Congrès Internationaux d'Architecture Moderne, which linked "architectural innovation, perceptual change, and social transformation in a utopian mode," seeing in "built form" the "beachhead of a new society within the existing order of things."[111] The texts in my archive develop different stances vis-à-vis the modernism of "clean-sweep planning" in ways that track formally, but only to an extent.[112] This interests me less because of what it can tell us about the politics of modernism, or rather, the politics of different modernisms, than because of what it can tell us about that desire, which Scott terms modernist, to "wip[e] the slate utterly clean and [begin] from zero."[113] What does it mean, for example, that such a desire should find expression on both sides of the fiction/documentary divide?

In other scholarly work on the interwar politics of sex and reproduction, literature emerges as more than just another venue in which anxieties about fertility, intimacy, or sexual continence get acted out. Thus, for example, in his account of the "Nausicaa" trial, Adam Parkes shows how the role literature plays in intimate life, the model it offers for intimate life, marks it out as at once an object of special anxiety and a site of counter-hegemonic possibility.[114] Donald Childs has traced the ways in which modernist writers "appropriate the language of eugenical biology as a metaphor in aid of ostensibly non-biological cultural projects," and so extend "the imperial sway of the scientific discourse of the body into a realm long thought most different from it (if not most hostile to it): the realm of the imagination," while Christina Hauck reads eugenics and (stylistic) modernism as parallel projects of biocultural renovation.[115] Although indebted to this scholarship, I want to consider the relationship of imaginative fiction to the world in a different light, through foregrounding the place of speculation, of the might-have-been, the not-yet-real, and the might-still-be, in crisis management. That is, rather than focus on the ways in which literature operates as a site where crises in the social order may be worked through, resolved, or transmuted, I am interested in reading across different orders of representation and action for the comparable or discordant way in which, in each, crises are resolved or made resolvable.

Consider once more the reception accorded *and what remains*. Recall that for *Dominion Post* critic Laurie Atkinson, "the ethnically cleansed New Zealand is impossible to swallow." In writing *Better Britons*, I have wanted to give the lie to Atkinson and Smythe's professions of incredulity by reminding readers that Miria George's science fictional scenario echoes multiple real-world instances. It is no accident that in Kim Scott's extraordinary second novel *Benang* (1999), the Nyoongar narrator Harley Scat, who represents the "successful end" of an unofficial experiment in "breeding out the colour," decides to "reverse that upbringing" by writing "a simple family history."[116] Harley recognizes that his grandfather's "clear diagrams and slippery fractions" have "uplifted and diminished me" (39). "You can meet a death," he says, "just knowing the paper talk" (428). And yet, amidst that same grandfather's "litter of paper, cards, files and photographs," Harley finds himself "settl[ing] and mak[ing] myself substantial," growing "from that fraction of life which fell" (30). It matters that Harley communicates what really happened to his family, because policies like "breeding out the colour" have so often seemed *un*real, exciting incredulity that anyone should have attempted such a thing. Responding to John Smythe's review of *and what remains*, Māori literary critic Alice Te Punga Somerville proposes reframing the question of plausibility – do I find this play believable? – as a question about plausibility: why am I inclined to find the play (un)realistic?

> *Why* is it not such a leap to connect these dots in this way and what does this tell me about myself and about this country? [Conversely,] *why* do I feel so comfortable dismissing this? *Why* do I feel so confident in my sense of how things work in N[ew] Z[ealand] that when someone offers a different vision I can dismiss it so absolutely?[117]

The George controversy suggests that the inconceivability of "breeding out the colour" constitutes the mode of its forgetting, at least by settlers. The extent to which it presents as fantastic, unimaginable outside of a work of imaginative fiction, therefore demands our attention. It could be argued that the implausibility of "breeding out the colour" reflects the policy's toothlessness: it appears unreal because it never had much impact in the real. Indeed, because the scheme to "breed out colour" was overseen by unelected bureaucrats, and did not have the effects that were promised, it has been dismissed as unrepresentative of Australian Aboriginal policy between the wars, negligible. Arguably, however, the scheme's failure makes it more, not less, worthy of scrutiny, bespeaking the overreach that is characteristic of projects of reproductive reform, which depend on control of the dimension of life many consider least amenable to the exercise of reason: sex. Perhaps, in fact, this sort of speculative overreach is fundamental to the project of "breeding out the colour," and not (just) a symptom or cause of its derailing. What might we learn from insisting on rather than lamenting the proximity of policies like "breeding out the colour" to speculative fictions like *Brave New World*?

Thus, my forays into the real world of policy are not intended to provide context for the fictions that I explore elsewhere. But neither do these fictions serve as context for the statements of bureaucrats and other real world actors, as if their fictionality rendered them somehow less real. Refusing the text/context dyad, I prefer the more flexible and evocative term "project." For Nicholas Thomas, thinking in terms of projects avoids "any polarization of material and ideal aspects of colonial (and anti-colonial) endeavours": it forces us to recognize that "colonial intentions are frequently deflected, or enacted farcically and incompetently," that colonial projects are often, well, "projected rather than realized."[118] In her work on Canadian settler femininities, Jennifer Henderson describes settler colonialism similarly: Canada, she says, is a "project of rule ... the precarious and contested realization of a scheme to extend the government of 'freely' self-governing individuals (and the exclusion of deficient remainders) across a new space and into an indefinite future."[119] To read memoranda and literary texts as likewise engaged in elaborating projects is not to deny the circumstances of enunciation that render the misfired fantasies of a bureaucrat consequential in a way that the reflections of an Aldous Huxley or even a Francis Galton simply are not. In any case, few novelists desire for their speech acts the sort of real-world efficacy that Thomas's colonial administrators presumably desire for theirs. It is novels' weakness (but also their power) that they tend, as Dominick LaCapra writes, "to be transformative – at least with reference to social and political contexts – in general, suggestive, and long-term [rather than immediate and concrete] respects."[120] They do nonetheless function pedagogically, offering up new and transformative ways of conceiving the world. Thinking in terms of projects, then, allows me to register continuities between the distinct ways in which different actors – states and individuals, writers and scientists, historical figures and fictional characters – imagine and pursue social change, while attending to the difference genre makes in the reproduction of national life.

There is another reason to prefer the term project. Like the verb "to project," "project" derives from the Latin verb "proicere," meaning "to throw forth." Schlegel calls projects "fragment[s] of the future."[121] As a number of scholars have argued, our thinking about futurity is bound up with our thinking about reproduction. To paraphrase the anthropologist Marilyn Strathern, the "procreative process" functions as a potent model for understanding how we move in and through time, from the past to the future.[122] "What we think of as 'the child,'" writes James Kincaid, "has been assembled in reference to desire."[123] Here, Kincaid suggests that the child represents a – perhaps even the – telos of desire. But this statement may be more provocative and consequential than even Kincaid implies. In *No Future*, Lee Edelman argues that we are unable to "conceive of a future without the figure of the child."[124] A model of procreative process helps us chart the distance between where (or when) we are now (desiring) and where it is we want to be (fulfilled), regardless of whether what we desire has anything to do with sex at all.[125] If desire implies a future, according to Edelman, it almost inevitably implies the child. Nor do children only embody the future. More than just a resource to be nurtured and protected through legislation, educational theories, and literature for children, the child is frequently ascribed a special capacity for imaginative play and fantasy that makes her indispensable to the dreaming of new worlds. Children are thus burdened with both futurity and responsibility for its coming to pass. To be sure, not all projects centre on the administration of reproduction. But if, as I have suggested, projects are "throwings forth," attempts to bridge the gap between an unsatisfactory now and that glittering to come, this is doubly true of reproductive projects. I noted earlier that a sense of unreality has crept into the historiography of "breeding out the colour." We should resist this derealization, I suggested, because it constitutes a kind of forgetting. It may be, however, that projects such as "breeding out the colour" have always been in a sense unreal. This in no way diminishes the consequentiality of the policy, its violence, but it does suggest that its facticity is complex, necessitating a methodology flexible enough to cross generic boundaries.

The utopianism of early-twentieth-century discourses of reproduction is the focus of chapter 1. Here, I read *Brave New World*, a dominant presence in contemporary debates about reproductive technology that is almost never situated in relation to the reproductive debates of its own era, alongside Eleanor Dark's 1934 novel *Prelude to Christopher*, in which a young Australian scientist founds a eugenicist colony on an island in the Pacific, and with a backwards glance at H.G. Wells's 1896 novella *The Island of Dr. Moreau*. Through juxtaposing Australian and British fictions in this way, I seek to show how an imperial imaginary that makes use of antipodean islands as staging grounds for utopian experiments is redeployed – repatriated – by metropolitan and Antipodean utopian nationalisms. Instead of dismissing these texts as mere science fictions, of little use in deciphering early-twentieth-century thinking about reproduction, I reflect on the use each makes of the tropes and forms of the utopia. Not only, I argue, do writers deploy utopian narratives to think through crises of national reproduction, but crises of reproduction may function to consecrate the utopian as the ideal form of the national. The history of the utopia has long been entwined with the histories of the island and the laboratory as spaces characterized by enclosure and apartness, and structured by an anxiety of origins; it is no coincidence that the island nations of Australia and New Zealand have consistently been described as social laboratories and utopias, "the new earth that will make the old heaven unnecessary."[126] Chapter 1 traces the spatial stories of reproductive utopianism as they work to insulate the nation from colonial bodies and histories, tethering national futures to the possibility of beginning again, (as if) sui generis. In this way, utopian solutions assuage concerns about the fate of a too mobile and too extensible British identity, which they strive to represent as always already particularized.

In chapter 2, I turn to a historical project of reproductive reform, the Australian state policy known as "breeding out the colour." In a section of the manuscript that does not appear in the published version of *Prelude to Christopher*, Eleanor Dark indicates that the protagonist's eugenicist commitments originate in frustration with the limitations of the "White Australia" policy: how, asks Nigel Hendon, can you build "the ideal white race in a black man's country?"[127] Where Nigel relocates the effort to build the "ideal white race" elsewhere, to another, apparently uninhabited, island, "breeding out the colour" disdains such island solutions. At the same time, it is itself a kind of island solution, animated by logics of excision, enclosure, and re-beginning. In 1938, Godfrey Huggins, then prime minister of Southern Rhodesia, likened "the European in this country … to an island of white in a sea of black."[128] What might it mean to conceive of whiteness as an island, or as a property of islands?

During the first part of the twentieth century, what Marilyn Lake terms an "emergent identity of the 'white man'" came to "complement, and then displace, the figure of the Britisher in Australian cultural and political discourse."[129] As a consequence, one historian has argued, Australian eugenicists "exhibit[ed] remarkably little interest in the 'Aboriginal problem,' or the 'peril' of Asian immigration," campaigning instead for "white racial improvement."[130] But in what did this whiteness consist? Beginning in the 1920s, governments in the north and the west sanctioned programs of miscegenation, tasking officials with procuring white husbands for women of Indigenous and white descent. Advocates of such policies hoped to "breed … the colour" out of the nation, and so advance their dream of a "White Australia."[131] Chapter 2 reads "breeding out the colour" with the grain, tracking the disavowals that allowed miscegenation to stand as the saviour of Australian whiteness. Citing government reports and memoranda, newspaper articles, and fiction, I situate the policy as part of a complex of efforts defending settler claims to Australian territory from the argument of Aboriginal priority. "Breeding out the colour" divorced belonging from descent, I suggest, undercutting genealogically-derived – that is to say, Indigenous – claims to the land while dismissing as irrelevant the remoter provenance of white settlerdom, its routedness. In this way, the dream of whiteness instantiates what Spivak, following Heidegger, calls a "worlding," the "reinscription of a cartography that … (re)present[s] itself as impeccable."[132] If the settler is indigenized through being whitened, it is insofar as whiteness manifests as forgetting, as the capacity to start all over again – all over again.

In each of the first two chapters, fantasies of re-beginning emerge as central to post-imperial projects of nation building. In the second part of the book, I take up fantasies of (fore)closure, in which not reproducing, even the end of reproduction, emerge as volatile sites of national meaning making. Chapter 3 reflects on the politics of abortion through readings of F. Tennyson Jesse's 1934 novel *A Pin to See the Peepshow* and Jean Rhys's 1934 novel *Voyage in the Dark*. As subjects who do much of the labour of reproduction, women are at once key to, and a key source of anxiety for, the experiments discussed in chapters 1 and 2. The object of intense surveillance in colonial Australia, women's reproductive labour, in the speculations of Wells and Huxley, is dispensed with altogether. This helps to explain the ambiguity that suffuses especially Rhys's representation of abortion in *Voyage in the Dark*. In seeking an abortion, Rhys's Caribbean-born protagonist, the white creole Anna Morgan, might be said to challenge the terms of women's belated enfranchisement, whereby admission to the charmed circle of meaningful citizenship hinges on their adherence to restrictive standards of sexual behaviour. At the same time, *Voyage in the Dark* brings into view the differential operations and effects of reproductive discourses of citizenship, their exclusion of certain kinds of reproductive bodies – the bodies, for example, of the poor or the mad – and certain kinds of familial ties – that cut across racial lines, for example – as endangering the right reproduction of Britishness. To a significant degree, the abortion doesn't challenge expectations of Anna as a reproductive subject, since not reproducing is what it is expected – desired – she will do. Importantly, it enables Anna to "start all over again, all over again."[133] But the foreclosure of abortion also contests the logic of re-beginning that equates futurity with disremembrance insofar as it moves Anna to recall the histories of violence that condition bodies in colonial contexts, including her own. Although Anna recoils from this legacy, the novel argues for a more robust engagement with the exigencies of genealogy, one which makes visible the involvement of national with colonial spaces, bodies, and histories.

In 1937, the British government convened an enquiry to investigate the incidence of abortion in Britain and consider the prospects for abortion law reform. When feminist Stella Browne appeared before the enquiry, its chairman, Norman Birkett, asked whether she would consider it a calamity for "the race" if "all women decided they would not have children." Browne answered, "I think that rather depends upon the prospects before the race, if it went on. I think if all women were unwilling to bear children it would be much better that no children should be born."[134] Here, Browne rejects the eugenicist presumption that women's bodies must bear the responsibility of perfecting the race, nation, and species, preferring no future at all to one women refuse to populate.

No Future is the title of Lee Edelman's much more recent polemic against forms of sociality guaranteed by reproductive futurism. In chapters 4 and 5, I ask what comes after death: is there a future in imagining the end?

In chapter 4, I ponder the uses of apotropaios, foregrounding narratives in which children are secured against a threatening future through being denied any future at all. Thus, for example, in the final pages of *Wednesday's Children*, a 1937 novel by the New Zealand writer Robin Hyde, the eponymous children are revealed to exist only in their mother's imagination; the eleventh section of *The Book of Nadath*, a long prose poem Hyde completed in 1937 but never published, envisages a grim future in which New Zealand has been taken over by Asian invaders. Written at a time when world war seemed likely, even inevitable, both works see children as so menaced by this prospect that even death seems preferable. The nation appears doomed. But is it? In fact, I argue, Hyde's necrophilic nationalism repeats, in a melancholic mode, the indigenizing move that also structures "breeding out the colour," rooting settler claims to Indigenous land in the ability to perform the role, usually reserved for Indigenous people, of a dying race. Acknowledging settler complicity in histories of Indigenous dispossession, *The Book of Nadath* recasts dispossession as an experience that the colonizer shares in potentia with the colonized. Death, Hyde suggests, annihilates the difference between colonizer and colonized. In this way, the nation achieves a belated legitimacy through being doomed. To paraphrase Eliot: in the end, perhaps, is another (re-)beginning.[135]

The endings discussed in chapter 5, while more comprehensive in scope, traffic in a similar sense of possibility. Leaving behind the interwar decades that are the focus of the four preceding chapters, chapter 5 turns to the second half of the twentieth century, when the pace of decolonization intensified, and its scope was radically broadened. Much of the legislation that disassociated Britain from its empire dates from this era, contributing to a sense of crisis about Britain's place in the post-war world order that continues unabated. Arriving at the University of Edinburgh in the early 1980s, Simon Gikandi was astonished to discover that "here in Great Britain, in the heart of civilization itself, the nature and destiny of the country were being discussed in terms previously reserved for the former colonies."[136] To Paul Gilroy, such a "fixation with the fluctuating substance of national culture and identity" appears "morbid."[137] If the structures of feeling that animate such discussions are very much of their moment, the predicaments they describe and rhetorics they invoke have long genealogies. As Alison Bashford observes, there is a "popular and, in some instances, scholarly narrative that Nazi eugenics and its assessment (or presumed assessment) in the so-called doctors' trials, the genocide convention, and in the

United Nations human rights convention collectively marked the end" of eugenicist thought.[138] In chapter 5, I enquire into the afterlife of eugenics, reading the late-twentieth-century resurgence in Britain of panics about demographic decline in relation to post-war developments in citizenship and nationality law.

More particularly, I ask how panics about the end of the nation double as fantasies about what the nation could or should become. How do they help to produce the communities they also represent as doomed? Apocalyptic scenarios in which Britain is overrun by a variety of spectacularly fertile foreign bodies (including, but not limited to, immigrants) proliferate in post-war British political discourse and cultural production. The narratives of engulfment that organize John Wyndham's 1951 novel *The Day of the Triffids*, Enoch Powell's 1968 speech "Rivers of Blood," and Danny Boyle's 2002 film *28 Days Later* do not merely reflect either demographic trends or territorial givens. Rather, they work to confine Britishness within sharply defined borders, anchoring the nation in the certainty of distinguishing between (menaced) insides and (menacing) outsides. Thus, in *28 Days Later*, Boyle abandons the tropical setting of his earlier film *The Beach* (2000) for a pastoral English landscape, pitching values of intimacy, domesticity, and containment against the horror of unruly fertilities and unnatural proliferations, including the global networks of travel, trade, and dissemination laid down by empire.[139] A similar trend is discernible in post-war immigration and nationality legislation. As I noted above, until the 1960s, all persons born or naturalized in British territories shared the common status of "British subject." In 1971, however, Westminster established the principle of patriality, withholding the right of abode from all British subjects save those with British-born parents. If, as most scholars observe, the 1971 Immigration Act rearticulated British citizenship as a function of whiteness, it did so, I suggest, by retracting the borders of Britishness. This account of the way in which the repatriation of Britain's island story frames Britishness as an embattled whiteness, excising the overseas happening of its history, helps to make sense of one of the xenophobic and white supremacist British National Party's more outrageous recent claims: that in opposing immigration, it is defending the right of "indigenous" Britons to resist "colonization," as established by the United Nations Declaration on the Rights of Indigenous Peoples.[140] The three major political parties, the Liberal Democrats, the Conservatives, and Labour, eschew the indigenist rhetoric that the British National Party (BNP) deploys in the service of white supremacy. As I show in chapter 5, however, the BNP's articulation of whiteness with indigeneity only exaggerates, or makes visible, mainstream attempts to suture British national identity to the singular space of the British Isles, to whiten Britishness by indigenizing it. In effect, Britain emerges as yet another "brave new world" to which, following the end, settlers may be introduced to start all over again.

The familiarity of the logics that underwrite twenty-first-century conceptions of British identity is depressing to contemplate. There is an urgent need for conceptions of British and settler identity that do not consign some of us to forms of social death. Reproductive models of belonging would seem irrecuperable, impossible to unbind from race, patriarchy, or heteronormativity. No wonder that Donna Haraway, "sick to death of bonding through kinship and 'the family,' and [longing] for models of solidarity and human unity and difference rooted in friendship, work, partially shared purposes, intractable collective pain, inescapable mortality, and persistent hope," calls for "an 'unfamiliar' unconscious, a different primal scene, where everything does not stem from the dramas of identity and reproduction."[141] Arguably, however, the problem with the post-imperial identities discussed here is that they accord too little weight to genealogy, not too much, especially as this articulates and grounds claims to land. In the settler nations, fractionalizing measurements that "mark one's generational proximity to a 'full-blood' forebear" have proxied for genealogy in ways that are destructive for Indigenous people, whose diversification they frame in terms of dilution and disappearance.[142] If "ties through blood … have been bloody," not mobilizing genealogy may eviscerate Indigenous political struggles. Indigenous and allied feminists and queers caution that Indigenous conceptions of genealogy and kinship will require decolonizing if they are not to reproduce "the colonial status quo with its attendant heteropatriarchy."[143] In doing so, however, they refuse a totalizing view of genealogy and kinship as inevitably complicit with biopolitical regimes of governance.

Finally, there is a risk that in prioritizing belonging in communities constituted through acts of affiliation and the work of solidarity, we will lose touch with the ways in which we are oriented to and by that set of forces we call the past, including genealogy. This is the point: to be freed from those "genealogical inheritances [that] threaten to determine the present by the past and reason and the conscious by unreason and the unconscious."[144] But if writing *Better Britons* has taught me anything, it is to query the impulse towards rupture. Is it necessary to break with the past in pursuit of a more just futur(ity)? Might it not be imperative, rather, to recognize and reckon with our inheritance of the histories of dispossession, genocide, and disavowal detailed in this book? As a settler resident on stolen Indigenous land, I am privileged by this inheritance. As a Canadian citizen, I make use of its disbursements every day. Such inheritances are not of my choosing – they were, as Sara Ahmed writes in *Queer Phenomenology*, "the condition of [my] arrival into the world" – but I, whom they shape, am nonetheless not compelled to reproduce them, or not exactly.[145] In settler contexts, Scott Morgensen contends, any critique of reproductive models of identity, belonging, and citizenship that fails to "examine settler colonialism as a condition of its own work" will be limited in its transformative reach.[146] In our efforts to imagine our "*world-making* and *kin-aesthetics*" as not just separate from, but counter to, the state's straightening projects, settler critics must take care not to "disown the ways their status as U.S. [or Canadian or Australian] subjects implicates them in the ongoing dynamics and imperatives of settlement," including state-sponsored reproductive interventionism.[147] In a brief envoi, then, I ask how else we might configure the relationship between the inheritances that condition our arrivals, and the modern impetus towards departure, returning to *and what remains* for the insights it affords into the politics of departure. How might we rethink the labour of inheritance so as to remain open to the unsettlement of the past and the difference of the future alike?

PART ONE

Beginnings

Chapter One

An Island Solution: Utopian Forms and the Routing of National Identity

In 1932, Aldous Huxley published his fifth novel, *Brave New World*. A dystopian fiction, *Brave New World* speculates about the consequences of a revolution in reproduction, depicting a future in which humans no longer reproduce but are rather produced to specification in laboratories, like cars on a factory assembly line. A year later, the Australian federal government circulated a memorandum outlining "Government Policy with regard to Aboriginals in [Australia's] Northern Territory."[1] The document evinces the state's commitment to regulating most aspects of the day-to-day lives of Northern Territory Aboriginals, but shows it especially keen to intervene in their sexual, reproductive, and familial lives. Thus, for instance, the memorandum stipulates that no "female aboriginal (or half-caste)" should marry "any person other than an aboriginal (or half-caste)" "without the permission, in writing, of a [local] Protector authorised by the Government Resident to grant permission in such cases."[2] Although permission was never granted "for a white or a half-caste to marry an aboriginal woman," in practice, as one bureaucrat noted, women of mixed white and Indigenous descent ("half-castes") were "encouraged to marry whites approved by the [Territory's] Chief Protector."[3] By tasking officials with procuring white husbands for women of mixed Indigenous-white descent, the Northern Territory had, in effect, instituted a program of compulsory miscegenation. To what end? A whiter Australia, delivered from colour.

On the surface, Huxley's bottled babies have little to do with "breeding out the colour." Indeed, their juxtaposition here invokes a host of commonsensical oppositions: between literature and history; between utopia and nation; between future and past; between metropole and colony. While the dystopian drama of *Brave New World* takes place against the backdrop of a post-national Britain, "breeding out the colour" refers us to the (ex-)colonial space of Australia. *Brave New World* is a science fiction, set six hundred years in the future. A "persistent and authoritative presence" in debates about biotechnology, consumerism, and totalitarianism virtually since its publication, it is read – still – for its prophetic relevance.[4] In contrast, "breeding out the colour" is history. It names a project of colonial rule actually essayed by interwar Australian governments with concrete consequences for Indigenous and non-Indigenous people alike. For all their apparent differences, however, it is productive to read "breeding out the colour" together with speculative fictions like *Brave New World* – *Better Britons* is built around that assumption – and not just because *Brave New World* shares with "breeding out the colour" the conviction that shifts in reproductive practice can alter social organization. Attending to precisely those details of genre and geopolitical location where *Brave New World* and "breeding out the colour" might seem to diverge brings key elements of their projects, I suggest, into sharper relief. How does it matter, for example, that Huxley's anti-reproductive Brave New World is a utopian polity? What would it mean to describe White Australia as a utopian project? What light might "breeding out the colour," which aims to secure national homogeneity against the threat of deviant colonial reproductions, shed on the centrality of the New Mexico Savage Reservation to the plot of *Brave New World*?

In this chapter, I focus on fictions about experiments in the production of new kinds of humans, before scrutinizing "breeding out the colour" in chapter 2. In all the texts discussed in chapter 1 – *Brave New World*, *The Island of Dr. Moreau* (1896), an earlier science fiction by H.G. Wells, and *Prelude to Christopher*, a 1934 novel by the Australian modernist writer Eleanor Dark – crises of reproduction impel scientists to implement radically transformative programs of reform. Thus, *Prelude to Christopher* tells the story of Nigel Hendon, a young Australian scientist who founds a eugenicist colony on a tropical island called Ti-Noon. In *The Island of Dr. Moreau*, the eponymous scientist attempts to obviate the necessity for reproduction by carving animals into humans through a bloody process that includes radical surgery and hypnosis. Meanwhile, as we've seen, *Brave New World* looks forward to a world in which reproduction has been done away with altogether. My aim is to understand not only the nature of these experiments and the crises they are designed to manage, but the techniques they employ in establishing regimes of reproductive control. Although not all three novels conform to the typology of the literary utopia – even *Brave New World* is, strictly speaking, a work of dystopian fiction – the projects they anatomize can all be described as utopian, extravagantly ambitious ventures that mobilize the tropes and forms of the political genre of the utopia. In lectures published in 1911 and 1912, the British eugenicist Karl Pearson worked hard to distance eugenics from utopian curricula that would make over the state as "a great matrimonial agency."[5] He counselled pragmatism: rather than attempt direct control over the reproductive decisions of their fellow citizens, "practical eugenists," he suggested, should work to remove legislative barriers to "the reproduction of the fit."[6] It is easy – too easy – to follow Pearson in dismissing bolder projects (like "breeding out the colour," for example) as crankeries with little capacity to illuminate either early-twentieth-century thinking about sex and reproduction or its import for changing conceptions of national identity and belonging. However, the work of scholars like Fredric Jameson and Phillip Wegner, who approach the utopia as a genre, a kind of text or polity whose politics inheres as much in its form as in its content, encourages us to move on from evaluating utopian modes of thought as impractical or absurd to working out the implications of desiring utopia, of what Jameson calls "the desire called utopia." As I suggest in this chapter, not only do writers like Huxley use the literary genre of the utopia to think through crises of reproduction and national identity, but crises of reproduction may function to consecrate the political genre of the utopia as the preferred form of the nation.

Pearson's dismissive references to crankism notwithstanding, utopianism constitutes a central theme in early-twentieth-century British and British diasporic thinking about reproduction and the nation. This signifies more than that calls for radical reproductive reform can entail a wholesale transformation in the way societies organize and perpetuate themselves. Rather, I argue, would-be reformers make use of utopian tropes and forms to develop powerful claims about the kinds of bodies, histories, and spaces that are proper to the nation. The history of the utopia has long been entwined with that of the island, suggesting that a utopian inflection might be discovered in many of the projects of empire.[7] In each of *The Island of Dr. Moreau*, *Brave New World*, and *Prelude to Christopher*, however, the voyage *out*, to an insular site marked for, or already given over to, colonization, occasions a voyage *in*, to an insular site marked as metropolitan. It is the anxiety generated by this traffic among colonies and between the colony and the nation, I suggest, that animates the utopian dream of total reproductive control. Such a reading may not jive with prevailing understandings of the Brave New World or, for that matter, *Brave New World* itself, whose critics have tended not to ask whether the novel's treatment of the Savage Reservation and its relationship with Utopia might reflect (on) interwar anxieties about the global career of Britishness. Critics of *The Island of Dr. Moreau* likewise under-read the significance of the novella's English coda, which invites us, I think, to see in Moreau's island laboratory a (deeply flawed) model for not just colonial but national projects of uplift and improvement. In *Prelude to Christopher*, not Aboriginality but madness and female autonomy – the madness of female autonomy – are the menaces claiming the attention of the eugenicist Nigel Hendon. But if thinking about the utopianism of Nigel's experiment or Moreau's makes legible their preoccupation with the contact zone as the site where national reproduction is most likely to go awry, it also explains how *Prelude to Christopher*, for example, can seem untouched by any such anxiety, a utopian tactics of containment extending even to the texts themselves. For what makes utopia so appealing an objective to the reformers in these fictions is the spatial story it tells, of apartness, enclosure, and self-sufficiency, promising sequestration from genealogical contamination and disseminatory drift, and from the risks of geopolitical entanglement. Re-imagined thus, the nation seems, as Paul Gilroy writes, to give birth to itself, but ceaselessly, as sequestration fails and is re-instigated, over and over again.[8]

Reproducing Utopia

In describing as utopian such an experiment in selective human breeding as Nigel Hendon's in *Prelude to Christopher*, I do not mean either that Nigel's aims should please us (they shouldn't) or even that they please Nigel (although they presumably do). The term "utopia," first used by Thomas More in his portrayal of an imagined island polity possessed of social, economic, and political structures and mores different from England's own, derives from the Greek words "no" and "place." In the poem that concludes *Utopia* (1516), however, Utopia's poet laureate, Anemolius, insists that it should be called Eutopia, or the good place, instead. According to Fátima Vieira, "by creating two neologisms which are so close in their composition and meaning" and, I would add, sound, "More created a tension that has persisted over time and has been the basis for the perennial duality of meaning of utopia as the place that is simultaneously a non-place (utopia) and a good place (eutopia)."[9] If many utopias are also eutopias, attempts to improve on the current state of things, they may present as not so good places, even the very bad place we call dystopia. Witness the early-twentieth-century eugenicists, whose dreams no longer seem especially eutopic. What, then, does it mean to categorize them as utopian? In framing Nigel's eugenicist project as utopian, I aim to move beyond the question of whether it is good or bad (or neither) to ask what it means to desire, as I am suggesting Nigel desires, utopia.

Much recent work on utopia is devoted to reclaiming "the desire called utopia" from precisely the kind of grandiose program of social overhaul with which the term is conventionally associated – and with which I'm concerned here.[10] Indeed, it is worth distinguishing between something like Bloch's utopian impulse, which Ruth Levitas defines as "the expression of desire for a better way of living," and what I will term the desire for utopia, in part so as to retain as open a sense of utopian possibility as is feasible, in part because it is useful to consider what programmatic utopias share as objects of desire.[11] What happens, in short, when we conceive of the utopia as a political genre? Fredric Jameson depicts the utopia as "an imaginary enclave within real social space."[12] An "aberrant by-product" of processes of "spatial and social differentiation," utopian "possibility is dependent on the momentary formation of a kind of eddy or self-contained backwater within the general differentiation process and its seemingly irreversible forward momentum" (15). In this space, this eddy or backwater, "new wish images of the social can be elaborated and experimented on" (16). Other scholars have recognized the utopian impetus towards closure, with Phillip Wegner drawing attention to "the deep relationship [with] the concept of *totality*" that informs utopian renderings of the world as a "fundamentally closed whole," and Jill Dolan opposing her vision of "a utopia always in process" to the "contained, self-reliant, self-determined system" of tradition.[13] Utopias, Antoine Hatzenberger writes, are "far away, closed, apart, and self-sufficient."[14] In an important sense, such accounts suggest, closure does not just enable "new wish images of the social" to be elaborated and experimented with; the desire for utopia is also, I want to suggest, a desire for the enclave, self-sufficiency, containment, and totality characteristics as well as conditions of the utopian dreamer's "new wish images of the social." Describing utopia in terms of closure, a word whose primary meaning is distinctly spatial, might seem to leave some utopias, located at a temporal rather than a spatial remove from the present, unaccounted for. For example, Vieira distinguishes between utopias "confined to remote islands or unknown places," which cultivate ahistoricity, and utopias projected into the future, whose inhabitants "envision their lives as a process of becoming."[15] But differentiating between spatial and temporal utopias in this way can obscure the extent to which, in each case, forms of spatial articulate with forms of temporal closure, telling us something critical about the political project of utopia: at stake is utopia's relationship with the geopolitical and historical contexts from which it emerges.

A utopian politics, Jameson writes, "aims at imagining, and sometimes even at realizing, a system radically different from this one," often through the extirpation of some evil from which all others are thought to spring (xii). For Wegner, "the staging of the closure of space offered in utopian fiction" inaugurates "an original modern sense of temporality, for which the supreme event is that of *revolution*: the rupture or break located in time between what are in fact two different worlds."[16] Huxley's treatment of historical and narrative causality, both as this is understood in the Brave New World and as it is represented in *Brave New World*, reinforces this sense of the historical inaccessibility of utopia, even if the "revolution" thus represented is unlikely to please Wegner. In his 1946 foreword to the novel, Huxley explains that although he initially "projected

[Utopia] six hundred years into the future," today "it seems quite possible that the horror may be upon us within a single century."[17] He's speaking of the text's prophetic accuracy, as though, given a set of propitious historical developments, the Brave New World would come inevitably to pass. At the same time, in that Utopia will someday simply be "upon us," it appears not as the product of actions and events, the effect of some set of causes, but as an imminence. Utopia's emergence is therefore to an important degree un-narratable. In the novel's opening chapter, Mustapha Mond, the Resident Controller for Western Europe, delivers a historical sketch to students on a tour of the Central London Hatchery and Conditioning Centre. In doing so, Mond appears to defy his own precepts against the teaching of history. However, as Mond speaks, the otherwise straightforward narrative begins to stutter, taking on a stichomythic rhythm as it darts ever more quickly between Mond's lecture, conversations among the Hatchery workers, and Bernard Marx's bitter mutterings. Information about "the famous British Museum Massacre," in which "two thousand culture fans are gassed with dichlorethyl sulphide," is bracketed by a detailed description of Lenina Crowne's outfit (50). Mond's history telling studiously avoids verbs and active subjects, eschewing rigorous attention to "roots and fruits" in favour of the incantatory power of the proper name (the British Museum Massacre, the Nine Years' War, Shakespeare) (104). The messiness of Mond's chronology points up the inadequacy of historical time and historical narrative to adequately explain not only Utopia but utopias more generally. In a world committed to the principle that "history is bunk," the only way to narrate history is to de-narrate it, to obscure, if not outright sever, the relationships of causality and consequence that conventionally motor the telling of history (34). The past need not be disposed of altogether: in the Brave New World, the contents of the past, while made to seem disposable (in the dual sense, that is, of being readily done without and lending themselves to easy disposal), serve in their very contemptibility to chart utopian transcendence. Any continuity between the less-than-perfect past and the resplendent now must, however, be disavowed. Perfection cannot have a future; how, then, can it have a history?

If all (programmatic) utopias must attempt such a "secession," as Jameson puts it, from the past, the claims of history emerge as a particularly pressing concern for those utopian projects that target reproduction for reform (85). Jameson calls "the gender turn of the Utopian imagination," its "reroute[ing] and deviat[ion] along the lines of gender and sexuality, rather than those of class dynamics and the mode of production," an "unhappy outcome for the Utopian and SF genre" (140). However, to the extent that modern thinking about time is bound up with thinking about reproduction (and vice versa), the reorganization of gender and sexuality may be fundamental and not eccentric to the promise of nineteenth- and twentieth-century utopian thought. As Marilyn Strathern explains, the reproductive model of futurity "plays off heredity and development through a contrast between the relationships implied in parenting and ancestry and the individuality that must be claimed by and for the child as the outcome of these relationships."[18] While the child originates physically and genetically in the bodies of her parents, and is assumed to develop along continuous lines (Nadine at three is the same person as Nadine at thirty-three), at no point does she merely replicate her parents or her previous selves; as an evolving composite, she is unpredictable. Reproductive futurism thus inheres simultaneously in the continuity embodied by the child and in the promise of its difference: without the guarantee of continuity, there is no guarantee that the individual, family, or community will persist as such; without the guarantee of change, there is no possibility that things will get better for what persists. In this sense, the child, like Jameson's utopia, "combines the not-yet-being of the future with [an] existence in the present," embodying desire and fantasy (xv–xvi). Noting the multiplicity of political positions that invocation of the child then helps shore up, Lee Edelman argues, "We are no more able to conceive of a politics without a fantasy of the future than we are able to conceive of a future without the figure of the child."[19] There can be no politics without futurity, without hope, without the possibility of affirmation. If the child functions as "the perpetual horizon of every acknowledged politics, the fantasmatic beneficiary of every political intervention," utopian thinking is necessarily reproductive thinking.[20] At the same time, rethinking reproduction must spark a concomitant rethinking of futurity. What is then striking is not that the Brave New World (for example) hitches its utopian star to the abolishment of reproduction, but rather that, as Jameson himself admits, the bourgeois family persists virtually unchanged in so many nineteenth- and twentieth-century utopias.[21]

The ostensible aim of each of the experiments in reproduction described by Dark, Huxley, and Wells is a more perfect humanity: better Australians, better workers, better humans. Arguably, however, what is really being sought is a more perfect mode of reproduction. In *Prelude to Christopher*, for example, it is the messy way in which humanity goes about reproducing itself that rouses Nigel Hendon to action: struggling to communicate his vision to Linda Hamlin, the woman he plans to marry, Nigel lauds

> the marvels of efficiency that humanity had perfected, the breeding of animals, the standardisation of machinery, the cataloguing of libraries, the miraculous precision of science. All in order, all beautifully in order, except itself! There it seethed and crawled over the whole face of the globe, like … this pest that was devastating all the orchards and gardens of the State – like thrip! A man who bred his sheep

> with infinite care would marry a tuberculous wife and rear an infected family; a man who grew his fruit trees undeviatingly true to type would beget a brood of half-caste children.[22]

In order to obviate such egregious reproductive miscalculations, Nigel plans to establish a colony to which he will admit only those "passed by himself and [his friend] Pen as mentally and physically sound" (49). In this way, Nigel believes, he can ensure that only "healthy children" are bred and reared (49). For Nigel, then, perfection is not only a set of traits – non-tubercular, white, sane – but the deliberate, systematic, *orderly* fashion in which one sets out to achieve them.

As reproduction is remade, Strathern and Edelman suggest, we can expect that our conception of time, the way in which we apprehend and experience the relationship between the past, the present, and the future, will change as well. Consider the Brave New World. Huxley's Utopians are, famously, laboratory productions, immaculately conceived.[23] Harvested from excised ovaries, ova undergo artificial insemination, replication, and comprehensive chemical conditioning, all within the grey walls of a Hatchery and Conditioning Centre. In Huxley's vision of the twenty-sixth century, not only does reproduction no longer motivate conventions of social organization, but with the assistance of Malthusian Belts and Abortion Centres humans effectively no longer reproduce at all. As a result, Utopians find the word "father" "gross, a scatological ... impropriety," while "to say one was a mother ... was past a joke: it was an obscenity" (151; 153). Relocating reproduction from the body to the laboratory allows for the standardization and specialization of Utopian bodies and minds: the Brave New World produces individuals with an aptitude and liking for work as intellectuals or janitors, depending on the need. But if the eradication of maternity makes possible a population tailored to need, it also contributes to and consolidates an ideological "campaign against the Past" that commenced with "the closing of museums, the blowing up of historical monuments," and "the suppression of all books published before A. F. 150" (51).[24] Their horror of maternity therefore bespeaks the horror with which Utopians view all forms of human continuity. Even the state's distribution of the drug soma promotes a historiography of discontinuity by suspending users in the inconsequential moment (110). When the misfit scientist Bernard Marx is threatened with transfer to Iceland, his technician lover Lenina Crowne chants, "was and will make me ill[,] I take a gramme [of soma] and only am": "five minutes later," the narrator remarks, "roots and fruits were abolished; the flower of the present rosily blossomed" (104). According to Mustapha Mond, the turn to ectogenesis capped a series of ideological battles over the shape and direction of Utopia: abandoning the past as a repository and generator of meaning helped fuel the culture of conspicuous waste and mandatory consumption that the World State wished to engineer. But if the World State's "campaign against the Past" was central to its utopian becoming, helping to establish rupture as the condition of its origin, ahistoricity is also specific to the project of *this* utopia, discontinuity the exemplary temporal experience in a world without reproduction.

At first glance, Dark's eugenicist appears uninterested in any such radical reorganization of the experience of time. Indeed, the science of eugenics makes sense only if the (biological) past is seen as affecting the present and future in vastly consequential ways that can be predicted and therefore harnessed. Francis Galton, an early proponent of eugenics, encouraged scientists to consider "each human or other personality [not] as something supernaturally added to the stock of nature, but rather as a segregation of what already existed, under a new shape, and as a regular consequence of previous conditions."[25] The narrative structure of *Prelude to Christopher* reflects this concern with the ramifying past. Dark sets *Prelude to Christopher* twenty-two years following Nigel's discovery of Ti-Noon. Now middle-aged, Nigel and his wife Linda inhabit a quiet rural community called Moondoona, where they sound a minor note of scandalous eccentricity. As the novel opens, Nigel is involved in a serious car accident, in the aftermath of which we, along with the Hendons and the local community, are invited to confront the legacy of his colony. The island is then available only in retrospect. A novel about a man who set out to found "the earthly paradise," *Prelude to Christopher* originates in the need to trace a route through – and out of – the detritus of memory (42). Grappling post-accident with the "vast inimical burden which was his life," Nigel woozily decides to pull at his memories of the past, "this little thread[,] like the unraveling of wool, till the mass was gone – finished – conquered" (9–10). Many years earlier, he had complained to Linda of the "Guilds, Institutes, Committees, Charities, [and] Cults" that, seeking to ameliorate humanity's diseased condition, pick "with feverish industry at the middle of the tangle, while the end [that is, Nigel's eugenic solution] hung in plain view and they dared not see it" (26). Nigel frames his experiment, as Dark frames her narrative, as an exercise in clarification: the past is to be ordered, its effects monitored and managed. The figure of the tangle invites more dramatic action, however. Daniel Kevles has described eugenics as a chiliastic pursuit because it seeks "the elimination of original sin by getting rid biologically of the original sinner."[26] Nigel means to dissociate select individuals and communities from the contaminations of an imperfect past, from the past as contamination. He intends, significantly, that the colonists' children should hear of "the world [their parents] had left as if it were history, a legend of bad days long past" (49). Even as it relies, then, on the fact of generational continuity, Nigel's project aims at the production of bodies "supernaturally" disconnected, as it were, from "the stock" of human nature.

The past is also *sous rature* on the island of Dr. Moreau. With his Beasts seemingly incapable of reproducing themselves – they bear offspring, which soon die – and this function arrogated to himself, Moreau eliminates the sense of continuity, of a connection between past, present, and future, that is proliferated through forms of viviparous reproduction.[27] What counts as human in Moreau's laboratory, moreover, is whatever has been purged of the animal past. As Moreau explains to the narrator, the shipwreck survivor Edward Prendick, "each time I dip a living creature into the bath of burning pain, I say: this time I shall burn out all the animal, this time I will make a rational creature of my own. After all, what is ten years? Man has been a hundred thousand in the making" (59). Moreau subjects his beasts to a violently compressed evolutionary process that leaves them, at least initially, "with a clean sheet, mentally," purged of inconvenient species memories (57).

In all three texts, then, utopian difference is constituted through a break with the past. This is not to say that utopian secessionism does not also manifest spatially, even in *Brave New World*. Among the rhythmic refrains broadcast to Utopian children in their sleep is the following concise statement of Utopian principles: "Civilization is sterilization" (110). The slogan hints at Utopia's dependence on a radical sexual hygiene. It is intended, however, to convey a "lesson in elementary hygiene" (110). By twinning contraception with cleanliness, the slogan draws attention to the laboratory space in which it is broadcast, inviting readers to reflect on the extent to which, in the Brave New World, the spheres of life and the hygiene-conscious laboratory overlap. Laboratory space does more than just figure Utopian discontinuity. It is in the laboratory, after all, that Utopians are – literally – made. The novel itself opens here. By turning life into a laboratory production – the light that enters through the windows of the Fertilizing Room at the Central London Hatchery and Conditioning Centre is "frozen, dead, a ghost," borrowing "a certain rich and living substance" "only from the yellow barrels of the microscopes" – the Brave New World insinuates its own sterile origins (3). In *Brave New World*, utopia, far from taking the form of an enclave, is everywhere. Still, might the laboratory, which the *Oxford English Dictionary* defines as a "building set apart for conducting investigations in natural science," not be read as a utopian enclave, a space, as the sociologist of science Bruno Latour says, in which to raise a world?[28]

Since laboratories need not be buildings, what seems crucial about the *OED*'s definition is its stress on the laboratory's being "set apart." Sociologists of science have shown how the laboratory's apparent detachment from "the real world," that is, from the entanglements of (identity) politics, ethics, and economics, is in fact enabled and sustained by a complex network of socio-political interests.[29] No one can say, argues Latour, "*where the laboratory is* and *where the society is*."[30] This is not to say that its sequestration does not serve an important purpose. Historical case studies reveal an insistent concern on the part of laboratory planners and architects with "control of both external and internal sources of disturbances to the measuring process."[31] Laboratories must incorporate accurate means of accounting for or preventing such disturbances as oscillations in temperature or geological shifts. Scientists wishing to determine the etiology of a given disease must filter out local idiosyncrasies – the weather, soil composition, dirt, age – so as to isolate a cause that, as Latour puts it, "is there for all to see": a microbe, a virus.[32] When Louis Pasteur moved the study of anthrax from the farm to the laboratory, he took with him only the microorganism he believed caused anthrax, and not the farm's smell or the vulnerable cows. In the laboratory, phenomena like diseases are remade into stable systems whose "output," as Jean-François Lyotard explains, can be accurately predicted "if all variables are known."[33] Such a model of causality reflects a Newtonian view of the universe as governed by a small number of invariable, predictive laws. What appears complex in situ – the causal apparatus of a disease like anthrax – scientists must simplify and make comprehensible by creating and maintaining conditions in which *x* always leads recognizably to *y*, in which causality is clear, nameable, and predictable. Of course, it is impossible to isolate causality as definitively as is required if the scientist does not know exactly what is coming in and out of her laboratory, if the latter is not a bounded space, its every contact with the world open to observation and regulation. But laboratory space does not only enable the historiographical operation in which scientists pair discrete causes with particular effects. Moving the study of nature from "outside" to "inside," the laboratory permits a parallel move from the particular to the universal. As David Gooding, Trevor Pinch, and Simon Schaffer explain, "experimental reasoning will try to get rid of any feature of a trial which ties it to a particular setting."[34] The laboratory is thus also a space in which the particular is made universal and usable through being extracted from the world.

The project of eugenics rests on the belief that heredity, like disease, is transmitted and, more important, expressed in predictable, recognizable ways. Whether the science of heredity will ever be anything but an actuarial science, providing probabilities but not certainties, is unclear. But it cannot help that it is more difficult to isolate the workings of heredity from factors loosely termed "environmental" than it is to isolate the bacterial agent responsible for anthrax. In "The Groundwork of Eugenics," one of a series of brief introductions to the science of eugenics that he published in 1912, Karl Pearson wonders whether "a biological science of the evolution of human societies [can] exist? … Can we place ourselves outside the community of which we form a part, and study the effects upon it of environment, of occupation, of nourishment and of breeding in the same judicial manner as the owner of a herd of shorthorns approaches the like problems?" (3). According to Pearson, a real "biological science" requires that its practitioners place themselves "outside the community" or "herd." Pearson means, he goes on to explain, that eugenicists must "repress sternly the personal," but in urging that his colleagues hew to a scientific ideal of "dispassionate" detachment, he also alerts us to the detached character of the geography of experiment, its singularity and self-integrity (3). Can scientists place themselves "outside the community of which we are a part," he asks? Put another way: is it possible to enclose entire communities within the *cordon sanitaire* of the laboratory? Pearson is not optimistic: although we can "observe those experiments which mankind is every day on so vast a scale making upon itself," that is, the perfectly unexceptional choices men and women make in the conduct of their sexual and reproductive lives, we cannot carry out "direct experiments on our fellow-men, and study training and nurture and parentage as it is possible for the owner of a thoroughbred stud to do" (4–5). It is perhaps to Pearson's credit that, unlike Josef Mengele and his peers, he does not propose employing forms of segregation developed for other purposes, such as the prison or the reservation, for this sort of "direct" experimentation. But without extracting communities of inheritance from the world, Pearson worries, scientists will fail to subject the complex and contingent processes of heredity to the kind of simplification necessary for a successful eugenics.

Enter the island. Like Karl Pearson, Dark's eugenicist cannot initially see how "the miraculous precision of science" is to be applied to marriage and reproduction (26). Then Nigel happens upon an old sailor, who tells him of an island Eden in the Pacific: "The old man's words turned a key in his brain – flung open a door. 'It's like being in a little world of your own'" (11). The island, called Ti-Noon, becomes "his symbol of attainment," a "half-translucent vision … born of pictures all but forgotten, of tales told in childhood, even, perhaps, of some remote ancestral legend of Hy-Brasil, the lost Eden, the island of the blessed" (22). He soon leads an expedition of the eugenically fit to settle the island. When scandal drives Dr. Moreau from London, he too opts to site his new laboratory on an island in the Pacific. It is no accident that islands prove central to the experiments in both texts. As Frank Manuel observes, "the early utopia was usually restricted to an island or similarly isolated environment"; such twentieth- and twenty-first-century fictions as Huxley's *Island* (1962) and the recent blockbuster film *The Island* (2005) testify to the persistence of the convention of utopian insularity.[35] Even the Brave New World, Huxley's utopia-gone-global, derives its forms and mores from insular models, including Ireland, Cyprus, Samoa, and the Trobriand Islands. Scholars have also noted islands' conscription as "natural" laboratories by a multitude of (especially Western) scientific, economic, and military endeavours, from evolutionary biology to nuclear development. Thus, Charles Darwin garnered crucial insights into the evolutionary process by studying the biota of islands – the Galapagos, the Falklands/Malvinas, Mauritius. The foundational ethnographies of Bronislaw Malinowski and Margaret Mead focus on the island societies of New Guinea and Samoa. Between 1946 and 1980, more than two hundred nuclear bombs and devices were detonated in the Pacific, many near inhabited islands. More positively, as Richard Grove has argued, the realization that "the economic demands of colonial rule on previously uninhabited island colonies threatened degradation" sparked conservationist practices and ideologies.[36] Islands don't then just happen to preponderate in novels about utopian reproductive projects, providing a picturesque backdrop against which the real action of remoulding humanity can be observed taking place. Rather, the peculiar character of island space enables Nigel Hendon and Dr. Moreau to manage – or at least contemplate managing – the relationships a community contracts with its "good" and "bad" pasts. Recall Karl Pearson's uncertainty as to whether a "biological science of the evolution of human societies" is possible: can we place ourselves, he asks, "outside the community of which we are a part?" Not only do islands manifest (ostensibly) self-evident "outsides," but they manifest *as* self-evident "outsides" (to the mainland), rendering thinkable what to Pearson seemed an impossible act of separation.

In *Brave New World*, Utopia relocates reproduction from the body to the laboratory in order to manage the transmission and expression of heredity in its citizenry. In addition, however, the sterility of the laboratory provides a model for Utopia's ruthless approach to those things – mothers, the past, the Savage Reservation – it considers undesirable. In the interwar years, Christina Cogdell notes, cleanliness "often referred as much to having a pure hereditary lineage and unblemished moral record as to keeping oneself and one's home free from dirt."[37] If one's house could not be relied upon to keep itself clean, why should the national gene pool not undergo a thorough cleansing? Terms such as "racial hygiene" and "ethnic cleansing" point to the genocidal uses of the discourse of cleanliness, which has been mobilized in the service of programs of human experimentation, sexual violence, and mass murder. Even Wells's Dr. Moreau describes pain as "a bath" (59). Island geography performs a similar function, alibi-ing, by naturalizing, the acts of selection and excision through which Moreau and Nigel Hendon pursue their dreams of population perfection. In the "Groundwork of Eugenics," Pearson insists that

> the conception of the destruction of the less fit as a beneficent factor of human growth must become part of our mental atmosphere, we must look upon it as the chief cause of the mental and physical growth of mankind in the past, not as a blind and hostile natural force carelessly crushing the single life, but as the source of all that we value in the intellect and physique of the highest type of mankind to-day ... There are religious faiths which look upon pain as a divinely administered good – as a beneficial discipline. May not something of the same kind be realised by those who stand on the firm platform of evolutionary science in the fiftieth year of its life? (23–4)

Destruction, wrote Pearson's American contemporary Charles Davenport, is a "conflagration" clearing the way for new growth.[38] Strikingly, in these excerpts, violence emerges as a natural event, akin to a divine visitation; violence is something that happens to people (or animals) rather than something people do. Siting his experiment in bio-social engineering on an island allows Nigel to displace responsibility for his calculations of fitness onto geography: lacking the Brave New Worldians' ability to manipulate genetic material directly, Nigel can simply leave the unfit behind, on the mainland. With the exclusion of the "less fit" re-imagined as the product of geographical circumstance, and their destruction re-articulated as a natural event, the violence of eugenicist selection may be denied or disavowed – for a time.

Striving to distance "the earthly paradise" from the corruption of provenance, Nigel insists, like the Brave New World, that civilization is sterilization (42). Geography frees Nigel to celebrate the immaculate origins of his "little Eden" (10). The past nonetheless remains recalcitrant. As David Cahan has shown, it is impossible to protect laboratories permanently against the threat of disturbance; the *cordons sanitaires* that help define laboratory space must rather be made and remade.[39] Containment comes no more naturally to islands. Because the congruities between island space, laboratory space, and utopian space appear so self-evident, scholars do not often explain why islands should function as "natural" laboratories and sites of utopian development, and thus fail to observe that they in fact do not, but must rather be made so to function. Greg Dening, an anthropologist and historian of the Pacific, has theorized islands' curious ambiguity as at once diverse and bounded, vulnerable and impregnable, through the near-binary of islands and beaches. The "beach" is that "marginal space where everything is relativized a little, turned around, where tradition is as much invented as handed down, where otherness is both a new discovery and a reflection of the old, where expediency is likely to prevail rather than principle."[40] The beach is a boundary place, a place of "beginnings and endings," and a liminal space, where encounter and exchange provoke and disarm the very effort to draw boundaries.[41] Meanwhile, Dening's islands, "less physical than cultural," connote closed systems of meaning.[42] The "islands" "men and women make by the reality they attribute to their categories, their roles, their institutions" include, I want to suggest, islands themselves.[43] By definition, all islands are insular, that is, island-like. But not all islands, and not only islands, are insular in the more colloquial sense of seeming narrow, cut off, and isolated. Some islands are beaches. Indeed, writers from the archipelagos of the Pacific and the Caribbean have tended to refuse dominant Anglo-European narratives of island isolation and confinement, foregrounding instead narratives of transoceanic migration and inter-island contact.[44] Thus, islands become "islands" in Dening's sense only through a never-ending process of filtering, purging, and excising.

More locates the eponymous society of his *Utopia* on an island. It appears, however, that the land was not always surrounded by the ocean.

> But Utopus, who conquered the land and named it after himself (for before that time it had been called Abraxa) and who brought its crude and rustic mob to a level of culture and humanity beyond almost all other mortals, after he won the victory at his first assault, had a channel cut fifteen miles wide at the point where the land adjoined the continent, and thus caused the sea to flow all around the land.[45]

That Utopia's origins can be traced to an act of severance enabled by the violence of conquest forcibly suggests the temporal paradox of utopia, which is that it both is, and cannot be, isolated from the contamination of the past. The fate of Moreau's Beast People dramatizes this irrepressibility of origins. Within Moreau's laboratory enclosure, elaborately sealed against the possibility of intrusion and outbreak, humanity is produced through the purgation, the cutting away, of animal flesh(liness). Yet despite Moreau's initial sense that "these creatures of mine" are "indisputable human beings," he soon observes "one animal trait, then another, creep[ing] to the surface and star[ing] at me" (58–9). Moreau must continually re-establish the laboratory as an immaculate zone by expelling those Beast People whose humanity falters. In the end, even this is not sufficient to sustain his purgative project. As we shall see, a similar recrudescence threatens the utopian enclaves in *Prelude to Christopher* and *Brave New World*. The "island" of utopia is thus revealed as, to quote Louis Marin, less "a point of origin [than] a fiction of origin."[46]

Reproducing the Nation

That the fictionality of the utopian origin should have something to tell us about conceptions of the nation is not perhaps obvious. After all, both Nigel Hendon and Dr. Moreau are forced to pursue their utopian experiments in exile. In Wells's novella, Moreau arrives on Noble's Isle fleeing scandal in England: Prendick recalls that Moreau, a "prominent and masterful physiologist, well known in scientific circles for his extraordinary imagination and his brutal directness in discussion," was forced to leave England following a gruesome exposé of his "wantonly cruel" methods (23). In *Prelude to Christopher*, Nigel seeks to distance Ti-Noon from the degenerate Australian mainland, only to watch as the mainland repudiates in its turn the extremity of his eugenicist gamble. Following the collapse of the settlement on Ti-Noon, Nigel, only ever at most a reluctant patriot, returns to Australia a reprobate. The Brave New World, meanwhile, is resolutely post-national.

Easier to see, thanks to the island excursions that drive the narrative action in *The Island of Dr. Moreau* and *Prelude to Christopher*, is the entanglement of utopian with colonial projects. The search for islands emerges as a central theme in the history of European expansion.[47] As Elizabeth DeLoughrey points out, "countless explorers directed their efforts towards the discovery of the 'Antilles': utopian counter-islands or ante-islands that … offer a deeper historical model for what Antonio Benítez-Rojo refers to as the 'repeating island' (1992)."[48] Conceived as utopian sites of progress, development, and Anglo-European futurity, the settler colonies seem to belong to a different imaginary than the one DeLoughrey outlines in her discussion of the Caribbean and Pacific. Still, that the island nations of New Zealand and Australia have enjoyed reputations as "the social laboratories of the world" confirms conceptions of the Pacific as a site of fantasy.[49] Where New Zealand writer Jane Mander saw "utopia materialised" and her compatriot Pember Reeves heaven on earth, others discerned a "Better Britain"; James Belich follows the lead of fellow historian J.G.A. Pocock in describing the settler colonies as "neo-Britains."[50] Michel-Rolph Trouillot notes that *Utopia* appeared in the same year as the first "paraethnographic account of the Antilles," a fortuitious "chronological convergence" that symbolizes, he says, "a thematic correspondence now blurred by intellectual specialization and the abuse of categories."[51] The coincidence of *Utopia*'s contemporaneity with the *Decades* of Pietro Martire d'Anghiera has implications for literary history, surfacing the shared desire that links the nascent genres of the utopia and ethnography. But it also configures the imperial venture as utopian in impulse, drawing attention to the longing for a better (or at least different) way of life that drives some of its manifestations, as well as the closures these perpetuate in pursuit of perfection. What might we now make of Leslie Fiedler's description of the Europeans sent across the ocean by "a dream of innocence … to build a new society" as "carriers of utopia"?[52]

Elaine Showalter has drawn attention to the colonial dimensions of Moreau's experiment, identifying "the Beast People who do all the labor of the island" with "the colonized, the oppressed slaves who revolt against their master."[53] Noting that Dr. Moreau is accompanied to the island by six "Kanakas" whose invisible labour – "the stores were landed and the house was built" – erects Moreau's compound, Cyndy Hendershot emphasizes the Kanakas' role as colonial subjects who come, in a sort of object lesson, to be replaced by the (initially) more promising, because non-reproductive, Beast People (56).[54] I want to qualify this interchangeability of Kanaka with Beast, of the colonial with the utopian endeavour by suggesting that Moreau's utopian experiments at once replicate and derealize colonial projects of man-making. Wells juxtaposes Moreau's regime of pain, which inscribes humanity literally onto his subjects' bodies, with the civilizing mission undertaken by the Kanakas, who assume the colonizer's responsibility of teaching the Ape-Man religion, as well as basic literacy and construction skills. On the one hand, Moreau's experiments reproduce, in brutally material and hence hyper-visible terms, the colonial work of man-making. In addition, they proliferate structures of oppression, as the erstwhile colonized – the Kanakas – take up the colonial work of man-making in their turn. On the other hand, Moreau's experiments bespeak a determination to improve upon such colonial strategies of reformation, which inevitably prove dissatisfactory.

It is impossible to accurately pinpoint the origins of the Kanakas. "Kanaka" is the native Hawaiian (Kanaka Maoli) word for "(hu)man" or "people." However, by the nineteenth century, "kanaka" had come to designate all Pacific Islanders regardless of origin. It was especially popular as a term for Pacific Islanders working, often under compulsion, on the sugar plantations of Queensland. So what originated as a locally specific term for "human" was transformed into a strategically non-specific term for a spectrum of peoples whose full humanity was (thereby made) open to question.[55] Moreau's account of the expedition's arrival on the island repeats this obfuscation of kanaka specificity: Moreau "remember[s] the green stillness of the island and the empty ocean about us, as though it were yesterday. The place seemed waiting for me" (56). The slip from "us" to "me" is telling. Although Moreau invests his island arrival with a felicitous serendipity – "the place seemed waiting for me" – and stresses the region's visible lack of animal or aquatic life – he notes the stillness of the land, the emptiness of the ocean – it's hardly plausible that he'd manage to stumble across this superbly suitable piece of real estate without Kanaka guidance. The island, rather than "waiting" to be discovered in an "empty ocean," actually circulates in global networks of trade, governance, and cultural production. Who is to say how "Noble's Isle" figures in the Kanakas' map of the Pacific, what Epeli Hau'ofa calls "our sea of islands"?[56] Moreau's utopian experimentalism depends on a set of relations that is always being obscured and that is finally, conveniently, obliterated by the Beast People. The suppression that Moreau explicitly strives for – "I will burn out all the animal" – both repeats and conceals another: the eradication of the Kanakas. One could say, then, that the pliable Beast People do not replace the Kanakas as colonial subjects inasmuch as they promise to eliminate the need for messy intercultural contact altogether. Why hire Kanakas, after all, when you can make Beast People? At the same time, I want to insist on the colonial uses of this sort of (attempt at) transcendence, which I read as only an extreme form of what we might call colonial amnesia, that is, the will to forget that allows a British scientist to see, in an "empty ocean," an island "waiting for me."

Until recently, Rod Edmond and Vanessa Smith observe, Western voyagers "thought of islands in terms of paradise or utopia, either an ideal inhabited island or else an empty island on which to start again."[57] If Edmond and Smith are correct to suggest that the utopian endeavour requires an *empty* island on which to start again, categorizing an island as utopic may constitute an example of utopian closure to the extent that it figures the island, more or less meretriciously, as empty. Would-be colonists have tended to define "inhabitants" rather narrowly, disregarding non-human forms of life, including, as the fiction of terra nullius makes clear, those humans whose mode of inhabitation they deem unsatisfactory. In *The Tempest* (1611), Gonzalo's plans for the island presuppose both the empty canvas of the island and his own generative presence therein.[58] And yet, Gonzalo's island is already inhabited, claimed by a series of usurped and usurping figures: Ariel, Sycorax and Caliban, and Prospero and Miranda. The emptiness of "his" island is produced and re-produced through suppressing its history as a site of encounter between Indigenous and non-Indigenous people. That it is to *start again* that the utopian endeavour requires an empty island points, meanwhile, to the iterative character of colonial settlement projects, the way in which, as Elizabeth DeLoughrey puts it, "Great Britain is discursively refashioned as a repeating island throughout its colonies in the Caribbean and Pacific, as suggested by the toponyms New Albion, New Britain, New Hebrides, New Ireland, and 'Little England,' or Barbados."[59] Repetition might indicate prior success: why not do again what worked so well before? As Moreau reminds us, however, one also "start[s] again" those ventures that look like failing: "each time I dip a living creature into the bath of burning pain, I say: this time I shall burn out all the animal, this time I will make a rational creature of my own." Either way, the new venture is a do-over rather than a continuation of the old, which it effectively effaces in what appears as yet another instance of utopian closure.

In the last section of *The Island of Dr. Moreau*, Prendick flees Moreau's island, but for England rather than another antipodean island. Arrived home, Prendick pens the narrative published as *The Island of Dr. Moreau*. A preface appended by Prendick's nephew notes that the veracity of his uncle's narrative remains in doubt because the island cannot be located with any certainty:

> The only island known to exist in the region in which my uncle was picked up is Noble's Isle, a small volcanic islet, and uninhabited. It was visited in 1891 by H.M.S. *Scorpion*. A party of sailors then landed, but found nothing living thereon except certain curious white moths, some hogs and rabbits, and some rather peculiar white rats. No specimen was secured of these. So that this narrative is without confirmation in its most essential particular.

And yet, the island of Dr. Moreau cannot simply be dismissed as "out of human knowledge," a fantasy space remote from the metropolitan civilization of turn-of-the-century England. Unaccountably convinced that the men and women he meets in the London streets are "another, still passably human, Beast People, animals half-wrought into the outward image of human souls" who would "presently begin to revert," Prendick flees London as he once fled Moreau's island (102). This time, he retreats to the English countryside. Underscoring Prendick's centrality to the narrative as a whole, the novella's English ending suggests that *The Island of Dr. Moreau* is ultimately less about the impact of colonial projects of man-making on the colonized than it is about the fate of Britishness (or Englishness) in the volatile theatre of encounter.

Here I want to return to the proposition with which I opened this section, only to dismiss it: that the fictionality of the utopian origin has something to tell us about conceptions of the nation. To assume that the nation falls into that class of things utopian thinkers and makers aim to render anachronistic is, I think, to repeat the error of reading the (ex)islic geography of utopia as a point of origin rather than, following Marin, a fiction of origin. In *Imaginary Communities*, Phillip Wegner tracks "a continuous exchange of energies between the imaginary communities of the narrative utopia and the imagined communities of the nation-state, the former providing one of the first spaces for working out the particular shapes and boundaries of the latter."[60] Thus, for instance, the "cut-offness" of the utopian enclave also characterizes the nation state insofar as the latter is normatively imagined as territorially bounded. (In fact, Zygmunt Bauman concludes, the utopia is so much a product of the way in which the nation-concept articulates territoriality with sovereignty that the concept lacks purchase in a world where "territorially-confined powers look anything but sovereign.")[61] This is not to say, as Wegner sometimes implies, that utopia is not also about empire. Rather, colonial relationships organize – and are organized by – the "exchange of energies" between the nation and the utopia. Wegner argues that "More's Utopia represents an England transformed and not," as other critics have argued, More's attempt to come to terms with the newness of the New World.[62] Utopia may "really" be here rather than, as it appears, there, a vision of the Old World rather than the New. What, then, is accomplished by the move to a New World setting? How is Britain constituted through being translated? What does it mean, conversely, when a society clearly located in the New World can be read as representing Britain and not a skewed version, even, of itself? For if More's New World Utopia represents an England transfigured, it is at the cost of not representing its New World self (or selves), as well as the relations of power that make such a displacement thinkable. Notably, Jameson derives the closure of primitivism, which remakes (colonized) cultures as, in the words of James Buzard, "the utopian preserves of disaffected moderns," from the same utopian root as the closure of nationalism.[63] What More's bifurcated utopian geography suggests, however, is that the closure of nationalism sometimes depends upon the closure of primitivism (and, perhaps, vice versa).

In the eighteenth century, writes historian Kathleen Wilson, the "circulated stories of [Cook's] voyages to the South Pacific" renewed "an important component of English ethnicity – that of England as a unique 'island race' – ... as central to Britain's national identity and imperial mission."[64] The island society of England (or Britain) could be compared with other island societies – Māori, Tahitians, Nuu-chal-nuth – and the comparison used "to promote the idea that humankind had risen stage by stage from a lower to higher form of existence, a progression in which primitive peoples demonstrably lagged behind."[65] The supposed backwardness of Pacific island peoples would later come to be seen – by some – as a virtue, a measure of the enviable degree to which they had managed to escape modernity and its alienations.[66] Thus revalued, the imputed lushness of Pacific spaces and indolence of Pacific peoples combined to transform the Pacific into "a place of dreams."[67] Through the exoticisms of disdain and longing, Trouillot argues, "Savagery [is transformed] into Sameness by way of Utopia."[68] To be sure, the genealogy that links the spatial utopia with the exotic travel narrative, seeding utopias in the Pacific or the Caribbean or the Americas, draws attention to the routed and uneven history of nation formation. At the same time, utopian secessionism obscures the networks in which nation states are actually embedded. Re-imagined along utopian lines through a kind of spatial hygiene, the nation is cleansed of its origins in the difference of intra-imperial encounter and comparison. Or almost. For even as texts like *Utopia* work to render difference as sameness, Turtle Island as the New World, Barbados or Ichirouganaim as Little England, the re-presentation is never complete. There is always some difference left over.

Thus, in *The Island of Dr. Moreau*, anxiety builds about how and whether Britishness can survive being reproduced globally, culminating in a (re)turn towards insularity. Wells's narrator witnesses the Beast People's reawakening into beastliness, which is confirmed by the murder of Moreau and Montgomery and accompanied by the accidental firing of the doctor's laboratory enclave. Although Prendick is horrified by the Beast People's regression, in fact, he not only enables but participates in it. It is, for instance, Prendick who, believing the Beast People to be men whom Moreau has enslaved and "infected with some bestial taint," fatally undermines Moreau and Montgomery's aura of invulnerability by revealing "that [they] could be killed" (49). That Prendick should confuse outcomes with origins, or at least hint at the difficulty of distinguishing neatly between the two, isn't surprising, since Prendick's own origins are suspect. As an "uninvited" guest whose presence on the island is only grudgingly agreed to by Moreau, Prendick represents the threat of an unsympathetic world (21). For this reason, his knowledge of Moreau's activities, like his access to the compound, must be judiciously controlled. But Prendick is also a shipwreck survivor: his narrative begins with an evasive account of his eight-day sojourn aboard an ill-provisioned dinghy, during which he is spared the horror of cannibalism only by the conveniently accidental deaths of his fellow survivors. Rescued by Montgomery and the crew of the *Ipecacuanha*, Prendick is dogged by allegations of cannibalism. Montgomery longs "to hear how you came to be alone in the boat"; upon arriving at Moreau's island, the captain of the *Ipecacuanha* dumps his passengers and cargo and so, he says, "clear[s] his ship" of "beasts and cannibals, and worse than beasts" (4; 14).

The suspicion with which Prendick is regarded suggests that the line between the beastly and the human is neither so easily nor so definitively drawn as Moreau, for one, would like. Hence, Moreau finds that his "man-making" efforts must target humans as well as beasts (54). Moreau imagines that he can "burn out all the animal" through the infliction of pain (59). Pain also seems to stand in for what is being purged, for the animal past. But as Moreau tells Prendick, "so long as visible or audible pain turns you sick, so long as your own pains drive you, so long as pain underlies your propositions about sin, so long, I tell you, you are an animal, thinking a little less obscurely what an animal feels" (54). Since "this store men and women set on pleasure and pain" is "the mark of the beast from which they came," the beasts' immersion in the bath of pain is to some extent performed for the benefit of human observers like Prendick or Montgomery, who are to be made more "rational" (and hence more "human") by being made less vulnerable to the claims of pain (55). To Moreau, desensitization to the spectacle of pain appears as much an evolutionary advance as the transformations undergone by the beasts.

Prendick challenges even Moreau's progressivist narrative of beastly development, asking whether humans might not one day re-emerge as beasts. It is true that, contrary to what Prendick initially believes, Moreau has vivisected animals, not humans. But Prendick's reasoning – "they talk, build houses, cook. They were men" – also contains a germ of truth: they were men, however briefly and unsatisfactorily (50). In a similar way, it doesn't matter whether Prendick's readiness to join the Beast People in their recitation of "the Law" signals, as he claims, the "contagion of these brute men" or the degradation already evinced in the primal dinghy scene, when Prendick comes near to drinking human blood (43). What matters is precisely that it isn't clear whether Prendick is the source or unfortunate victim of a contagious beastliness; what matters is the reality of indiscriminate, ubiquitous contagion. That uncertainty is what constitutes the mark of the beast. If we don't know where anything is coming from, how can we know what to excise? With his unreliable memory, his recurrent feeling of having "already encountered" each startling new thing, Prendick unsettles the belief in the possibility of beginning afresh, of expunging the past, of pinpointing, even, what needs to be expunged, that underwrites Moreau's gruesome experiment (6).

Peter Hulme has shown how the gradual metamorphosis of "cannibal" from a term designating an Indigenous people of the Caribbean to a figure for savagery effectively refracted European anxieties about the savagery of colonialism.[69] Thus, while Prendick's descent into "dumb, quadrupedal, hairy," and potentially cannibalistic animality signals his corruption in and by an alien environment – he's gone native – it also testifies to the always-already presence of the beast within, troubling the taxonomic and dichotomous logics that underwrite man-making projects like Moreau's (97). We might understand this ubiquity of the beastly in evolutionary or existential terms as the common inheritance of humanity, that "remote kinship" whose claims so fascinate Charlie Marlow in *Heart of Darkness*.[70] In contrast, Hulme's work encourages us to read Prendick's latent cannibalism as the sign of a ravening violence that is not innate but rather historical, a defining feature of modern European imperialism. In *The Island of Dr. Moreau* as in *Heart of Darkness*, narratives that position metropolitan subjects as the victims of contaminating environments co-exist with narratives that position metropolitan subjects as sources of contamination. Indeed, self-consciousness appears as a kind of contamination, a disease endemic to colonial spaces and situations.

In returning to England, Prendick strives to suppress the (contaminating) knowledge of his own contamination by exiting the revelatory space of the contact zone. As Carey Snyder notes, that "Prendick does not [in the end] set off to explore new lands and cultures," instead cloistering himself from "the possibility of any human encounters," constitutes one of Wells's most significant revisions of the adventure script.[71] Back in England, Prendick dedicates his life to reading, to conducting experiments in chemistry, and to the study of astronomy, asserting, in an echo of Moreau, that "whatever is more than animal within us must find its solace and its hope" in the "vast and eternal laws of matter" (104). With Moreau's example burned into his memory, Prendick yet retains enough faith in the laboratory to end his days braced by its illusion of antiseptic control. This is in many ways a puzzling outcome. Has Prendick failed to understand the lessons of his own narrative, the dangers that attend Moreau's quarantine-and-cure approach to the animal within? Are we meant to disdain Prendick's horror of Londoners as the singular mania of a traumatized kook? Or does Wells mean us to celebrate Prendick's pastoral solution? In fact, Prendick's obsessions are not quite Moreau's: his experiments are analytical rather than productive, dedicated to understanding rather than altering the operations of matter. It is possible that, for Prendick, Moreau fails not in his commitment to experimental rigour, but in not being rigorous enough. "Each time I dip a living creature into the bath of burning pain, I say: this time I shall burn out all the animal, this time I will make a rational creature of my own": despite being represented as a fiery purification, a biological scorched earth, Moreau's "humanising process" entails grafts and transfusions, admixture, adulteration, and miscegenation (50). Like Moreau, Prendick sees immurement as a necessary condition for human advancement. However, his retreat to the English countryside and to consideration of "the laws of matter" bespeaks a more rigorous devotion to purity, the conviction that civilization is (to quote Huxley's Utopians) sterilization and not the cross-fertilizations that accompany human contact, interracial, interspecies, or otherwise. Where, for Moreau, humanity is to be secured through the encounter with – and forced assimilation of – difference, Prendick believes that humanity can emerge only, if at all, through the contemplation of English nature, physical and psychological.

Prendick's utopian project may be doomed before it even begins. The beastly contagion whose spread he both records and facilitates effectively collapses the distance between London and the island of Dr. Moreau: why should he find safety from his own cannibalism in London any more than in the Pacific? Still, Prendick's retreat is worth highlighting because it anticipates the "turn" in twentieth-century conceptions of Britishness delineated by scholars such as Alison Light and Jed Esty. According to Fredric Jameson, imperialism involves an extenuation of national life, as "a significant structural segment of the economic system as a whole is relocated elsewhere, beyond the metropolis, outside of the daily life and existential experience of the home country."[72] In the British imperial instance, national identity was also in a sense relocated, since Britain did not officially discriminate between subjects born in the British Isles and subjects born or naturalized in British overseas territories until the 1960s, well into the era of decolonization. It is Jed Esty's wager that British divestment must therefore have affected (British-born) Britons' experience of national life. Imperial diminishment, he argues, permitted – or forced – national consolidation; with British economic, political, and cultural resources less and less diverted (or, of course, supplemented) overseas, a truly national culture might be (re) discovered, compact, independent, knowable, at home. Thus, in their late writings, modernists like Forster, Woolf, and Eliot "absorbed the potential energy of a contracting [i.e., decolonizing] British state and converted it into the language not of aesthetic decline but of [English] cultural revival."[73] Alison Light discerns a similar, essentially conservative, concern with Englishness in the interwar fiction of women writers like Agatha Christie and Daphne du Maurier.[74] Esty and Light seek to backdate, as it were, the "anthropological turn" that "Colin MacCabe, following a more conventional periodization, describes as having made postwar English culture into 'an object of study like any other, privileged only by historical accident and not by some immanent qualities.'"[75] Intriguingly, James Buzard has identified in Victorian fiction an auto-ethnographic project similarly devoted to locating and localizing Britishness (or Englishness).[76] Here the impetus is not the necessity of coming to terms with imperial decline and the loss of colonial resources, but rather the sense that imperial success is stretching Britishness nearly to the point of dissolution. As the "anthropological turn" recedes into the nineteenth century, we need not conclude that Esty and MacCabe are wrong, or that the phenomenon resists historical explanation altogether. I see instead a multiplicity of "turns," as Britishness is alternately particularized and universalized, localized and diffused, not always in accordance with the changing fortunes of empire.

It makes sense that the contraction of Britishness as a category of identity conferring particular rights and privileges should have been formalized around the middle of the twentieth century, in response to the accelerated post-war pace and scale of political decolonization and global migration: in 1971, hoping to reduce the number of "coloured" migrants seeking entry to Britain, the British government introduced legislation that differentiated among British subjects based on their degree of "belonging" to the United Kingdom. Still, the relationship between the contraction of Britishness as "a territory of affect" (the term is Ian Baucom's) and the contraction, real or prospective, of British territorial sovereignty is not a simple one.[77] Although the British empire underwent no significant diminution in the last decade of the nineteenth century – quite the opposite, in fact – contemporary observers expressed unease about its present impact and future prospects. The Second Boer War (1899–1901) aroused anxieties about the fitness, physical and otherwise, of the British populace that also resonate throughout a text like *Heart of Darkness*. In *Imperialism*, J.A. Hobson implies that Britishness cannot be reproduced just anywhere, and certainly not in places currently inhabited by individuals "destitute of real power of self-government" and unsuitable for "genuine white settlement of any magnitude" (328). Every enlargement of Great Britain in the tropics is," he warns, "a distinct enfeeblement of true British nationalism" (362). In *The Island of Dr. Moreau*, fear of imperial entropy and decline drives Edward Prendick to rethink Britishness along emphatically post-imperial, insular lines. Prendick's solution to the puzzle of British identity, its status as a simultaneously national and imperial commodity, may not signal a definitive shift in metropolitan conceptions of Britishness, but it does anticipate the legislative denouements of the later twentieth century, which I treat in greater depth in the final chapter of *Better Britons*.

It is possible to read in the Brave New World's insular turns a similar geopolitical motif. For it is not true that there is nothing "outside" Utopia. Huxley's utopian enclave is not quite coextensive with the globe. In the second act of the novel, Lenina Crowne and Bernard Marx travel to the New Mexico Savage Reservation, where they meet John, a blonde, blue-eyed man who is the son of Thomas, the Hatchery Director, and a Brave New World woman called Linda. Twenty-five years previously, Thomas had taken Linda to visit the Reservation; when she disappeared, Thomas was forced to leave her behind. Stranded without access to an Abortion Centre, Linda gave birth to John. Sensing an opportunity to revenge himself on the scrupulous Director, who has threatened his difficult employee with transfer to Iceland, Bernard convinces Linda and John to return to the Brave New World. Here, as Mother and Savage, they cause a sensation that recalls the historical exhibition of such "savages" as Rebecca Rolfe (Matoaka or Pocahontas), the Raiatean Mai (known in Britain as Omai), and the "Hottentot Venus." It is in this encounter between John Savage and the Utopian couple, between Reservation and Utopia, that the novel contracts its uneasy debt to *The Tempest*. Steeped in the Shakespearian canon – at the age of twelve, he is given *The Complete Works of Shakespeare* by his mother's lover Popé – Huxley's Savage greets the prospect of visiting London with Miranda's famous exclamation: "O brave new world that has such people in it" (139). As the child deprived of his birthright (including, ironically, the right not to be birthed) only to be confronted, years later, by the glittering spectacle of his mother's lost civilization, John plausibly assumes Miranda's mantle. That we may consequently locate Shakespeare's enchanted island in the Savage Reservation shows Huxley surprisingly attuned to the colonial and specifically New World resonances that have occupied latter-day readers of the play.[78]

Initially, the New Mexico Savage Reservation appears to function as Utopia's ghastly, unassimilable other. As the narrative unfolds, however, it becomes evident that the Reservation might more accurately be seen as Utopia's double. Thus, like the utopia, the Reservation is defined by its boundedness. The boundaries of the Reservation are demarcated by "upward of five thousand kilometers of fencing at sixty thousand volts" arranged in straight lines, or what the narrator calls "the geometrical symbol of triumphant human purpose" (101; 105). The mesa on which stands the pueblo of Malpais is "like a ship becalmed in a strait of lion-coloured dust" (107). As the Reservation Warden informs Lenina, individuals born within this double enclosure "are destined to die there" (102). Since to "touch the fence is instant death," there is "no escape from a Savage Reservation" except by air; free movement across the line of progress is reserved for those coming from the outside, the "civilized" (102). Tourists like Bernard and Lenina are fascinated by the Indians' "superstitious" rituals, by the spectacle of their religious, disease-prone and viviparous lives, by their performance of the past. Although the Indians themselves resist the spectacularization of their lives, greeting the intruders with indifference, contempt, and outright hostility, they are nonetheless made to inhabit the hermetic time-space of a museum exhibit.

It is not obvious why the Brave New World should go to such lengths to preserve an (Old) New World reservation when it so readily resorts to the destruction of historical monuments. In the geography room at Eton (another "primitive" survival?), John learns that "a savage reservation is a place which, owing to unfavourable climatic or geological conditions, or poverty of natural resources, has not been worth the expense of civilizing" (162). In this definition, savage people become a savage place that the authorities may choose to civilize or not. What this slide between people and place leaves unclear is why the savage place must be maintained as a reservation for savage people. Why not remove and "civilize" the people, and leave the wasteland (if indeed it is of no conceivable use) untouched?

In fact, the weak logic John encounters at Eton stems from a grotesque historical amnesia that it is worth pausing to rectify. In the United States, expanding white settlement forced Indigenous peoples to establish considerably constricted homelands on reservations administered by the government, frequently located at great distance from traditional homelands, and vulnerable to further settler incursion. The administration of reservations was guided both by a desire to protect Indians from European interference and by assimilationist aims. Joseph Herring argues that it was never the intention of Indian removal policy "to exile Indians to desert wastelands," though one might be excused for thinking so, given settlers' persistent (and often successful) attempts to strip reservations of valuable resources such as timber.[79] Rather, as Melissa Meyer notes, "the assimilationists had always thought of Indian reservations as temporary phases in a process whereby American Indians," having tasted the benefits of the Euro-American education system and agrarian economy, would "meld completely into U. S. culture."[80] The legacy of the reservation system for Indians is mixed. Thomas Biolsi suggests that the Lakota Reservations at Pine Ridge and Rosebud "served as homelands or 'sustained enclaves' allowing the maintenance of modified traditional ways of life that would have been liquidated if the Lakota had been directly exposed to the market forces of the agrarian economy (assimilationist discourse notwithstanding)."[81] On the other hand, the current controversial practice of bioprospecting, in which researchers target isolated populations in search of new pharmaceuticals, rare genetic material, and insights into the workings of diseases such as diabetes, suggests the evolving possibilities for abuse the reservation system facilitates. Spokane/Coeur d'Alène writer Sherman Alexie's 1997 speculative poem sequence "The Farm" sketches a particularly horrifying scenario in which the bone marrow of American Indians is discovered to contain a cure for cancer. In response, the American president issues Executive Order 1492, which confines Indians to reservations and subjects them to an intensive program of breeding and marrow-milking. In this instance, the state's destructive investment in Indian cultural and biological purity coincides with and is enabled by its strict enforcement of reservation boundaries. Regardless of how one assesses the risks and possibilities of a reservation-based politics, all reservations, Huxley's included, bear the marks of a long history of encounter, conquest, and exchange. The Reservation Warden includes Spanish and Christianity in his list of the "extinct languages" and "monstrous superstitions" still spoken and professed on the Reservation, while the film John views in the Eton geography room records the (Spanish) signs of Christian missionary activity (103). The Brave New World nonetheless persists in characterizing the Savage Reservation as "a place which ... has not been worth the expense of civilizing," and so represses the extent to which a civilizing project – that is to say, colonialism – drove Indians onto reservations in the first place (162). Thus, the Reservation's significance rests not only in how it functions as a repository for the past and for superseded modes of temporal experience but also, perhaps paradoxically, in its dampened historicity, the appearance it gives of being static and unchanging. By preserving the Reservation as an ethnographic exhibit, the Brave New World stages this latest moment in an ongoing history of contestation and entanglement as an encounter with the new (old) and exotic. Stripped of its history, the Reservation, like Utopia itself, is radically decontextualized.

The Reservation's transmogrification from a civilizing space for uncivilized peoples into an essentially savage space only extends the Americas' long history of (re)discovery, the reiterated re-Newal of the (Brave) New World. As John Gillis points out, "because European voyagers had set out to recover an old world it took a long time before the notion of a New World sank in and the idea of recovery was replaced by the modern notion of discovery."[82] Even today, "first contact" remains a compelling fantasy peddled by anthropologists, tour companies, and environmentalists (among others). On the one hand, then, the emergent utopia of the Brave New World appears to have learned from "savage" societies as rendered by the closure of primitivism. Utopian sexuality is modelled on the promiscuity of Samoan and Trobriand Islander life (as described by Malinowski and Mead): "among the savages of Samoa, in certain islands off the coast of New Guinea," children tumble "promiscuously," and "nobody had ever heard of a father" (39). Details of Utopia's origins in the suppressed ventures of an unremembered colonialism emerge elsewhere in the novel. Mond informs John, for instance, that the Brave New World's commitment to a caste system and to the careful management of leisure was sharpened by failed experiments on the islands of Cyprus and Ireland, both erstwhile British colonies.[83] On the other hand, the closure of utopia turns out to depend on the closure of primitivism, the extent to which the messy history of cross-cultural encounter, exchange, and rule on display throughout the Savage Reservation can be sanitized, obscured. It is no accident that the Savage's arrival in the Brave New World surfaces the "discreditable" secrets of the past, as well as the past as secret (97).

Whether, like Moreau's utopian experiment, Utopia should be read as *in the first instance* a project of imperial disremembrance is, I think, not clear. It is interesting to note, however, just how much satirical animus Huxley reserves for the Savage and the Savage Reservation. Twenty-first-century readers are likely to find Utopian innovations in intimate and reproductive life less appalling than Huxley appears to think we should. Still, the narrative successfully evokes what Huxley elsewhere describes as the "horror" of Utopia through yoking these innovations to voracious consumerism, mindless presentism, and a rigidified system of social reproduction modelled on the Fordist assembly line ("Foreword" xvii). In *Brave New World*, Huxley offers a cautionary tale about the poisoned offerings of industrial modernity, which he codes as American.[84] At the same time, he warns against turning to the primitive in response. Critics have convincingly demonstrated Huxley's growing disenchantment with Lawrencian primitivism.[85] Thus, for example, the Brave New World's frenzied response to the Savage parodies D.H. Lawrence's faith in the redemptive power of America's "dark, aboriginal" spirit.[86] But even as Huxley's satire betrays something of how "the primitive" is made and consumed, his distaste for primitivism shades into a distaste for primitivized peoples and cultures.

I read *Brave New World*, then, as a utopian call to preserve Englishness from *both* industrial America, the America, that is, of Fordism and the consumer society, *and* primitive – that is to say, Indigenous – America, from the endless presents of future-oriented consumer capitalism and nostalgic primitivism alike. Of course, this is just the sort of preservation the novel otherwise intimates is impossible. For although John Savage performs "savagery," the savagery he performs isn't (only) the savagery of the caricatured native. John's mother Linda doesn't inspire the kind of Utopian interest John does, partly because she is a mother, an "obscenity," partly because she is grossly unattractive, but also because, we're told, "she wasn't a real savage, had been hatched out of a bottle and conditioned like any one else: so couldn't have really quaint ideas" (153). Although savagery implies the possession of "really quaint ideas," it inheres in the stigma of birth. If "civilization is sterilization," savages are not made but born – literally (110). Birthed, John threatens Utopia with the resurgent savagery of genealogy and reproducibility. As the Reservation Warden makes clear, however, all Reservation children "are born, yes, actually born" (102). Why then does Huxley go to the trouble of inventing a character with so complicated a parentage? John's whiteness matters, I want to suggest, insofar as it makes visible the biological as well as the cultural continuity Utopia has mostly done away with. In their conversations, Mustapha Mond introduces John, already familiar with Shakespeare, to an Anglo-American tradition of religious writing in the form of a vernacular Bible, Thomas à Kempis's *The Imitation of Christ*, and works by William James and Cardinal Newman. John's command of Shakespeare may appear to validate a primitivist understanding of culture: although it is Popé who gives John *The Complete Works of Shakespeare*, only John may make use of them, as though any successful claim to the cultural patrimony of the anglophone Atlantic must be biologically derived. Huxley fails to imagine, here, how the Indians might have made use of *The Complete Works*; John's whiteness tends to diminish the centrality of non-white and Indigenous actors, and hence of colonization itself, to the Reservation's history.[87] Nevertheless, because *The Complete Works* are discovered in the Antelope Kiva (or sacred chamber) by Popé rather than John, a cross-grain reading of *Brave New World* might re-render "Shakespeare" as a sign of encounter and (coerced) exchange. Like the invisible "half-breeds," John's complex origins insist on the history of incursion and visitation that has made the Reservation into a Reservation, the historicity that is denied in the old Etonian description of the Reservation as "a place which ... has not been worth the expense of civilizing" (103). His return to London, like Prospero's to Milan, or *The Tempest*'s to Europe, testifies in turn to the routedness of the Anglo-European tradition, its mobility and malleability, unsettling the closure of utopianism by disrupting the closure of primitivism. I don't know that Huxley is especially interested in what a latter-day scholar might term John's hybridity. Still, if *Brave New World* baulks at the Americanization of civilization, doubling down on the utopian project it in places condemns, the figure of the Savage lingers as a reminder that Englishness, far from "giv[ing] birth to itself," is the product of a "hiss hiss history happened overseas."[88]

Island Solutions

In the search for "an empty island on which to start again," it might have been hoped that Australia would suffice, utopia materialized. If the "whole process of settlement can be seen as a type of utopianism," Australians have nonetheless subsequently made many additional attempts to "put utopia in place," both in Australia and elsewhere.[89] *Prelude to Christopher* depicts one such effort. Nigel may deplore the claims of nationalism. But although Nigel's experiment takes place offshore, as it were, it isn't therefore disengaged from the utopian project of Australia. On the contrary: the Ti-Noon venture stages contemporary debates about the composition and character of the new Australian nation. Thus, for example, it is likely that Dark based Nigel Hendon's "paradise" on Cosme and New Australia, the experimental colonies established in Paraguay along broadly eugenicist lines by the Australian nationalist labour leader William Lane.[90] Although descendants of Lane's two hundred colonists still live in Paraguay, the experiment collapsed around 1904, twelve years after its inauguration. By delaying the foundation of her utopian settlement until 1910, Dark sets Ti-Noon on a collision course with the Great War, the crucible in which, it is often argued, Australian national identity was forged.

In 1915, five years after the colony's founding, news of the disastrous ANZAC landings at Gallipoli Cove crosses Ti-Noon's creamy beaches. Eager to return home to fight in the war, the colonists provoke a bloody confrontation with the pacifist Nigel that culminates in murder and the colony's dissolution. One could argue, to be sure, that the war only forces to the surface sentiments that have been percolating for years. When, at the crucial moment of confrontation, Nigel asks the mutineers to observe the conditions under which they joined the colony, one snarls, "You and your conditions! 'Mentally and physically fit!' What about your wife?" The colonist is referring to Linda's family history of insanity. According to Linda's biologist uncle Paul Hamlin, "My brother [Linda's father] has it in a particularly intense form. Our father, of whom you may have heard – his book on Eugenics is practically a classic – had no taint of it whatever; but *his* brother, my uncle, was, for a short time before his death, under restraint" (46; emphasis in original). Linda, Hamlin concludes, "is the final blossoming of all the Hamlins" (31). Informed of this genealogy just as he is on the verge of announcing the expedition to Ti-Noon, Nigel is torn: as Linda's lover, Nigel is convinced of her brain's present and "future normality," but "what I believe," he tells her, "isn't the point; I'm working on a theory, I'm taking science as my foot-rule. Scientifically you don't – you *can't* come up to the standard" (51; 91; emphasis in original). In the end, he allows Linda, last in a meticulously recorded line of lunatics, to join the "up to the standard," the "mentally and physically fit," on Ti-Noon (91). Although Nigel refuses to father her children, Linda's presence among the colonists not only breaches the *cordon sanitaire* through which the island experiment was to be maintained, but dents the principles that were supposed to have underwritten its creation. What does Linda's exhaustive knowledge of her family history – Linda's gloating guardian has carefully instructed her in reading "the family tree which he had so painstakingly compiled and so beautifully set out on a great sheet of yellowish parchment, with the names of the 'afflicted' in red ink, appearing like plague-spots here and there" – actually mean (35)? Is it certain that Linda's family history of insanity guarantees her own affliction? But if it does not, what justifies Nigel's eugenicist project? Linda's inclusion in the expedition to Ti-Noon thus highlights its vulnerability. It is the war, however, that catalyses its collapse. A colonist challenges Nigel, "There's a war, and your country's in it. Do you want to see it beaten? Haven't you any patriotism?" (163). But which country? Dark's colonists express their discontent with Nigel's regime by singing "Rule Britannia." At the same time, Gallipoli was memorialized as a specifically Australian calamity, and rapidly assumed the dimensions of a founding national myth. If settlers entered the war as Britons, they exited it as (to a degree) Australians. The war's arrival on Ti-Noon provokes Nigel's colonists to a nationalism increasingly Australian in orientation that Nigel experiences as murderous: in their desire to join the war effort, the colonists assassinate Nigel's friend Pen.

The war reveals the would-be makers of the "earthly paradise" to be in thrall to the past and to the Australian mainland, their progressive ambitions self-sabotaged (42). As he watches the mass of "picked human beings" beat a man to death, Nigel is

> frozen with horror of a knowledge you could not deny – that somewhere beneath the soundness of these picked human beings of yours a dark current ran silently, a blood-lust, a savagery, a sadistic joy in battle ... Even more destroying was the fury in yourself that made of you, for the first time, a slave to some almost prehistoric ancestry. You were not, any longer, that self which you had so jealously controlled. You were a male animal driven by a sole desire to kill. You were, God help you, what Linda feared to be, a homicidal lunatic. (68)

Nigel cannot escape the "fury in yourself," but he will not partake of the colonists' frenzied nationalism: patriotism, he exclaims, "is not enough" (163).

Nigel's disdain is reciprocated by the Australian public, which greets a post-war account of "his fantastic experiment" with outrage (71). Ti-Noon nonetheless enjoys a shadowy afterlife on the mainland. The action of *Prelude to Christopher* is divided between a present set in the small rural community of Moondoona and the past as it is recalled by Linda, Nigel, and Nigel's mother. Now home to the middle-aged Nigel and Linda, Moondoona remembers the scandal of Nigel's "Eugenics, his birth-control, his sex-hygiene," and is faintly, righteously disturbed by Linda's oddness (71). Yet respectable Moondoona, Linda says, is not so different from Ti-Noon. In the first place, the war that everyone celebrates has something in common with Nigel's island experiment, not so much its opposite as a close cousin. Although Nigel mourns what he sees as the war's dysgenic effect on population quality, he also envisions war as a sort of hothouse, a "manure-heap where the fine flowers of human behaviour" are forced and goaded, blooming gloriously until they die and fall back "into the filth that fed them" (178). The violence of war, in other words, offers a "short cut to a perfected humanity" for which the price is death (63). Still more significant is the Christopher whom the novel's title – *Prelude to Christopher* – announces to be forthcoming. Christopher isn't the name of the child Linda wants, the child she believes would cement her hold on normality. Rather, Christopher is the child the young nurse Kay dreams of having with Nigel, the child she seems likely to have following Linda's suicide at novel's end. Kay is "normal," leading Nigel's mother to hope that "still at this eleventh hour, his life might be mended, and led by Kay into quieter and more orthodox paths" (87). Linda too imagines Nigel finding "the rightful ending of his stormy life" in Moondoona, "growing things. Wheat and sheep; and children, with the blue-eyed nurse [Kay]" (173). In this projection of the novel and nation's linked futures, "growing things," especially children, strengthens the settlers' bond with the land. Dark's women suspect that "in *their* brains and bodies so irrevocably earth-chained, rather than in the soaring dreams of their menfolk, lay the ultimate salvation of the human race" (63; emphasis in original). Christopher may then be seen as a gendered rejoinder to the hothouse approach pursued by Moreau and Hendon. Yet although "growing things" is explicitly contrasted with Nigel's divergent experimental path, both advance a creed of normality and quietly uphold the importance of the cull. Since Nigel refuses to contemplate fathering either a legitimate child with Linda or an illegitimate child without her, Christopher's birth requires Linda's death; as the prelude to Christopher, Linda's suicide is the logical consequence – and cost – of Nigel's principles. Indeed, she has often imagined herself "cutting the thread of her own existence with the cool detachment of a scientist exterminating some dangerous bacterial growth" (202).

In this way, *Prelude to Christopher* draws attention to the high price assessed women by settler projects of nation building. It obscures almost totally the devastation levied on Indigenous peoples. That this is a significant omission is indicated by changes Dark made to the manuscript of *Prelude to Christopher*. First, she eliminated the suggestion that Ti-Noon is inhabited when Nigel's colonists first arrive, thereby freeing Nigel from the necessity of repressing this aboriginal inhabitation himself.[91] Second, she decided that Nigel would not explain his removal to Ti-Noon by asserting, "You can't build the ideal white race in a black man's country."[92] Dark's focus on a character with a family history of madness is era-appropriate, reflecting the preoccupation of many Australian eugenicists with the "problem" of feeble-mindedness. According to Jane Carey, Australian women eugenicists prioritized white racial improvement, "exhibiting remarkably little interest in the 'Aboriginal problem.'"[93] As Nigel's (excised) comment suggests, however, anxieties about whiteness cannot be comprehended outside of the colonial situation in which they arise and propagate. It is worth remembering, moreover, that whereas Australia never approved a policy of forcible sterilization for the "feeble-minded," Australian governments did target the sexual and reproductive lives of Indigenous people for intervention. This is the context in which *Prelude to Christopher* was written and published; this is the context that Dark deliberately obscures.

Recall Nigel's determination to leave the world behind "as if it were history, a legend of bad days long past" (49). By locating his eugenic experiment on an "uninhabited" island rather than on Australian soil, Nigel bypasses the problem of White Australia's black history altogether: on Ti-Noon, he is able to realize the fantasy of terra nullius, of settlement, that is, uncomplicated by the resistant presence of Indigenous peoples. Meanwhile, by choosing to leave unspoken the extent to which Nigel's quest to evolve a perfected humanity is driven by the exigencies of living in a "black man's country" – there remains only that passing mention of "half-caste children" – Dark isolates Nigel from the contemporaneous efforts of Australian administrations to "breed the colour" out of the nation (26). Where Nigel excises Aboriginals from his fantasy of the Australian nation, Dark tacitly excises the excision itself. Recovered, Dark's editorial decisions therefore specify – and duplicate – Nigel's flight from "history" as a flight from Australia's black history. In the end, then, *Prelude to Christopher* is haunted not so much by the threat Linda's genetic inheritance poses to the linked projects of eugenics and nationalism as by the broader significance of its suppression. Linda's (self-)excision both stands for and extravagantly obscures a reticence about the crisis of settler identity that motivates the expedition to Ti-Noon and the imperative to reproduce normality. How to build "the ideal white race in a black man's country"? It would be a mistake to see in Nigel's failure even to articulate his despair only a tacit admission of bafflement. This reticence, and indeed the novel's reticence about this reticence, are rather calculated, permitting a re-articulation of the state's embroiled utopianism that is the more characteristic, not to mention effective, for being disavowed and displaced. That Nigel turns to Ti-Noon in his quest to build "the ideal white race" suggests, in other words, both the weakness and the strength of Australian utopian nationalism. According to Elizabeth MacMahon, Australia's "island territories [have often] assume[d] the synechdochic function of representing the 'island' in the paradoxical locution of *island continent*."[94] In *Prelude to Christopher*, the island of Ti-Noon, and not only the colony it briefly shelters, simultaneously figure and light the way to Nigel's symptomatically repressed ideal, which is also the ideal of "breeding out the colour": an Australia delivered from its black history, that is, made insular.

In the literary texts examined here, utopian projects of reproductive reform do significant spatial work, charting new, insular, geographies of national belonging. Borrowing from Rod Edmond, I call these "island solutions."[95] Of course, island solutions do not belong in the realm of imaginative fiction alone. In 1973, the Australian prime minister Gough Whitlam offered control of the Torres Strait Islands to Papua New Guinea. Three decades later, Canberra, in a panic about refugee landings in the Torres Strait Islands, sought once again to eject the islands (and hence any refugees who might alight there in future) from national space by retracting Australia's territorial boundaries.[96] Britain too has resorted to island solutions. By redefining most British overseas subjects as (potential) immigrants, for instance, the Commonwealth Immigration Act of 1971 effectively ejected imperial space from what was thereby reclaimed as national space. In the next chapter, I take up a historical example contemporary with *Brave New World* and *Prelude to Christopher*: "breeding out the colour." No island removals were contemplated by advocates of the policy. And yet, "breeding out the colour" too constitutes a kind of island solution, I want to suggest, and not only insofar as it depended on, and even proliferated, the carceral geography of the Australian colonial state, which segregated black from white Australians via a variety of social, educational, and territorial projects. In the more recent examples cited above, spatial engineering converges with biosocial engineering as the threat subaltern contaminants pose the national body is countered through the simplification of national space. In pursuit of territorial legitimacy, "breeding out the colour" proposes to subject whiteness itself to a form of utopian closure. "You can't build the ideal white race in a black man's country," Nigel insists. Out of a "sea of black," some Australians nonetheless gambled, might emerge "an island of white."[97]

Chapter Two

Whiteness for Beginners: An Australian Experiment

It is difficult to make sense of "breeding out the colour," and not just because the policy was eliminationist in rhetoric and intent.[1] Most of the eugenicist programs implemented globally took a negative approach to improving racial health, restricting immigration, sterilizing the "feeble-minded," and promoting abortion (for some), all in the name of national fitness. To be sure, eugenicists came to play an important role in the development of marriage and family counselling services during the middle decades of the twentieth century.[2] Still, as an attempt to avert catastrophic reproductive outcomes by orchestrating desirable ones, "breeding out the colour" stands out. More striking yet is the way the policy harnesses miscegenation to the project of white supremacy. Racial theorists, including eugenicists, have tended to equate racial mixture with degeneracy. Miscegenation has sometimes been proposed as a solution to alleged crises of Indigenous decline or recalcitrance. In New Zealand, for instance, "the recommendation of miscegenation as a solution to racial [that is, Indigenous] decline seems to have been fairly common."[3] Conversely, late-nineteenth- and early-twentieth-century Brazilian thinkers framed miscegenation as a path to national whiteness. In both cases, however, what is known in the Brazilian context as the "whitening thesis" less encouraged systematic state-sanctioned miscegenation than explained what already seemed to be happening. If, as Thomas Skidmore points out, the "whitening ideology squared with one of the most obvious facts of Brazilian social history – the existence of a large 'middle caste,' generally called 'mulatto,'" Australia has never possessed a "middle caste" of individuals claiming mixed racial descent, making "breeding out the colour" a more radical, because more interventionist, proposition than *branqueamento*.[4]

Because "breeding out the colour" was proposed by unelected officials rather than any legislative body, historians have questioned the extent to which it can be held to reflect official or even mainstream Australian conceptions of whiteness, indigeneity, and national identity. That "breeding out the colour" was not implemented everywhere in Australia, but only in the frontier jurisdictions of Western Australia and the Northern Territory, appears to further diminish its significance as a government project of colonial governance and nation building. Indeed, "breeding out the colour" affected few Australians, Indigenous or otherwise, directly. Cecil Cook, who served as the Northern Territory's Chief Protector of Aboriginals between 1927 and 1939, claimed that during the first ten years of his tenure "between 40 and 50 coloured girls have married whites."[5] According to the annual reports filed by the administrator of the Northern Territory from 1931 to 1939, when the policy was quietly dropped (along with Cook himself), no more than seven such marriages were approved yearly in a population comprising (roughly) 4000 Europeans, 800 "Asiatics," 900 half-castes, and perhaps 20,000 Aboriginals.[6] On this point, it is instructive to compare "breeding out the colour" with the practice of removal, which gained traction in all regions of Australia, and remained operative as a program of enforced assimilation long after "breeding out the colour" was shelved. Reporting in 1997, the Australian Human Rights and Equal Opportunity Commission Inquiry into the Forced Separation of Aboriginal and Torres Strait Islander Children from Their Families calculated that from 1910 to 1970, "between one in three and one in ten Indigenous children were forcibly removed from their families and communities," to be fostered or adopted out, often to non-Indigenous families, or to be institutionalized.[7] In that time, the inquiry stressed, "not one Indigenous family has escaped the effects of forcible removal."[8] In the aftermath of the inquiry's report, *Bringing Them Home*, removal has emerged as a national trauma, the Stolen Generations among the most visible legacies of Anglo-Australian colonialism.

Why, then, should we care about "breeding out the colour"? "Breeding out the colour" is interesting and important, I argue, for precisely the reasons that it seems inconsequential. If it is tempting to dismiss "breeding out the colour" as the pet scheme of powerful crackpots, namely, Cecil Cook and his Western Australian counterpart Auber Octavius Neville, what does this tell us about how the work of governance, including attempts to govern (through) intimate relationships and experiences, entangles individuals with institutions, the personal with the official? If miscegenation seems a strange method of "realizing the objective of the conservative purist who demands an All White Australia," what does this "perversity," as Russell McGregor terms it, tell us about the whiteness of White Australia?[9] That the architects of "breeding out the colour" failed to achieve their stated aims does not mean that the policy has left no trace in the real. It may be that in attending to a narrow range of substantive effects – How many marriages did Cook oversee? Did generations of children progressively "whiten"? – we misrecognize the signs of a policy's failure and success.

Commentators have tended to frame removal as a program of "cultural extermination" and not, like "breeding out the colour," an attempt at biological absorption. Keith Windschuttle, whose 2002 book *The Fabrication of Aboriginal History* sets out to demonstrate that Australian scholars have routinely exaggerated and even invented the evidence of settler colonial violence, pooh-poohs the notion that "the removal of children was somehow part of the project for breeding out the colour. That was never true. As the words of the phrase said, it aimed to control breeding. It was solely a proposal about fostering the marriage of part-Aboriginal women to white men. It was not a policy to remove children, forcibly or otherwise."[10] But removal and "breeding out the colour" cannot be quarantined from one another in so literal-minded a way, especially since both target the sexual, reproductive, and familial lives of Indigenous people. This was well understood at the time. When, in 1934, the federal government announced that it was arranging for "fifty octoroons, sons and daughters of quarter-caste [Northern] Australian natives and white men" to be adopted by white families living in the southern cities, the National Council of Women of Australia wondered at a policy that would, it claimed, "ultimately allow [octoroon girls] to marry white people."[11] Writing in 1947, A.O. Neville made the connection between "breeding out the colour" and removal explicit, insisting that "the success of our plan of assimilation is [closely] allied with the question of who shall marry whom."[12] The line between absorption and assimilation, between a focus on "biology" and a focus on "what was inside people's heads," is less clear-cut than is commonly supposed, the logic of "breeding out the colour" lingering long after the policy itself became an embarrassment.[13] "Breeding out the colour" is no anachronism, a relic of older, more brutal forms of colonial governance, but a component – and an arguably key component at that – of Australian modernity.

In this chapter, then, I read photographs, newspaper articles, fiction, reports, and government memoranda in order to explore the ideas about whiteness, indigeneity, reproduction, national identity, governance, futurity, and the archive that underwrote "breeding out the colour." I begin by reading the archive of "breeding out the colour" for what it can tell us about how and with what consequences the state takes control of reproduction. How do individuals, texts, and institutions interact to produce a "state" that controls – or tries to control – reproduction? What are the mechanisms, conceptual, textual, and institutional, by which an individual's fantasies become official policy, an individual's actions the actions of that construct "the state"? How, conversely, is intimate life made into a site of state action? How do regimes of reproductive control organize the relationship between individual agents and institutional ones? In the second part of the chapter, I read the archive of "breeding out the colour" as elaborating a set of stories about whiteness, indigeneity, and settler colonialism, taking as my starting point the disavowals that allowed miscegenation to stand as the saviour of White Australia. Like the Immigration Restriction Act of 1901, which was used to prohibit Asian would-be immigrants from entering the country, "breeding out the colour" confirmed that racial others – Asians and, in this case, Aboriginals – had no place in the new nation, which was reserved for whites and those who could be made white. As first peoples, however, Aboriginals posed a different kind of challenge to the nation than did either Chinese or Japanese immigrants, threatening not only its racial integrity but its territorial sovereignty. As I show throughout the chapter, the way in which "breeding out the colour" figured whiteness and the whitening process worked – perversely – to suppress genealogically derived rights of belonging and, importantly, land ownership, thus strengthening settler claims to Australia against the argument of Aboriginal priority. Indeed, Indigenous priority and settler belatedness cease to matter at all, as the state retraces, on bodies this time instead of maps, the impeccable lying cartography of terra nullius.

In Their Own Words

Neville's plans were all talk.

Keith Windschuttle, "Manne Avoids the Real Debate"

You can meet a death just knowing the paper talk.

Kim Scott, *Benang*

Proposing that "insights into the social imaginaries of colonial rule might be gained from attending not only to colonialism's archival content, but to the principles and practices of governance lodged in particular archival forms," Ann Laura Stoler describes colonial archives as both "transparencies on which power relations were inscribed and intricate technologies of rule in themselves."[14] I thus begin my investigation of "breeding out the colour" with a reading of the government archive, showing how archival practices, and the practice of archiving itself, further the projects of reproductive control they are supposed only to document by turning private life into official business. The government archive of "breeding out the colour" makes visible the entanglement of the personal with the public, the intimate with the official, in a number of ways. I reflect, first, on the way in which the fantasies of someone like Cecil Cook achieve traction and authority as part of the process of becoming government policy, before exploring how and with what consequences the state makes the sexual, reproductive, and family lives of Indigenous people its business.

Although I also draw on manuscripts and documents housed by the National Library of Australia and the Australian Institute of Aboriginal and Torres

Strait Islander Studies, the bulk of the material that I cite in this chapter is archived at the National Archives of Australia, the central repository for the records of the Commonwealth (i.e., federal) government. That so much material relating to "breeding out the colour" can be accessed in Canberra speaks to the complex circuitry of settler colonial governance during the interwar period. Each state set policy for the Aboriginals living within its borders, except in the case of the Northern Territory, which did not become fully self-governing until 1978.[15] Because the Commonwealth administered Territorian affairs from Canberra, officials like Cecil Cook reported not only to an administrator in Darwin, but to the Canberra-based bureaucrats employed by the Ministry of the Interior. The more junior of these bureaucrats would assemble Cook's memoranda and supporting documents into dossiers for passage up the bureaucratic food chain, sometimes including newspaper clippings or information about Aboriginal policy in other jurisdictions for purposes of comparison, inspiration, and instruction. The bureaucratic dossier is thus the nucleus around which the National Archives has grown: when you order a document for use in the Reading Room, it is the dossier, more or less, that arrives at your station. According to its website, the National Archives of Australia exists for the benefit of the public, helping to keep the work of governance transparent by, on the one hand, "promot[ing] good records management in Australian Government agencies" and, on the other, "manag[ing] the valuable records of our nation and mak[ing] them accessible now and to future generations."[16] If, as Stoler points out, "transparency is [nevertheless] not what archival collections are known for," it is partly because archives and the documents that constitute them do not – cannot – record the work of governance in any simple – transparent – way.[17] The "sources" we discover in the government archive "are not 'springs'" of truth, but must be read with the kind of attention to voice, rhetorical choice, genre, audience, and situation, that we tend to reserve for more obviously crafted documents, like poems and novels.[18]

Like all texts, moreover, government records inhabit a variety of contexts, some of which we can reconstruct, some of which we can't. Individual documents are organized into dossiers under subject headings such as "The Marriage of White Men to Half-Caste Women," or "Education of Aboriginals Northern Territory." In many archives, the dossiers are themselves organized into series by jurisdiction and date, indicating who – Aboriginal Affairs, say, rather than Education – took an interest in what, when, where, and why. As a result, Stoler says,

> navigating the archives is to map the multiple imaginaries that made [in the Dutch colonial contexts with which she is largely concerned] breastfeeding benign at one moment and politically charged at another; that made nurseries a tense racial

> question; that elevated something to the status of an "event"; that animated public concern or clandestine scrutiny, turning it into what the French call an "*affaire*." In short, an interest in European paupers or abandoned mixed blood children gets you nowhere, unless you know how they mattered to whom, when, and why they did so.[19]

It is important to recognize that what matters to whom changes over time. Documents, and the "events" they record, acquire new meanings through being resituated and recontextualized, as when they are invoked in policy discussions remote from the time of their creation, or cited as evidence of government wrongdoing by a body such as the Human Rights and Equal Opportunity Commission (HREOC). Many of the records that I looked at had been indexed by HREOC's Inquiry into the Forced Separation of Aboriginal and Torres Strait Islander Children from Their Families as sources of information not only about Aboriginal policy but about Aboriginals themselves, reflecting the inquiry's recommendation that "all government record agencies be funded as a matter of urgency by the relevant government to preserve and index records relating to Indigenous individuals, families and/or communities and records relating to all children, Indigenous or otherwise, removed from their families for any reason."[20] Each time I opened a file, a sheet of paper informed me of this indexing project, and hence of the violence that had demanded it. Some documents, especially those pertaining to identifiable or living individuals, have been sheathed in opaque covers meant to secure them from the prying eyes of strangers like me. How did these records read before they testified to the Human Rights Commission, or were allowed to fall silent? Several points emerge from this discussion of the way in which the Australian government archive is organized and signifies. First, the government archive is made; it should not be taken as found. At the same time, however, the archive is not (only) a repository of texts documenting the actions of governments past and present, but, as HREOC's attention to archival practice suggests, a site of state action in itself. Leaving aside, for the moment, the injustices to which the archive, or the practice of archiving, gives rise, I want to explore the part played by the archive in government processes of decision making.

In *Broken Circles*, her magisterial history of Australian state intervention in Aboriginal family life, Anna Haebich draws on the work of Michel Foucault and Nikolas Rose to argue that "the process of governing or 'governmentality' … is not a matter of implementing an 'idealized schema in the real by an act of will' but of negotiating and juggling a host of often conflicting 'strategies, techniques and procedures' … in accordance with the 'materials and forces to hand … the resistances and oppositions anticipated or encountered.'"[21] Not only did

Aboriginal policy vary from state to state, as chief protectors pursued different solutions to, for example, "the half-caste problem," but administrative units – the Western Australian Aborigines Department and its satellites, say – were themselves riven by personal rivalries, divergences of opinion, even small acts of resistance. Where, as in the removal of half-caste children to institutions in Western Australia and the Northern Territory, a chief protector based in Perth or Darwin relied on the cooperation of men and women living thousands of kilometres away, the efforts of a single police officer could check an order given on high, at least temporarily. Haebich writes that "the problems of distance and lack of police cooperation must have driven the staff at head office to tear their hair at times."[22]

Chief Protector Cook, meanwhile, was never so certain of his superiors' support for "breeding out" as the confident tone of his memos, letters, and speeches would seem to indicate. In the midst of an uproar sparked by the *Brisbane Daily Herald*'s June 1933 report that the "Commonwealth Government is to give cash bonuses to white men who marry half-caste women," the secretary of the interior, H.C. Brown, circulated a memo in which he voiced his reservations about the policy.[23] "My own view," Brown wrote, "is that half-castes who have been given certain rights and enjoy the franchise, should have the same privileges in respect to selecting their husbands or wives, as are enjoyed by other citizens of the Commonwealth."[24] A year later, J.A. Carrodus, a career bureaucrat who filled various posts in the Ministry of the Interior throughout the 1930s, outlasting Cook as well as several ministers and administrators, also expressed scepticism about "the scheme for the encouragement of the marriage of half-caste girls to whites," though he did not frame his opposition in Brown's terms of rights.[25] Few did. Citing the reservations expressed by Brown and Carrodus, Keith Windschuttle argues that the federal government never approved the policy of "breeding out the colour," thus, he says, "absolutely refut[ing] any claim that the government sought to put an end to Aboriginality."[26] Loath as I am to engage Windschuttle and the denialism that he purveys, it bears pointing out that, in the mid-1930s, the Department of the Interior, Northern Territory Administrator Robert Weddell, and the chief protector publicly agreed that "the present policy of the Northern Territory Administration is to encourage the marriage of half-caste girls to approved white men."[27] I highlight Brown and Carrodus's uncertainty about the legitimacy and efficacy of "breeding out the colour" not to absolve them of responsibility for the policy, which they publicly supported, but rather to invite reflection on the relationship between private dissent and public approval. The writings that constitute the government archive bear the traces of their authors' unease, distaste, anger, and disappointment, helping us to see the work of governance as negotiated and contested. But writing is also critical to the process by which consensus – or a consensus-effect – is achieved, debate and dissension transmuted into the monolith we call government policy. This may explain Adam Ashforth's assertion that "the real seat of power [in modern states] is the bureau, the locus of writing."[28]

"Breeding out the colour" is most closely associated with the chief protectors in the jurisdictions where it was implemented, Cecil Cook and A.O. Neville. But while it is important to acknowledge the limited scope of state and even Commonwealth policy, as well as the reservations of senior Commonwealth bureaucrats, I think we should be wary of claims that "breeding out" was merely the "pet scheme" of two powerful men. How much more productive to ask, with Ashforth, how "this fictitious and magical 'thing' we term a 'state' is brought into being over and above the myriads of relationships between real human beings organized in the *name* of the state."[29] Allegations of inappropriate personal interest were frequently launched Cook's way during the controversies of 1933 and 1934. In the 23 June 1933 edition of the *Northern Standard*, Fred Thompson contends that "any public employee who subordinates the best interests of the taxpaying public to his own self-invested autocracy should look to himself for his salary and not be permitted to interfere with the individual liberty of any protégé of the taxpayers – no matter what colour their skin."[30] In 1934, the Member for Melbourne Ports, Ted Holloway, attacked Cook during a routine parliamentary debate. According to Holloway's unnamed Territorian sources, "socially and as a private citizen, Dr. Cook was an estimable gentleman, but … officially, he was an absolute crank, his pet scheme being to breed all the half-castes in the territory back to white people." Holloway went on to suggest that "because he wishes to demonstrate his theory is scientifically sound, Dr. Cook wishes to have all the half-caste women married to white men and thus solve the half-caste problem in the Northern Territory."[31] What these commentators find offensive about "breeding out" is Cook's emotional and intellectual over-involvement in the plan. Policy should not be (obviously) shaped by ego or the pursuit of scientific glory. In the formulation of policy, the good public employee is disinvested of self.

However much we might invite our political representatives to demonstrate their hard-won convictions and heartfelt opinions, I doubt we'd find much wrong with this idealized understanding of public service. At the same time, what the archive suggests is that the selflessness of the public servant is maintained, if indeed it is not produced, through institutionally sanctioned practices of writing. Years after my first visit to Canberra, what I recall is the sheer iterative excess of the Commonwealth archive, the irritation, bemusement, with which I would contemplate a memo I was sure I'd read, just now, or was it yesterday? And I had too, only the dates had changed, along with the signature at the bottom of the page. My "archive fever" sent me looping through the carbon evidence of what I couldn't help feeling constituted a form of plagiarism.[32] Take two memoranda composed on 7 and 27 February 1933:

(1)

His Honour,
The Administrator of the
Northern Territory,
DARWIN.
PERMISSION TO MARRY ABORIGINALS.
With further reference to previous memoranda in which I have called attention to the very grave problem which has been developing in Northern Australia owing to the intermarriage of alien coloured races with aboriginals and half-castes, it is strongly recommended that the Commonwealth take action to have the States, particularly Queensland and Western Australia, adopt a policy uniform with that of the Commonwealth.

For years it seems that Protectors of Aboriginals have regarded it as undesirable that a half-caste or quarter-caste aboriginal should be mated with a white. On the other hand mating with Japanese, South-Sea Islanders, Chinese and hybrid coloured aliens has been regarded as a very desirable solution to what was regarded as the marriage problem of coloured girls some of whom have over seventy-five per cent white blood. The result has been the accumulation of a hybrid coloured population of very low order. I am unable to speak for Western Australia and Queensland but these coloured individuals constitute a perennial economic and social problem in the Northern Territory and their multiplication throughout the north of the continent is likely to be attended by very grave consequences to Australia as a nation.

In the Territory the mating of aboriginals with any person other than an aboriginal is prohibited. The mating of coloured aliens with any female of part aboriginal blood is also prohibited. Every endeavour is being made to breed out the colour by elevating female half-castes to white standard with a view to their absorption by mating into the white population. The adoption of a similar policy throughout the Commonwealth is, in my opinion, a matter of vital importance.
Cecil Cook [signed]
(C. E. Cook).
Chief Protector of Aboriginals.

(2)

The Acting Secretary,
Prime Minister's Department.

Marriage of Half-castes and Aboriginals.

> The Chief Protector of Aboriginals of the Northern Territory has reported that a grave problem is developing in Northern Australia owing to the inter-marriage of alien coloured races with aboriginals and half-castes. He states that these coloured persons constitute an economic and social problem in the Northern Territory and expresses the view that their multiplication throughout the North of the continent is likely to be attended by grave consequences to Australia as a nation.
>
> In the Northern Territory, the mating of aboriginals with any person other than an aboriginal is prohibited. The mating of coloured aliens with any female of part aboriginal blood is also prohibited. Every endeavour is being made to breed-out colour by elevating female half-castes to white standard with a view to their absorption by mating into the white population.
>
> It is understood that, in some of the States, it is regarded as undesirable that a half-caste or quarter-caste should be mated with a white. The mating of such females with Japanese, South Sea Islanders, Chinese and other coloured aliens is considered to be a desirable solution of the marriage problem of coloured girls. The result has been the accumulation of a coloured population of a very low order.
>
> My Minister is of the opinion that the policy adopted by the Commonwealth in the Northern Territory might, with advantage, be adopted by the States, particularly the contiguous states of Queensland and Western Australia. He realizes, however, that the State Departments will have their own vision on the matter and consequently suggests that this proposal be listed for consideration at the next Premiers' Conference.
>
> (Sgd) J. A. CARRODUS [stamp]
> for Secretary.[33]

The authority that Cook claims in his 7 February memorandum derives in part from the institutional positions (doctor, scientist, chief medical officer, chief protector) that he is fortunate enough to occupy. Cook carefully delineates the scope – or limits – of this authority, his admission that "I am unable to speak for Western Australia and Queensland" confirming that he is otherwise speaking on behalf of the administrative unit called "the Northern Territory." Typically, however, Cook also draws attention to the "I" who speaks, so that while his recommendations gain legitimacy and force by seeming to emerge from an institution rather than an individual, they also represent "my opinion." If Cook speaks *for* or *as* the Northern Territory, he seems nevertheless anxious to remind us that it is *he* who speaks for the Northern Territory. But who speaks for or as the Commonwealth? On 27 February, substantial portions of Cook's memorandum are transposed, rearranged, and integrated into a new memorandum, "signed" by Carrodus on behalf of his secretary, H.C. Brown. Changes to Cook's wording are introduced so as meticulously to isolate opinion – "the

Chief Protector … *expresses the view* that their multiplication … is likely to be attended by grave consequences" – from what is then construed as a fait accompli, namely, the endeavour to "breed out colour." Although the views presumably motivate the policy, they are rhetorically differentiated in an attempt to de-link individual subjects from the practices they initiate or condone. Carrodus's plagiarism – the possessive is singularly inappropriate – authorizes itself precisely by overturning the authority that attends the attestation (via the signature) of the speaker's presence in language. It constructs certain practices as without need of authorization; authority (as power over people, things, beliefs) begins to inhere, paradoxically, in the capacity to dispense with authority (as issuing from, guaranteed by, a subject-author-actor). The Commonwealth, at least in this instance, isn't an actor, but the set of actions or ideas it choose to own, and then denies owning. The ubiquitous Carrodus here takes refuge in institutional authority, an authority devolved onto a set of apparently anonymous texts that act in the world as though of their own volition.

Such repetitions produce a consensus-effect, whereby recommendations, what the government should do, get turned into policy, what the government says it is doing. Thus, throughout 1933, Carrodus publicly insisted that the policy of the Commonwealth was to encourage the mating of half-castes and whites, as though this was happening on a large scale. In fact, between June 1931 and June 1934, eleven such marriages were approved. On the one hand, the discrepancy between what the government says it is doing and what is actually happening underscores Haebich's point that the "process of governing … is not a matter of implementing an 'idealized schema in the real by an act of will.'" Like the royal commissions Stoler discusses in *Along the Archival Grain*, the government's apparent predilection for talk over action reflects its uncertainty about how best to act, or an unwillingness or even inability to act at all. If nothing else, "breeding out the colour" shows the colonial archive to be, as Stoler writes, a site "of the expectant and the conjured," where "dreams of comforting futures and forebodings of future failures" jostle with diktats and trim tables.[34] Their verbal assurances notwithstanding, it is possible that Cook lacks the support he needs, from his superiors in Canberra or from his subordinates in the field, to carry out his project of "breeding out the colour." Their recalcitrance may be, but need not be, principled. On the other hand, in that it removes action from the field to the bureau, not so much replacing action with talk as turning talk into action, the textualization of governance is critical to regimes of reproductive control, which work in part through capturing intimate acts and relationships in language, in numbers and diagrams and bureaucratese. Neville's plans may have been, as Windschuttle puts it, "all talk." I am arguing here for the significance of "talk."

In Western Australia and the Northern Territory, the exigencies of administering "Aboriginal affairs" generated an extraordinary amount of information about Indigenous subjects and their histories. In Western Australia, as Anna Haebich explains,

> the [Aborigines] Department came to focus on surveillance and control of individuals and families. The instrument of rule became the personal dossier. From 1915 the Department developed a file and card system based on individuals and families, recording details on relief, blankets and clothing issued, any crimes and breaches of the Aborigines Act, family histories and department decisions relating to the subject's life.[35]

Cook sent charts to the Ministry of the Interior recording the names, ages, skin colour, and institutional whereabouts of the half-caste children in the branch's charge, and may have maintained similar registers for the wider Indigenous population. Such registers render – or attempt to render – people into collections of categories, statistics, and other data that can be compared, moved around, and manipulated, or at least more easily than intelligent flesh. As James C. Scott writes in *Seeing Like a State*, "the simplified, utilitarian *descriptions* of state officials" have – or are ascribed – "a tendency, through the exercise of state power, to bring the facts into line with their representations."[36] Thus, in Kim Scott's 1999 novel *Benang*, Ernest Scat plots out his experiment in "breeding out the colour" on paper: in Ern's study, the narrator, his grandson, discovers "photographs of various people, all classifiable as *Aboriginal*," "a page of various fractions, possible permutations growing more and more convoluted," and a "couple of family trees … All leading to me," "the first white man born" (25–7; 10; italics in original). In addition, however, as people are rendered into data, archived, the state assumes the authority to manage their lives.

A National Archives folder labelled "(Mrs) C. Odegaard (1) Classification as an Aboriginal. (2) Proposed retention of daughter in Aboriginal compound" is particularly revealing in this context.[37] Beginning in 1933, a woman named Christine Odegaard waged a fierce battle with the Northern Territory Administration for custody of her thirteen-year-old daughter Florence. Writing to her parliamentary representative, Mr Martens, Mrs Odegaard explained that "Mr. Cook Chief Protector of Aborigines has classed me as an abo, also my daughter Florrie and wants to take Florrie from me and place her in the Compound among a lot of half castes and blacks."[38] In 1933, the Northern Territory crown law officer, E.T. Asche, explained that "the Chief Protector is the legal guardian of half-caste children under the age of eighteen years, notwithstanding that any half-caste child has a parent or other relative living."[39] A

Commonwealth statement from roughly the same time further specified that "every [honorary] Protector is, within his district, the local guardian of such children."[40] According to Tony Austin, "women could remain under guardianship indefinitely, while Protectors could assume guardianship for men if they felt it was needed."[41] The vesting of custody in protectors was standard in most states, and frequently served as the legal basis on which removal was allowed to proceed. As the daughter of a half-caste woman and a Norwegian man, however, Florence Odegaard would not automatically have been subject to the Aboriginals Ordinance. Hence Cook's declaration ("[he] has classed me as an abo"), and Mrs Odegaard's resistance. Odegaard wrote letters to Martens and the minister of the interior, obtained a statement from her daughter describing her ill-treatment, retained a lawyer, and finally applied for a writ of habeas corpus. Her efforts were in vain: Judge Wells decided that although the chief protector, as Florence's legal guardian, could not keep her in the Darwin Convent against her will, and although Florence "did not have any idea at present as to what she wanted to do except to go back to her mother," "it would [nonetheless] be a disadvantage to [Florrie] to be returned to her mother."

In writing to the Ministry of the Interior, and taking her case to court, Christine Odegaard evidently hoped to bypass the authority of the government official who had recently reasserted his guardianship not only of her daughter Florence, but of Christine herself. What authority did she imagine she was calling upon? The archival dossier includes reports submitted by the chief protector and local superintendent of police. These reports are peppered with careful demonstrations of personal knowledge: Cook narrates an incident in which he "saw this girl inadequately clothed in conversation with a Chinese" and reprimanded the mother for her negligence. In a later memo, Cook claims that "Mrs. Odegaard is one of Darwin's outstanding liars and I have frequently had occasion to tell her so." The accusation of dishonesty, bolstered by its having been allegedly communicated in person, is preceded by information likely gleaned from a police report, dated the day before, in which Superintendent Stretton describes one of Odegaard's letters as a "tissue of lies." Cook may be reporting hearsay. Carrodus certainly was: in making a recommendation on the matter to his minister, he asserts, "Mrs. Odegaard is a most undesirable character. Her daughter is much better off where she is," thus delivering judgment on a woman he has never met. An appeal to her parliamentary representative having failed, Christine Odegaard seems to have believed, not unreasonably, that a distant Canberra bureaucracy might, in tandem with the juggernaut of European law, counter the interference of a self-invested autocrat. But at the time, at least, Cook's arrogant pronouncements could be, and were, taken up by a discourse of disinterestedness that simply reproduced, stripped of all markers of intimacy, his judgment of unfitness, and approved continued separation. In that Darwin court of law, nothing Christine or Florence said could trump official versions of their lives past and future.

Wells's 1936 ruling denied Odegaard authority over her own body and child. The Aboriginals Branch had effectively supplanted her. It seems clear that in the Australian system of protection paternalism, while providing the conceptual framework within which the half-caste could be "only a grown-up child who will have to be protected and nursed," also took on a literal dimension.[42] If, as mission worker and activist Mary Montgomerie Bennett asserted, "no department in the world can take the place of a child's mother," protectors sought nonetheless to play the father.[43] Sometimes they were the (biological) fathers. The *Northern Standard* routinely printed letters hinting at sexual misconduct on the part of Northern Territory protectors and other white men of status, giving rise to pleas that the administration hire only married men, and scorn at the naivety such pleas disclosed. Through the character of Humboldt Lace, the married protector who fails to preserve his ward from the lust of white men, including himself, and the father who abandons the product of that failure, Xavier Herbert's 1938 novel *Capricornia* savages the split-level machinations of a paternal(ist) order whose promise to protect is always at the same time a promise to betray. There are decent white fathers in *Capricornia* – Tim O'Cannon (though he treats his Aboriginal wife Blossom abominably) and Peter Differ – but they too, in their inevitable deaths, are finally unable to defend their daughters against the predations of other, more powerful, Fathers. Thus, the articulation of the protector's authority in terms of paternity did not buttress, but replaced or overturned, claims made on the basis of alleged biological and other forms of paternity.

In a 1932 memorandum devoted to "the Half-Caste Problem," Cook notes that since half-caste youths had "no kin and no dependents," they were more likely to be forced into contracts that provided inadequate benefits: "The employer may and often does claim to be his father and profess to be actuated solely by interest in the boy's welfare. In such a case well-meaning persons including Protectors may be persuaded to compel the youth to uncongenial employment and the exercise of these powers of ownership, which constitute slavery, is not disputed."[44] Here, Cook warns "well-meaning persons" against allowing the claims of biological kinship to supersede their mandate of care. Cook sought to undermine Christine Odegaard's credibility by similarly maligning her maternity. In 1936, with the case headed for court, Cook resorted to increasingly tortuous insinuations, explaining that "it is only in the last few months that Mrs. Odegaard has become so persistent in her application for restoration of her daughter, and it happens that these few months coincide with the period of her cohabitation with a white man who is equally ardent in his efforts to remove the girl from the Convent." The interest Christine Odegaard's latest lover shows in Florence is compatible only, the Protector goes on to imply, with an intent to pimp the girl. There is no doubt that many half-caste boys were tapped as sources of cheap labour by their station-owner fathers, or by men eager to take advantage of tangled Territorian genealogies. It may even be true, as Cook claimed, that Florence's mother and stepfather meant her to "become a prostitute in an environment of coloured aliens and low-grade whites" (though in light of the effort Christine expended this seems unlikely). Nevertheless, it is also true that with paternal neglect and abuse said to be widespread, and maternal care believed non-existent or insignificant, the half-caste could simultaneously be declared without biological kin, and claimed, in the words of Aborigines' Friends' Association secretary J.H. Sexton, as "the white man's child."[45]

The full implications of this rhetorical move will become clear in the next section of the chapter. Here, it serves to highlight the importance of state authority and action to the reformist project of "breeding out the colour." If the half-caste was both the white man's child and not, it is in part because, although the architects of "breeding out the colour" located the nation's future in the production and reproduction of miscegenated bodies, they also foregrounded the state's role in managing reproduction, suppressing the ties forged through reproduction as irrelevant, and indeed inimical, to their plans. In a 1930 letter to the government resident at Alice Springs, Cecil Cook wrote, "Just as it is impossible to convert raw hide into leather by officially proclaiming their identity, so it is impossible to adapt a camp bed half caste to our civilization by means of a gazette notice proclaiming his full citizenship."[46] In fact, however, adaptation by gazette notice is an apt figure for "breeding out the colour," a policy informed by a reliance on government intervention and, as I shall demonstrate, a preoccupation with representation. Speaking in April 1937 at a gathering of state and Commonwealth officials involved in Aboriginal affairs, A.O. Neville strove to maintain the fiction of a "dying race" and talk up the government's capacity to ensure a future for that race, with confusing results: "In my opinion, no matter what we do, they [full-blooded Aboriginals] will die out. It is interesting to note that on the department cattle stations established in the far north for the preservation of these people, the number of fully-blooded children is increasing, because of the care the people get."[47] Significantly, whether or not "the people" will "die out" is posed as a question of government care: either they'll survive, as a result of care, or they won't, despite care. The future is for the government to bestow, though it may be refused, incomprehensibly. The incompatible halves of Neville's statement thus teeter between conceding the over-determining force of racial inheritance and asserting the transformative power of government action. In the end, only the state could successfully (i.e., legitimately) harness reproduction to the national fantasy of a White Australia.

The White Man's Child

> Despite all his training, the doctor's nostrils wrinkled at the smell. He saw a grey sheet, a wasted body. Gloom. His eyes flickered over the woman, the creamy-skinned boy. His vision tripped him and he was looking into hazel eyes. His high thoughts circled and descended to the carcasses left by dead men's minds; notions of genetics and of breeding. What he'd read before the war. It was true, you could see it.
>
> Kim Scott, *Benang*

Advocates of "breeding out the colour" understood – and embraced – the centrality of whiteness to early-twentieth-century conceptions of Australian national identity. Alfred Deakin, who became Australia's second prime minister in 1903, explained federation as a product of "the desire that we should be one people, and remain one people, without the admixture of other races."[48] Deakin's notion of a "united race" composed of men and women able to "intermarry and associate without degradation on either side" and "inspired by the same ideals, and an aspiration towards the same ideals, of a people possessing the same general cast of character, tone of thought, the same constitutional training and traditions," linked whiteness with Britishness, so that it was never clear whether White Australia had room for, say, the Irish or the Italians (qtd. in Willard 189). What is clear is that, drawn together through what one New South Wales premier (Henry Parkes) called "the crimson thread of kinship," and fear of what another (Jack Lang) called "an Asian tidal wave," the new Australians were white, and, much more importantly, would continue white, without any admixture of "Black, Brown and Brindle."[49] The Immigration Restriction Act, which sought to restrict non-European immigration to Australia through administering language tests to would-be immigrants, was among the first pieces of legislation passed by the new Commonwealth.[50] Colonial legislation had earlier imposed a poll tax on Chinese immigrants and halted the practice of blackbirding, that is, the importation of Pacific islanders to work in the northern sugar industry.[51] By the 1920s, the White Australia policy was well established, and had even inspired a mostly glowing history, Myra Willard's *History of the White Australia Policy to 1920* (1923).[52]

Willard concluded her book by admitting that "the history of a White Australia is so far mainly, if not entirely, the history of a negative policy ... The development of the White Australia policy in its positive form may be said to be a movement scarcely yet begun" (212–13). In order to secure White Australia, Australians needed to actively pursue the development of the land and its people, its white people. Officials were especially concerned to develop the country's sparsely inhabited – and resource-rich – centre and tropical north. And yet, measures enacted in the name of a White Australia had left northern plantations unable to rely on cheap (often forced) alien labour from Asia and the Pacific.[53] "By the exclusion of non-European peoples who were willing to come to the Southern land, Australians," asserted Willard, "were aware that they would probably retard the material development of their country" (200–1). What was desired was not development of the Northern Territory per se, since the "progress of Australia" ought not to be accelerated "at the expense of the future nationality of Australia," but instead development by and necessarily of whites, for whites (Labilliere qtd. in Willard 201). Whether white men and women could thrive in tropical climates was, however, unclear. Throughout the interwar period, as Warwick Anderson and Alison Bashford have shown, researchers in the field of tropical medicine repeatedly took up the question of whether white men and women were physiologically constituted to survive in the tropical climates of Northern Queensland and the Northern Territory.[54] And what of the Indigenous inhabitants, whose presence no amount of immigration legislation was going to dispel? Although Indigenous population levels were everywhere hit hard by settler colonization, in the 1930s, Indigenous people still made up a significant proportion of the population in Western Australia (approximately 6 per cent), and an outright majority in the Northern Territory, unlike in the southern states, where urbanization and the longer standing and greater scope of white settlement had taken their toll.

Whereas New Zealand's founding document, the Treaty of Waitangi/te Tiriti o Waitangi (1840), explicitly recognizes Māori sovereignty over the land, Australia was settled as terra nullius, as, that is, land belonging to no one.[55] In practice, of course, New Zealand has not always lived up to its treaty obligations, more often acting as though it too was settled as empty land. Still, Britain's inconsistent approach to settlement in the Pacific is worth noting both because of what it tells us about how Europeans viewed Aboriginals as opposed to Māori, and because of its consequences for Indigenous land claims: te Tiriti at least establishes that Māori once "exercise[d] or possess[ed]" "the rights and powers of Sovereignty" over "their respective territories" (it is the question of whether or to what extent Māori ceded this sovereignty in consequence of the treaty that is a matter of judicial, legislative, and academic debate), while Indigenous Australians have had to establish that the country they want returned to them was theirs in the first place.[56] Like that other convenient myth, the myth of the vanishing savage, the fiction of terra nullius bespeaks "the lack of a lack or, in other words, ... a wished-for lack that is instead an all-too-real obstacle to identification. Rather than absences, primitive races such as the Australian 'black-fellows' were and remain presences disturbing the process of national unification and identification."[57]

Deakin's "united race" might stretch to include the Irish, but it could not assimilate Aboriginals. At the same time, so long as Indigenous people remained to assert the "distinct, defined, and absolute rights of proprietary and hereditary possession" that, as the governor of South Australia acknowledged in 1840, they had held "from time immemorial," the legitimacy of settler claims to the land would continue in doubt.[58] Where the fiction of terra nullius works to resolve "the Aboriginal problem" by redefining Indigenous-controlled territories as "desert and uninhabited," "breeding out the colour" can be read as an attempt to rectify "the lack of a lack" in a more material way, through reproduction.[59] For Cook, marriages between whites and half-castes were important insofar as they ensured a continued "influx of white blood" into the Aboriginal population.[60] Promising to erase the traces of earlier miscegenation, "breeding out the colour" envisioned the half-caste's conversion into a trustworthy labourer and "white citizen," while perpetuating the myth of imminent Indigenous decline.[61] Soon, Australia really would be "All-White." Or would it? We are unused, I think, to the claim that whiteness may be produced through miscegenation. Does "breeding out the colour" then purchase the extinction of natives and native title at the expense of racial purity?

A set of photographs taken in 1922 by the anthropologist Sir Baldwin Spencer offers an approach to this question. Invited to survey the effects of Commonwealth policy on Indigenous peoples living in the Northern Territory, Spencer embarked on a fact-finding tour of central Australia, releasing in due course a report accompanied by photographs of individuals resident in the institutions he investigated. I reproduce three here. In the first photograph (Figure 1), Harry Ross sits against a plain, light background, flanked by Maggie and a boy, Henry. In the second (Figure 2), a young girl called Agnes Draper rests her forearms on a windowsill. The room behind her is a darkness framed by the rough wood of the window frame and a wall made, we can just see, from corrugated metal. She is wearing a light-coloured long-sleeved dress with ribbons at the wrists, and sports a light-coloured ribbon in her hair. In the third photograph (Figure 3), Norman Bray stands, body turned slightly away from the camera, arms held loosely at his sides, hands curled. What little Spencer knew of his subjects is written below or inscribed on the backs of the photographs. He carefully notes his subjects' mixed Indigenous-white descent. Thus, Harry and Maggie Ross are "half-castes" and Henry is their son.[62] Of Harry Ross the photographer has remarked, "this man speaks English well, is most capable in

Figure 1. Harry, Maggie, and Henry Ross. Photo by Baldwin Spencer. Courtesy of the National Archives of Australia (A1 1930/1542).

Figure 2. Agnes Draper. Photo by Baldwin Spencer. Courtesy of the National Archives of Australia (A1 1930/1542).

dealing with stock & quite equal to taking his place amongst white workers." However, "the [same] photograph does not do justice to the half caste woman." She is, it is true, out of focus, and, of the five individuals here captured on film, appears most distressed by the experience of posing for a photograph. But do her blurred features constitute the (only) injustice referred to by the photographer? In fact, I want to argue, the photographic "justice" Spencer demanded but couldn't always achieve for his subjects is bound up with Cook's goals for the subjects of what the *Sydney Morning Herald* called "the greatest experiment in native administration the Commonwealth has ever undertaken."[63] This might seem a stretch. After all, Spencer tabled his report ten years before Cook's project of managed miscegenation achieved notoriety. Indeed, like some of Cook's colleagues, Spencer maintained that "there is little probability of an average white man marrying a half caste woman on account of racial prejudices," while "no white woman, or at all events very rarely, will marry a half caste man." "In justice to the half castes," and particularly to save half-caste women from the

Figure 3. Norman Bray. Photo by Baldwin Spencer. Courtesy of the National Archives of Australia (A1 1930/1542).

"degradation" of marrying a "blackfellow," he proposed segregating half-castes from both whites and blacks and encouraging them to marry among themselves. Still, I think that Spencer's caution expresses not so much disapproval of a "breeding out"–type scheme as a lack of confidence in its practicability: in the report, intermarriage between whites and half-castes appears as a negated possibility before the marriage of half-caste with half-caste is even considered, suggesting that intermarriage represents an ideal but sadly impractical solution to the "half-caste problem." More important, Spencer's photography draws on a visual discourse that also provided "breeding out the colour" with some of its terms and premises.

Spencer took photographs of half-castes. But what does this mean? Racial science, as Deborah Poole, James Ryan, and Nancy Stepan have all made clear, was a "visual and diagrammatic science par excellence – that is, it depended on an elaborate visual language to make its points."[64] Stepan notes, however, that "diagrams of race could not be compared to the 'real things' of race since the races became coherently visible only as a function of the representations themselves."[65] In other words, visual media such as photography do not document the existence of race, but rather produce and mark out the differences that constitute race. Thus, in Ann Stoler's Foucaultian reading of the Dutch colonial racial order, it is "cultural competencies and sexual practices" that signal "the lines of descent secur[ing] racial identities and partition[ing] individuals among them," identities scientists seek to make visible in the human body, available for comparison, and hence classifiable.[66] The difference that is being made visible isn't necessarily an already visible difference, but may inhere in ascriptions of cultural difference that in turn imply forms of inherited and inheritable difference. Scholars have stressed the instability of visual and other forms of representation, suggesting that "the fixity of the species" could never finally be secured "against the outward appearance of flux that constantly threatened to blur distinctions between types and so break down the classificatory grid."[67] If racial science was a visual science, Stepan argues, it was nevertheless not a photographic science: "Instead of selecting the visual evidence of the body so that it could be pared down to a recognizable type, the camera produced a plethora of visual detail without selection, and therefore a multiplicity of plausible meanings."[68] Various representational techniques – introducing a ruler into the frame of the photograph, manufacturing sharp contrasts, captioning – helped direct signification. But the fact that recourse to such measures was thought to be necessary suggests that even photography, with all its promise of optical realism, failed of itself to deliver unmistakable types. The recalcitrance of the photographic medium is of course crucial to current attempts, personal and academic, to decolonize the photographic archive.[69] However, my readings of Spencer's photographs and "breeding out the colour" also suggest that "the half-caste," the racial type Spencer, Cook, and Neville invoked in order to eliminate, named a category of being defined by flux, by the capacity for change.

Born in Britain, Spencer trained as an anthropologist, undertaking pioneering fieldwork in Australia from the 1890s on. He was among the first to photograph and film Indigenous people in central Australia. It's perhaps inevitable, then, that his 1922 photographs – full body shots of colonized subjects against largely neutral backgrounds, accompanied by notations of descent – should recall the spectre of the ethnographic type.[70] Ethnography has been described as a funereal science, devoted to the salvation, in text if not in deed, of peoples and cultures it construes as ever vanishing. With its impressive capacity for forensic truth telling, photography is accorded a critical role in this salvage project: ethnographic photography tends to type individuals, engineering a graphic sameness within and between populations that (ostensibly) testifies to their lack of evolutionary progress and potential. Salvage photography captures individuals in the temporal field of loss, their difference made visible as backwardness and the expectation of extinction. But of course, Spencer's photographs are not just ethnographic artefacts. They are also policy instruments. As Spencer's commission indicates, because of the patchwork nature of early-twentieth-century colonial administration, anthropologists, along with missionaries and medical professionals, remained crucial to the kinds of data collection efforts outlined above. The oft-suggested appointment of a government anthropologist to oversee Aboriginal affairs in the Territory never materialized. Anthropology and public administration were nonetheless bound through the exchange of letters and advice, promises of support, patronage, and employment, overlapping personnel, and the activities of the humanitarian lobby. Thus, in 1930, Cecil Cook, who later proposed "equipping [the Aboriginal Branch's] responsible officers with a knowledge of anthropology," himself took a short course in anthropology designed specifically for public servants.[71] A.P. Elkin, a professor of anthropology based at the University of Sydney, periodically intervened in Northern Territory Aboriginal affairs, not always to Cook's satisfaction. Although the Spencer photographs were not themselves publicly circulated, photographs like Spencer's, along with language calculated to arrest the eye, provided interwar humanitarians with potent weapons in their struggle to expose and ameliorate conditions that Aboriginal activist William Cooper termed "shocking beyond words."[72]

In 1929, commenting on photographs produced under similar circumstances as Spencer's, the *Adelaide Register* warned that

> it would not do to permit this revelation [of the living conditions endured by Aboriginals in the Northern Territory] to leave Australia. Such proof of our neglect

> of our elementary duty towards the survivors of the primitive race dispossessed of this country by the act of British settlement, such appalling evidence of the consequences of that neglect, such an indictment of official ineptitude and public apathy, if presented to the world, would be placed on record to our everlasting shame.[73]

As this excerpt makes clear, the thin skin of the camera lens, the immediacy it appears to promise, allow photographs to stand as "appalling evidence" and "indictment" all in one. There is no need for additional judgment (i.e., interpretation), because they proffer judgment in their transparent veracity. They are true because they are photographs. Concerned with saving face, the *Register* would like to acknowledge the facts, including the fact of their insupportability, and dismiss the matter altogether. But photographs can also compel action on the facts that shame us. Pointing the way to redemption, photographs can even become sites of redemption in themselves. The evidentiary claims of photography have been radically undermined in recent years; scholars no longer look to a photograph for a record of some moment as it "actually" happened. Yet for all our talk of the image's ability to "reconfigure its referent," to operate as a space of fantasy and desire, we still, I think, tend to treat photography in relation to a past reality it both does and does not record.[74] As Elizabeth Edwards suggests, photography deals not only in facts but possibilities, registering our fantasies about the future as well as the past.[75] For Roland Barthes, not just ethnographic photography but the medium itself is characterized by deathliness: "By giving me the absolute past of the pose (aorist), the photograph tells me death in the future … Whether or not the subject is already dead, every photograph is this catastrophe."[76] Reading Barthes against the grain, I focus here on the photograph's capacity to tell the future (anterior). To take a banal example: in *Words of Light*, Eduardo Cadava points out that the temporal transparency of a photograph – it appears to show us an event in the moment of its happening – conceals the laborious extenuations of development.[77] A print may be produced and displayed seconds or years after light hits film. In its record of a moment, a developed photograph looks back at itself. Doesn't this mean, conversely, that in the moment of recording, the photograph looks forward to itself (or, as Barthes would have it, to death)? Even salvage photography is proleptic, since it aims to record the inevitability of its subjects' extinction. Temporal flux is thereby built into photographic fixity.

In a similar way, the Spencer photographs modulate between the nominally incompatible lexicons of futurity and futurelessness, ghosting the half-caste even as they capture her essential futurity. It is striking that although he also visited the Mission at Hermannsburg, managed by the Lutheran Church for the care and spiritual uplift of the Arrernte, Spencer's photographs are without exception of individuals he encountered at the Alice Springs Bungalow, a government-administered institution established specifically to care for half-caste children. Spencer's choice of photographic subjects reflects his positive assessment of half-castes' capacity for development: unlike the Hermannsburg managers, who he says "flatly and absolutely refused to have anything at all to do with the half-castes" in the conviction that "they are a hopeless people to deal with and much inferior to the full blooded aboriginals," Spencer insists that "the half castes are capable of reaching a higher stage of development than the pure-blood blacks." He goes on to point out that "the somewhat widely spread belief that half castes, if inter-married, will not have children is quite erroneous. They do." At the 1937 Canberra Conference of Commonwealth and State Aboriginal Authorities, A.O. Neville also distinguished between "full-bloods," who he believed would die out "no matter what we do," and "the coloured people of various degrees," who, he argued, constituted a "problem of the future."

Neville's statement is ambiguous. In claiming that "coloured people" constitute a "problem," Neville taps into a strain of orthodox racial theory that equated racial mixture with degeneracy. In the eighteenth and nineteenth centuries, uncertainty over how best to characterize difference among humans centred on the "problem" of admixture: were races (like) species, fundamentally distinct varieties whose crossings bore no fruit? "Mulatto," a common term for individuals of mixed descent, takes its point from the usual infertility of the mule, product of the "unnatural" union of a male ass and a mare. Miscegenation discourse often manifested as a form of extinction discourse, offering, in settler contexts especially, "a relatively comforting explanation for some vague but large fraction of mass extinctions."[78] Miscegenation was sometimes even cast as a means of ensuring extinction. In the Brazilian writer Afrânio Peixoto's 1911 novel *A Esfinge* (*The Sphinx*), a character claims that the Portuguese colonists had "another advantage [over the Indians and Africans] – cross breeding with the Negro, thereby eliminating it with the successive infusions of white blood."[79] Where the fertility of mulattos could not be denied, the proliferation of categories expressing percentages and kinds of mixture buttressed assertions that the descendants of interracial unions did not reproduce themselves but rather an alarming heterogeneity.[80] Miscegenation, that is, produced no new race. Even in countries (Australia or Brazil, say, rather than the United States) where individuals of mixed descent were strategically recognized as constituting a separate racial group requiring special treatment, half-castes were not usually seen to possess a future as half-castes per se. For many thinkers, then, racial hybridization appeared to embody the degeneration threatening society. At the same time, miscegenation was said by some, including Arthur de Gobineau, to play a positive role in the development of mature societies. Australian officials preached both positions simultaneously. Certainly, Neville and Cook saw no future for the half-caste qua half-caste. Still, given Neville's insistence on the inevitability of Indigenous decline, that he could imagine "coloured people" as part of the future, problem or no, is significant. The establishment, however dubiously intentioned, inadequately funded, and disastrously managed, of state-run and state-sponsored "educational" institutions like the Bungalow further testifies to official interest in half-caste development.

It is this exciting potentiality, metonymically alluded to in discussions of half-caste fertility, that appears to warrant half-castes' increased visibility to the public eye. I speak both figuratively and literally here. Recall that Harry Ross is "quite equal to taking his place amongst white workers." Baldwin Spencer attributes his aptitude for working amongst whites to his good English and his talent for stockwork. However, by juxtaposing the commendation with the photograph, Spencer implies that Ross's being "quite equal" is something we should be able to see. Indeed, alerting his readers to the presence and placement of the photographs in his report, Spencer writes, "I append a few photographs (Nos. 1,2,3,4,5,6,7,8) that I took at the Bungalow which will show, more than any words could express, that the children are entirely different from the true blacks, in fact it would be difficult, in the case of some of the quadroons especially, to distinguish between them and white children."[81] In other words, what a viewer sees in these photographs – on the one hand, an utter difference between half-caste children and "true blacks" and, on the other, the difficulty of recording difference between half-caste children and "true" whites – should testify to the truth of Spencer's claim that "the half castes are capable of reaching a higher stage of development than the pure-blood blacks," validating his recommendation that half-castes be provided for separately from full-bloods. Although Harry and Maggie Ross are not children, they are photographed with a child we are encouraged to assume is theirs. The photographs therefore assert connections between half-castes' potential for development, their reproductive potential, and the promising extent to which they approximate, or might be imagined to approximate, whiteness. Perhaps, then, it is because Spencer's photograph of Maggie Ross fails to adequately highlight her capacity to live and work among whites, fails, that is, to showcase her "whiteness," that he considers it "unjust."

Spencer was not alone in seeking to prove half-castes' potential for advancement by drawing attention to their "white" skins. In 1931, for example, a correspondent styling himself "Araunah" contributed an article to the *West Australian* in which he urged approval of "breeding out the colour." In order to prove his argument that "the aborigines would ultimately become absorbed, blending insensibly into the white stock with which they had mated and leaving in their descendants no physical trace of a mixed origin," Araunah detailed "some actual observations made on [a] recent tour" of Aboriginal camps:

> There are in each of the camps visited quarter-castes so white as to be indistinguishable from Australians of purely British parentage. Even the finger nails (sure indication of mixed blood even where the British strain has mingled with the Aryan races of India) betray no dark circle of pigmentation, and in many cases the noses are aquiline and all the features characteristically European. In one camp we saw several children with flaming red hair! Dozens of people, taken out of the squalid setting of the camp and seen differently clad in a wholly white environment, would be accepted without question as people of white parentage.[82]

In 1934, newspapers reported that the Commonwealth was arranging for "fifty octoroons, sons and daughters of quarter-caste [Northern] Australian natives and white men," to be adopted by white families living in southern cities.[83] Then minister of the interior J.A. Perkins explained to the *Melbourne Herald* that the families' identities would remain secret, so as to give the children "every chance to grow up as whites."[84] "In appearance," he stressed, "the children show no traces of aboriginal ancestry. They are as white as any other children" "except in their surroundings."[85] Perkins, Araunah, and Spencer assume that "actual observations," preferably authenticated by photography, reveal truth. That truth might be forensic, as when, in his report to the 1934 Western Australian Royal Commission, H.D. Moseley referred his readers to a photograph for proof that "no half-caste child has been born on the [Violet Valley] station during the last 18 years."[86] Sometimes, however, what we are meant to see is a projection, a future truth. Out of the "pathetic sight" of nearly white children made to endure beastly conditions, Araunah constructs the satisfactory sight of a white setting inhabited by consequently white children, a fantasy that prospectively vindicates his support for "breeding out the colour." Similarly, because Perkins's potential adoptees are apparently white, they may "grow into normal white men and women."[87] Asking us to detect the signs of future progress in the present, the images conjured by Perkins, Araunah, and Baldwin Spencer collapse the "before" and "after" photographs of Indigenous children that are among the most compelling visual legacies of the American and Canadian residential school systems. Presented as a form of self-fulfilling prophecy, "breeding out" could claim defence of conservative purity because it assumed the future achievement of whiteness.[88] The half-caste you saw, in other words, was also her future, her *white* future.

The terminology employed to describe individuals of mixed Indigenous descent confirms that half-caste futurity was characteristically judged a function of half-caste whiteness.[89] As was sometimes pointed out, because of the Northern Territory's history of immigration from Asia and the Pacific, mixed-race family histories might include Malays, Afghanis, Chinese, Japanese, African-Americans, Cingalese, Māori, and so on. Although, in daily usage, "half-caste" served as a conveniently capacious descriptor for all individuals of mixed Aboriginal-European descent, the term did not generally extend to individuals with non-white backgrounds. Cecil Cook distinguished half-castes from "crosses of lower alien races" or "hybrid coloured aliens," regardless of whether such "aliens" could claim Indigenous parentage or not.[90] For Cook, a diverse mixed-race population could be divided into those who (re)presented a problem of colour – individuals descended from non-white and non-Indigenous peoples – and those who might prove its solution – individuals of Indigenous and white descent.

Whiteness played a similar role in contemporary American debates about whether native Hawaiians of mixed racial descent should qualify for United States citizenship. According to Kēhaulani Kauanui, Hawaiians of mixed white and Indigenous descent were more often recognized as "practically white" and therefore deserving of citizenship than were individuals claiming Hawaiian and Chinese or Japanese ancestry. Although Kauanui's description of whiteness as "*the* critical solvent" illuminates the distinction Cook draws between half-castes and "hybrid coloured aliens," her liquid metaphor works best in a context where race is determined through a calculus of blood.[91] In the United States, the contradictory logics of racial formation function such that "one drop" of black "blood" is enough to make me black, regardless of how I look, but a blood quantum of 49 per cent may not suffice to identify me as native Hawaiian. In contrast, as Araunah's article makes clear, "breeding out the colour" construed whiteness as something to be seen, a surface to be read. What the half-caste would be tomorrow was indicated, even pre-emptively corroborated, by what she looked like today. In this way, "breeding out the colour" exposed a tension at the heart of racial thought itself, between a synchronous focus on race as type, as a primarily visual aid to classification, as phenotype, as *outside*, and a diachronous focus on race as lineage, as an expression of descent lines, as genotype, as *inside*.[92] Problems arise when, because "individuals of similar 'race' [are believed to] look alike," "similarity of appearance is attributed to [a] common descent" that does not exist or that the community would normally not acknowledge, as when Americans of African descent "pass" for white.[93] In framing the half-caste's white appearance as a sign, guarantee, of her future whiteness, "breeding out the colour" blurred the line between "apparent" and "real" whiteness: if you could see today what she'd be tomorrow, what separated looking like from being?

White resistance to "breeding out the colour" suggests the controversial extent to which the project offered to re-imagine not only the half-caste's place in the Australian nation but whiteness itself. In a 1933 letter to the Darwin *Northern Standard*, a correspondent calling herself Mother All White condemned Cecil Cook's "definite policy of uplifting (?) the half-caste of the North by encouraging, by gentle measures, intermarriage with the white men."[94] Mother All White concludes her letter by asserting that "if some of the finances used to support the halfcaste concubines were used to give young white men a financial start to establish a home that would be a credit to himself and his country, we would soon prove to the Southern States we were their equal in every way and neither a white elephant nor a Cinderella." Here, by denying that "we" are "a white elephant," Mother All White challenges the common contemporary view of the Northern Territory as something in which much has been invested with little or no return.[95] At the same time, however, the slip, in Mother All White's letter, from "the Northern Territory" to "we Territorians admits a complicated anxiety about whiteness that resonates, oddly enough, with the career of two actual white elephants. Their story is worth a brief detour into Barnum country.

In 1884, the American entertainer, museum director, circus manager, and fraud P.T. Barnum exhibited a sacred Burmese white elephant in London and New York City.[96] From the first, the public's attention focused on the elephant's whiteness, which was felt to be at best a disappointment – "It is perfectly clear," conceded one correspondent, "that the skin of an elephant could not under any circumstances present the milky whiteness some of us have lately been picturing to ourselves" – and at worst a sham.[97] Scandal erupted in April, when a Philadelphia newspaper claimed that Barnum's rival, Adam Forepaugh, had whitewashed one of his own alleged white elephants. The truth of the controversy is uncertain. Barnum was a notoriously efficient publicity-monger, and there is a strong possibility the scandal was engineered. Still, the stunt, if that's what it was, is instructive. Once Forepaugh's hoax had been exposed, Barnum took the extraordinary step of commissioning and exhibiting his own fraudulent white elephant.[98] In an equally extraordinary article, the *New York Times* considered the far-reaching implications of what it called "an interesting experiment":

> Mr. BARNUM's plan of making an elephant white by artificial means in order to contrast it with the dark and genuine white elephant is an ingenious one, but it is of less interest to elephants than it is to another class of our population. The inventor of the process of bleaching elephants claims that it can be applied without the slightest injury to colored people, and that it furnishes a complete answer to JOB's famous inquiry as to the possibility of whitening an Ethiopian. The experiment now making with the elephant is watched by the entire population of Thompson-street with the

> utmost interest, and if it succeeds, the colored man will be as rare among us as the sacred white elephant himself.[99]

The piece goes on to describe a situation in which the "ex-colored man" will be whiter than the "original white man," thus necessitating civil rights for whites.[100] The anonymous author concludes by hoping that the inventor of the elephant-whitening formula, "Paul DeSpotte," "will find some way of accurately imitating the Caucasian complexion," for "in that case all distinctions between the two races will at once disappear, and the negro question will vanish from our politics, never to reappear."[101] To look at, the "genuine white elephant" is not so white as the artificial white elephant, but it is more authentically white. Its whiteness, in fact, is not for the eye. This seems clear, in a paradoxical kind of way. But from the grotesque scenario of a whiter than white "colored man," whose perfection signals his inauthenticity, the *New York Times* moves to imagine a "colored man" who is as white as a white man, inhabiting a world without a colour line. "All distinctions between the two races will at once disappear": the *Times* envisions a white-man-whiteness that is available to all, untethered to whatever "inner" criteria one might propose. This whiteness is visible, even if, by failing to coincide with "the milky whiteness" conjured by some dictionary definitions, it remains a figure of speech.

Even before the Forepaugh scandal broke, a clever and timely ad for Pears soap had appeared in the 8 March 1884 issue of the *Illustrated London News*. A man in "native" dress stands next to an elephant, his rag suggestively poised over a large white marking on the animal's forehead. The ad discloses "THE REAL SECRET OF THE WHITE ELEPHANT – PEARS' SOAP. *Matchless for the Complexion.*" Just as "An Interesting Experiment" envisioned a human market for Paul DeSpotte's whitening technique, so a later Pears ad (also from 1884) substitutes a black child for the elephant, and a white child for its keeper.[102] Although the head of the soaped child remains black, the slogan nonetheless continues to declare Pears "Matchless for the Complexion." The temporal layerings and manipulations of commercial advertising model, even as they also mine, the temporal paradox of whiteness. Barnum's elephant, white and whitewashed, performs the lag between the future advertising promises (your white child will be cleaned white/r) and the reality advertising corrects or constructs as in need of correction (your child isn't clean or white), a lag for which consumers contract to pay, over and over again. In the Pears ads, these two moments are conflated as the exposure of inadequacy is made to coincide with its partial amendment, a future of daily washing obfuscated by advertising's temporal glamour. Thus, where the black body is soaped by the white, it appears white, an effect that reverses the usual pattern of contamination in transmitting whiteness rather than blackness. Sex – miscegenation – is both suggested and denied by the hygienic context. Whether we are witnessing a revelation of shared whiteness (deep down we're all – or could be – the same), or the application of a new and better whiteness, both does and doesn't matter, since what we are buying (into) is precisely a transposability of surface and depth such that every surface is also its own meaning, and that meaning always whiteness. If the scandal of the elephant is that its whiteness is not the right one, giving rise to fears of (racial) fraud – they're trying to pass it off on us as the real thing – then at their most radical, the soap ads seek to make such fraud meaningless. All legitimate ways of being become ways of successfully passing for white. That in both ads whiteness is carefully circumscribed does not exclude the possibility of future diffusion, even as it denotes the incomplete nature of the civilizing project.

Barnum's white elephant haunts Mother All White's letter as the possibility, raised by "breeding out," that all whiteness is spurious, a form of passing. According to Mother All White, Cook's proposals threaten to produce an inferior brand of white settler incapable of developing the land as desired. As an alternative, Mother All White calls on the government to help young white men establish homes "that would be a credit to [themselves] and [their] country," homes run, that is, by white women.[103] Mother All White's letter suggests, somewhat confusedly, that the presence of white women will enable pioneers to retain "decency and some refinement" and so check further racial mixture. Or perhaps, rather, it's that the reproduction of whiteness as decency and refinement depends upon the reproduction of white bodies. Either way, whiteness emerges as much a matter of morality as it is a function of appearance or even biology. But this leads to a problem: if "we" white Australians are not the "white elephant" that "breeding out" is sure to manufacture, why do we need to prove it by "uplift[ing our] standards of purity?" Why should a Mother All White require purifying?

On the whole, opponents of "breeding out the colour" sought, like Mother All White, to resolve the ambiguity in conceptions of whiteness by emphasizing inner criteria, including genetics as well as intangibles like "decency and refinement." "Black blood," they insisted, was a stain not easily removed, though it might be made invisible. Not only was race not something you could altogether see, but what you saw might not be any guide to a person's race at all. Supporters of "breeding out" sometimes cited contemporary scientific evidence of the "Australian aboriginal … being a forerunner of the Caucasian race" rather than of the "Negroid" in order to dismiss fears of atavism.[104] Cook drew on the history of miscegenation in Victoria, New South Wales, and Tasmania to argue that the "risk of 'sports' and similar manifestations of atavism in later generations" was insignificant.[105] Opponents firmly rejected such reassurances: the secretary of a women's political organization wrote, "Those of us who have lived in Eastern countries ... have seen the unhappy results of mixing the white & black races, of the awful consequences which can occur even in the third & fourth generations."[106] In a 1933 *Sun* article, the anthropologist W. H. Stanner warned that "it is impossible by looking at an individual to say what his or her hereditary constitution is ... What has *apparently* happened in a racially mixed population is no necessary guide to what has *actually* happened."[107] Suspicious of miscegenation's alleged long-term potential, Stanner insisted that "superficial observation" over "a short period of a few generations" could not prove "characters" to have been "bred out."[108] You might not be able to see "the primitive Australian features," but that didn't mean they weren't "lying dormant," waiting for the "right conditions" to show.[109]

From a perspective that stressed insides over outsides, as well as the purity of racial types, miscegenation could never result in anything like whiteness, since an individual's genetic make-up would always retain the memory of racial mixture. But note: even Stanner couldn't resist including in his article a photograph of a woman holding a child as "an example of miscegenation in which the white blood predominates in the child."[110] If blackness was the "well-guarded secret" that Stanner hoped to expose through "strict genealogical examination," it seems that whiteness could nonetheless be discerned by "superficial observation."[111] In a similar way, despite their reliance on the scientific discourse of heredity (Cook and Neville always spoke of first and second crosses, à la Mendel), proponents of "breeding out the colour" ultimately concerned themselves not with hidden causes like blood or genes or genealogy, but rather with surfaces, with the visible evidence. Absorption, as Russell McGregor puts it, "sought not to make fitter people, but to make people better fit in."[112] Cook's peculiar approach to whiteness seems to have been driven more by pragmatic considerations than by anything else. If, to realize White Australia, we have to ignore how some of our white brethren came to be white, so be it. Better, he implies, "a white population with the problematic risk of an occasional sport" than "a particoloured population in which the half-caste and the coloured alien rapidly attain a position of dominance."[113]

This sort of disinvestment in the biological past has serious consequences for white settlers and Aboriginals alike, especially as it informs a disinvestment in the past more broadly. Let's revisit, for a moment, Araunah's article for the *West Australian*. In order to be accepted as "people of white parentage," the "quarter-castes" Araunah heralds as "so white as to be indistinguishable from Australians of purely British parentage" must be removed from "the squalid setting of the camp" into "a wholly white environment." Make no mistake: what Araunah is saying here is that in order to be accepted as "the white man's child[ren]," Aboriginals must be removed *from their families*, with whom, presumably, they live in the camps. Removing half-castes from their families, detaching them from kin and other networks, does not just enable their accession to whiteness, but in a sense constitutes them as white. This is borne out by the experience of Emily and David Nannup, whose young children were removed to the Moore River Native Settlement north of Perth in the early 1930s.[114] Their attempts to regain custody were brought to the attention first of Mary Bennett and then of the 1934 Moseley royal commission. Believing the Department of Native Affairs would have to reconsider its decision if they could show themselves and, more important, their children, "clean from the blood of an aboriginal," the Nannups painstakingly traced their respective genealogies through stories gathered from friends, relatives, and employers. The result is a heartbreakingly complex calculation of racial inheritance that adds up, the Nannups argue, to their exemption from the Aborigines Act and hence from the articles used to justify the removal of their children. When, in official eyes, the word "Aboriginal" has meaning only "for the purposes" of the Aborigines Act (or the Northern Territory Aboriginals Ordinance), exemption from those "purposes" does not even serve as a permanent racial designation, offensive as this would be, since it can be revoked at any time. To be deemed "not Aboriginal" for the purposes of the act is not the same as being deemed "white" or even "clean from the blood of an aboriginal." Even so, exemption requires the interruption or outright denial of genealogy: David Nannup says,

> I am not ashamed to own my aboriginal relations though I have not lived with them. The nearest I have lived to them is 300 to 200 yards about 20 years ago … I have always kept away from aboriginals because I knew that people would try to bring me under the Aborigines Act. The reason I did not want to come under the Act is that they take your children and hunt you down and move you for no reason, but just when they please.

Although David and Emily Nannup may never have been subject to the act, continued exemption required individuals to meet shifting standards of intelligence, culture, and overall European-ness, in large part by "choosing" not to associate with other Aboriginals. In the end, the Nannups' attempt to prevent separation from their children by enduring separation from their families and communities failed. What interested the department, apparently, was the dismantling of families, generation by generation: so that half-castes might have a future, they had to be divested of their past, black and white. In 1941, the scientist Norman Tindale pointed out that

> some folk who have aboriginal blood in their veins could not be proved to be of aboriginal descent within the meaning of the Act, while others with less amounts of aboriginal blood, by reason of their accidental preservation of a more complete genealogical history, might be compelled to admit their liability and be forced to seek exemption from the provisions of the Act before being able legally to regain the status they enjoy at present as "white" citizens.[115]

It is as though knowledge of genealogy is itself a potential marker of Aboriginality. This is so even where, as in the Nannups' case, that genealogy demonstrates, in the terms of the times, a "breeding out of colour." The half-caste was the "white man's child" only insofar as he was nobody's – nobody's, that is, but the state's.

The fate that David Nannup fears – that the state will take his children and hunt him down and move him for no reason, but just when it pleases – is horrific enough. In addition, however, by sidelining the claims of descent, policies like removal and "breeding out the colour" degrade, sometimes permanently, the relationship between Indigenous people and their homelands. Their efficacy in doing so is evinced by the difficulties that dog Indigenous land claims today. In 1995, the Australian Federal Court concluded that

> native title can be enjoyed only by members of an identifiable community who are entitled to enjoy the land under the traditionally based laws and customs, as currently acknowledged and observed, of that community … The only persons entitled to claim native title are those who can show biological descent from the indigenous people entitled to enjoy the land under the laws and customs of their own clan or group.[116]

As submissions to the HREOC inquiry continually stressed, however, it is difficult for victims of removal to participate in land claims because knowledge of biological descent relations and traditional responsibilities is precisely what has been taken from them. A man whose mother had been removed from Lake Tyers as a child told the inquiry,

> I have no legal claim to come back here [to Lake Tyers]. I can't speak on the board of management, I'm not a living member out here on this mission. What right have I got to speak out here? And this is the way that a lot of the Aboriginals living on this mission see me – as a blow-in, a blow-through. Yet I've got family that are buried out here on the mission … and I have no rights. As an Aboriginal I don't have any rights out here.[117]

As the Reverend Bernie Clarke concluded, the Stolen Generations "have been removed from the very link which most land rights legislation demands in order for your rights to native title to be recognised. So in effect their removal in that way from their own family and context was also to deprive them of certain legal rights that we later recognised."[118] It is unlikely the architects of removal and "breeding out the colour" foresaw their use in disrupting future Indigenous land claims. Regardless, that survivors find it difficult to return to country indicates the extent to which the anti-genealogical thrust of removal and "breeding out the colour" serves settler projects of territorial control. "Following the theft of land," Kay Torney has written, "must come the theft of family."[119] In a sense, however, the theft of family is simply the theft of land by roundabout means.

If the ideas about whiteness and genealogy that inform "breeding out the colour" facilitate the extinguishment of native title, the policy bolstered settler claims to the land in more positive ways as well. That Cook did not consider "hybrid coloured aliens" suitable material for his program of miscegenation is telling in this regard.[120] According to Russell McGregor, "[Cecil] Cook's fear of hybrid Asian-Aboriginality suggests that absorptionist strategies were directed against colour rather than Aboriginality per se."[121] It is certainly true that Cook was keen to check what he termed "the multiplication of multicolour humanity by the mating of Halfcaste with alien coloured blood."[122] Nevertheless, Cook never suggested that, for example, women of mixed Asian-white descent might profitably be encouraged to marry white men. Non-white, non-Indigenous Australians did not come under his mandate. But perhaps Cook's violent suspicion of "alien coloured blood" might be read as evidence of a positive investment in Aboriginality. By positive I don't necessarily mean affirmative, although contemporary responses to "breeding out the colour" often interpreted the Commonwealth's position in that light. While some women activists defended "racial mixture" as neither preventable nor "bad," the Metropolitan Branch Women's Section of the United Country Party "deplored that the Federal Government is so far lost to the knowledge of our deep rooted sentiments and pride of race, as to attempt to infuse a strain of aboriginal blood into our coming generations."[123] This was not how Cook generally pitched "breeding out the colour," and there is nothing to indicate it's what he secretly desired.[124] However, like his contemporary Xavier Herbert, Cook may have thought indigeneity worth assimilating.

Herbert, whose first novel about the Northern Territory, *Capricornia*, won the Sesquicentennial Literary Prize in 1938, served as acting superintendent of the Kahlin Aboriginal Compound in Darwin between October 1935 and June 1936. In a letter written at Kahlin to the broadcaster Arthur Dibley, Herbert wondered,

> Am I mad? Do you know what I've been dreaming of doing? Why, no less than dreaming of teaching the Aboriginal Race to accept citizenship & win a place in the Nation, ~~so that they may cross with the Invaders~~, & honourable place, so that they may cross with the invaders & enrich the new Nation with their blood. Already I have founded a Euraustralian League, the members of which are Halfcastes & Quartercastes whose blood is pure Aboriginal & European, the aim of which is to teach pride of race to these people & to teach others to honour them & ultimately to found a Nation. Fantastic, is it not, to teach people to feel proud of Aboriginal blood? But is it mad? Truly, I've come to envy these Halfcastes their heritage, so much so that, for all my love of the soil & all my pride in being born of it, I must confess that I'm simply an invader & that there is no hope of my ever being able to claim the right to live in this land ~~unless I infuse my blood~~ unless I infuse my my [*sic*] blood into the Aboriginal race.
>
> Oh it's difficult to explain while I am tongue-tied. There is no hope in my dreaming. There never was. I am mad. Surely the rest of the world cannot be insane & I sane?[125]

In this passage, Herbert struggles to articulate his vision of an Australia enriched by Aboriginal "blood," calling for the colour to be, as it were, bred in rather than out. He is usefully open about the feelings of (territorial) illegitimacy that fuel his quest to establish a miscegenated "True Commonwealth": "I'm simply an invader," he confesses, and "there is no hope of my ever being able to claim the right to live in this land … unless I infuse my … blood into the Aboriginal race." What this entails, practically speaking, is sketched out by Andy McRandy, a minor character in *Capricornia*. A vicious satire of Territorian society, *Capricornia* charts the progress of a fatherless half-caste named Norman Shillingsworth. From McRandy, Norman learns that "a feller aint been in this country unless he's tried the Black Velvet," sex, that is, with an Aboriginal woman.[126] Although the desire Herbert expresses for Aboriginality is nowhere echoed in the archive of "breeding out the colour," both Herbert's fantasy and "breeding out the colour" pivot on sex between white men and black women. But how do sex and reproduction guarantee one's authentic "being" in country, one's "right to live in this land"? How might the body be imagined to mediate the relationship between a nation and the territory it claims for itself?

All subjects, as Radhika Mohanram points out, "have a close relationship with the landscape that surrounds them, a relationship which shapes their bodies and perceptions, forms their knowledge and informs their sense of aesthetics."[127] Still, some subjects are seen as more embodied and emplaced than others. Noting that the term "native" usually designates only persons "native to" places at a remove from the West, Arjun Appadurai suggests that the figure of "the native" is defined by his confinement, expressed not only in his "mysterious, even metaphysical attachment" to a physical place but in his total adaptation to the demands and possibilities of that environment and consequent inability to function anywhere else.[128] The "ecological immobility of the indigenous person as a discursive botanical construct functions," writes Mohanram, "to locate the [European] settler as mobile, free."[129] As Elizabeth DeLoughrey observes, these tropes of incarceration and mobility complement rhetorics that "position the native in a homogenous, prepositional time antecedent to the narrative of European, linear-based progress": Manichean spatial and temporal orders get "mapped" onto one another, as peripheries are attributed anachronism, centres dynamism and contemporaneity.[130] At times, space is altogether subordinated to time, representing the static condition against which progress is to be measured. These tropes are importantly gendered as well as raced. Rajagopalan Radhakrishnan notes, for example, that women frequently serve as "the mute but necessary allegorical ground for the transactions of nationalist history."[131]

The ascription of rootedness may work, as Mohanram argues, to produce the native as an embodied other to the settler's unmarked, disembodied, mobile, self. At the same time, the native threatens to disappear into the landscape with which she is identified to the extent of being unimaginable apart from it. (Mobility confers its own risks: the race maps of the late nineteenth and early twentieth century register a considerable anxiety about the degenerating effects of displacement upon European settlers, travellers, and colonial officials.) In colonial contexts, the black female body functions "as a mediator for male citizens [in this case, settlers] to experience the landscape and the nation as nurturing, comforting, familiar," whatever the estrangements they may otherwise feel and inflict upon others.[132] More pragmatically, in societies where property is vested in men, marriage functions as a way for men to gain access to a variety of kinds of property, including land. The mediating body may vanish altogether, as the land itself is feminized, made figurally available as a nurturing and potentially productive (and exploitable) body. Thus, one of the characters in D.H. Lawrence and Mollie Skinner's novel about the West Australian outback, *The Boy in the Bush* (1924), suggests that "she" – that is, Australia – is "waiting for real men – British to the bone – … Wait for a few of *us* to die – and decay! Mature – manure – that's what's wanted. Dead men in the sand, dead men's bones in the gravel. That's what'll mature this country. The people you bury in it. Only good fertilizer. Dead men are like seed in the ground. When a few more like you and me, Bell, are worked in –"[133] Mr George imagines "real men," settlers, springing up, like the *sparti* of Thebes, from land fertilized by their forefathers' decaying bodies. The settler's desire for the land manifests as a desire to become indigenous to the land by becoming the land. At the same time, Mr George's peculiarly necrophilic conception of settlement occludes the very real – and prolific – encounters between settler and Indigenous men and women that help to constitute the contact zone. If the slippage between the Indigenous female body and the land-as-body allows settlers to understand sexual intercourse with Indigenous women as a form of territorialization, women's bodily connection with the land must nonetheless be repressed lest it undercut those claims to territorial legitimacy it is made to underwrite. Herbert's apparently progressive dream of a miscegenated nation also tends to obviate the Aboriginality upon which its legitimacy, even existence, would depend. In *Capricornia*, McRandy's advice is delivered to Norman Shillingsworth in the presence of the swagmen Jack Ramble and Joe Mooch. As the four men sit by a campfire, McRandy demands a "good Australian tune – one't expresses the Spirit of the Land," so Ramble and Mooch oblige with "Waltzin Matilda," "The Red Flag," and "Black Alice" (328). "Black Alice" opens "Oh don't you remember Black Alice," suggesting that the Aboriginal woman has in fact been forgotten, her presence erased, her body dis(re)membered (331). Significantly, the choice of "Black Alice" reveals "Jack Ramble" to be Norman's absconding father, Mark Shillingsworth: we last saw Mark "roaring *Black Alice* with Chook [aka Mooch]" (14–15). Although Norman does not recognize "Jack Ramble" as his father until much later (only the reader is in a position to make the necessary connection), Mark's assertion of paternity through a song about a forgotten "gin" parallels white male attempts to assert a filial relation to the land through relations with women who, like Black Alice, are quickly forgotten.

Like the fiction of terra nullius, "breeding out the colour" instantiates what Gayatri Spivak calls a "worlding," rewriting the history of Indigenous dispossession as the history of mere settlement, and in such a way that the revision appears not only invisible but unthinkable, "a reinscription of a cartography that … (re)present[s] itself as impeccable."[134] It depends upon, and perpetuates, an amnesia about the colonial past and present, targeting Aboriginality and the Aboriginal body for disremembrance. At the 1937 gathering of State and Commonwealth Aboriginal authorities, A.O. Neville pitched "breeding out the colour" to delegates by posing a question: "Are we going to have a population of 1,000,000 blacks in the Commonwealth, or are we going to merge them into our white community and eventually forget that there ever were any aborigines in Australia?"[135] Neville's own preference was clear: through "breeding out the colour," which promised "the ultimate absorption into our own race of the whole of the existing Australian native race," white Australians might learn to forget "that there ever were any aborigines in Australia." "Breeding out the colour" thus gives new meaning to the pernicious myth of the dying savage, as the "passing of the aborigines," to use the phrase coined by the Australian ethnographer Daisy Bates, comes to refer not – or not only – to their passing on, their extinction, but to their passing for white.[136] In this sense, Sir Baldwin Spencer's photographs can be said to ghost the half-caste even as they celebrate her futurity. But even the forgetting had itself to be forgotten. White parentage, Araunah had suggested, could be acquired through a simple change of scene. The implied corollary: a change of scene could obliterate the signs of black parentage. It's not that supporters of "breeding out" believed they could simply declare or photograph half-castes white. Nevertheless, conceiving of whiteness as an aesthetic category and whitening as a surface transformation allowed Cook, Araunah, and others to cast "breeding out" as the legitimate saviour of a White Australia because it allowed them to pass over, to forget, the means – miscegenation – by which "breeding out the colour," the "forgetting" of Aboriginality, would actually take place. When the half-caste became truly white, she would never have been, and would never again be, black, her Aboriginality, as J.A. Perkins hoped, a "forgotten chapter" in the achieved narrative of whiteness.[137] White Australia's black history would be no more.

Aftermath

Their maker dead, the policies they helped to inspire abandoned and discredited, the photographs remain. Should I have reproduced them here? I'm not sure. I include the photographs for the same reason that I quote from Commonwealth memoranda: because I want you to see what I'm talking about. In fact, what I'm most anxious for you to see is precisely the centrality of seeing itself to the project of "breeding out the colour." Inviting you to see for yourself is thus a loaded invitation, in part because it repeats an invitation I've argued the photographs themselves extend. As Jonathan Culler points out, the practice of quoting, of drawing on the language of a text, even a photographic text, in order to further an argument one is making about the text, represents an attempt to frame the text, as it were, from the inside: we feel most "securely outside and in control … when [our] discourse prolongs and develops a discourse authorized by the text, a pocket of externality folded in, whose external authority derives from its place inside."[138] What should occupy a position of distance from the object, the critical frame that comments upon and explicates the texts in question, is instead implicated in (and by) the object under study. Who, then, is framing whom? Am I perhaps being framed? Worse: am I guilty?

Like this book, Tony Austin's 1993 history *I Can Picture the Old Home So Clearly: The Commonwealth and "Half-caste" Youth in the Northern Territory 1911–1939* includes reproductions of the Spencer photographs. Pointing to a tonal difference between the limbs and faces of especially Agnes Draper and Norman Bray, he suggests that Spencer's photographs of half-castes were materially altered to produce the effect of whiteness. That is, the children were whitened either through the judicious application of cosmetics or during the development process itself. This is in some ways an irresistible hypothesis; I'll confess that it helped focus my thinking about "breeding out the colour." Spencer's doctored photographs, we could say, fed the fantasy that half-caste children could be whitened without recourse to expensive social welfare programs, unpopular emancipation projects, or continued miscegenation.[139] Deborah Poole notes that facial whitening, achieved either by tampering with the emulsion or through the use of cosmetics and flour, was a common practice in nineteenth-century Andean studio photography, allowing families to "translate their aspirations into enduring material artifacts."[140] So the practice is not unheard of. At the same time, to speculate about the children's whiteness – can they really be as white as they seem? – is, it seems to me, to succumb to the odious logic of the photographs, since it is in the movement between suspicion and belief that their meaning inheres and "breeding out," as we've seen, finds its rationale. There is the danger, then, in reconstructing a set of viewing practices whose implications and consequences are frankly genocidal, of renewing their power and participating in an ongoing campaign of hurt. But surely photographs are not so easily framed as that. "No totalization of the border is … possible," Derrida has written.[141] If, as Christopher Pinney says, photographic images, perhaps more even than words, are able to "perform radically different work" in different epistemes, there is a risk (to my authority, that is) that you won't at all see what I mean, but something rather different.[142] This is a risk I take with pleasure, however, because it means that other ways of seeing are indeed possible. That they are necessary is indisputable.

Through rendering people into data, I've argued, the state assumes the authority to manage their lives. In *Benang*, the narrator Harley Scat, wondering at his belief that "I should be able to find my way out of even here" because "I could read and write so well," observes that his "family, at the end of which line I dangled, learnt to read and write very early on. My [Aboriginal] great-grandmother signed her own marriage certificate. We have certificates, of marriage, death, birth. We got caught that way, on paper" (425–6). At the same time, as Harley's great-great-grandfather understands, paper talks: Sandy One wants to register his child, Harley's great-grandmother, because "then it would be murder when they took, used, killed like they did … There would be the certificate. It'd be written down, there'd be words saying who there was" (178). Indeed, these "words" aid Harley in his quest to (re)trace the contours of genealogical and geographical belonging by writing "a simple family history" (10). If, through such initiatives as forcible removal and "breeding out the colour," Australian governments sought to dismantle Indigenous kinship networks and disperse Indigenous geographies of home, the need to know who was birthing whom and where, to calculate the permutations, the lessening fractions, proliferated documentation of genealogy and, indirectly, of individuals' allegiance to country. There have been calls, among Indigenous and other colonized peoples, for all such documents to be destroyed. In the compromise agreed to by the National Archives of Australia, many photographs, especially of or pertaining to identifiable or living individuals, are sheathed in opaque covers, and so have attained a measure of long-denied privacy. According to some activists and scholars, however, it isn't so much that such records are too readily accessible, overexposed, but that they are not, in fact, easily accessed by the individuals whom they most concern. *Bringing Them Home* recommends loosening stringent privacy regulations and developing measures to help Indigenous people looking to reconnect with family negotiate the archival maze. Restitution and recuperation may require that artefacts be brought home, literally (as in the case of human remains) or figuratively. Pinney describes recuperation as a kind of particularization, the "enclosing in a new space of domesticity and affection of images formerly lost in the public wilderness of the archive."[143] In the Australian Institute for Aboriginal and Torres Strait Islander Studies' copy of A.O. Neville's *Australia's Coloured Minority* (1947), for example, typewritten insertions identify Neville's photographs of half-caste "types," thereby staging, partly from the inside, a multilayered interruption of standard archival practice: not only have some of ethnography's constitutive erasures been made visible, but they have been made visible in the space of the text, small scandals on the public face of the archive. I first encountered the Spencer photographs in "the public wilderness" of the National Archives of Australia. I have seen them reproduced between the covers of twentieth- and twenty-first-century scholarly monographs. What if Norman Bray had children, and I came across his photograph in their living room? What would I see then? What do you see?

PART TWO

Endings

Chapter Three

"I kept on dreaming about the sea": Foreclosure and the Aborting Woman

All of the projects examined in previous chapters, from Moreau's experiments in vivisection to "breeding out the colour," bear especially heavily upon women as embodied subjects who do much of, and are identified with, the labour of reproduction. In *Prelude to Christopher*, Linda Hamlin Hendon is the hinge on which Nigel's eugenicist plot turns and comes undone. What renders Linda's possible madness terrifying is her reproductive autonomy, forcefully demonstrated when, wanting a baby and refused one by Nigel, she seduces his friend, the painter d'Aubert, and becomes pregnant anyway. In the pregnant female body, the reproductive process in all its aspects, biological, social, cultural, political, is made visible and vulnerable. The actions of a single woman threaten to derail an entire nation. Until recently, many nation states made it difficult for women who married foreigners to retain their citizenship, as though women's capacity to bear children was also a sign of their susceptibility to contamination by foreign others, as though each act of parturition produced not one new citizen but two, the child and his mother. Little wonder, then, that the scientists discussed in chapters 1 and 2 should seek either to control or circumvent the need for women's participation in the reproductive process.

Women's propensity for exercising their sexual and (hence) reproductive autonomy in contrary ways, whether by having children when they should not, or by refusing to have the children they should, figures prominently in early-twentieth-century discourses of reproduction as a key contributing factor to what was experienced as a crisis of reproduction: the decline in fertility that saw birth rates in many Western nations plummet between 1860 and 1940. This crisis of sexual reproduction seemed to presage a more general crisis in the workings of the nation state, women's apparent unwillingness or even incapacity to bear (the right kind of) children read as a reflection, expression, or cause of the state's inability to reproduce itself. Historians and demographers continue to ponder the reasons for and significance of the fertility decline, which Wally Seccombe describes as "among the most important and least understood transformations in the making of the modern world."[1] Between 1860 and 1940, the number of live births "experienced by each married woman in the [British] population [fell] from an average of nearly six to an average of just over two," a decline visible across class lines, if most marked initially among the upper and middle classes.[2] A similar fall-off has been documented for Australia and New Zealand. For such a decline to have taken place, Seccombe observes, a "widespread desire to prevent conception" must have converged with "the capacity to take effective action."[3] But whether the falling birth rate reflects the growing effectiveness and popularity of contraceptive devices such as the cap, or whether, in fact, most men and women, although convinced of the need for family planning, preferred to rely on abortion or attempt sexual self-control, is still debated.[4] Of course, understanding how the fertility decline was achieved is not the same thing as knowing why, around the turn of the twentieth century, so many men and women became invested in limiting the size of their families. The report of the McMillan Inquiry (1937), a committee tasked with investigating the incidence of abortion in New Zealand, suggested that "no social legislation, however generous," would prevent women from limiting their families, since

> the view, formerly widely accepted, that membership of a large family is in itself a valuable contribution to education, and to the training of responsible citizens, appears to be at a discount, and many parents now consider that advantages which can be *given* to a child as a result of family limitation, outweigh the natural advantages of a large family in which the children develop initiative through companionship.[5]

In an assessment largely echoed by historians, the McMillan Inquiry identifies the reasons powering New Zealanders' commitment to fertility control as at once economic – with the advent of universal state schooling, for example, the cost of raising children could no longer be offset by sending them out to work – and ideological, reflecting changing ideas about marriage, family, and the role of women and children therein, about sexual mores, and about class identity.[6]

Today, it is difficult not to see the mainstreaming of reproductive control as a positive development, especially for women. At the time, however, the falling birth rate was experienced as a crisis, arousing panic for what it said about the state of the nation, present and future. Both the McMillan Inquiry and its British counterpart, the Inter-Departmental Committee on Abortion established in 1937, framed the high incidence of abortion as the symptom of "an insidious canker in the body politic," expressing concern about the possibility of "race suicide," especially if the fertility decline should be unevenly distributed across class, national, or racial lines.[7] In *Social Insurance and Allied Services*, the 1942 document that is often celebrated as a blueprint for the post-war British welfare state, William Beveridge asserts that "with its present rate of reproduction the British race cannot continue."[8] Audible in statements like Beveridge's is the worry that Britain will lose the capacity to defend itself and its empire. The threat of Asian expansionism hovers over the proceedings of the McMillan Inquiry: in his statement, a representative of the Roman Catholic archbishop of Wellington warned, "if the English speaking peoples will not populate the land it will be the retribution of Divine Justice when English speaking people are in subjugation to prolific nations."[9]

This is not to say that it was then held to be desirable that all women, any woman, should have children. What was needed was not simply "plenty of children," but plenty of the right sort of children: the sentiments of Karl Pearson, who bemoaned the economic considerations that, he insisted, obliged middle- and upper-class families to practise birth control, even as government "legislation, municipal hygiene, state support, medical progress and unlimited charity" fostered high birth and low mortality rates among the poor, were widely shared.[10] Unmarried mothers became a popular subject of debate during the 1910s and 1920s thanks to an alleged rise in the number of illegitimate children born during and just after the war. On the one hand, the McMillan Inquiry deprecated measures that would deter "single women from allowing their pregnancies to continue," suggesting that its aim was to maximize the number of women having children, no matter their marital status.[11] During the First World War, Westminster considered reforming the laws concerning bastardy so that "war babies" could be legitimated retroactively, following the father's death if necessary. Although this may have reflected the special feeling aroused by the war, "the primary identity of the father as soldier ma[king] both these women and these children somehow acceptable," it helped broaden definitions of what was or could be considered moral behaviour.[12] On the other hand, the aversion commentators in both Britain and the settler nations displayed towards legalizing birth control seems to have reflected the conviction that access to birth control would increase promiscuity.[13] If the main cause of abortion among the unmarried was "a looseness of the moral standard" for which the "remedy must be educational," then the problem was less abortion per se than extramarital sex and pregnancy.[14] For some commentators, indeed, the existence of unmarried women seeking birth control, abortions, even having children, no matter if there were never as many of these as projected, indicated that British stock had already degenerated beyond repair. National suicide was not a threat, but a reality.

Although men also participated in the ideological shifts and behavioural adjustments that contributed to the early-twentieth-century decline in fertility, it was women's actions and beliefs, the figures of the sexless (or deviant) spinster, careless flapper, and aborting or feckless mother, that drew the attention of interested doctors, politicians, journalists, and activists.[15] Commentators characterized interwar women, alternately too and too little fertile, as quick to assert their rights of bodily pleasure and autonomy, thereby neglecting their duties to the nation state. Echoing Sydney Smith, who dismissed the aborting woman's claim of bodily autonomy as "illogical" because it denied the state its right to "exercise control over the destruction of its future citizens," Anthony Ludovici informed women that "your body cannot be your own to do as you like with so long as you live with other people in a state of more or less mutual dependence."[16] The authors of the McMillan Report thought it unnecessary even to comment on the assertion that a woman has the "right to determine for herself whether a pregnancy shall continue or not."[17] Woman must be put "back in her place – which is only another way of saving the world."[18] That many government efforts to improve infant and maternal health centred on alleviating maternal ignorance rather than, for example, the straitened material circumstances of women's lives, further testifies to the alacrity with which women were made to bear the burden of "saving the world." Thus, although the 1904 Inter-Departmental Committee on Physical Deterioration acknowledged the link between the failure of many Boer War recruits to meet the army's minimum health standards and the impoverished conditions in which they had grown up and lived, the government acted by providing girls with instruction in hygiene, cooking, and childcare.[19] Similarly, as Barbara Brookes points out, although many women "asserted that poverty had been the determining factor in their decision to abort," medical practitioners nonetheless declared education the key to combating the prevalence of criminal abortion.[20] The ignorance or fecklessness of the reluctant mother offered a more appealing target for the various and proliferating arms of scientifically minded state intervention than poverty.[21]

In this chapter and the next, I explore how women engaged with, inhabited, and reworked such narratives. Here, I focus on the practice of abortion, asking whether and how, through abortion, women rework maternalist frameworks of citizenship. Jean Rhys's 1934 novel *Voyage in the Dark* ends when Anna Morgan, its protagonist and narrator, undergoes an abortion that leaves her hallucinating on a blood-soaked mattress. Having travelled to England from her birthplace in the Caribbean, eighteen-year-old Anna makes a precarious living first as a chorus girl and then as the mistress of the much older, much wealthier bachelor Walter Jeffries. When Walter (or rather his cousin Vincent) terminates the relationship, Anna takes up residence with a masseuse named Ethel

Matthews, embarking on a series of brief affairs with men she meets in the streets, hotels, and eating establishments of London. One of these nameless men makes her pregnant. Aided by her capable friend Laurie and more materially by Walter and Vincent, Anna pays a Mrs Robinson fifty pounds to terminate the pregnancy, a procedure that almost kills her.

Mary Lou Emery hazards that *Voyage in the Dark* is "probably the only work of fiction in the early twentieth century that describes abortion from the woman's point of view."[22] In fact, however, *Voyage in the Dark* is only the most well known of a group of early-twentieth-century British novels that narrate abortion "from the woman's point of view." In F. Tennyson Jesse's *A Pin to See the Peepshow*, Julia Starling, pregnant by the husband she despises, visits a Mrs Humble to "ha[ve] something done"; Olivia Curtis, the middle-class narrator of Rosamund Lehmann's *The Weather in the Streets* (1936), ends her pregnancy when it is made clear to her that her married lover Rollo Spencer "could never … An illegitimate child would be quite out of the – quite unthinkable."[23] Other early-twentieth-century British literary works, if they do not all render, even cursorily, the experience of abortion itself, nonetheless turn on acts of abortion, including Elizabeth Robins's *The Convert* (1907), Leonora Eyles's *Margaret Protests* (1919), T.S. Eliot's *The Waste Land* (1922), A.S.M. Hutchinson's *This Freedom* (1922), Aldous Huxley's *Eyeless in Gaza* (1936), Christopher Isherwood's *Goodbye to Berlin* (1939), and Mary Lavin's *The House on Clewe Street* (1944). Two government enquiries, meanwhile, on maternal mortality (1923–37) and abortion (1937–9), bear witness to the state's interest in abortion during this period. Nor were Britons alone in their preoccupation with the "illegal operation." I have already noted the work of the McMillan Inquiry. According to Meg Gillette, more abortion fictions were published in the United States between 1929 and 1934 than over any prior five-year period; Nicole Moore notes a similar flurry for Australia, pointing to the numerous novels by major Australian women writers, including Dymphna Cusack, Eleanor Dark, Jean Devanny, Ruth Park, Katherine Susannah Prichard, and Kylie Tennant, that either spotlight acts of abortion or contain references to the practice.[24]

Rather than strive to account for the rich diversity of ways in which abortion signifies in early-twentieth-century fiction, polemic, and policy, this chapter pursues close readings of two narratives, *A Pin to See the Peepshow* and *Voyage in the Dark*, in which abortion plays a central role. Following the successful decriminalization campaigns of the 1960s and 1970s, fictional and non-fictional stories of abortion have usually been read (in the English-speaking West at least) as stories about the (in)eluctability of maternity, as stories, that is, about autonomy, choice, and the benefits and costs thereof. Besides insisting on the importance of speaking about abortion, its causes and effects, these stories argue for women's capacity to make considered and ethical choices in matters pertaining to their own bodies, and to negotiate the many, sometimes contradictory, responses such choices engender; or they seek to prove, trafficking in what Patricia Mann calls a "conservative drama of maternal goodness and nihilistic radical feminism," that abortion is a "thoughtless … choice," that "pro-choice medical communities have deliberately misled women to believe abortion is physically and emotionally painless, without consequences," that "women's fundamental instinct is maternal, and abortion opens a wound which only a return to maternity can heal."[25] Whether anatomizing or intervening in abortion debates, most scholars highlight their consequences for, and effects on, women, suggesting that reproductive behaviours, acts, choices, and rights have meaning for women primarily *as* women. Thus, for example, Drucilla Cornell claims that the right to abortion will only be secured, finally, if we can "find a way to resymbolize feminine sexual difference within the law" such that the "wrong in denying a right to abortion" is clearly understood as "a wrong that prevents [women's] achievement of the minimum conditions of individuation necessary for any meaningful conception of selfhood."[26] What interwar narratives of abortion reveal, in contrast, is the extent to which, in the first part of the twentieth century, reproductive acts and imperatives were held to constitute not only gender and sexual identities but racial and national ones as well. If abortion troubled interwar conceptions of women's identities and obligations qua women, it also challenged interwar conceptions of women's identities and obligations qua citizens and members of a national or racial community. In this sense, Sally Minogue and Andrew Palmer make a false distinction when they describe women like Anna Morgan as having to "choose between the public shame of unmarried motherhood and the private pain of abortion": abortion is always a public act, even, as we shall see, when it is literally unspeakable.[27]

In *No Future*, Lee Edelman identifies abortion with "the possibility of a queer resistance" to reproductive futurism as the "organizing principle of communal relations," urging queers to "stand *against* reproduction, *against* futurity, and so against life" by "com[ing] out *for* abortion."[28] In a deliberate echo of anti-abortion rhetoric, Edelman reads abortion as an act of refusal, even repudiation, that forecloses not only on a particular set of futures (the foetus' as a child, the woman's as a mother), but futurity itself. If Edelman's insistence on reading abortion as a heroic act of uncompromising resistance to the reproductive logics of citizenship is refreshing, still, it discounts the multiple ways in which such logics interpellate women as well as the overdetermined nature of the act itself, which speaks to the complexity of the social worlds within which and in relation to which women make decisions about their reproductive lives. The Child may embody "the citizen as an ideal, entitled to claim full rights to its future share in the nation's good," but as feminist and queer theorists of colour have pointed out, this does not mean that the state therefore embraces all children.[29] In 1930s Britain, it is true, abortion was prohibited in most cases, a proscription which might seem the logical product of the imperative to reproduce: the state wants women to have babies, not abort them. However, any discussion of the illegal operation must consider the multiple ways in which the law addresses aborting women, as guilty or innocent of the crime of abortion, certainly, but as embodied subjects positioned variously in and by a differentiated social landscape as well. It is easy to see how abortion might be imagined as "a grave national danger," what Christina Hauck calls "the most severe and least understood crisis of modernity."[30] The pregnant body can seem equally unruly, threatening the nation's capacity to collect and reproduce itself. There are contexts in which, persons for whom, illegality seems to stick as much to maternity as to abortion, compelling women to choose between effective and actual outlawry. As the African American feminist scholar Patricia Hill Collins observes, "for many women of color, choosing to become a mother challenges institutional policies that encourage white, middle-class women to reproduce, and discourage and even penalize low-income racial ethnic women from doing so."[31] Thus, while *A Pin to See the Peepshow* contests the maternalist terms on which women were admitted to the charmed circle of meaningful citizenship, wondering at a polity that disaccommodates the aborting woman, *Voyage in the Dark* draws attention to the exclusions that structure access to motherhood within maternalist citizenship regimes, whose coextension with projects of class, racial, and imperial consolidation it also exposes.

The chapter therefore departs from psychoanalytically inflected feminist approaches to Rhys's work that centre her protagonists' fraught relationships with "mad, spectral, distracted, or dying" mother figures, insofar as it reflects on the discursive and political mechanisms through which women, including Anna, come to be (un)recognizable as mothers in the first place.[32] Read in this light, abortion presents as more than a simple repudiation of reproduction or reproductive logics of time and citizenship. Certainly, in *Voyage in the Dark*, the foreclosure of abortion at once figures and is a consequence of the multiple foreclosures that have rendered Anna's life unapprehendable (to use Judith Butler's term) as such, as, that is, a life worth living.[33] This is not to say that it signifies only loss, lack, evacuation. The text highlights, rather, the complexity of foreclosure as a movement of encryption as well as expulsion, in which what is denied is simultaneously given substance.[34] Recall Jameson's description of utopian possibility as "dependent on the momentary formation of a kind of eddy or self-contained backwater" in which "new wish images of the social can be elaborated and experimented on" (15–16). Might abortion not be said to produce just such an eddy or backwater through the operation of foreclosure, which, like the rhetorical figure praeteritio, elaborates alternatives precisely through closing them off?[35] Late in *Voyage in the Dark*, Anna, pregnant but trying not to be, dreams repeatedly of her birthplace in the Caribbean, utopian desire manifesting once again in the form of an island excursus. Unlike the utopian projects described in chapters 1 and 2, however, the voyage home brings Anna face to face with those histories the nation is invested in forgetting: here, the histories of intimacy and intimate violence that have entangled not only British and Caribbean ecologies, economies, and cultures, but families too. It would be possible to read the final vignette of the novel, in which the doctor hired to treat Anna jocularly supposes that the abortion will allow her to "start all over again, all over again," as suggesting that this history has been or will be gotten over, moved on from (188). Her dreams linger nonetheless, not as guides to what might be, but as reminders of what was, arresting the work of re-beginning.

"The illegal operation"

Before the nineteenth century, Britons seem to have distinguished as a matter of course between abortions induced before and after "quickening," that is, the moment when the mother first feels the movements of the foetus.[36] (Even the Catholic church, which today anathematizes all forms of birth control, differentiated between abortions induced before and after quickening, which it termed "ensoulment," until 1869.) This distinction may also have been recognized under British common law. From the first decade of the nineteenth century on, however, the British state began to intervene more and more directly in women's reproductive lives, influenced by the opinion of medical men who, impatient with conceptions of pregnancy as a condition about which women were best equipped to judge, "sought to eradicate, firstly, traditional concepts such as quickening and secondly, the provision of treatment by other than medical practitioners."[37] Thus, the criminalization of abortion belongs to the story of the professionalization of medicine. Lord Ellenborough's 1803 Wounding and Maiming Bill proscribed (among other things) "the malicious using of means to procure the Miscarriage of Women" post-quickening. Abortion became a capital offence for abortionists if not for women themselves.[38] By 1861, the quickening test had been dropped, and women made liable. Although women of all classes and races continued to make use of abortionists and abortifacients such as slippery elm bark, they were not often prosecuted, in part because the "crime" eluded easy detection, in part because judges and juries proved reluctant to inflict "severe penalties for an act to which everyone involved consented."[39] Most of the prosecutions that did take place involved single women in service and amateur abortionists; women with the wherewithal to pay for the services of an accredited medical practitioner were less likely to attract the attention of the law by dying messily, while doctors "held advantages of status and skill" over their amateur colleagues that enabled them to more easily defend their actions.[40] For example, although the 1929 Infant Life (Preservation) Act conferred de facto legal status only on abortions performed by doctors for reasons of insanity or life-threatening physiological conditions, so-called therapeutic abortions could safely be purchased by women possessing the requisite social and economic capital even if they did not (strictly speaking) meet these conditions.

Between the 1861 Offences Against the Person Act and the 1967 Abortion Act, which decriminalized abortions performed under certain conditions, abortion did not simply vanish from the public eye. In fact, during the 1930s, abortion became the object of fierce public debate in Britain and elsewhere in the English-speaking world. During the interwar decades, Britain's Ministry of Health twice launched enquiries into the causes and effects of maternal mortality; when the report of the second enquiry (1937) adduced a connection between rates of maternal mortality and the incidence of abortion, the ministry convened an interdepartmental committee to investigate and propose measures for reducing the supposedly high incidence of abortion.[41] Many of the witnesses who testified before the Birkett Inquiry saw the practice of abortion as both a factor in, and the most shocking manifestation of, that crisis of sexual reproduction with which *Better Britons* has been so closely concerned. Not just the precipitous decline in the birth rate could be attributed to overreliance on abortion. Abortion was also thought to affect the quality of children being born insofar as it affected women's long-term physical, psychical, and moral health. Measures passed around the turn of the century and designed to ameliorate the conditions of childbirth, infancy, and early childhood had improved rates of infant mortality, which declined steadily throughout the first quarter of the twentieth century.[42] In contrast, the rate of maternal mortality held steady at approximately five deaths in every one thousand births and even rose slightly between 1923 and 1936, a trend that excited much public concern and was often ascribed to unsafe abortions.[43] In the public's mind, maternal mortality and abortion were closely linked.[44] Even if a woman did not die from puerperal sepsis following an induced abortion, or escaped infection altogether, some commentators believed the procedure to be inherently damaging to a woman's health, impinging on her capacity to bear and raise children in the future. According to Barbara Brookes, medical professionals tended to view the pregnant woman as "a case to be successfully completed by the birth of a healthy child."[45]

Few would have baulked at the still broader claim that *woman* was "a case to be successfully completed by the birth of a healthy child." Childbirth, wrote that misogynist extraordinaire Anthony Ludovici, is necessary to complete the sexual cycle.[46] As his contemporary Charlotte Haldane put it, "Every woman who refuses motherhood is curtailing her psychological as well as her physiological development in a manner which may have serious consequences to herself."[47] Meanwhile, the Inter-Departmental Committee on Abortion raised the possibility that easy access to fertility control of any kind would hasten national decline by increasing promiscuity.[48]

But abortion did not arouse panic only for its degenerative effects on the nation and race. It was also read as a sign of the degeneration of the British people, especially British women. For how could women's persistent recourse to abortion be explained? At least one commentator attributed the declining British birth rate to a sort of national malaise, a nervous exhaustion brought on by the exigencies of living in modernity. Testifying before the Birkett Committee, Beckwith Whitehouse, of the British College of Obstetricians and Gynaecologists, postulated that miscarriages were on the rise because "the artificial conditions of modern life set women's nerves 'on edge' and ... caused increased contractions of the uterus."[49] Whitehouse's focus on spontaneous abortions was, however, unusual, with most of his peers preferring to foreground women's agency in actively refusing, rather than being denied, the burden of motherhood. A 1914 essay in the *British Medical Journal* expressed concern at what it termed women's "rebellion against the imposed self-sacrifice of the mother's lot."[50] To a meeting of the Edinburgh Obstetrical Society, Sydney Smith noted disapprovingly that "the modern woman had her own point of view, and that was that she had control of her own body, and if she was not inclined to go through the trouble and inconvenience of childbearing there was no moral right to compel her to do so."[51] Women who thus claimed "to have sole right over [their] own bod[ies]" thereby demonstrated their status, asserted the gynaecologist Geoffrey Theobald, as "biological rejects."[52] The government's 1937 *Report on the Investigation into Maternal Mortality* noted the "increased nervous tension" exhibited by women in the post-war era, but linked this to the "fashion of 'slimming' and the habit of cigarette-smoking."[53] In this way, Stephen Brooke argues, policymakers consciously situated abortion (and maternal waywardness more generally) as indicative of the "apparent and lamented erosion of traditional values and sexual mores" in the wake of the First World War and the progress made by women in gaining access to the public spheres of work and politics.[54] For Haldane, the "determination to have no children" was only one of the "psychological diseases of the time" against which young women needed to be safeguarded, which also included "the craving for stimulants, for excitement, for drugs."[55] The use of "artificial aids" to arrest the "elaborate natural process" of reproduction might lead to the effective or even actual death of the race, but it also bolstered Ludovici's conclusion that "the population he sees about him – the people who are regarded as well and healthy, not the people who crowd our hospitals, asylums, and homes for cripples and incurables! – are sub-normal, or sub-human."[56] Even the ignorance that was sometimes adduced for women's willingness to abort showed, Ludovici felt, how "completely broken is the tradition which, once upon a time, was handed down from mother to daughter."[57]

In many ways, Julia Starling, the young married protagonist of F. Tennyson Jesse's novel *A Pin to See the Peepshow*, conforms to the stereotype of the aborting woman disseminated by writers like Anthony Ludovici and Charlotte Haldane. A self-involved, over-avid consumer of sentimental fiction who enjoys her work in a smart dress shop but is bored, even disgusted, by her older husband, Julia enters into an affair with Leonard Carr, an aircraft fitter-mechanic six years her junior. When he stabs her husband in the street outside their suburban flat, the police arrest Julia on a charge of conspiracy to murder. The two are tried, convicted, and hanged. Despite the disclaimer that fronts the novel, *A Pin to See the Peepshow* pretty obviously riffs on one of the most notorious murder cases of the interwar years. In October 1922, following the stabbing death of Percy Thompson, Edith Jessie Thompson and Frederick Bywaters were arrested on a charge of having conspired to murder her husband. Although Bywaters confessed to the crime, Edith Thompson's involvement had to be inferred from the sixty-five or so letters she wrote to Freddy over the course of their two-year affair, and in which she appeared to be plotting to injure her husband. Unable to convince a jury of Edith's innocence, Thompson and Bywaters were hanged the morning of 9 January 1923. The case was and remains controversial for a number of reasons: the ambiguity of the evidence used to convict Edith Thompson; a suspicion that, as James Joyce is reported to have said, inciting "is not quite the same as actually doing it"; the fact that no woman had been hanged in Britain since 1907.[58] It has inspired several literary treatments, including E.M. Delafield's *Messalina of the Suburbs* (1924), Dorothy Sayers's *Strong Poison* (1930), *A Pin to See the Peepshow*, and, of all things, an episode of *Finnegans Wake* (1940), and was cited in later campaigns to abolish the death penalty.

What is interesting about the Thompson/Bywaters case (and hence *A Pin to See the Peepshow*) is the extent to which Edith's crime was read, even at the time, as a species of sexual crime. During the trial, the judge and prosecution repeatedly censured the sexual conduct of the defendants, especially Edith's. In his trial notes, the judge dismissed the defence's characterization of the affair as a "great love," calling it "great and wholesome disgust," while in his summation, he instructed the jury to "bear in mind that illicit love may lead to crime," even if "you must not of course let your disgust carry you too far."[59] Decades later, a juror claimed that "it was my duty to read [the Thompson/Bywaters correspondence] to the members of the jury ... 'Nauseous' is hardly strong enough to describe their contents ... The jury performed a painful duty, but Mrs. Thompson's letters were her own condemnation."[60] Edith was felt to have transgressed in other ways as well: she was older, twenty-six to Bywaters's twenty, a fact that seems to have led many ordinary Britons to conclude that she had led him on; and she was a working woman, "the self-confident manageress of a dressmaking department in the city."[61] In *A Pin to See the Peepshow*, Julia clings to the achievements of her creative work at l'Etrangère, a small dressmaking shop in the West End, to the resentful confusion of her husband, who "wasn't, he told himself, the sort of man whose wife had to work" (171). During the Thompson/Bywaters trial, the Solicitor General linked Edith's continued employment at Carlton & Prior with her failure to fulfil her obligations as a woman and wife, suggesting that "perhaps because there were no children, or for other reasons, she was carrying on her employment."

In addition, however, Edith Thompson's crime, the crime of conspiracy to murder, has persistently been identified with, and even as, the crime of abortion. In his biography of Thompson, René Weis interprets some of Edith's queries about herbs, drugs, and poisons as allusions to abortifacients. During the trial, the Solicitor General drew Edith's attention to an incident documented in one of the letters, in which she laments that her husband "had the wrong porridge today." "I was referring to – I really cannot explain," she responded, but went on to acknowledge that she and Freddie had "talked about that sort of thing, and I had previously said, 'Oh, yes, I will give him something one of these days." What Edith cannot explain, Weis suggests, is that she was trying to abort, the unspeakability of the act being such that she would rather admit to culpability in the crime of murder than "admit in public that she had been trying to abort."[62] Although Edith Thompson does seem to have terminated a pregnancy in early 1922, Weis, like Freddy Bywaters before him, is not always persuasive when arguing that Edith was interested in poison only as a means of suicide or abortion. It is nonetheless striking that when Edith's contemporary F. Tennyson Jesse reimagined the affair, murder, and trial, she too read Edith's reticence on the stand as due to an unwillingness or inability to speak in public about abortion. In *A Pin to See the Peepshow*, Julia, refusing to bear what she believes to be her husband's child, tries an assortment of abortifacient methods – "she bought every kind of patent medicine that urged married ladies to end irregularities and delays now" – before consenting to visit Mrs Humble, who induces a miscarriage using an instrument of some kind (273). Listening to the letter "referring to what she had had done in Camden Town" read out in court, Julia thinks,

> they had warned her that she must not tell the truth about this. An English jury might think an illegal operation quite as bad as adultery – and adultery, apparently, was quite as bad as murder! It was awkward, because the letter, as this man read it, sounded just as though it referred to poisoning Herbert [her husband], as some of the other letters actually referred to poisoning him. (355)

If the jurors are likely to think "an illegal operation … quite as bad as murder," nothing in the novel or abortion debates of the period indicates that it is because they are likely to read abortion as a form of murder. Most scholars date the preoccupation with foetal life to the post–Second World War era. Rather, Julia's lawyers worry that a punishing moral economy will encourage the jurors to see Julia's sexual transgressions, legal and illegal, as a reason to believe her guilty of involvement in the murder.

Jesse draws attention to the slippage between Julia's alleged crimes of abortion and conspiracy to murder by emphasizing the moment during sentencing when the judge, in a parody of the marriage ceremony, asks whether "there [is] any question of law as to the sentence I have to pronounce?' and the woman sitting beside her leaned forward and whispered to her. It was something about – if she was going to have a baby, could she say so now, and everything would be all right" (366). Julia is conscious of a bitter irony: "if she had not got rid of Herbert's child, she would have been safe now" (366). The judge here affords Julia the opportunity to (temporarily) dodge the death penalty by "pleading the belly."[63] The logic underwriting "pleading the belly" suggests that the imperative to reproduce the nation trumps the imperative to safeguard it through eliminating malefactors: no citizen, male or female, is as valuable as a mother. It is less Julia's humanity or possible innocence that disturbs the men tasked with executing her, Jesse suggests, than her capacity to bear children. Wondering at the persistence of the idea that "it was somehow worse to hang a woman than a man," the prison doctor, a man called Ogilvie, reflects, "The dark consciousness of the womb was present with every man who had to do with the business, of the womb that was the holder of life, from which every living soul had issued in squalor and pain. Some deep awareness of the mother, the source of life, worked in the mind of every man" (392). In 1931, a decade after the events fictionalized in *A Pin to See the Peepshow*, the Sentence of Death (Expectant Mothers) Act codified Ogilvie's conviction that mothers should be exempt from the ultimate penalty, instructing that pregnant women facing execution should have their sentences permanently commuted. Julia's refusal to inhabit the role of mother – Ogilvie observes that Julia "had evaded the womb's responsibilities, while partaking of its pleasures" – thus condemns her twice over: it both figures and numbers among the moral transgressions for which she is in a sense convicted, but it also prevents her from escaping the zone of illegality to which these transgressions relegate her (392). Even at this late stage, motherhood could make "everything ... all right" for Julia. In this way, the abortion, Julia's attempt to foreclose on a future in which she is become the mother of Herbert's children, justifies the state in foreclosing on Julia via the finality of judicial murder.

Whether Jesse would have us, as readers, likewise foreclose on Julia, or deprecate Julia's execution, and the moral code that facilitates it, is not altogether clear. The third-person narrative is often focalized through Julia, creating sympathy for her, but it is also sometimes distanced from her, laying bare her flaws. Still, in noting that Julia's moral profligacy makes it easier for the jury to convict her of murder, Jesse implies that a more just justice system would recognize a considerably expanded repertoire of femininities, including, but not limited to, the aborting woman. If women must be hanged for murder, let them be hanged for murder, and not for having taken a job or a lover, or terminated a pregnancy. Decriminalizing abortion might help, but only in part, as the suspicion with which jury, judge, and prosecution regard the perfectly legal act of adultery forcefully suggests. Treating Julia's "greediness," which manifests alternately as an enormous capacity for physical pleasure and as a "thing which always made her reach out for the bright and shining bubble which was beauty," largely sympathetically, Jesse conveys the need for accounts of desiring femininity that do not frame female desire, sexual or otherwise, in terms of physiological abnormality, moral evacuation, or degeneration (12–13; 76).

Insisting that women who make use of contraception or avail themselves of the services of abortionists do not thereby violate the social contract is, to be sure, a worthy citizenship project. Note, however, that whereas abortion is the error that ejects Julia Starling from the respectable middle class, it only intensifies a criminal stench that already clings to women like Anna Morgan, whose colonial origins distance her even from those London women who, like her, engage in forms of what we might now call sex work. In this context, I want to look at two moments in Jesse's novel in which the narrative focus zooms out from Julia to encompass the plight of women more generally. When Julia arrives at the little newspaper shop where the abortionist conducts her business, she is appalled by the "dingy" "morality of the place," the "casual acceptance of depravity" suggested by its "so blatantly innocent air": "at least the Darlings [her family] were never dingy," she reflects (288). The narrator does not distance herself from Julia's fastidious response to Mrs Humble and the service she provides. Mrs Humble's greed – having set eyes on Julia's "spotless *crêpe de chine* underclothes," she regrets not charging Julia more for the abortion – is not sympathetic, unlike Julia's lust for beauty (287). Julia is notably upset, however, by the proximity with the "dingy" working poor into which her need for an abortion brings her, cleanliness being here associated with class in a way that is simultaneously materialist and not, since Julia fails to recognize the material conditions that make cleanliness difficult to achieve the further down the social ladder one travels. In the newspaper shop, it's harder to sustain the fantasy that she is "one of the great lovers of history" (276). Her situation is exposed as "commonplace and ordinary," not tawdry, as the prosecution will insist, but familiar territory for women of all classes and convictions. Jesse may be highlighting another of the misreadings of Julia that occur throughout her life, in which the particularities of her character and life are assimilated to a dreary narrative about the exigencies of working-class reproductive life that drive women to seek out the abortionist at ten pounds a pop. Still, it is striking that in the closing pages of the novel, with Julia awaiting execution, Jesse takes the time to twin her story with that of Mrs Humble, who has ended up in the same prison "doing ten years' for an abortion" (378). The Lady Superintendent of the prison reflects worriedly on what she finds difficult to think of as Mrs Humble's "crime":

> what, after all, had she done but help poor girls out of a trouble which civilisation would not permit to be anything else? Wasn't it, except in very rare cases, always economic pressure that had brought everyone into prison? Not merely women who were in for debt because they couldn't pay their rates ... but all the other women also, the street-walkers; the shoplifters; the members of thieves' gangs; the abortionists. They had all done what they had done because they hadn't any money; and the Mrs. Humbles could even think that they had been doing a good work as well. (378)

The lady superintendent's doubts about the righteousness of her calling indicts an economic system that drives the dingy to crime while criminalizing dinginess, highlighting the extent to which what is an exceptional experience for a middle-class woman like Julia, the experience of illegality, is a feature of life for the poor. If Julia associates abortion with poverty (it is what poor, dingy people do), and fears that getting an abortion declasses her, Jesse invites readers to consider why the poor might abort more, or more visibly, than other classes of Britons.

Here, the illegality of abortion emerges as something akin to the illegality of undocumented migration, as something that sticks to some but not other embodied subjects – "illegals" – succinctly denoting their ineligibility for inclusion within the community of the nation. The illegality that has obtained for undocumented migrants in the United States is, as Nicholas de Genova insists, historically distinct, produced through the conjuncture of particular histories of immigration, racialization, labour mobilization, welfare reform, and nation-formation.[64] Still, de Genova's work offers a useful model for thinking about the illegality of abortion, insofar as it foregrounds not only the classed, raced, and gendered operations of the law, but the role of the law in shaping how bodies are read and experienced to begin with.[65] Although the illegal act of abortion, unlike the illegal act of undocumented migration, says nothing officially about, nor has any official consequences for, one's citizenship status, attending to its illegality can nonetheless shed light on the extent to which access to the goods of citizenship is unevenly distributed. In Britain, where abortion has been a prosecutable offence since the early nineteenth century, the criminalization of abortion does not only mandate the prosecution, imprisonment, even execution of the aborting woman and her abortionist. It tars any refusal or failure to perform maternity as an affront to the sovereign authority of the state, turning an activity many people understand as "mundane" into an "illicit [act]."[66] Illegality, de Genova writes, has become a "constitutive dimension of the specific racialized inscription of Mexicans in the United States."[67] Where abortion is integral to the intimate life of the working poor, for example, its proscription has the similar effect of criminalizing working-class personhood. Conversely, the illegality of abortion waxes and wanes according to the existing (uneven) distribution of power.

Historically, prohibitions on abortion have been enforced differentially, with poor, working-class women more likely to be prosecuted than middle- or upper-class women. Does this mean that the state has more invested in the reproduction of the poor than it does in the reproduction of the rich? Not necessarily. The poor are targeted for medico-legal management for reasons that are in part pragmatic: in interwar Britain, the authorities were not normally alerted to cases of abortion unless something went badly wrong, a rare outcome for women who could afford the comparatively safe operations performed by medical professionals in sterilized surroundings. The visibility of the catastrophe of working-class morbidity and mortality inspired efforts to improve the health of the poor. But identifying the health of the poor as in need of amelioration could also lead to proposals for their extermination. In their testimony before the Inter-Departmental Committee on Abortion, representatives of the Eugenics Society claimed that decriminalizing abortion would actually bolster motherhood, since poor women in poor health were "quite unfit to carry out the responsibility" of, on the one hand, having children and, on the other hand, adhering to a daily regimen of birth control.[68] The illegality of abortion for the poor might then be said to be a product of their illegality, not a sign that the state wishes they would reproduce more, but a sign that it considers all their acts – including abortion, but also including reproduction – illegal, a flouting of its authority.

This complexity is adumbrated in a passage Virginia Woolf eventually removed from the manuscript of *The Years* (1937). The Pargiter cousins are looking down into the street:

> "Look at those wretched little children" said Rose …
>
> "Stop them, then" said Maggie. "Stop them having children."
>
> "But you cant" said Rose.
>
> "Oh nonsense, my dear Rose," said Elvira [who becomes Sara in the published version]. "What you do is this: you ring a bell in Harley Street. Sir John at home? Step this way ma'am. Now Sir John, you say, casting your eyes this way & that way, the fact of the matter is, ~~my husband~~" whereupon you blush. Most inadvisable, most inadvisable, he says, the welfare of the human race – sacrifice, private interests – ~~three~~ six words on half a sheet of paper. ~~A tip~~. [In the margin: Three guineas in his left hand]. Out you go – well, that's all. What I mean is, in plain language, ~~if that woman~~ Maggie ~~says she wont have a child~~, she wont [have] a child […] "We wouldnt have children if we didnt want them," said Maggie.
>
> "You wouldn't be allowed But you cant say that in public" said Rose. "You can say that here, to me, in private" […] "But how is that woman down there going to Harley Street? with three guineas?"[69]

In the strike-outs, the woman's (self-)censored exchange with Sir John; Rose's claim that some things can only be spoken about, if at all, in private; and the conversation's eventual excision from *The Years*, the passage betrays the cousins' insistence on "plain language" by registering its difficulty. This tension between the necessity and impossibility of speaking plainly pervades Woolf's work, where it speaks to the difficulty women experience in learning about the body, desire, and sexuality, including their own, but it gains added point from the illegality of the treatments under discussion. Only in private can women share (or not) information about birth control; in public, as the Bradlaugh-Besant trial had made clear, such speech is obscene and hence prosecutable. It remains importantly unclear, to be sure, just what is being purchased with the three guineas (a tantalizing sum, given the title of the major essay Woolf published in 1938, *Three Guineas*). Hermione Lee suggests that three guineas is the sum required for an abortion, but this seems low, given that the protagonist of *Voyage in the Dark* shells out three guineas for a box of worthless abortifacient pills and anticipates a charge of fifty pounds for the surgical procedure.[70] Still, at a time when unskilled labour was worth between one and two pounds a week, three guineas appears a substantial sum for any sort of treatment, and Harley Street the realm of privilege: as Rose says, "How is that woman down there going to Harley Street? with three guineas?" Rose's sceptical response to Elvira's Harley Street narrative stresses, perhaps even critiques, women's differential access to abortion services, the "clear class divide between the availability of safe, therapeutic abortion (curettage) and the more dangerous use of abortifacient pills, nonsurgical implements such as crochet hooks and knitting needles, and 'folk' remedies such as slippery elm bark."[71] But the cousins' insistence that the woman not have more children also reflects their more discomfiting conviction that her existing children are wretched, and that she must be stopped from having more.[72] Is it possible that *this* is what cannot be said in public? To the Pargiters, perhaps, the criminalization of abortion seems misdirected insofar as it impedes an open campaign to stop women like "the woman down there" from having children.

Accordingly, the norms at work in the pre-war world of *Voyage in the Dark* register Anna's pregnancy as a gross incompetence that disqualifies her from the race to "get on" – and from helping the race to "get on" (74). The newspapers, magazines, and cheap paperbacks that Anna and her chorus-girl friends devour project class advancement through marriage as, for women, the only future worth having, the only possible future. Whether it's Maudie soliciting a loan so that she can "smarten herself up a bit," or the capable Laurie knowing just who to contact in case of "accidents," Rhys's marginal women invest frantically in a futures market whose only prize is marriage (159; 74). Perversely, the moral failure to which Anna's pregnancy graphically testifies signals her unfitness to contribute to "our" future by reproducing (within the confines of marriage): that Anna is now pregnant proves that she should never have been permitted to have children. Nor is Anna's reproductive unfitness only a function of her sexual conduct. The dimensions of Anna's unfitness are rather multiple and intersecting. What Anna's flatmate Ethel describes as Anna's "pottiness" – "you're not all there; you're a half-potty bastard" (145) – threatens to class her with the "feeble-minded" whom commentators in Britain (and governments elsewhere) wanted targeted for sterilization. Molly Hite points to the "imputation of madness" that haunts all women "if they do not speak 'in character,' which is to say, in the wholly predictable ways that their role obliges," rendering their words and actions as "senseless," as when Anna burns Walter's hand with a cigarette (86).[73] Even her unconventional sexual behaviour is legible as madness. Pregnant and unmarried, Anna imagines "them," a disapproving chorus of common-sense critics, "watching you, their faces like masks, set in the eternal grimace of disapproval. I always knew that girl was no good" (164). Since, as Donald Childs explains, an incapacity for "exercising self-restraint; and for cherishing an ideal of virtue under any form" could be deemed a pathological condition ("moral insanity") too serious to risk passing on to one's children, "their" smug dismissal of Anna's goodness comments on her reproductive fitness.[74] In fact, "their" satisfaction at having a judgment confirmed – "I always knew" – suggests that Anna's moral decrepitude had been forecast long before any possibility of its manifestation, that her moral decrepitude is more the product of bad breeding than her propensity to breed badly is the result of moral decrepitude. Anna's poverty might be read in this way as well: eugenicists such as Francis Galton and Karl Pearson were not above arguing that the slum, rather than giving rise to the slum-dweller (in itself a problematic claim), was in fact produced by the slum-dweller, a distinctive biological type who sought out inferior environments. Since heredity and not environment or education was to blame for the appalling physical and mental condition of the poor, how could they be permitted to reproduce? Anna's ambiguous racial and national status presents as a final disqualifying property, seeming to testify to the degenerated fate of Britishness in colonial contexts.

Following a disaster with a massage client, Anna's xenophobic roommate Ethel raves, "I thought you were the sort of kid who'd take the trouble to be nice to people and make a few friends and so on and try to make the place go. And as a matter of fact you're enough to drive anybody crazy with that potty look of yours" (145). She continues, "the thing about you … is that you're half-potty. You're not all there; you're a half-potty bastard" (145). It's not unimportant that "bastard," with its connotations of illegitimacy and consequent lack of right to the ancestral hearth, is among the insults Ethel hurls at Anna, for Anna is creole, a white woman of British descent born in the Caribbean. In this, as most critics of the novel acknowledge, she is like Rhys herself. Jean Rhys was born Ella Gwendoline Rees Williams in 1890 in Dominica, then a British crown colony. She was the daughter of William Rees Williams, a Welsh doctor who had come to the island in 1881, and Minna Lockhart, whose family had owned plantations on Dominica for three generations. Rhys moved to England in 1907, returning to Dominica for a period of only eight weeks in 1936. Anna is similarly a fifth-generation "West Indian … on my mother's side," and follows her stepmother Hester to England only when her Welsh planter father dies (55). Anna's relationship to Britain is at once genealogical, racial, and cultural. Early in the novel, Anna confesses, "I had read about England ever since I could read," reminding us that the construction of England as home(land) occurs, in colonial contexts, primarily through the circulation of images of home in newspapers, photographs and books (17). On a train rushing through the English countryside, Anna is confronted by "things" she learns are the "haystacks" she's read about in books (17). A mobile national imaginary produces England as Anna's "real" homeland while relegating what seems real, the Caribbean-as-home, to the realm of the imaginary. Hence Anna's disturbing sense that "sometimes it was as if I was back there and as if England was a dream. At other times England was the real thing and out there was the dream, but I could never fit them together," a disturbance that then gets read as a kind of madness, as when Ethel tells her, "you're not all there" (8; 145).

The demand that one be nostalgic for a place one has never seen is not uniquely made, of course, of white settlers. In *A Map to the Door of No Return* (2001), the black Trinidadian-born writer Dionne Brand describes gathering with her family around the "ovular sound of the BBC": although the BBC "is the news from away," its voice tells the young Brand that she is the one who is "living elsewhere," who is "already mythic."[75] But there is a particular racial charge to the promise of belonging that England meretriciously extends to its colonial subjects: some British subjects, it appears, (should) find it easier to go "home" than others. Anna's limited capacity to recognize England bespeaks affinities that, although carefully cultivated, are understood to have been inherited. According to Angela Woollacott, many white settlers explained the appeal of the metropole in terms of a "call of the blood."[76] When Hester insists that she "did think when I brought you to England that I was giving you a real chance," it is clear that the chance inheres at least as much in removing Anna from a deleterious racial environment as in the greater range of educational and economic opportunities England may afford Anna (64).

For English settlers and their descendants, the route "home" was facilitated by a lingering conception of race as geographically and climatically as well as biologically determined. As Gillian Beer has pointedly observed, the Englishman is native only to England; conversely, only the Englishman can be native to England. Elsewhere, what is native is always what is not English.[77] Nancy Stepan notes that the ties between a given race and its geographical location were thought to be aboriginal and functional. Many of the maps produced from the middle of the nineteenth century onward were "therefore race maps, showing the global distribution of race types and positing the Caucasian or white race as superior in achievement, health and civilization, as well as firmly located in the temperate parts of the world."[78] But although claims that whites could live in the tropics only as a master race helped justify existing inequities of social organization, they also registered fears that whites were degenerating in tropical contexts, gone native through climate-induced disease. In response, British colonists worked to maintain sharp boundaries between themselves and the natives. This strict demarcation of native terrains was needed to ward off both the scarifying spectacle of the nativized Englishman and the deeply disquieting prospect of reverse colonization, of the chickens coming home to roost. The cultural instruction effected through radio broadcasts or the circulation of literary materials then betrays, as Vanessa Smith puts it, a "conflicted desire to produce colonial subjects and institutions whose identity confirmed their originals, while maintaining an equally affirming sense of difference."[79] The spectacle of the nativized Englishman or the anglicized native confirms that only disaster awaits those who stray beyond their native terrain.

This leaves white settlers, especially those born in the tropics, in an equivocal position. Late in *Voyage in the Dark*, Anna recalls an advertisement for "Biscuits like Mother Makes, as Fresh in the Tropics as in the Motherland, Packed in Airtight Tins" (149). Mothers make biscuits, but they also, of course, make people: the ad sells domesticity's capacity to secure as "Fresh" a reproduction of whiteness in "the Tropics" as in the metropole. But however optimistically secured from tropical predations and the effects of slow transport, the biscuits are only "like Mother Makes," suggesting abiding doubts about the authenticity of tropical reproductions and a recognition (or insistence?) that for English settlers and their descendants, "the Tropics" can only ever approximate a Motherland. The biscuits can be bought, but they cannot be made. In Rhys's later novel *Wide Sargasso Sea* (1967), the protagonist's English husband admits that the creoles may be "of pure English descent," but contends that "they are not English or European either."[80] Purity of descent notwithstanding, the colonial is not English (enough). Joe Adler, a friend of Anna's lover Carl, enrages Anna when he pretends to have known her father "Taffy Morgan [or] was it Patrick" (125). By invoking stereotypes of Welshness ("Taffy") and Irishness ("Patrick"), and refusing to distinguish between them, Joe asserts their interchangeability as equally inadequate versions of Englishness. Meanwhile, the other chorus girls call Anna the Hottentot, identifying the white creole with a nineteenth-century European icon of racialized sexual pathology.[81] These instances of misrecognition suggest how, as Peter Hulme writes, "the term creole seeps across any attempt at a manichean dividing line between native and settler, black and white."[82] Since, in the Caribbean, "the 'native' is either for the most part absent – if what is meant is indigenous – or 'creole' – if what is meant is 'born in the West Indies' – to distinguish between black and white creoles is already to blur the desired distinction."[83] I don't mean to suggest that there is no way to distinguish between groups yoked by a history of asymmetrical violence (here, slaves and slave-owners). Rather, the slippage tells us something about conceptions of whiteness and Englishness in this period, as subject to deformation as they are reproduced overseas. As Angela Woollacott demonstrates, even migrants from places like Australia, where whites made up an overwhelming majority of the population, found that they were thought to be "tainted by their (supposed) exposure to the violence inherent in colonial frontier expansion, [and] roughened by the hardships of colonial conditions and unrefined colonial social life."[84]

Rhys's nuanced, often agonized, treatment of white creole identity, both in *Voyage in the Dark* and elsewhere in her oeuvre, has been well plumbed.[85] Critics have rarely examined the relationship between Rhys's critical take on the failed promise of imperial Britishness and her interest in failed maternities, however, and then only as analogy or metaphor. On the one hand, it is argued, Rhys twins maternal deprivation with metropolitan disdain, "the alienation from the mother" becoming, as Laura Niesen de Abruna puts it, "a metaphor for the white Creole girl's alienation from the mother culture, England."[86] On the other hand, it is claimed, Rhys attaches "negative motherliness" to Dominica, aligning the "unsatisfying mothering she received as a child" with her sense of having been out of place from birth, even in her place of birth."[87] But the maternal relationship is not only a potent figure for the relationship of the metropole with its colonies, or the nation with its citizens. Rather, as Laura Ciolkowski observes in a reading of *Wide Sargasso Sea*, policing the "biological boundaries of Englishness" is one of the ways that anxious metropolitan subjects strive to "fix the difference between an 'English' core and an 'ethnic' periphery."[88] The pregnant creole body threatens this project of separation insofar as it manifests and threatens to proliferate the vagaries of imperial reproduction, exposing the relationships that bind Britain with its colonies as actually and not just figuratively familial.

To an important degree, then, Anna's refusal to see the pregnancy to term, far from thwarting hegemonic projects of national reproduction, helps to further them. In "choosing" abortion, she refrains from reproducing her criminality, confirming that maternity is a privilege reserved for those women whose citizenship, underwritten by various forms of material and social capital, reads as substantive. Arguably, abortion may help to preserve the illusion that the belonging of substantive citizenship lies within her grasp, offering Anna re-entry into the predatory economics of the city, a second chance at the future. And indeed, at the end of the novel, watched over by a doctor who moves "like a machine" and jokes about her imminent return to prostitution, Anna thinks "about being new and fresh. And about mornings, and misty days, when anything might happen. And about starting all over again, all over again" (187–188). At the same time, Anna's regeneration is characterized by repetition and mechanicity, the novel's looping closing lines, "starting all over again, all over again," echoing the opening of the novel. Elsewhere, Anna is acute about the way in which the promise of futurity held out by marriage and modern consumer culture works to regulate female sexuality, desire, and ambition. Walking down Oxford Street, she notes,

> The clothes of most of the women who passed were like caricatures of the clothes in the shop-windows, but when they stopped to look you saw that their eyes were fixed on the future. "If I could buy this, then of course I'd be quite different." Keep hope alive and you can do anything, and that's the way the world goes round, that's the way they keep the world rolling. So much hope for each person. And damned cleverly done too. But what happens if you don't hope any more, if your back's broken? What happens then? "I can't stand here staring at these dresses for ever," I said. (130)

If abortion secures for Anna the thin veneer of respectability – she's not, at least, an unwed mother – that is the minimal prerequisite for marriage, it's not clear that marriage is a future worth holding on to. Surely any respectability that the "illegal operation" secures for Anna will be spurious anyway. How, as Judith Butler asks in a related context, does one act "from within the presumption that one's acts are invariably and fatally criminal?"[89]

"A loophole of escape"[90]

Abortion leaves Anna in the untenable position of having to live.[91] It also opens a space, however, in which to challenge "their" monopoly on the future and its meanings, the "double and contradictory" movement of foreclosure affording glimpses of other futures, other futurities.[92] This is true not just in the sense that, as Sue Thomas argues in a reading of the abortion in *Voyage in the Dark*, pregnancy spurs women to imagine – or to attempt to imagine – themselves as mothers, a "projection of the future" Anna finds finally uninhabitable.[93] Intimations of more than this lost or inaccessible maternity are brought home to Anna through the act of abortion. From the time she acknowledges the pregnancy, Anna struggles to "do something about it," ingesting useless pills and powders before resolving to obtain the money necessary for a surgical abortion (166). Her pregnancy, in other words, is never not also an abortion, and vice versa. In the dream that marks the narrative place of this paradoxical temporality, Anna finds herself on a ship

> sailing very close to an island, which was home except that the trees were all wrong. These were English trees, their leaves trailing in the water. I tried to catch hold of a branch and step ashore, but the deck of the ship expanded. Somebody had fallen overboard.

> And there was a sailor carrying a child's coffin. He lifted the lid, bowed and said, "The boy bishop," and a little dwarf with a bald head sat up in the coffin. He was wearing a priest's robes. He had a large blue ring on his third finger. (164–5)

Anna thinks she ought to kiss the dwarf's ring, but instead walks the treadmill of the ship's deck, while the dream "rose into a climax of meaninglessness, fatigue and powerlessness" (165). After that, she says, "I kept on dreaming about the sea" (165).

It is tempting to read the dwarf as a version of the bolom, a figure of Caribbean myth who manifests in the form of a fetus with turned-in feet. In the literature of the Caribbean, the bolom is frequently ascribed origins in an act of abortion or infanticide. Thus, for example, in Derek Walcott's *Ti-Jean and His Brothers* (1957), a fabular play about three brothers tasked with outwitting the Devil, the Devil is accompanied by the Bolom, a child "strangled by a woman" "through the hinge of the womb."[94] In Dionne Brand's 1999 novel *At the Full and Change of the Moon*, Bola is the only member of the Convoi Sans Peur, a secret society of militant slaves, to survive their mass suicide. The bolom materializes what Claude Meillassoux terms the slave's "unborn-ness," that is, his social death.[95] But if the bolom materializes slave abjection, it also embodies slave defiance. The coercive and exploitative circumstances of slave reproduction furnish a powerful brief for abortion and infanticide. In *At the Full and Change of the Moon*, the slave Marie Ursule has "washed out many from between her legs … She had vowed never to bring a child into the world, and so to impoverish de Lambert [her owner] with barrenness as well as disobedience. Not one child born in that place for years, except what de Lambert could make himself with his own wife. Until one day, Marie Ursule made one with all itself intact."[96] That "one" is Bola. In Toni Morrison's 1987 novel *Beloved*, Nan tells "small girl Sethe" that her mother "threw them all away but you. The one from the crew she threw away on the island. The others from more whites she also threw away. Without names, she threw them. You she gave the name of the black man."[97] Later, Sethe will cut the throat of her youngest daughter. In the writings of black diasporic women, Caroline Rody claims, "instances of childbirth gone awry, of the deaths of mother or child, of mother-child separation, or of a woman's refusal of childbearing become tropes for the entrance of 'bad history' into women's lives, for female resistance to history, and for authorial inheritance of a traumatic past."[98] Thus, Xuela Richardson, the narrator of Jamaica Kincaid's *The Autobiography of My Mother* (1996), explains her childlessness by saying, "I refused to belong to a race. I refused to belong to a nation … The crime of these identities, which I know now more than ever, I do not have the courage to bear."[99] Born out of an unbearable history, Sethe's acts, or

Marie Ursule's, spell refusal, certainly. But as Paul Gilroy writes, "Such moments of violence" as Sethe's in the shed at 124 Bluestone Road also possess "a utopian truth content that projects beyond the limits of the present."[100] The children whose births punctuate but also, in different ways, result from the practice of abortion – Bola, the Bolom, Sethe – embody the promise of genealogical renewal: Bola, Marie Ursule's self-created child, is grandmother and great-grandmother to a diaspora, while Sethe, her mother's only daughter by a black man, breaks finally through to the possibility of "some kind of tomorrow" (Morrison 322). Walcott's play, which closes with the Bolom "*being born*," enacts a particularly spectacular fantasy of slave (re)birth (70). But even where no such rebirth seems imminent or possible, women's determined resistance to the brutalities of slavery through the violence of abortion and infanticide carries a utopian charge, an orientation towards an imagined future into which a bolom might eventually be born.

It is possible that Rhys learned about the bolom from the black caregivers of her Dominican childhood, in whose storytelling rituals she, like Anna Morgan, relished participating. This is not to suggest that the dwarf in Anna's dream *is* a bolom, or to claim for Anna's abortion a politics such as Walcott and Brand elaborate in their fictions, which is particular to the (post)slavery contexts of their production. Although slavery articulates with (other) gendered systems of subordination and exploitation, Anna's experience of illegality cannot be assimilated to the relentless assault on sexual, reproductive, and family life that is Marie Ursule's lot as a slave. As Anna struggles to "do something about [the pregnancy]," however, it is precisely this history of violence that comes to preoccupy her, especially as it intersects with the history of her slave-owning family (166).

Although fantasies of homecoming recur throughout *Voyage in the Dark*, these increase in number and intensity in the final section of the novel. Even before she will acknowledge the fact of her pregnancy, Anna dreams of the road to Constance, her mother's estate, where she recalls encountering "the woman with yaws" (152). Later, she remembers watching a masquerade "from between the slats of the jalousies" of her family's Dominican home (185). "Get on or get out, they say": since Anna's failure to "get on" bespeaks her dis-ease in the Motherland, no wonder that she seeks, instead, to "get out" (74). Anna's efforts to return to her Caribbean birthplace, if only imaginatively, invert metropolitan geographies of home and away by relocating the motherland from Britain to Dominica. Whereas Anna's father's money and second wife mediate Anna's relationship with Britain, Anna inherits her connection to the Caribbean through her mother: as she repeatedly informs Walter Jeffries, "I'm a real West Indian … I'm the fifth generation on my mother's side" (55). This matters because for all that mothers, as the biscuit ad makes clear, are charged with sustaining the spread of British goods, values, and people overseas, at the time *Voyage in the Dark* was published, the official mode of British cultural inheritance was patrilineal. Until the passage of the 1948 British Nationality Bill, for example, female British citizens lost their citizenship upon marriage to foreigners, while alien women who married British citizens automatically acquired their husbands' citizenship. Because women are figured as the soft edges of the race and nation, maternal inheritances are stripped of lasting legal or social value. This is even or especially true where what one inherits from one's mother is all-determining, as in the plantocracies of the Americas. Where the law made enslavement a condition inheritable from the mother regardless of whether the father was white, black, or coloured, free or enslaved, the condition of the mother signified legally to delegitimate the child. Indeed, Hortense Spillers wonders whether the condition of the mother that is "forever entailed upon all her remotest posterity" is in fact slavery, or the "'mark' and the 'knowledge' of the *mother* upon the child that translates into the culturally forbidden and impure. In an elision of terms, "mother" and "enslavement" are indistinct categories of the illegitimate inasmuch as each of these synonymous elements defines, in effect, a cultural situation that is *father-lacking*."[101] She calls for African Americans to claim the monstrosity of this mother as the basis for a radically different text of feminist as well as black empowerment. If the laughter, condescension, and suspicion to which references to her mother(land) expose Anna throughout *Voyage in the Dark* do not approximate the violence systematically visited upon slaves in the Americas, still, the fantasies of Caribbean homecoming that punctuate Anna's narrative reflect a comparable struggle to make meaningful "the 'knowledge' of the mother."

In taking up this inheritance, Anna contests the assumption that she should feel at home in England. Dominica is not thereby rendered a welcoming space, the true home to which she may now seek to return. It is not just that Anna's relationship with her mother is unlikely to have been idyllic. In Anna's case, making meaningful "the 'knowledge' of the mother" requires reckoning with a (family) history of cross-racial intimacy and violence. Indeed, Anna's memories of the Caribbean betray a preoccupation with sex, reproduction, and the workings of inheritance, and especially with what Hester calls "the sins of the father" (53). Recall the woman Anna encounters on the road to Constance estate. Although yaws is neither congenital nor transmitted through sexual contact, syphilis, the disease for which it is often mistaken (and to which it is related), is. Panics about syphilis, communicated through tragic narratives in which unsuspecting wives are infected by philandering husbands, were a major impetus for the late-nineteenth- and early-twentieth-century purity movements and contagious diseases acts that so shaped turn-of-the-century feminism and feminist conceptions of sex. Earlier in the novel, a song had reminded Anna of "Miss Jackson Colonel Jackson's illegitimate daughter – yes illegitimate poor old thing but such a charming woman really and she speaks French so beautifully she really is worth what she charges for her lessons of course her mother was –" (62). Miss Jackson's illegitimacy and racial ambiguity – it is implied that her mother was black, perhaps even a slave – play on those spectres of the "outside" families that haunt Anna throughout the novel. Thus, for example, Anna's stepmother Hester is scandalized by the spectacle of her brother-in-law's many illegitimate children "wandering about all over the place called by his name … And you [Anna] being told they were your cousins (64). A name Anna recalls seeing on an old Constance slave list, Maillotte Boyd, offers another reminder of planter proliferation, and the violence that enabled and accompanied it. Lying in Walter's bed, she thinks, "Maillotte Boyd, aged 18, mulatto, house servant. The sins of the father Hester said are visited upon the children unto the third and fourth generation – don't talk nonsense to the child Father said – a myth don't get tangled up in myths he said to me" (53). Categorized as "mulatto, house servant," Maillotte Boyd is not only likely the product of an interracial rape, the sort of routine sexual violence that enabled planters to increase their human capital, since the children of enslaved women "followed the condition of the mother," but herself likely a victim of the same routinized sexual violence. Indeed, noting that the "proper" name of Daniel Cosway, a key actor in the plot of *Wide Sargasso Sea*, is Boyd, Peter Hulme is prompted to a set of dizzying genealogical speculations: "If it were possible to use *Voyage in the Dark* as a way of reading *Wide Sargasso Sea*, then Daniel Boyd is presumably Maillotte Boyd's son by Antoinette's father. Maillotte is the name of Christophine's friend in *Wide Sargasso Sea*, the mother of Tia. If this is Maillotte *Boyd*, then Tia is half-sister to Daniel, who is half-brother to Antoinette."[102] This tightening of the genealogical screw has greater implications for a reading of *Wide Sargasso Sea*, in which Tia and Daniel play key roles, than for a reading of *Voyage in the Dark*. Maillotte's children are not mentioned in *Voyage in the Dark*. And although Constance, like Coulibri, is modelled on Rhys's family's estate, Anna cannot, even in the kind of impossible cross-fictional genealogy Hulme concocts, be a Cosway: Antoinette's brother dies early in the novel, while Antoinette herself has no children. Nevertheless, Maillotte's brief appearance in *Voyage in the Dark* recalls (presages?) her son's role in *Wide Sargasso Sea*, where he reveals, among other things, Antoinette's affair with another mixed-race Cosway cousin, Sandi. The name "Maillotte Boyd" invites Anna to reflect on her relationship with Walter:

to what extent is Anna like Maillotte, the enslaved mulatta like the white creole?[103] How free is each, ensnared within systems of sexual exploitation, to express and pursue desire? But it also highlights the familial ties, the inheritances, that bind Anna to the space of the Caribbean. Not syphilis but adultery, rape, and miscegenation are the "sins of the father" visited upon children like Antoinette, Daniel, and Anna. Might the monstrousness Anna fears for her child – she tells Walter's awful cousin Vincent, "Sometimes I want to have it and then I think that if I had it, it would be a … It would have something the matter with it" – be not (only) deformity, as the figure of the dwarf suggests, but miscegenation (173; ellipses in original)? In *Voyage in the Dark*, miscegenation is nearly always unspeakable. Miss Jackson's "mother was –" (62). Anna challenges Hester's insinuation "that my mother was coloured … You always did try to make that out. And she wasn't" (65). And yet it's always coming up. "I thought I had forgotten about her. And now – there she is" (152).

Elsewhere in the novel, it is true, Anna's longing for "home" is channelled through memories of Francine, the young black servant who tells Anna stories and counsels her through puberty, hinting at a form of belonging or affiliation that does not derive from genetics, genealogy, or generation, that is extra-familial, trans-racial, even queer. Her first night in Ethel's flat, Anna imagines waking up "back there": "I'll say Francine I've had such an awful dream – it was only a dream she'll say – and on the tray the blue cup and saucer and the silver teapot so I'd know for certain that it had started again my lovely life" (135). Francine's presence is needed to confirm that the economic and sexual degradation of Anna's adulthood has "never happened," that Anna has only dreamt England (135). This is in part because Francine, Anna imagines, is not subject to time in the usual (white) way. When Hester warns Anna that she'll "have a very unhappy life if you go on like that," Anna wishes to speak to Francine, "but I knew that of course she disliked me too because I was white; and that I would never be able to explain to her that I hated being white. Being white like Hester, and all the things you get – old and sad and everything" (72). Anna believes that Francine, not being white, will not grow old, and unlike Anna, need not worry about what others think of her life prospects. She may thus reasonably guarantee any attempt by Anna to turn back the clock, as it were. Repelled by the possibility of "being white like Hester, and all the things you get," Anna expresses a desire to be as she imagines Francine to be: impervious to time's influence, and thus, it seems, necessarily black. During the initial stage of the affair with Walter, Anna recalls, "I wanted to be black I always wanted to be black. I was happy because Francine was there … Being black is warm and gay, being white is cold and sad" (31). The three assertions – "I wanted to be black," "I was happy with Francine," "Being black is warm and gay" – are linked through their emphasis on feeling. The connectives we might supply – "I want to be black because I am happy with Francine and because being black is warm and gay," or even, "I want to be black because I am happy with Francine; I am therefore black because being black is warm and gay" – work to construe race as a matter of feeling desire or hatred, warmth or cold, as, in short, a matter of affect. In this fantasy of cross-racial identification, not only does Anna's desire for the Other imply a desire to be Other, but desire itself is enough to make her Other.[104] Since Anna's happiness at being with Francine makes her feel both at home and black, the relationship functions for Anna as a form of passing. Here, Anna traces the contours of "real West Indian" belonging in a transformative and importantly personal affiliation with blackness (55).

This has seemed to many readers a worthwhile project. Thus, for example, Urmila Seshagiri observes that "Anna's 'affiliation' with Francine … foundationally threatens the codes of white Caribbean plantocracy."[105] But does it? The limits of passing-as-belonging are multiple and contradictory. In Anna's fantasies of homecoming, her relationship with Francine stands in both for childhood and, I think, the possibility of a pristine encounter between individuals (momentarily) emancipated from histories of obligation and dependence, indeed from history itself. The impulse is utopian in the sense elaborated in chapter 1. As Sara Ahmed writes, however,

> encounters are meetings … which are not simply in the present: each encounter reopens other encounters … The particular encounter both informs and is informed by the general: encounters between embodied subjects always hesitate between the domain of the particular – the face to face of this encounter – and the general – the framing of the encounter by broader relationships of power and antagonism.[106]

Thus, a dismayed Anna knows, even as she attempts to prove otherwise, that Francine "disliked me too because I was white" (72). And with good reason, perhaps, for when Anna dreams of resuming her "lovely life," Francine appears not as the girl who explains menstruation to Anna or tells her stories in patois but as the servant called upon to comfort with tea and bromides. They are two girls, yes, but they are also servant and mistress, slave and planter, black and white. Their relationship is woven through and through with history, as Anna realizes when she sees Francine washing up, a scene Mary Lou Emery reads convincingly as disclosing "the trauma of labor."[107]

Francine recalls that history for Anna in another way as well. In a brutal exchange, the resolutely English Hester complains about Anna's "awful sing-song voice …! Exactly like a nigger you talked – and still do. Exactly like that dreadful girl Francine. When you were jabbering away together in the pantry I never could tell which of you was speaking" (65). Hester blames Francine and the "rocks and stones and heat and … awful doves" of Gerald Morgan's Caribbean estate for her failure to rear a "lady" (62). This, combined with her certainty that England will prove Anna's "real chance," exposes the class, colonial, and racial dimensions of Anna's bad breeding (62). But for Hester, the incorrigible ease with which Anna "catches" bad breeding in the form of a "jabbering" voice and unladylike behaviour can only be explained by a possibility she is unwilling to air openly: in response to Hester's observation that "considering everything," Anna "probably can't help" "the unfortunate propensities which were obvious to me from the first," Anna feels compelled to deny that "my mother was coloured" (65). Whether Anna's association with Francine makes her black or whether (for Hester) the relationship makes sense only given some prior taint is unclear, even irrelevant. If, as Ahmed has suggested, in seeking to pass for black, whites enact, among other things, "the fantasy of an ability (or a technique) *to become without becoming*," there is yet no escaping consanguinity, since even where no biological relation can be discerned, the contamination of blood is always adduced to explain the existence of relationships between blacks and whites.[108] No legal document can make Hester Anna's biological mother, but the possibility that Anna may care for Francine and vice versa casts doubt not only on Anna's whiteness but on her mother's as well.

On the one hand, that, for Anna, her family, and friends, affect raises the spectre of hidden genealogies reflects a suspect conception of belonging as describing, deriving from, the fact of racial identity, "the call of the blood." On the other hand, white expressions of anxiety about the possibility of racial contamination surface a history of familial mutilation, rape, and natal alienation that would otherwise go unacknowledged. In reading for miscegenation, Anna's white peers concede the history that, for whites in a post-slavery society, makes miscegenation a not unlikely family secret. It is as if the body were, or might be, as Nathan Stormer writes, "a repertory of memory, the surface on which history had inscribed itself."[109] Anna may not be "coloured" herself, but the suspicion of mixture is her legacy of an unforgivable past, the sins of the father come visiting. In this way, the attempt to identify contaminants within the community (here, "coloured" creoles seeking to pass for white) ends by giving the lie to the assumption that it is possible to definitively identify "what and who are contained (or belong) within its literal and figurative borders."[110] Britons, Ian Baucom suggests, have often turned to genealogical … principles of shared identity and rights" to suggest that "England was uninvolved, untroubled, unaffected by 'its' empire, and that the history of Englishness, consequently, is an entirely local affair."[111] In *Voyage in the Dark*, however, the genealogical ties that Anna seeks alternately to revivify and repudiate do not only lead her back to the space of the Caribbean, but surface the involvement of England with its empire at the most intimate of levels, tracing what we might describe as a counter-genealogy of Britishness in the aporias of her tangled family tree.

If Anna functions as an embodied reminder to Britons of this involvement, the "wrong" "English trees" with which "her" island is seeded offer incontrovertible evidence of Dominica's encounter with Britain. Here, I depart from readings of the novel that see Anna as effecting, in the closing section of the novel, a healing return to her island home, "evacuating [herself] into the collective enunciation of the West Indian social scene."[112] For Anna, it should be noted, does not in fact make it all the way "home": in the dream, she is prevented from stepping off the ship, not least by her realization that "somebody had fallen overboard." Andrew Thacker reads moments like these as "subvert[ing] any discourse of place as settled attachment." For Rhys, he says, "the voyage of subjectivity is always a little off course, and never arrives at its destination."[113] In *Voyage in the Dark*, home emerges as, to quote Sara Ahmed, "the impossibility and necessity of the subject's future (one never gets there, but is always getting there) rather than the past that binds the subject to a given place."[114] But Rhys emphasizes the historicity of this impossibility as well. After all, if Anna cannot go home, it is *because* of the past that binds her, and with her Britain, to the Caribbean.

For the body "fallen overboard" is, surely, another iteration of the image of the drowning slave that, as Baucom demonstrates in *Specters of the Atlantic*, haunts the transatlantic history of modernity, animating the work of Afro-Caribbean writers like Kamau Brathwaite, Édouard Glissant, M. NourbeSe Philip, and Derek Walcott.[115] For these writers, the Atlantic is the wound, rupture, unifying the black diaspora. But the trauma of the Middle Passage is likewise Anna's inheritance, dividing her from Francine, the slave descendant, to whom it nonetheless also sticks her. It would be possible to see in the dream an attempt to contest metropolitan codes of racial adequacy by giving weight to Anna's sense of "real West Indian" belonging that goes nowhere, sent off course by her preoccupation with the body overboard, or, alternately, by her refusal to acknowledge the indisputably miscegenated character of her family, to acknowledge that the miscegenated character of her family matters. Perhaps what is required is for Anna to get over the shame that, Sue Thomas suggests, leads her to abort the pregnancy rather than pass on the taint of her uncertain class and racial position.[116] I want to resist the assumption, however, that Anna's being stuck signals failure, a prelude to some more satisfactory resolution. In other words, I want to resist pathologizing the experience of impasse that, as numerous commentators have observed, she shares with other Rhys protagonists.

"Metaphors of paralysis and directionlessness" abound in *Voyage in the Dark*, Seshagiri notes, conjuring a sense of entrapment it is difficult not to want (Anna) to break free of.[117] I'm not sure, however, that we don't more often need to get stuck in (on?) the past, to be with those bodies overboard, the brutality of whose deaths conditions our being in the present. If Anna is caught between islands and identities, this in-between, which is also the Atlantic, may be precisely where Anna needs to be, learning how to inherit, how to *bear*, that "atrocious history" that was born and is interred in its "abyssal … abysmal" depths.[118] "The sea is history," Walcott writes.[119] What if, in moving on, we also hung on, "kept on dreaming about the sea"?

Hanging On

I first read *Voyage in the Dark* over a decade ago. That encounter started me down a path that has led here, to a book about reproductive projects of citizenship and nation building. Like Mary Lou Emery, I was stunned by Rhys's representation of abortion, which I had not expected in a novel published in 1934. I was unsure how to read Anna's abortion, given the pre-decriminalization contexts of its writing and publication. And so, following in the footsteps of historians like Barbara Brookes, Stephen Brooke, and Joanna Schoen, I began to reconstruct the meanings ascribed to abortion and other reproductive acts in the first part of the twentieth century.[120]

I remain convinced of the need for nuanced accounts of how reproductive acts have signified at particular moments of the twentieth century. At the same time, the gap between pre- and post–Second World War discourses of reproduction can be overstated. In particular, we tend not to recognize, or not sufficiently, the extent to which reproductive acts and imperatives continue to articulate gender and sexual identities with racial, national, and civic ones. Regarding abortion as a practice with serious consequences for the (racial) health of the nation that reflects, almost always poorly, on women's capacity for citizenship registers, to be sure, as an anachronism, a relic of eugenicist-era thought. How much more compelling seem the rhetorical tactics of someone like Stella Browne, one of only a handful of interwar feminists to explicitly advocate for decriminalization on the grounds that this would "extend the rights and happiness of women."[121] And yet, something is lost when the right to abortion is delinked from conversations about citizenship altogether. This is not to say that neither reproductive rights nor citizenship contribute anything to "making life more bearable and more interesting and better and bigger for the majority of women."[122] But in foregrounding the exclusions that structure access to citizenship within maternalist citizenship regimes, the representations of abortion in interwar texts like *A Pin to See the Peepshow* and *Voyage in the Dark* urge readers to the difficult work of rethinking how the goods of citizenship, as well as the good that is citizenship, are defined and distributed, among women but also across differences of race, class, nationality, religion, and ability. Sadly, as contemporary feminist and queer activists of colour can attest, this is no less urgent a project in the twenty-first century than it was in the 1930s.

Chapter Four

Apprehending Loss: Maternity at the Margins

Race suicide, if you will, is the policy of the mothers of the future. Who shall blame us?

Maternity, ed. Margaret Llewellyn Davies (1915), Letter 20

In *Three Guineas* (1938), Virginia Woolf ponders a question that, she drily supposes, no "educated man" has ever before asked a woman: "How in your opinion are we to prevent war?"[1] In the main text of the essay, Woolf develops a gendered critique of militarism, linking women's education and professionalization with the pacifist cause whose importunities provide the occasion for the essay. In her copious notes, however, she proposes a more succinct solution to the problem of war. Having ruefully concluded that "we [women] have no weapons with which to enforce our will," Woolf appends a footnote:

> There is of course one essential that the educated woman can supply: children. And one method by which she can help to prevent war is to refuse to bear children. Thus Mrs. Helena Normanton is of the opinion that "The only thing that women in any country can do to prevent war is to stop the supply of "cannon fodder." … The fact that the birth rate in the educated class is falling would seem to show that educated women are taking Mrs. Normanton's advice. It was offered them in very similar circumstances over two thousand years ago by Lysistrata. (127; 275)

As Susan Grayzel notes, "The maintenance of gender order via an appropriate maternity [is] a fundamental tactic of [modern] war."[2] To refuse to be a mother, then, is, from one point of view, to shirk one's patriotic duty and decline one's responsibility as a (female) citizen, but it is also to decry the nation's murderous need of mothers. That women might protest war by refusing to bear children could appear as Woolf's wry jest, or overwrought fantasy. Anthony Ludovici's 1924 book about the coming spinster take-over, which concludes with a truly bizarre vision of a dystopia in which ritualized infanticide is practised and men, become superfluous, are periodically culled, is, after all, called *Lysistrata*. Still, it seems telling that New Zealand and Britain, in 1936 and 1937, should have established committees to investigate the incidence of criminal abortion just as preparations for war were ramping up. Responding to suggestions that "fear of war," whether in "the form of a) conscious visualization of the horrors of war or, b) subconscious fear evidenced by excessive anxiety about the future," was acting "as a powerful deterrent from child-bearing," a witness who spoke before the McMillan Inquiry thought it important that "there should be no thought behind state legislation on birth control or abortion, … of encouraging the production of children" as either "potential soldiers, i.e. of potential killers of other people's children," farm and industrial workers, or "even as a means of filling up the empty spaces of our land and so maintaining it for ourselves versus other nations."[3] In interviews conducted by the Joint Council of Midwifery at British municipal hospitals between 1937 and 1939, working- and middle-class British women, many of them mothers already, explained their recourse to abortion by citing "the uncertainty of [a] future" darkened by chronic ill health, economic pressures, and looming war.[4] They would be happy, they insisted, to have children, if only there was more money, or they hadn't been warned they'd die carrying another child to term, or their children could be kept from the front lines.[5]

Such statements exude foreboding. On the one hand, commentators worry that a drop in the birth rate and concomitant decline in vitality and optimism will handicap the British empire in the fight against expansionist and nakedly pro-natalist fascist states like Germany, ending in the end of empire. On the other hand, women, schooled by the Great War in the demographic effects of modern war, baulk at the thought of their children given over to the military machine to become cannon fodder, or subjected to the horror of aerial bombing campaigns and foreign occupation. The assumption that they can be counted on to produce "killers of other people's children" turns women from the maternal path. If British men and women are unlikely to have practised birth control out of fear of war and anti-war sentiment alone, still, these feature prominently enough in such accounts as we have of working- and middle-class sexual, reproductive, and family life as to demand our attention.[6] In either case, a loss that is feared but has yet to take place – the loss of one's nation or child – precipitates a set of pre-emptive actions that have loss as their result: the imperilled nation sacrifices individual children to the imperative of collective survival; the reluctant mother refuses to bear the children she might otherwise welcome. "To castrate oneself *already*, always already, in order to be able to castrate and repress the menace of castration, to renounce life and mastery in order to assure oneself of them; to put into play, by ruse, simulacrum, and violence, the very thing that one wishes to conserve; to lose in advance that which one wishes to erect; to suspend that which one raises": Derrida describes such logic as apotropaic.[7]

In chapter 3 I read the closure of abortion in terms of the futures and futurities it nonetheless, I argued, projects. Through readings of texts by the New Zealand–born writer Robin Hyde, this chapter reflects on the exigencies and uses of a projected future imagined in terms of closure, focusing on women's attempts to rethink maternalism along pacifist and anti-imperialist lines. Treating forms of maternity that often go unrecognized – the maternity of the single mother, of the mother who is not yet a mother, of the bereaved mother – works such as *Wednesday's Children* (1937) and *The Book of Nadath* (written in 1937 but published only posthumously in 1999) feature children whose vulnerability at once bespeaks the high cost of, and encodes an alternative to, settler sovereignty projects. Hyde's willingness to contemplate the end of (national) reproduction, to envision a New Zealand bereft of children, might seem a praiseworthy approach to national, even civilizational, ruin, one which resists the temptation to view any weakening in the existing order as a calamity to be raged against, by whatever means necessary. What Sarah Trimble calls "the economy of survival" can demand too much of us.[8] Indeed, as Stella Browne asserts, "if all women were unwilling to bear children it would be much better that no children should be born."[9] Apprehensions of decline interrupt the progressive flow of settler time, muddying a distinction between "backward" indigenes and "forward-thinking" colonists long of use in upholding the territorial claims of the latter. In so doing, however, they also forward settler projects of territorial control, albeit in a new, minor, key, elaborating (national) self-mastery, as Kathleen Marks observes in her work on apotropaios, "through the anticipation of threat and an attendant self-projection that represses aggression."[10] For what are such narratives but a perverse form of "proleptic elegy," the term Patrick Brantlinger applies to that "nation-founding discourse" which justifies European settlement projects by heralding the imminent – immanent – extinction of Indigenous people, situating "the vanishing savage" in a time prior to the nation, and the settler as his rightful heir?[11] Hyde's Pākehā characters lament their own impending deaths along with the violent history of settlement, seeking indigeneity via the medium of the grave, in which bodies merge with, or rather, are converted into, the land. In these texts, finally, death inaugurates a new order of settler national being.

"The fewcher of the waarld"[12]

Robin Hyde was born Iris Wilkinson in Capetown in 1906. She was the second daughter of George, an Anglo-Indian veteran of the Boer War, and Nelly, an Australian nurse working in a military hospital.[13] In 1909, the Wilkinsons relocated to Wellington, New Zealand, where George took up a position as a postal clerk and mail sorter, and developed literary and political interests inimical to the more conventional Nelly. In late 1922, having graduated from the Wellington Girls' College, Iris Wilkinson commenced work for the Wellington paper *The Dominion* and its country cousin *The Farmer's Advocate*; she wrote columns on society events and parliamentary goings-on. Journalism would always provide Wilkinson with a precarious source of income: over the next fifteen years, she contributed, sometimes regularly, to newspapers in Wellington, Wanganui, Christchurch, and Auckland, as well as to the *New Zealand Railways Magazine*. But she also had literary ambitions, submitting poems and short stories throughout the 1920s to literary pages and journals in New Zealand and Australia. In 1929, she published a collection of poetry under the name Robin Hyde. Two more collections of poetry would follow, as well as five novels and two books of non-fiction. This is not to mention a considerable body of work left unpublished at her death in 1939: memoirs, short stories, plays, and at least two major poetic sequences.[14]

In 1937, following one of a number of stays at an Auckland-area mental hospital, Hyde completed the "queerest little book of my days": a manuscript entitled "The Book of Nadath."[15] In its current form, *The Book of Nadath* is a long prose poem divided into fourteen named sections, each spoken by Nadath, a self-described "false prophet."[16] If the diction, syntax, and speaking voice suggest a biblically inflected mysticism, Nadath's concerns, set down in the looming shadow of war, are urgently contemporary.[17] Thus, for example, the eighth section of the poem is given over to a critique of "The Iron Child," or war, drawing attention to the way in which jingoistic and militaristic projects of national self-aggrandizement harness processes of social and biological reproduction. Because women's sons, "upright and tall," are given over at birth to the iron child ("we shall take him from you"), procreation fulfils the imperative to breed soldiers and soldiers' mothers, to reproduce the iron child. War also feeds directly on women's bodies in the form of sexual intercourse with the enemy, forced and consensual. According to the men who defend the iron child from Nadath's condemnation, guarding the iron child means saving our "hearths," "lest that earth Nadath has called sacred be ravaged, and the face of the field stream blood": the spectres of rape and consequent miscegenation are here invoked in the images of desecrated hearth and ravaged earth, as they are earlier in the figure of "the iron child of another race [who] shall come against us, to break in twain the gates" (31).

While children are at once war's favourite victims and its preferred prosecuting agents, it is nonetheless at women that Nadath directs his ire and pleas. "You feed [the iron child], you flatter him, you comfort him. You have surrendered to him the heritage of your sons, and your daughters' pittance": Nadath accuses women of betraying their patrimony by sanctioning the death of the legitimate heirs and producing, under whatever coercive circumstances, illegitimate children (30). He goes on to wish that women "had hated your husbands so dearly [as you claim to hate the iron child]; for then your beds were not empty this night: and if you had cherished your sons as well, there were not a red clay stamped into a sodden field" (30). Women must love rather than hate the iron child, Nadath implies, since they seem prepared to stand by while war engulfs their men. And indeed, an old woman is provoked to respond, "There is no need to mock at us: our [way] is love, and we must follow where it leads us" (31; insertion in text). Nadath refuses to acknowledge, ultimately, the sexual charge of war, the opportunities for pleasure war affords both men and women, elaborating a rigid morality that, in condemning women for their promiscuity, doesn't seem much of a departure from the jingoism that leads to women being tarred and feathered, their hair razed, for sleeping with the enemy. Still, "The Iron Child" commands attention for its suggestion that only women can articulate an effective pacifism. In her 1940 essay "Thoughts on Peace during an Air-Raid," Virginia Woolf notes the cruelly painted faces of women shopping in wartime and thinks, "If we could free ourselves from slavery we should free men from tyranny. Hitlers are bred by slaves."[18] Similarly, in the fourth section of *The Book of Nadath*, the prophet despairs, "Oh slaves, is it out of the wombs of slaves that the new world can be born?" (13). If women continue slaves, their children will not bring a new world into being.

Throughout "The Iron Child," Nadath repeatedly commands his reluctant auditors to slay "the father": "In the kingdoms of earth there are strange things seen and done, but not this: that a child be born without a father … If the father of the iron child be a man, slay that man (31–2). He later concedes, "If the women will hear, and will forsake the iron child utterly, it may be that this is enough" (33). Because the law of the iron child is "sterner" for mothers, only their compliance has "borne him up," and therefore only their determination to "drop the iron child from your arms" can save the young from being "torn and broken" (28; 31; 30). As I've suggested, the iron child is both war and the real child conscripted by war, so that it's unclear – deliberately so, I think – whether Nadath means women to reject war or their own children. It may be that there is no child who is not already the iron child, no fathers who are not already "fathers." On the one hand, then, Nadath urges the destruction of those persons and structures that make war possible, the "fathers" of war. On the other hand, Nadath seems to be advising precisely what he insists is inconceivable: the birth of children without fathers. If women could birth children without fathers, whether by abolishing a patrilineal order of naming and inheritance or through biotechnological proxy, they might remove their reproductive labour from the service of the iron child and so force a new order of life. Taken to its logical extreme, the birth of children without fathers, because (so far) impossible, implies Woolf's half-serious solution of an end to reproductive labour altogether. Such fantastic scenarios aside, what is evidently required is a change in the way women birth and raise children, for without willing bodies, coercible bodies, without any bodies at all, the iron child will surely perish.

Just such a change might be thought to have been achieved by the protagonist of Hyde's 1937 novel *Wednesday's Children*. By the time we meet Wednesday Gilfillan, she has spent the previous decade living on an island in Auckland Harbour with her five illegitimate children – Attica, Dorset, Naples, and the twins Limerick and Londonderry – and Māori nanny Maritana. Once a quiet presence in the house of her half-brother Ronald, Wednesday Gilfillan commenced her "degraded" career at the age of twenty-seven by winning a fortune in a manner, to quote Ronald's insufferable brother-in-law, "that must have been pleasing to the Devil. An Australian lottery ticket. Twenty-five thousand pounds" (36). She then left the Gilfillan household to move in with the man who sold her the lottery ticket, Constantine Agropolous. He abandons her just before the birth of their daughter Attica. Each of Wednesday's subsequent lovers – an Englishman named Edward, an Italian man called Beppo, and the Irishman Michael – desert Wednesday when they learn she is pregnant, leaving her to raise the children on a small island with only Maritana to help. To the horror of Wednesday's middle-class Pākehā family, the births of her children are each announced in a local newspaper. Ronald's wife Brenda and brother-in-law Crispin are not amused: "Behold Wednesday," reflects a hysterical Brenda, "suddenly a boa-constrictor, slipping from Brenda's reach, and coiling herself gaily in the most conspicuous positions" (30). However, Wednesday, her children, and island prove attractive to the Englishman Mr Bellister, whose ward Derwent is engaged to Brenda and Ronald's daughter Pamela. Intrigued, even in love, Mr Bellister seduces Wednesday, and promises (threatens?) to marry her and take her to England.

In describing a retreat to a tiny island paradise that culminates in a kind of muted disaster, Hyde, like the authors discussed in chapter 1, taps into a long tradition of locating in the Antipodes utopian possibilities for redemption and revitalization. At the same time, it is likely that Nigel Hendon, in particular, would find Wednesday's island experiment anathema (and vice versa), insofar as the island in Auckland Harbour welcomes precisely those individuals whom the nation-as-laboratory will not accommodate. Whereas Linda Hendon is burdened with a suspect genealogy that prohibits her full participation in her husband's eugenicist endeavour, Wednesday's spinsterhood, she feels, "edge[s her] off the earth" and turns her "unreal" (274). We have seen how especially feminine reproductive (mis)behaviour became a matter of public concern in the first decades of the twentieth century. Historians Leonore Davidoff, Megan Doolittle, Janet Fink, and Katherine Holden note that "a tradition of concern about the problems of the 'redundant' or 'superfluous' woman" intensified in the 1920s and 1930s, as single women, metonymically represented by their supposedly empty wombs, came to emblematize all that was wrong with the post-war world.[19] Outrageous as always, Anthony Ludovici warned that the nation must not tolerate the "bungled and the botched" bodies of spinsters.[20] At best, spinsters were felt to be irrelevant, external to the workings of the nation, this despite the fact that, as Davidoff et al. point out, unmarried and childless women contributed a significant portion of the labour needed to sustain the so-called nuclear family. In *Wednesday's Children*, Hyde strives to mobilize this marginality: where New Zealand's utopian potential is bound up with its geographic marginality, Wednesday's utopian efforts are motivated and enabled by her social marginality, the fact that she is, as she puts it, "an unwanted woman" (261). As the New Zealand writer M.H. Holcroft wrote in 1943, "Always there are the margins which seem to contain the great potentialities of the future."[21]

The British writer Sylvia Townsend Warner offers a queerly subversive take on the spinster in her delightful 1926 novel *Lolly Willowes*. Caroline Willowes, a happily married, satisfactorily procreative, and frighteningly competent housewife, initially categorizes the novel's eponymous spinster heroine as an "unused virgin," "passed from one guardianship to another."[22] Caroline's pitying stock-taking condemns Laura Willowes to "a state of Aunt Lolly," needed by her nieces and nephews ("Caroline did not know what the children would do without their Aunt Lolly"), or to being "my sister-in-law Miss Willowes" (61–2). As Caroline sees things, Laura is the "extra wheel" in the well-oiled mechanism of her healthily reproductive family (47). She is defined – diminished – by the children and unions of others. Understandably fed up, Laura longs "to have a life of one's own, not an existence doled out to you by others, charitable refuse of their thoughts, so many ounces of stale bread of life a day" (243). She retreats from her sister-in-law's London townhouse in Apsley Terrace to a snoozy hamlet called Great Mop, where she makes a pact with the Devil and becomes a witch. Groping after something "that lurked in waste places," Laura claims for her own what others have refused (for her): a life on the margins, emancipated from and thankfully superfluous to the mechanisms of Apsley Terrace (78; 239). She insists that "one doesn't become a witch to run round being harmful, or to run round being helpful either, a district visitor on a broomstick," but rather to be "passive and unnoticed," to "sit in [a] doorway and think" (243; 240).

In Wednesday Gilfillan, who supplements her lottery winnings by working as a fortune-teller, Robin Hyde imagines a different sort of "white witch": unlike the utterly unproductive Laura, Wednesday offers comfort and advice to "snipped-off, faded bit[s] of tapestry" like herself, and helps brace a community fractured by poverty and unimpressed by "tepid soup and tepid salvation" (*Wednesday's Children*, 113; 375; 112). What is more, although Wednesday distances herself from her sister-in-law's impeccably middle-class brand of domesticity, unlike Laura, she does not disavow its constituent parts: reproductive sex, children, and a comfortable home.[23] None of Wednesday's lovers pass the "test" of pregnancy, instead abandoning her to her growing brood of children: "She heard herself saying to [Michael], in a slightly raised voice: 'Michael, I am going to have a baby.' For the fraction of a second, the razor hung suspended, flashing as Wednesday's oar flashed now when she raised it out of the sleek dark water against the moon. Then it came down, sword of Damocles. She knew that Michael wasn't going to pass the test" (58). It may seem surprising that Wednesday's fantasy love life should revolve around a series of defaulting fathers-to-be. But Wednesday's victory, as Mary Edmond-Paul puts it, "is that she hasn't had to be dependent on [the] disappointing responses" of men like Michael.[24] As an unmarried working mother who fostered out her only surviving child, Hyde was well acquainted with the narrow range of options facing single women who got "caught," or chose maternity without the safety net of marriage. According to Edmond-Paul, Hyde envisages, here and elsewhere, "a maternal future, a future in which a woman would have the financial independence to refuse marriage or to manage without it and keep her baby."[25] The lottery frees Wednesday for unconventional sexual behaviour by enabling her to "sustain the consequences" singly, reliant on no one – save, of course, Maritana.[26]

But Wednesday's children represent more than their mother's sexual and economic emancipation. Or rather, it is what the children represent that makes their mother's – and indeed all mothers' – emancipation so critical. Fleeing conscription to the Italian campaign in Abyssinia, Naples's Italian father Beppo returns to the island midway through the novel with his brother the Elf. When the Elf wonders "what makes me come to this funny little island," Wednesday responds,

> What made America have a shot at a Peace Plan, and League of Nations, however much it went wrong and we all let ourselves down? … It's just that there's

something in people that can't take itself out in gramophones and automobiles and tall buildings, and the fascinating amours of the machine. And, of course, it's just as much satisfied with its truly filthy industrial record in Europe. It hasn't got a country. So in the meantime, it becomes naturalized on my island. You're here for precisely the same reason that President Wilson went to Paris. (257–8)

Housed in the aptly named L'Entente Cordiale, Wednesday's children embody her commitment to pacifism and internationalism. By selecting as fathers for her children absconding men of different nationalities, she defies (to an extent) the racialist adherence to hearth and sacred earth *The Book of Nadath* insists animates militarism. Struggling to explain his sister's disgrace to Mr Bellister, Ronald Gilfillan cries, "The fact is, she's a sort of international thingumabob," which Crispin characteristically translates as "harlot," but which makes Wednesday sound like a female James Bond, saving the world through sex (33).

This is not to say that hearth and earth retain no relevance for Wednesday. True, Wednesday advances a considerably expanded definition of family as organized around matrilineal rather than patrilineal conceptions of descent and inheritance. It's no coincidence that the establishment of L'Entente Cordiale requires Wednesday to break away from the household of her half-brother, with whom she shares only a father. The language of reproduction, family, and domesticity nonetheless remains important to her project. No Lysistrata, Wednesday reworks but does not reject the contemporary tendency to view reproductive bodies as national assets or liabilities, and reproductive acts as nationally significant. (Nor, importantly, does she defy contemporary taboos proscribing intimacy across the lines of colour. On this point, L'Entente Cordiale might just as well be situated in England as in the Pacific: although Wednesday, dreaming of India, expresses a desire for a "white child" whom she intends to call "Amber," no Asian, Pasifika, or Māori men join her on the island [60].) Whatever it is that "made America have a shot at a Peace Plan, and League of Nations" may not have a country, Wednesday explains, but it has become "naturalised on my island": pacifist internationalism takes shelter on Wednesday's island, in L'Entente Cordiale, rooting itself in, but also itself rooting, a nascent utopian nationalism. In this respect, *Wednesday's Children* echoes the oft-cited autobiographical fragment Hyde wrote following a 1933 suicide attempt, in which she stresses the importance of "home" as a ground in which to root efforts at international cooperation. She explains,

I know now what I am looking for. It is a home in this world. I don't mean four walls and a roof on top, though even these I have never had, the attic at the asylum and the stilt-legged Maori cabin where I spent three weeks at Whangaroa

> constituting my nearest approach to habitations. As often as not, though, four walls and a roof get in the way, are the very point where one is fatally side-tracked from ever having a home in this world.
>
> I want a sort of natural order and containment, a centre of equipoise, an idea – not a cell into which one can retreat, but a place from which one can advance: a place from which I can stretch out a giant shadowy hand, and make a road between two obscure villages in China, teach the Arab and the Jew how to live together in Palestine, tidy up the shack dwellings and shack destines of our own thin Maoris in the north.[27]

Here, Hyde imagines individuals rather than nation states or multi-state organizations intervening in conflicts overseas. At the same time, not only is the end of intervention peace within or between groups, within or between nations and nation states (China, Palestine, Israel), but in proposing home as a "place from which one can advance" rather than a "cell into which one can retreat," Hyde tags local attachments as the sine qua non of effective international action. Internationalism, conversely, may provide the nation with a founding set of principles. It's worth noting that although New Zealand's entry into the First World War automatically followed Britain's, the Pacific country not only signed the Treaty of Versailles independently of Britain, but joined the League of Nations as a founding member. In context, participation in the League might be seen as signalling a nascent national assertiveness. Indeed, as Elleray notes, Britain feared that New Zealand's independent membership in the League would lead to "an unseemly airing of linen in public should Britain and her former dependency ever disagree over policy," a fear that was realized, precisely, in the contretemps over Abyssinia: New Zealand favoured sanctions, while Britain counselled lenience.[28]

Ultimately, whatever home Wednesday constructs on her island is short lived, if it ever existed at all. The novel ends with the outrageous revelation that the children Wednesday claimed to have birthed and raised are fabrications. In a letter addressed to Hugo Bellister, she explains that she spent her lottery winnings in financing the Anstruther Children's Home, "which was small but good, and where they used it in an experimental way, sunlight and funny, flowery lessons, and painless growing up" (274). When Ronald and Mr Bellister visit Wednesday's island, they discover not the comfortable family home she (and the narrator) had described but an empty wooden shack. Wednesday herself appears to have committed suicide. In the next section, I reflect on the significance of this late turn: what is the point of imaginary children? Exposed as fantasy, Wednesday and the children lost to us, L'Entente Cordiale need not be accounted a failure, I suggest. Rather, this relegation of Wednesday's island experiment to the realm of the fantastic should be read as an apotropaic gesture, in which the experience of loss is called upon to preserve that which threatens to be lost.

Full of Woe

In 1990, the New Zealand poet Fleur Adcock offered a tempered appraisal of *Wednesday's Children*, acknowledging its "historical" importance but lamenting its recourse to "the whimsical, baby-talking habits of J. M. Barrie and A. A. Milne."[29] For Adcock, the novel's fantastic elements weaken its "idealistic protest against the imprisonment of women." Fantasy – the names "Barrie" and "Milne" suggest its essential childishness – is insufficiently weighted by real-world concerns to sustain even estimable political agendas like Hyde's, which are in any case already diminished by their lack of pragmatism. The disclosure that concludes the novel can appear to concede this point, Susan Ash notes, suggesting that Wednesday has been indulging in a "'childish' evasion of reality through fantasy."[30] The sympathy with which Wednesday and her children are rendered throughout the novel, however, makes it unlikely that Hyde's project is so disciplinary. Like Crispin, one could find Wednesday's deception embarrassing or enraging. Instead, I want to read the derealization of her children in a more positive light, as telling us something about the promise they embody, as well as the challenges she faces trying to rear father-free children in a patriarchal world.

Although reciprocated by Wednesday, Hugo Bellister's declaration of love caps a series of increasingly threatening male interventions into island life that begins with Beppo's return to Auckland and picks up steam with Great-Uncle Elihu's decision to will Wednesday's children all of his money. Wednesday wonders, with apparent inconsequence, whether Mr Bellister "practiced Yoga. At the moment, it was easy to imagine him spending months in a solitary hut with a cow-dung floor, contemplating his navel, that he might the better learn how to Will" (260). Like Elihu, Mr Bellister seeks to bring Wednesday within the compass of his will, promising her "protection and safety and independence of the world": "We'll all live together at 'Fawns' [his English estate] … Possibly we'll have more children. Who cares?" (265; 269). To be sure, Elihu and Hugo are hardly the patriarchy's most sinister representatives. And yet, Wednesday tells Hugo, it is Great-Uncle Elihu, and not Brenda or Crispin, who has made "the worst trouble, … leaving that money, that wretched money, to my children" (265). We sense, moreover, that while Wednesday's children may not matter to Hugo "in an obstructive way," they also don't matter very much at all (269). Menacing Wednesday's achievement, the production of children in whom are invested utopian principles of pacifism and internationalism, the step-father-to-be's promise of care threatens indifference at best.

To insist, however, that the incursion of too much reality in the rigid person of Mr Bellister turns Wednesday and her children unreal perpetuates a view of fantasy as pathological that the novel takes some pains to disrupt. If *Wednesday's Children* offers readers "a 'childish' evasion of reality through fantasy," well, children are central to Wednesday's pacifist agenda. Could fantasy, rather than the sign of its failure, be similarly central to the novel's utopian politics? Contemplating the "peace and security" of spring evenings on her island, Wednesday thinks about the migratory birds flying "back to New Zealand from the North":

> Sometimes the poor brave sillies flew straight into the Polyphemus-glare of the lighthouse windows. A thud of soft breasts, a crackle of tiny hollow bones, and down they plumped, journey's end a quieter thing for them than the urgent racial memories had whispered. If that had happened to Beppo and the Elf – if there hadn't been the island for them to fly to – one could easily imagine the thud that so small a migrant as Beppo would have made, breaking against the great blind eye of Reality. (139–40)

In an essay on the utopian fiction of Katherine Burdekin, a British contemporary of Hyde's, Daphne Patai conjures a similar image, watching as birds come up against windows they imagined they might fly through. For Patai, this arresting scene – this scene of arrest – represents a problem that "writers of literary utopias" must confront as they "labor to illuminate their own society by imagining alternatives": "what these writers are doing is attempting *not* to hit the glass walls of their habitual frames of reference … If they face the glass head-on, they cannot make it out. Where, then, can they situate themselves so as to allow the glass to become visible?"[31] Patai's "birds" deploy the indirection of utopian writing to shed light on the real. Apprehending "Reality" isn't the aim of Hyde's godwits, however, who wish, rather, to avoid getting smacked up against it. By 1937, as Wednesday admits, the capacity of international organizations like the League of Nations to broker peace, even the desire for peace itself, appeared irredeemably compromised, not just idealistic but damagingly so. As against the world's descent into war, Wednesday's internationalism can seem anachronistic, parochial, futile. But it is precisely what David Harvey calls "the doctrine that 'there is no alternative,'" the inevitability of the "Reality" with which we, like poor Beppo, are always being urged to come to terms, that Wednesday and her fellow island residents are trying to resist.[32] The island can then be said to function as a refuge for not only internationalist but utopian currents of thought more generally, as a place where alternatives remain imaginable, however improbable their translation into reality. It harbours the unreal(istic): talking lions, peaceniks – and fantasy. The children themselves appear as avatars not only of pacifist internationalism but of the island nation's utopian potential.

The fantastic then finds a home on Wednesday's island. But it is also fantasy (albeit of a different sort) that makes the island community possible in the first place. "Like blood," writes Jacqueline Rose, "fantasy is thicker than water."[33] That is, like blood (and also unlike blood), fantasy underwrites forms of social cohesion and continuity. In *Wednesday's Children*, the terms "fantasy" and "reality" organize ideas about the proper conduct of women's lives. Presided over by her sister-in-law Brenda, the home Wednesday flees for L'Entente Cordiale is a miracle of starchy linen, impeccable landscapes, and curtains with "no fantasy about them" (28). Along with the "English flowers planted in a long, narrow bed outside the dining-room windows," the presence of a bona fide butler rather than the "virulently independent" "raw girls" who suffice the rest of middle-class Auckland codes as English the middle-class norms of domesticity to which Brenda is determined to adhere (28). As against Brenda's domestic choreography, Wednesday's island, site of illicit affairs and home to a mongrel brood of illegitimate children, conjures a freer, less hierarchical New Zealand, liberated from the necessity of hewing to the standards of the old country. In this sense, it appears fantastic even before the novel's closing coup de grâce. And yet the novel slyly hints at the dependence of even (or especially?) the stolid middle-class home upon a species of fantasy. Brenda "had very nearly created Beagle [the man-servant]. She made him, not in her own image, but in the image of the ideal butler ... The whole of it, for that matter, ... was Brenda Gilfillan's doing. She had made it. She had made also Pamela" (27–8). Children as well as servants are integral to the creation of the perfect home, which is achieved largely without the aid of Brenda's hapless husband. What's exceptional about Wednesday's domestic idyll, then, is less its fantastic character than the explicitness of its fantastic character. Not only does Wednesday develop a utopian vision of the New Zealand nation (as pacifist, as internationalist, as mongrelized, and so on), but she strives to transform New Zealand into a home for fantasy, a place, that is, where fantasy is at home in every home.

That the nation is made and sustained through acts of imagination is an uncontroversial claim, the idiosyncracy of Hyde's fantastic stylings notwithstanding. In the now classic *Imagined Communities*, Benedict Anderson foregrounds the fictionality of the nation-form, linking the emergence of the "imagined political community" of the nation with the novel's emergence as a dominant literary form.[34] Both nation and novel, he explains in the later *Spectre of Comparisons*, were spawned by the simultaneity made possible by clock-derived, man-made "homogeneous empty time," and thereafter, of Society understood as a bounded intrahistorical entity. All this opened the way for human beings to imagine large, cross-generational, sharply delineated communities, composed of people mostly unknown to one another, and to understand these communities as gliding endlessly towards a limitless future. The novelty of the novel as a literary form lay in its capacity to represent synchronically this bounded, intrahistorical society-with-a-future.[35]

Fiction "seeps quietly and continuously into reality, creating that remarkable confidence of community in anonymity which is the hallmark of modern nations."[36] Jonathan Culler has cautioned literary critics against the "dubious" claim, sometimes derived from Anderson's work, "that the novel, through its representations of nationhood, made the nation."[37] He prefers the "less shaky" claim "that the novel was a condition of possibility for imagining something like a nation."[38] What is intriguing about *Wednesday's Children* is that in representing the nation, the novel stages the nation's – and, for that matter, its own – imagining. The novel opens,

> At precisely 7.30 on the night of June 22nd a small woman in a fur coat entered the advertising department of a newspaper office (*The Comet*) in the city of Auckland, New Zealand.
>
> There are still some Flat-Worldians, or, as Swift called them, Big-Endians, who have not been trained by crossword puzzles, the increasing strangeness of politics, or the mystery of the League of Nations (which is so rapidly replacing that of the Holy Trinity in modern life), to use their imagination. To these, such a statement as the above will convey nothing …
>
> At a karma-stage slightly higher are those who, hearing mention of actions in a strange city, a strange country, will lay down their newspapers, saying vaguely, "Auckland? Auckland?" Is New Zealand in Australia, they will wonder, or is it the other way about? But they will go no further with the matter.
>
> By elimination, we come thus to the ideal type of listener … the man who knows a bit, and can believe or imagine much more. (13)

The narrator then proceeds to delineate what such an ideal type would see – Wednesday, the street, the awful architecture, the lawns of Albert Park, and taxis – smell – "at least three different scents" – and hear – "the ghostly whispering of rain" (15). He would know, the narrator slyly suggests, a fact not grasped by many a dweller in the Northern Hemisphere: in New Zealand, June 22nd is the "shortest day of the year" (14). And he would see Wednesday Gilfillan bumped by the door as she enters the office. This is Hyde's way of schooling us in the protocols of being a local, an Aucklander, a New Zealander. But it is also Hyde's way of schooling us in the protocols of fiction reading, of reading this fiction, the novel *Wednesday's Children*, as well as of constructing the fiction that is Wednesday's life. We are asked to draw on the skills developed in us by "modern life" in order to participate in the construction of a fantasy. For it is only if we can "believe or imagine much more" than that a woman walked into a newspaper office that the novel can unfold, that "*The Comet* doors [can] open before Wednesday Gilfillan," that we can seem to be meeting Maritana, Attica and co., that we can believe, in short, in Wednesday, her four lovers, and five children (16).

In a sense, the children have always been fantastic, at once embodying and guaranteeing those commitments of Wednesday's that her peers dismiss as absurd and impractical. To re-render Wednesday's children as fictions, scraps of the imagination, is then only, perhaps, to literalize what has always been most true and promising about them. Such a reading appeals to the extent that it takes seriously rather than pathologizes Wednesday's and the novel's turn to fantasy. At the same time, reading *Wednesday's Children* thus minimizes Mr Bellister's role in the novel's coup de grâce. Wednesday's valedictory letter frames her death as an expression of loyalty to the children, whom it will somehow function to preserve: "there has to be loyalty, hasn't there," she tells Hugo (277). Believing that marriage to Mr Bellister will make her fantasy children and lovers seem "misty and faraway …, a stupid discarded toy," she decides to kill herself as a way, precisely, of preserving fantasy's force, its significance in and for the real (277). With marriage threatening to edge Wednesday off the earth, making her, as spinsterhood did before, "unreal," she kills herself, embracing one form of derealization in the attempt to avert another, an apotropaic act if ever there was one (274). It would be absurd to deny how impoverished seem the choices Wednesday allows herself: so that Wednesday may forestall the loss of the children, she must succumb to the self-loss of death. Is there no alternative? The children cannot but appear differently to readers once their ontological status has been clarified, growing as misty and faraway as Wednesday fears she will find them post-marriage. We must experience what happens to Wednesday and her children as a loss. Surviving through (and as) Wednesday's fidelity to the principles they were supposed to have embodied, the children yet cease to exist in the (textual) real, a removal that encourages pessimism about the capacity of this world to nurture alternatives to the status quo. That their preservation is purchased with loss is made clear on the very last page of the novel, when Mr Bellister writes the names of Wednesday and her five children on six "white fan-shaped shells," which he stands "in a row, their pointed ends digging into the sands. They glistened like tiny tombstones" (286). Re-rendered as fictions, scraps of the imagination, Wednesday's children must be accorded (some of) the rituals conventionally performed for the dead, including interment. However, if loyalty to the children entails giving them up, could it be that giving them up isn't just an unfortunate outcome of that loyalty, but a central element in it? According to the old saw, Wednesday's child is full of woe. In *Wednesday's Children*, perhaps, the better "fewcher" the children appear to promise is secured through being relocated to the space of loss, encrypted.

"A death at the heart of it"

Prolepsis emerges as likewise critical to the formal and political workings of "The Greenstone Shadow," the eleventh section of *The Book of Nadath*. Here, however, it is provided with a genealogy that underscores its utility to the project of settler nationalism. "The Greenstone Shadow" describes a near future in which "the yellow man" rules over "the people of Nadath," who have "learned to endure the yoke" but refuse the yellow man's "talk of brotherhood"; rejecting the yellow man's medicines, his "good counsel," they also withhold their "secrets from his understanding" (43–4). Anthropologists "goad on the people of Nadath, that they should work in their ancient ways and make their songs, as in the time unconquered," while the anthropologists themselves "wrote many books about the people of Nadath, and painted pictures, or went into savage places to find relics and a trace of the story" (44–5). Meanwhile, sexual unions between "Nadath's sisters" and the yellow man result in cities overrun by abandoned mixed-race children (43). In imagining a New Zealand governed by yellow men, "The Greenstone Shadow" reflects the fears of Asian expansionism that circulated throughout the Pacific during the interwar years, as Japan took over greater and greater swathes of eastern and southeastern Asia. But it seems clear that "The Greenstone Shadow" also describes a historical invasion: the colonization of Aotearoa by the British. How indeed could we fail to recognize, in the yellow man's deployment of physical force and sexual coercion, of ethnography and science, the characteristic tactics of European colonial governance projects? This story of yellow men and the people of Nadath is also, then, a story of Pākehā and Māori.

Although the Māori characters in her fiction and poetry can appear cartoonish (see, for example, Maritana), Hyde's biography, journalism, and letters reflect (for the period) an unusually marked interest in and sensitivity to Māori concerns, past and present. In 1935, she, along with the young poet Gloria Rawlinson, took Māori language instruction from Maungatai Babington of Ōrākei, while in 1937, she began serving as secretary for the Association of the

Friends of Orakei. The Ōrākei land block, located in what is now Auckland, has long been a flashpoint in relations between Māori and Pākehā. After signing the Treaty of Waitangi in 1840, a Ngāti Whātua hapū (local kinship group) living in the Tāmaki Makau Rau region of the North Island invited British settlers to establish the township of Auckland on 3000 acres of land. Over the next two decades, Ngāti Whātua lost control of much of their land in the Tāmaki Makau Rau. In the late 1860s, determined to reserve at least the papakāinga (home base) at Ōrākei, Ngāti Whātua asked the Native Land Court to confirm its collective ownership of the 700-acre Ōrākei Block. Although the court agreed that the Ōrākei Block should be "absolutely inalienable to any person in any manner absolutely," it divided the title between thirteen Ngāti Whātuā individuals, thus paving the way for a century of further depredation. Coercive government purchasing practices culminated in the evictions of 1952, at which point the marae (community meeting place), homes, and buildings were destroyed. Already by 1937, however, the affluent city had declared the residents' tenure on the flat illegal and proposed their removal.[39] Members of the Orakei Village Protection Committee and the Auckland Clergy Association, Pākehā all, formed the Association of the Friends of Orakei to register their disapproval of the Auckland city council's actions. On 18 August 1937, a week after the association's first meeting, Hyde penned an animated letter to her friend and Labour MP John A. Lee on the subject of socialism's responsibility to Māori and the land-rights movement. In a note dated 10 August, Lee had termed Hyde's concern for Māori "almost" pathological, and relegated Ōrākei to the status of a "side issue."[40] Hyde now asserted, "I am there [on the side of the Ōrākei Māori] because I am a Socialist, not because I'm not one."[41] Importantly, she also cited a poem she was then writing: "We came as guests and traders: we stayed under [the] Treaty [of Waitangi]: we picked quarrels, or mishandled them, for land. 'Let him learn, he who sleeps in a conquered land beds himself with a corpse, which shall take its own time to rot." This last is from "The Greenstone Shadow," except there, of course, it is the yellow man who pays conquest's stomach-churning price.[42]

If the poem's futuristic scene allows Hyde to grapple with the Pākehā legacy of conquest and crafty treating, this is not to say that "The Greenstone Shadow" is not therefore concerned with the threat of Asian invasion, which it seeks, rather, to situate historically. Hyde invites her Pākehā readers to see themselves in Māori, as similarly vulnerable to conquest. Pākehā too, Hyde seems to be saying, may suffer the kind of violent incursion that will make it impossible for them ever again to claim to constitute a people. Acknowledging that "generalized condition" of precariousness that renders all of us, as Judith Butler has written, vulnerable to violence (among other sensuous experiences) promises a more ethical politics of encounter.[43] Contemplating the finitude of their own supremacy, Pākehā may be forced to recognize the enormity of what they have done to Māori. Recognizing themselves in the aggression of the yellow man, they may find it more difficult to dehumanize him. But the poem does not only work by analogy, encouraging readers to compare white settler with Asian invaders. It implies, in addition, that Pākehā are vulnerable to Asian invasion *because* they once dispossessed Māori, framing settler colonialism as a sin for which Nadath's people must now atone.

As I noted in chapter 2, settlers have often framed intercourse with colonized female bodies as a means of bolstering claims to the land. In "The Greenstone Shadow," the sexual relationships into which Nadath's people are coerced, even forced, result in offspring that the women refuse to acknowledge as their own. The invaders are not untouched by this violence, however:

> They [Nadath's people] did not dream of an uprising and a revenge: they were their own revenge ... They said, Is it for Abel to ask favours of Cain? But Abel was struck down by his brother. Now let Cain find the burying-place, and dig deep through rock, since his nostrils are uneasy. Let him learn, he who sleeps in a conquered land beds himself with a corpse: which shall take its time to rot. (44)

Indeed, the yellow man comes to feel alienated not only from the people he helps to rule but from his fellows:

> What curse has fallen upon me? I have come to hate my race and my companions.
> We are too loud in these streets: but beyond is the echo of a voice that was beautiful, singing its death-rune in loneliness to the abiding stars.
> When we go among the defeated we are hypocrites, and we bring back only that pretence which we deserve,
> For we do not love them in their defeat, but only the shadow of their days without challenge, that greenstone shadow. (45)

Nadath knows what comes next: acknowledging that his people too were "watched by the greenstone shadow," Nadath identifies the yellow man's sense of alienation – from himself, from others – as "the burden of the conqueror, the heavy price of an empire" and, finally, the cause of his downfall: "we cannot be ourselves, we cannot know ourselves, for shame at the watching of the greenstone shadow" (46). Thus do the invaders render themselves vulnerable to invasion in their turn. The yellow man laments, "Layer upon layer, the story turns to rock, with a death at its heart": relations in the contact zone petrify; violence proliferates (46).

In the concluding section of "The Greenstone Shadow," Nadath, pondering "how the plans of a few make water-carriers of the children, before their limbs are grown: make of the race a slave, and call it a conqueror," cries out, "If there be still in the world a place where the feet of children dance, let Time hang it with mists, with the snowy fleeces of clouds, and close around it a cordon of young trees with raven locks, / Lest it be known, and evil come to it: lest it find the face of its greenstone shadow" (46–7). Whether Nadath fears proliferating "the burden of the conqueror, the heavy price of an empire," or the doom of conquest, the poem belies his hope that any children may be saved from these fates. Or does it? Might not Nadath's proleptic gambit, to the extent that it functions apotropaically, in fact contrive a kind of refuge? According to Kathleen Marks, apotropaic gestures work by "anticipat[ing], mirror[ing,] and put[ting] into effect that which they seek to avoid."[44] "The Greenstone Shadow" mitigates the catastrophe of future civilizational death by projecting it into the past, as having already taken place. In effect, it makes a sanctuary of the grave.

The poem's turn on the genre of the proleptic elegy is critical to this project. In *Dark Vanishings*, Patrick Brantlinger reflects on the myth, prevalent in the late nineteenth and early twentieth centuries, of imminent (and immanent) Indigenous extinction, identifying such anticipations of loss as part of a "nation-founding discourse" that positions the settler as a legitimate successor to the (soon to be dead) Indigene.[45] Although late-nineteenth- and early-twentieth-century racial theorists heralded Māori as superior in intelligence, educability, and general capacity to other savage peoples, they were not therefore less likely than Aboriginals, for example, to be thought on the brink of extinction. As James Belich points out, the dying race meme persisted until at least 1930, "a generation after census evidence showed conclusively that Maori were on the increase."[46] In *Wednesday's Children*, the fantasy of locatedness into which the reader is inserted at the beginning of the novel also conceals a death at its heart: the narrator notes "a certain awful sameness about these [Auckland] buildings" which might suggest "that their architect was Cain, and that the corpse of Abel would probably be discovered in an advanced state of decomposition somewhere beneath them, if one went snooping" (14). The narrator nowhere identifies this body. Elsewhere, however, Hyde transforms the story of Cain and Abel into an allegory for the dispossession of Māori by Pākehā.[47] "The only good Indian is a dead Indian," one of the American generals tasked with prosecuting the Indian Wars is reputed to have said. Perhaps, conversely, only the dead are truly indigenous.[48] Read in this light, Mr George's exclamation in *The Boy in the Bush* passage cited in chapter 2 makes a different kind of sense: "She's [Australia's] waiting for real men – British to the bone – … Wait for a few of *us* to die

– and decay! Mature – manure – that's what's wanted. Dead men in the sand, dead men's bones in the gravel. That's what'll mature this country. The people you bury in it. Only good fertilizer. Dead men are like seed in the ground" (22–3; emphasis in original)." Trusting in post-mortem insemination to produce a mature, prosperous population bypasses the problem of settler belatedness, and matches, even trumps, Indigenous peoples' claim to the land. "The Greenstone Shadow" seeds the land with the corpses of ex-settlers in a way that echoes Mr George's necrophilic fantasy, except that here, the land's vengeance is that of a dying or dead race. If, as Dana Luciano suggests, the myth of the vanishing savage translates Indigenous people into "a past tense" that is prior to, even outside of, national time, it does so, Brantlinger insists, by imagining a "funereal future" bereft of Indigenous people that has, " in a sense, always already taken place."[49] In the "funereal future" Nadath conjures, the settler's death, proleptically imagined, actually confirms his inheritance of Indigenous land, literalizing his claim to be tangata whenua (people of the land).

Marks describes apotropaios as a "dangerous and yet fruitful way of confronting a painful past," insofar as what we remember of the past conditions our expectations of, and especially fears about, the future.[50] Certainly, "The Greenstone Shadow" anatomizes the violence of settler colonialism, cataloguing – condemning – its effects on colonizer and colonized alike. And yet, as we've seen, "The Greenstone Shadow" remains committed to that project of indigenization that constitutes a foundational element in the architecture of settler sovereignty. It is a guilty conscience, perhaps, that leads Nadath to fear invasion, surfacing the painful history of Māori–Pākehā relations. But "The Greenstone Shadow" also under-reads the complexity of this history to precisely the extent that it continues to proleptically, and therefore inappropriately, elegize Māori.

Consider the image of the greenstone shadow. "We do not love [Nadath's people] in their defeat," the yellow man sighs, "but only the shadow of their days without challenge, that greenstone shadow." That greenstone, or pounamu, is of particular importance to Māori, who wear pounamu both in honour of their ancestors and as a kind of ancestor itself, suggests that "that greenstone shadow" refers to Māori, or to New Zealand's deplorable treatment of Māori. Even if the yellow man, in invoking greenstone, means to denote what remains of Pākehā culture, that greenstone was originally of significance only to Māori hints at the way in which settlers arrogate Indigenous objects, rituals, and beliefs to themselves in the effort to discover or invent the national tradition they assume they lack. Settler artists and designers have often turned, as Nicholas Thomas notes, to a "distinctive environment" and "native productions" for inspiration.[51] In the late nineteenth and early twentieth centuries,

New Zealand–born writers like Jessie Mackay and Ronald Finlayson drew on local Indigenous culture and themes in their poems and stories to provide "the descendants of settlers with a history peculiar to themselves."[52] In the preface to *The Spirit of the Rangatira and Other Ballads* (1889), Mackay wonders "where indeed could patriotism find a fitter shrine than the land that contains the majesty of the sounds and the glory of Aorangi; the land that contains the wonders of Rotomahana and the tomb of Te Terata, marvellous even in its desolation?"[53] Aorangi, Rotomahana, and Te Terata are all natural features of the New Zealand landscape, but in pointing to "the majesty of the sounds … of Aorangi," in using, especially, the mountain's Māori name instead of its loaded European moniker (Mount Cook), Mackay implies that the distinctiveness of the land inheres partly in how it has been marked by Māori. Naming, as the geographers Robin Kearns and Lawrence Berg suggest, is a form of norming, providing (at least potentially) "normality and recognition to those who dominate the politics of place representation."[54] The persistence of Māori place names can be taken to signal the failure of a toponymical colonialism. However, the use of Māori place names by Pākehā has also sometimes permitted a simultaneous drain on two sets of nativist cultural capital – the distinctiveness of the land and Māori cultural production – while seeming to eliminate the need to confront the problematic presence of Māori themselves. Often, writers and painters deny that Māori have marked the land in any way at all. In *Wednesday's Children*, for example, Hyde has Wednesday describe Māori as "wandering careless things that don't count [as having set foot on the island] and don't set anything down in register except the natural warnings and welcomes of the place" (277). In his 1940 essay "The Deepening Stream," M.H. Holcroft claims that "the forests of yesterday" cast a "shadow within the New Zealand mind" that should fuel nationalist cultural production. It does not seem a stretch to connect Holcroft's "shadow" with Nadath's "greenstone shadow."

Certainly, Māori mana whenua was severely tested in the decades following the signing of the treaty: in a 1939 parliamentary debate, the Māori MP Sir Apirana Ngata quoted a chief who'd said, a century earlier, that "under Waitangi, the shadow of the land went to the Queen, but the substance remained with Maoris. Now [said Ngata] they had only the shadow."[55] At the same time, figuring Māori as shadows misrepresents the vitality of their continued inhabitation of the land, a form of rhetorical attenuation that doesn't just register, but actually participates in, the ongoing assault on mana whenua. In a similar way, the ascription of shared futurelessness that leads Hyde to identify Māori with Nadath's people obscures the fact of Māori survivance. Given Hyde's interest in and sympathy with Māori concerns, it is hard not to hear in Nadath's call to protect the place "where the feet of children dance" a reference to a pair of violent incidents: one at the Taranaki settlement of Parihaka in 1881, in which Pākehā attackers found themselves skirting dancing Māori children; the other at Hiruharama in 1917, involving Tuhoe, upon whom the ethnographer Elsdon Best would eight years later bestow the moniker "Children of the Mist."[56] That the encounters between Pākehā and Māori "children" in the Taranaki and Urewera were devastating for Māori cannot be denied. And yet, the self-governing prosperous, syncretic, and intertribal communities of Parihaka and Hiruharama (a transliteration of Jerusalem) also cannot be understood as refuges untouched by colonialism or unengaged with modernity. Nor did the children of Parihaka and Hiruharama give up the ghost, or even give up. Wednesday Gilfillan fears that it is "too late" for Ma(o)ritan(g)a to have children (19).[57] (At least Hyde doesn't deny that inequitable social relations affect birth rates: Maritana isn't childless because she belongs to a dying race but because, as the narrator remarks, "babies of her own would have taken up her time" [19].) Hyde (sometimes) knew better: in a March 1937 letter to parliamentarian Downie Stewart, she recalled a Māori man quoting "Rewi Maniapoto's message, 'Friends, we will fight against you for ever – for ever,' and [saying] that had always gone on, but the pakeha [*sic*] had never noticed it."[58] There may be a corpse waiting to be discovered – reanimated? – somewhere beneath the buildings of Auckland (the Treaty of Waitangi, perhaps) but it is not, in any case, the dead body of Māoritanga. Premised on "the lack of a lack or, in other words, on a wished-for lack that is instead an all-too-real obstacle to identification," the doubly elegiac project of "The Greenstone Shadow" inaugurates a kind of mourning that is really a conjuration, a ritual performed, as Derrida writes, to ensure that "the dead will not come back" but will remain "localized, in a safe place, decomposing right where [they were] inhumed."[59] After the end, the settler nation is reconstituted in the utopian space of the grave.

Chapter Five

Shrunk in the (White)wash: Britain at World's End

With the Second World War, this study seems to reach a natural stopping point. Cecil Cook was removed from office in 1939; A.O. Neville retired in 1940. Thereafter, absorption disappeared as an explicit aim of Australian Aboriginal policy. The Inter-Departmental Committee on Abortion filed its report in 1939, recommending against any liberalization of the law on abortion. The outbreak of war temporarily stifled further debate about the relationship between femininity, maternity, and citizenship. The Abortion Law Reform Association continued to press for the liberalization of British abortion law, but as Stephen Brooke notes, "it did not regain momentum until the 1950s," at which point, "with full employment and greater welfare provision, the context of abortion reform had changed considerably." Although critiques of eugenics and racial science were circulating as early as the 1930s, advanced by prominent British scientists including J.B.S. Haldane and Julian Huxley, the revelations of the Nuremberg Trials are usually assumed to have discredited eugenicist thought once and for all, laying bare its genocidal implications. Scholars have complicated this narrative in a variety of ways, drawing attention to the entangled histories of genetics and eugenics, and highlighting the "eugenic arguments that justified eugenic sterilization policies [in the United States and elsewhere] and that stood behind the 1960s push for family planning programs."[1] Eugenics did not then die with the Nazi regime. Less clear is the nature of the relationship between early-twentieth-century eugenicist thought and the "new eugenics," that is, contemporary medical genetics. "As a result of ongoing developments in the field of genetics that have led to biotechnology, genetic engineering, cloning, and proposals that soon the human 'germline' will be able to be 'enhanced,'" Christina Cogdell writes, "today, eugenics is back."[2] However, Donna Haraway distinguishes between the "old" eugenics' commitment to the collective and the "new" eugenics' foregrounding of "reproductive investment decisions and individual genetic health."[3] According to Nikolas Rose, although many states are, "once more, regarding the specific hereditary stock of their population as a resource to be managed, these endeavors are not driven by a search for racial purity," but in the interest of creating "biovalue."[4]

The biological citizenships under construction in the twenty-first century cannot, I suspect, be so sharply distinguished from the earlier, more explicitly racialized, conceptions of citizenship current in the first decades of the twentieth century. The Māori writer Patricia Grace forcefully suggests this imbrication of contemporary with historical regimes of biovalue in her 1998 novel *Baby No-Eyes*, which aligns late-twentieth-century projects of bioprospecting with colonial policies of appropriation and dispossession. Rather than pursue such continuities here, however, I want to attend to another survival of the interwar era: demographic panic. In recent years, reports of falling birth rates have generated lurid headlines, of which the German tabloid *Bild*'s "Baby Shock: Germans Are Dying Out" may stand as a representative example. Australia is among several OECD states to have introduced "baby bonuses" in the hopes of shoring up the low birth rates that, it is claimed, threaten national prosperity and well-being. Introducing a 3000 AUD maternity payment in 2005, then treasurer Peter Costello urged Australians to have "one for Mum, one for Dad, and one for the country." In 2006, the British novelist Martin Amis expressed alarm at the fertility gap separating "us" from "Islamists": in an interview with *The Times*'s Ginny Dougary, he exclaimed, "they're … gaining on us demographically at a huge rate. A quarter of humanity now and by 2025 they'll be a third. Italy's down to 1.1 child per woman. We're just going to be outnumbered."[5] The British fertility rate now hovers close to the magic replacement number of 2.1 babies per woman, up from a 2001 low of 1.73 babies per woman. Such sentiments as Amis's remain unexceptional.

As Dougary's interview with Amis suggests, contemporary anxieties about the declining fertility of (some) Italians, Germans, or Britons cannot be separated from anxieties about the place of racial and religious others – and especially Muslims – in European cultural, economic, and political life. There is no denying the specificity of the post-9/11 situation out of which such fears emerge. For the "new school of conservative opinion in Europe and the United States," whose depiction of "Europe as a doomed continent" has gained traction since 9/11, Matt Carr says, "the fatal confluence of declining fertility rates and loss of civilizational confidence" has set Europe on the path to becoming an Islamicized "Eurabia."[6] Writers like Oriana Fallaci, Niall Ferguson, Melanie Phillips, and Mark Steyn bemoan the "slothful senescence of Europe," no match for the "youthful energy" of Islamic societies with their superabundance of young men.[7] Eurabianists predict that Muslims' share of the European population, currently at 3 per cent, will rise to 40 per cent within fifteen years. Few are hopeful that Europe can reverse this trend: in an article that compares Ahmadinejad-ruled Iran to Nazi Germany, Ferguson hypothesizes the "twilight of the West" at the hands of a Sino-Islamic alliance.[8] The rhetoric of demographic engulfment that at once fuels and is fuelled by twenty-first-century Islamophobia is nevertheless not new, but recycled from other historical and geopolitical contexts.

Certainly, the Eurabianists' sensationalist scenarios echo those early-twentieth-century warnings of race suicide that, as we saw in earlier chapters, expressed fears of engulfment by degenerate class and racial others. However, their currency in Britain also bespeaks the enduring influence of one of the most divisive British political figures of the post–Second World War era, the Conservative MP Enoch Powell. On 20 April 1968, Powell delivered the speech now known as "Rivers of Blood" to the Conservative Political Centre in Birmingham. Early in the speech, Powell cites the despair of a constituent who has decided to leave the country. The man tells Powell, "I have three children, all of them been through grammar school and two of them married now, with family. I shan't be satisfied till I have seen them all settled overseas. In this country in fifteen or twenty years' time the black man will have the whip hand over the white man."[9] Immigrants' reproductive potency, this working man implies and Powell insists, renders them a "national danger":

> As time goes on, the proportion of [Commonwealth immigrants and their descendants] who are immigrant descendants, those born in England, who arrived here by exactly the same route as the rest of us, will rapidly increase. Already by 1985 the native-born would constitute the majority. It is this fact which creates the extreme urgency of action now, of just that kind of action which is hardest for politicians to take, action where the difficulties lie in the present but the evils to be prevented or minimised lie several parliaments ahead.

Powell's views are often dismissed as extreme. The opinions articulated in "Rivers of Blood" were largely disavowed by the mainstream political parties of Powell's day (including his own), while the speech itself effectively ended his political career: he held his parliamentary constituency until 1987, but was never again named to a cabinet position. In fact, however, as Kathleen Paul reminds us, the positions staked out in "Rivers of Blood" register a post-war shift in mainstream thinking about the racial and spatial meanings of British identity.[10] Thus, if Powell's paranoia adumbrates Amis's, the intimations of demographic engulfment and even collapse that animate "Rivers of Blood" returning in Amis's assertion that "we're just going to be outnumbered"; if the last ten years have seen Powell partially rehabilitated, "Rivers of Blood" acclaimed, even from within the ostensible mainstream, as a prophetic call to action;[11] we are reminded that twenty-first-century panics about demographic decline and overwhelmment must be read not just through the lens of contemporary geopolitics but as informed by earlier struggles over the content and location of Britishness in the aftermath of empire.

Whereas earlier chapters examined responses to the threat of demographic collapse, this chapter, like chapter 4, highlights the fantasy of demographic collapse itself, as not just a reflection of and on demographic data, but, in its own way, a fantasy about what the nation could or should become. This may seem counterintuitive: unlike the texts that I examined in chapters 1 and 2, which describe efforts to breed better kinds of national subjects and communities, fantasies of demographic collapse project national, even species, death. And yet, as Amis's use of "we" to differentiate Italians from "Islamists" indicates, forecasts of demographic disaster – "we're just going to be outnumbered" – help produce the communities of belonging they also represent as doomed. If, as Carr astutely observes, "in many parts of Europe, Muslim communities live besieged existences, but the Eurabian nightmare reverses these dynamics," to what end?[12] I pursue this question through readings of post–Second World War apocalyptic and post-apocalyptic British science fictions, focusing on *28 Days Later*, a 2002 film directed by the acclaimed British filmmaker Danny Boyle from a script by Alex Garland. By foregrounding speculative fiction in this way, I aim to take seriously Carr's observation that the "contemporary vision of Europe's decline is often reinforced by sensationalist science fiction scenarios."[13] Thus, for example, in a 2006 exercise in speculative history published by the *Daily Telegraph*, Ferguson imagines how a "future historian might deal with the next phase of events in the Middle East," a four-year war ushered in by "the devastating nuclear exchange of August 2007."[14] The 2008 documentary film *Demographic Winter* (produced by the conservative Family First Foundation) deploys the visual grammar of apocalyptic cinema – "the disappearing bodies [of children] a gentle rendition," as one reviewer puts it, "of nuclear flash incineration; the snow that replaces them at once evoking atomic and crematorium ashes, as well as emblemizing the frostier demographic death the filmmakers envision" – to convey a warning about "the decline of the human family."[15] How do such "sensationalist science fiction scenarios" configure national belonging?

Reading apocalyptic and post-apocalyptic fictions as animated by anxieties about not just the Cold War, or the prospect of nuclear Armageddon, as is commonly assumed, but imperial divestment and immigration, I develop a critique of the rhetoric of demographic collapse by situating panics about engulfment and disintegration in relation to projects of post-imperial reconstruction and (dis)remembrance. In moving from pre- to post-Second World War–era discourses of reproduction, I aim to draw attention to the continuities (often disavowed) that link these different moments in the still unfinished history of decolonization, while bringing out a family likeness in settler and post-war metropolitan ruses of identity.[16] For the most part, scholars have read post-war developments in British immigration and nationality law as signalling the ascendancy of race-based conceptions of community. Thus, for example, Ian Baucom argues that Englishness has "defined itself *against* the British Empire … by largely abandoning spatial and territorial ideologies for a racial 'discourse of loyalty' and coidentity."[17] Interventions such as Baucom's are important, since the reforms he discusses were deliberately packaged in such a way as to obscure their racializing effects. In this chapter, however, I suggest that the racial turn in British discourses of identity encodes not a move away from, but a shift in, place-based definitions of British belonging. It is the spatial stories of demographic apocalypticism that, insofar as they disclose an impulse towards indigenization, or repatriation, work to exclude British overseas subjects from the British body politic. Not only racial but spatial difference, as well as the imperial history that has disseminated Britishness overseas, is expelled thereby.

Darkening Island

Although its origins predate the twentieth century, the subgenre of apocalyptic fiction gained traction following the Second World War. (It is worth noting that *The Last Man*, the Mary Shelley novel whose 1826 publication may be said to have inaugurated the modern apocalyptic literary tradition, slipped out of print in 1833 and remained so until 1963.) Structuring many apocalyptic and post-apocalyptic fictions is a sense of besiegement, as a survivor or group of survivors struggles to ward off civilizational or species extinction. Enoch Powell describes the immigrant "problem" as a "cloud no bigger than a man's hand, that can so rapidly overcast the sky." In M.P. Shiel's 1901 novel *The Purple Cloud*, a deadly cloud really does overcast the sky, ultimately enveloping the globe and sparing only a single regenerative couple. In Anna Kavan's *Ice* (1967), published nearly seventy years later, a tide of ice renders the world uninhabitable for all save, briefly, a sparring couple. Nevil Shute's *On the Beach* (1957) spotlights the inhabitants of Melbourne as they await the fatal approach of nuclear radiation from the war-wracked North. Vegetable aggression accompanies alien invasion, decimating the population of the British Isles, in H.G. Wells's *War of the Worlds* (1898) and John Wyndham's *The Day of the Triffids* (1951). In *Fugue for a Darkening Island* (1972), refugees from an African nuclear Armageddon swarm Britain, while ad hoc family units strive to hold off the infection that ravages Britain in *28 Days Later* and ramifies globally to conclude its sequel, *28 Weeks Later* (2007).

The fictional Armageddons of especially the immediate post-war period are usually read as responses to fearsome developments in the technology of war. But more than atomic bombs "made the bridge across which," as one American sociologist (rather apocalyptically) remarks, "apocalyptic fantasies, marching from their refuge among fringe groups, invaded all society" in the 1950s.[18] While apprehension of both imminent war and the immanence of war certainly marks British apocalyptic and post-apocalyptic fictions as products of the Cold War and, latterly, of the War on Terror, they also need to be read in relation to decolonization and the efforts to reconstitute British identity in its wake. This is in part because the history of the Cold War is entangled with that of decolonization. Embarking on a study of "the Cold War" in "the Third World," political scientist Odd Arne Westad concedes that these terms – Cold War, Third World – might initially seem antithetical: "the term 'Cold War' signals Western elite projects on the grandest of possible scales, while the term 'Third World' indicates colonial and postcolonial processes of marginalization (and the struggle against these processes)."[19] This is no accident. The very term "Cold War" bespeaks a determination to hold these projects and histories apart. It recentres Europe and the old Atlantic relationship by exiling the violence of armed conflict to a reconstituted periphery. The "hot" wars fought in and over Afghanistan, Angola, Ethiopia, Guatemala, South Africa, and Vietnam function as proxies for, rather than fronts in, the "cold" war that organizes relationships among American and European polities. In fact, however, not only did "US and Soviet interventionisms" shape the "international and the domestic framework within which political, social, and cultural changes in Third World countries took place," but "Third World elites often framed their own political agendas in conscious response to the models of development presented by the two main contenders of the Cold War, the United States and the Soviet Union."[20] And of course, hot wars, no matter where they play out, have a tendency not to stay put, their traumatized participants and material by-products (including radiation) circulating globally. Westad refuses to subordinate one set of projects to the other. The map of the Cold War does not, argues another scholar, "provide the essential context" for the map of decolonization.[21] Nor is the reverse true. Westad nonetheless suggests we see the Cold War as a struggle to decide which of the United States and the Soviet Union should claim the mantle of European modernity, and therefore understands superpower interventionism in the South as "a continuation of European colonial interventions and of European attempts at controlling Third World Peoples."[22] For Britain, meanwhile, a more and more obviously *former* seat of empire, the threat of omnicide, is, I think, necessarily articulated with the story of its own global decline, and the ascendancy of the United States and Soviet Union.

In the 1950s, crises in Egypt and Kenya delivered blows to Britain's post-war hopes of hanging on to its empire. With consciousness of the indefensibility of the imperial project strengthening at home as well as abroad, and the economic costs of empire growing less and less supportable, Britain returned self-determination to most of its colonies over the course of the 1950s, 1960s, and 1970s. In conjunction with these events, increasing numbers of British overseas and other migrant subjects made their way to Britain to study and work, changing the demographic, socio-cultural, and political landscape of Britain in ways that some Britons, at least, have found deeply troubling. Although the post-war surge in immigration to Britain was not, or not only, a consequence of decolonization, their historical convergence, as well as the peculiar structure of British nationality and immigration law, inevitably articulated debates about immigration, race, and national identity, about the competencies necessary for accession to Britishness, together with debates about Britain's relationship with its (history as an) empire.

Of course, one of the ways in which post-war debates about immigration, race, and national identity engaged with Britain's history as an empire was to insist on the irrelevance of this history, denying that decisions about who should and should not be permitted to live in Britain should be informed by any history of shared (imposed) belonging. The narrator of Christopher Priest's 1972 novel *Fugue for a Darkening Island* rehearses this gambit in his account of a Britain wracked by civil war. When multiple nuclear devices are detonated on the African continent – why, where, and by whom are left unspecified – rendering it uninhabitable, the survivors flee for places like Britain, where they are not welcome but nonetheless stay, battling government-backed white supremacist forces for control of the country. The narrator, a former university lecturer named Alan Whitman, recounts his struggle to survive amidst military confusion and a crumbling infrastructure. Tellingly, Priest suppresses the history that might help to explain why Britain should appear an especially appealing destination to the refugees, and the refugees unappealing candidates for inclusion within the body politic. It is striking, for instance, that Whitman acknowledges, but will not explicate, the existence of official and popular racism prior to the Afrim landings. As a young man, Whitman tended bar in an East End pub whose diverse clientele over time grew younger and whiter: listening to the pubgoers' talk, Whitman gathered that "their prejudices and information on subjects such as race and politics were as conservative as those attitudes implied by [their] dress."[23] Several years later, he adds, "John Tregarth and his party were to gain a substantial electoral backing from areas in which different races were mixed freely" (49–50). The spike in racism that manifests in the homogenization of the pub's clientele and the electoral success of Tregarth's "neo-racist" agenda appears unmotivated. To the extent that it prevents us from rationalizing racism as something that, in certain situations, "makes sense," the narrative's failure to elucidate the reasons for the pub's changing character doesn't altogether seem a bad thing. But such a move also tends to elide the complex interplay of economic factors and immigration policy in the post-war rise of sentiments that would have made the election of a Tregarth-style government in Britain seem, by 1972, not inconceivable. In this way, Priest's narrative simultaneously gestures towards and obscures the local and global histories that would help account for the presence in Britain of both racially mixed neighbourhoods and racial tension before the arrival of the Afrim. Rather than any turmoil within Britain or its erstwhile empire, it is an invasion from without that, in *Fugue for a Darkening Island*, explains and warrants British "neo-racism."

Although the account *Fugue for a Darkening Island* offers of the rise of British white supremacism is evasive and tendentious, Priest's interest in the effects of decolonization and immigration on conceptions of Britishness is unmistakable. Many British apocalyptic and post-apocalyptic fictions do not so explicitly thematize racial diversity as a sign of, or answer to, the apocalypse. Take, for example, the two fictions that are the focus of this chapter: *28 Days Later* and *The Day of the Triffids*. In Wyndham's novel, a comet sighting blinds over 90 per cent of the world's population, sparing, among others, biochemist Bill Masen and socialite Josella Playton. Having met and then lost track of Josella in the chaos following the catastrophe, Bill travels the English countryside in search of her, fighting off hostile fellow survivors as well as attacks by the titular triffids, huge mobile carnivorous plants once cultivated for their oil. The couple is reunited at Dennis and Mary Brent's Sussex farm-turned-country-house, Shirning, where they attempt to live self-sufficiently, before removing, finally, to a larger settlement on the Isle of Wight. Alex Garland, who wrote the screenplay for *28 Days Later*, has acknowledged his debt to Wyndham: "Our male protagonist, waking up in hospital to find an entirely new landscape outside, will be familiar to anyone who has read *Day of the Triffids*."[24] Directed by Danny Boyle, *28 Days Later* opens with a rescue: a team of animal-rights activists infiltrates a Cambridge research facility and liberates a passel of chimpanzees, one of which is infected with a virus called "Rage." Twenty-eight days later, Jim (Cillian Murphy), a comatose young Irish bicycle courier, awakens in a deserted London hospital, a scene that, as Garland concedes, echoes the opening of Wyndham's novel. Jim wanders the streets of the capital, bemused by their air of desertion and the "missing persons" flyers pinned to the walls, but soon attracts the violent attentions of Rage-infected men and women, from whom he escapes only with the aid of Rage-free Selena (Naomie Harris) and Mark (Noah Huntley). That night, while sheltering in the Underground with Mark and Selena, Jim learns that Rage, which transforms those it infects into mindless hemorrhagic bundles of murderous appetite, has spread throughout Britain, perhaps even globally. The film then tracks Jim and Selena's struggle to survive – Mark is killed early on – concluding weeks later with their apparent rescue by military jet from a cottage in the Lake District. In neither text, then, is demographic collapse explicitly articulated with the threat of racial diversification and imperial divestment, as it is in Priest's novel. Nevertheless, like *Fugue for a Darkening Island*, *The Day of the Triffids* and *28 Days Later* stage dramas of invasion and of annihilation that, their evasions excavated, tell us something about post-imperial articulations of what it means to be British.

In *28 Days Later*, the agent of social dissolution, the Rage virus, is pointedly home-grown, not an invader from without. To this extent, the film realizes the scenario H.G. Wells's narrator dreads at the end of *The Island of Dr. Moreau*: the (re)emergence of the murderous beast in British-kind. Returned to England, Prendick lives in terror, shaken by his encounter with the Beast People and awareness of his own cannibal urges. While "at most times the terror of that island"

> lies far in the back of my mind, a mere distant cloud, a memory and a faint distrust, … there are times when the little cloud spreads until it obscures the whole sky. Then I look about me at my fellow men. And I go in fear. I see faces keen and bright, others dull and dangerous, others unsteady, insincere; none that have the calm authority of a reasonable soul. I feel as though the animal were surging up through them; that presently the degradation of the Islanders will be played over again on a larger scale … When I lived in London the horror was well-nigh insupportable. I could not get away from men; their voices came through the windows; locked doors were flimsy safeguards. I would go out into the streets to fight with my delusion, and prowling women would mew after me, furtive craving men glance jealously at me, weary pale workers go coughing by me, with tired eyes and eager paces like wounded deer dripping blood, old people, bent and dull, pass murmuring to themselves, and all unheeding a ragged tail of gibing children. Then I would turn aside into some chapel, and even there, such was my disturbance, it seemed that the preacher gibbered Big Thinks even as the Ape Man had done; or into some library, and there the intent faces over the books seemed but patient creatures waiting for prey. Particularly nauseous were the blank expressionless faces of people in trains and omnibuses; they seemed no more my fellow-creatures than dead bodies would be, so that I did not dare to travel unless I was assured of being alone. And even it seemed that I, too, was not a reasonable creature, but only

> an animal tormented with some strange disorder in its brain, that sent it to wander alone, like a sheep stricken with the gid. (Wells 102–3)

Is it possible that the island adventure narrative has, in the twentieth century, developed along apocalyptic lines, Prendick's Moreau-inspired dread of the coughing, mewing, bleeding crowd, the as-if-undead commuters, his own possibly disordered brain, blossomed into the sense of besiegement that so permeates apocalyptic films like *28 Days Later*?[25] As I argued in my reading of Wells, the mobility of savagery, its ubiquity, wreaks havoc with the racial hierarchies and ideological pieties that once sustained the imperial project. In *The Island of Dr. Moreau*, Edward Prendick discovers that beastliness is a contagion that the imperative to categorize cannot contain: just because Prendick isn't a Kanaka, or one of the Beast People, doesn't mean he can't also be a cannibal. Whereas the adventure narratives of the nineteenth century – *The Coral Island* (1857) establishes the paradigm – purvey fantasies of education, domestication, and Christianization, proliferating European civilizational norms throughout the savage periphery, apocalyptic fictions like *28 Days Later* flirt with the inverse scenario, in which it is civilization, rotted through, that is shown to be in need of salvation.

Like *The Island of Dr. Moreau*, however, *28 Days Later* suggests that the contagion of savagery, although it emerges at home, is nonetheless not at home there: it remains an intruder, attributed origins elsewhere. The immediate etiologic agent for Rage is a virus so fantastically contagious that only a single drop of infected blood is required to effect the irreversible and virtually instantaneous transformation that constitutes enRagement. But the film also develops a series of etiological narratives that move beyond the virological to the political in explaining the origins of Rage. To begin with, although the virus itself evades the visualization regimes of science and cinema – the film enlists neither microscopes nor "contagion-cams" to make the virus visible – the bodies that it remakes do not.[26] There are in fact two outbreaks of Rage in *28 Days Later*: the first coincides with the release of the chimpanzees from the Cambridge research facility, while the second occurs within the confines of the fortified compound managed by soldiers under the command of a Major West (Christopher Eccleston). The source of infection is in the first instance a chimpanzee and in the second a black soldier named Mailer (Marvin Campbell). Analysing the cinematic representation of disease in the 1980s and 1990s, when AIDS and Ebola emerged to monopolize public epidemiological consciousness, Kirsten Ostherr notes how films like *Outbreak* (1995) racialize and sexualize contagion, positing "a teleological progression from the diseased 'premodern' world [of Africa] to the modern, sanitized 'First World,' under increasing threat of infection in a historical period characterized by fluid national boundaries and transnational bodily movement."[27] Lines are drawn – between species, between the First World and the Third – even as they are shown to be porous. The fear that viruses may, like HIV or Ebola, jump species articulates, naturalizes, and fuels the fear that these viruses may jump "worlds," from what Richard Preston, whose 1992 article "Crisis in the Hot Zone" "introduced" Ebola to (*New Yorker*–reading) Americans, calls "the silent heart of darkness" to the centres of modernity.[28] Its biological origins in English bodies notwithstanding, Rage is likewise embodied in ways that recall the rhetorical and iconographic conflation of Africa, primitivism, and contagion prevalent in the contemporary discourse of disease. Through succumbing to contagion, Priscilla Wald observes, "First World" nations like Britain are seen to undergo "thirdworldification."[29]

Its mediated origins also suggest a properly global provenance for Rage, suggest, indeed, a provenance for Rage in the globalization of violence. As the film opens, we are treated to grainy news footage of a series of violent clashes between security forces and civilians in different parts of the world. The camera pulls back, revealing a bank of video screens on which loops the footage we have been watching. Strapped to a table, a vivisected chimpanzee watches with us. On a security monitor, meanwhile, a team of masked activists enters the research facility, bent on animal rescue. From Selena's perspective, "it started as rioting. And right from the beginning you knew this was different. Because it was happening in small villages, market towns. And then it wasn't on the TV anymore. It was in the street outside. It was coming through your windows. It was a virus, an infection."[30] In Selena's account, "it" – like the film itself – begins not with "a virus, an infection," but with rioting on television. In fact, the closest referent for Selena's "it" is "the bad news" a sardonic Mark has just said he's got for Jim. The film implies that violent rage is a communicable disease transmitted through "bad news," through, in other words, the agency of communicative media, including, and perhaps especially, film and television: just as Rage jumps from the infected chimpanzee to its human would-be liberator, so rage jumps from the screen into the street and into living bodies. In indicting the too easy circulation of (images of) violence through the media, Boyle and Garland lament both that violence is everywhere and that violence is, in particular, here and not only there, where it belongs. In his screenplay, Garland writes that the film should open with looped "images of stunning violence" showing "soldiers in a foreign war shoot an unarmed civilian at point-blank range; a man … set on by a frenzied crowd wielding clubs and machetes; a woman … necklaced while her killers cheer and howl" (3). The images that Boyle selects include a public hanging involving keffiyeh-wearing men; Korean police beating half-naked men; crowds being gassed and beaten by police on horseback; Filipino police clad in riot gear retreating before hostile civilians; and a necklacing. That the choice of footage is significant beyond its "stunning violence" is indicated by the quite different video footage that opens the comic book *28 Days Later: The Aftermath* (2007).[31] Written by Steve Niles under licence from Fox Atomic, which distributed the Boyle-Garland film, *The Aftermath* tells four interlinked stories about the Rage outbreak.[32] The first of these, titled "Development," supplies yet another explanation for how Rage came to be: two scientists, Warren and Clive, develop an agent that ostensibly inhibits human anger and aggression, but graft it to a section of the Ebola genome that "unexpectedly" mutates, giving rise to the Rage virus (18). Clive, disgusted, contacts the Animal Freedom Front, setting in motion the events of *28 Days Later*. We are first introduced to Warren and Clive when, in their search for a human test subject, they visit a police facility that collates CCTV footage of criminal violence, and are treated to film of a series of brutal physical and (it is implied) sexual assaults. What *28 Days Later* hints at – that media like film function as vectors of violence – Clive makes explicit when he asks the monitoring officer "how [he] look[s] at this all day," adding, "it can't be good – watching too much of this, I mean" (4). Indeed not: soon after, Warren murders one of his rent-a-criminals. Both film and comic book foreground acts of spectacular violence that take place in public spaces like city streets (rather than, say, in the private space of the home). But where the violence of *The Aftermath* takes place on British soil (it is in this sense domestic), Boyle and Garland stress the foreignness of the violence – machetes, for instance, conjure the horrors of tropical(alized) violence, of jungle warfare and African genocide – which the film depicts taking root at home.

Panics about metropolitan degeneration are not new, inspiring the urban exploration and apocalyptic invasion narratives of the late nineteenth century, including George Chesney's *The Battle of Dorking* (1871), Margaret Harkness's *In Darkest London* (1889), and any number of novels by H.G. Wells. Still, this threat was rendered more immediate in the post-war era, in part because of the instability of the global political landscape, which the (perceived) political recalcitrance of many former colonies, their resistance to toeing the Western line, seemed only to exacerbate, in part because of the greater numbers of British overseas subjects seeking entry to Britain. I want to draw a line, then, from the outbreak narrative Selena tells in *28 Days Later* back to the invasion narrative Powell rehearses in the (in)famous closing section of "Rivers of Blood." Powell's fable features an elderly constituent resident on a formerly "respectable" Wolverhampton street:

> With growing fear, she saw one house after another taken over [by people of colour]. The quiet street became a place of noise and confusion. Regretfully, her

> white tenants moved out ... The day after the last one left, she was awakened at 7am by two negroes who wanted to use her phone to contact their employer. When she refused, as she would have refused any stranger at such an hour, she was abused and feared she would have been attacked but for the chain on her door ... She is becoming afraid to go out. Windows are broken. She finds excreta pushed through her letter box. When she goes to the shops, she is followed by children, charming, wide-grinning piccaninnies. They cannot speak English, but one word they know. "Racialist," they chant.

The speed with which this once majority white neighbourhood has become majority black – eight years – testifies to what Powell, like Alan Whitman, sees as the contagiousness of blackness, blacks' capacity to spread like an overcasting cloud through a district – or nation – when once they gain a toehold. The "allegories of trespass" that recur in Enoch Powell's speeches of 1968, where they simultaneously celebrate the spatial nature of English identity, its inherence in the old woman's "quiet" street, in the integrity of her domesticity and essential privacy, unbroached by shit and savage children, and lament the contamination of English space(s) by incursive black bodies, echo throughout post-war British debates about nationality and immigration, driving the substantive changes to nationality and immigration law that were undertaken between 1962 and 1982.[33] Throughout this process of reform, it was claimed that Britishness needed to be made a more exclusive property, not available to every overseas subject alike, if Britain was not to be overrun by people of colour. In memoranda and parliamentary debates, bureaucrats and politicians alike spoke of the need to restrict non-white immigration by restricting the entry of British subjects. In November 1958, *The Economist* reported that "the liberal line – uncontrolled immigration – can be held for a few more years, but not indefinitely. Far from thinking that the British people will get used to colour ... this school of opinion in Whitehall and beyond feels that when the tide of colour rises to a certain, as yet unspecified, point, the mass of British voters will demand that some check be imposed."[34] According to Margaret Thatcher, a desire to assuage the public's fear "that this country might be rather swamped by people with a different culture" inspired the 1981 Nationality Act.[35] This sort of rhetoric has not disappeared: in her work on emotions, Sara Ahmed notes that twenty-first-century British politicians, including David Blunkett and William Hague, continue to deploy words like "flood," "swamped," and "overwhelmed" to describe the arrival of refugees in Britain.[36] Apocalyptic fictions may focus on remoter threats (aggressive vegetation, for example). They nonetheless register the sense of overwhelmment that British politicians and commentators have persistently conjured in justifying restrictive immigration laws, giving material and apocalyptic form to the threats racialized others pose Britons and Britain, not only because of their "different culture," but because of their anger and violence.

It could be argued, as Sarah Trimble suggests in her work on *28 Days Later*, that "by articulating the visual grammar of rioting with zombified bodies," the film opens the door to a counter-reading of the violent rage it codes as incomprehensibly other, one that frames rage as the artefact of a transatlantic history of injustice in which Britain is assuredly implicated.[37] The viability of such a counter-reading rests on the use this relentlessly citational film makes of the figure of the zombie. Introducing the screenplay for *28 Days Later*, Alex Garland names as one of his inspirations the zombie apocalypse films of George A. Romero:

> The scene in which our heroes loot a supermarket is a set piece of post-apocalyptic wish-fulfilment, probably most brilliantly achieved by the empty mall of *Dawn of the Dead* ... Selena's race – specified as black rather than just happening to be black – is a kind of reference to George Romero's Night-Dawn-Dead trilogy [that is, *Night of the Living Dead* (1968), *Dawn of the Dead* (1978), and *Day of the Dead* (1985)], which was notable for the black leading characters.[38]

True, Garland and Boyle's "zombies" are frenziedly mobile, not the shuffling, groaning undead of American filmic tradition. Like Romero's Night-Dawn-Dead trilogy, however, *28 Days Later* depicts an apocalypse of catastrophic demographic collapse, as whole swathes of the population cease to be enumerable among the fully human, that is also an apocalypse of overwhelmment, as the zombified masses swarm in an attempt to turn (murder) the unInfected. The blackness of Romero's leading characters – Ben in *Night of the Living Dead*, Peter in *Dawn of the Dead*, John in *Day of the Dead* – which Garland notes but does not explicate, signifies in complex ways. If the calculus of post-apocalyptic survival(ism) draws attention to the uneven distribution of power across the racially differentiated social landscape of the post-war United States, the zombies who force our protagonists to such revelatory acts themselves unveil, as Trimble puts it, the "exploitative power relations still unfolding from European contact."[39]

Although the etymology of the term cannot be traced with precision, it was as a component of African diasporic religious practices that zombification first drew the interest of scholars, government officials, and cultural agents. In the post-slavery societies of the Caribbean, the zombie signifies politically as well as religiously, embodying the injuries that constitute enslavement. Recall Claude Meillassoux's description of the slave as "marked by an original, indelible defect which weighs heavily upon his destiny. This is, in Izard's words, a kind of 'social death.' He can never be brought to life again as such since, in spite of some specious examples (themselves most instructive) of fictive rebirth, the slave will remain forever an unborn being (non-né)."[40] If, as I suggested in chapter 3, the bolom embodies this ever-unborn-ness of the slave, the zombie embodies the living death that is slavery. On the one hand, then, the figure of the zombie concentrates attention on the depredations of "the peculiar institution," while encouraging audiences to reflect on the equivocal place of individual agency, authority, and autonomy in capitalist labour regimes, even liberal polities. When, for instance, in the 1932 film *White Zombie*, a Haitian plantation owner (Robert Frazer) asks the local – white – voodoo master "Murder" Legendre (Béla Lugosi) to facilitate his marriage to a young white woman (Madge Bellamy) by transforming her into a zombie, the structure of consent upon which the sexual and social contracts both rest is thrown into crisis – can a zombie engage itself matrimonially? – and loss of autonomy shown to be rather the fate of all modern subjects than the unique property of the slave.[41] On the other hand, the figure of the zombie arouses anxiety about the nature of the subjectivities produced within and for capitalist labour regimes and liberal polities. Thus, in post-apartheid South Africa, argue Jean and John Comaroff, stories about zombies express fears of "being reduced to ghost labor, ... being abducted to feed the fortunes of a depraved stranger," which fuel hostility to a "growing mass, a shadowy alien-nation, of immigrant black workers from elsewhere on the continent," foreclosing on the possibility of solidarity with the undead.[42]

Romero's contribution to the cultural lexicon of the zombie, its alarming reproducibility, achieved virally, further moderates the figure's critical potential. Where control of the zombie's post-mortem actions remains vested in a necromancer or bokor, the living death of zombification foregrounds the slave-master's role in maintaining the slave in her enslavement. If the living death of zombification manifests the loss of agency that accompanies slavery, the zombie-master manifests the something – the law, the person – that is responsible for taking that agency away. Once the agent of zombification is made a blood-borne virus rather than a powerful embodied actor, however, once zombies are no longer produced, that is, but rather reproduce, the living death of slavery is re-imagined as catching, the zombie-slave an agent of the doom of which it was formerly only the victim. A perverse politics is the result. To be sure, some aspects of the peculiar violence of slavery are better represented by Romero's self-replicating zombie than by the cartoonish plotting of Béla Lugosi's zombie-master in *White Zombie*. In the American South, slaves were required to reproduce their enslavement by bearing children whose status, as the law put it, followed the condition of the mother. Slavery thus transformed the reproductive body from a guarantor of black biological and cultural continuity into the very mechanism through which that continuity was broken. But even as the self-replicating zombie draws attention to the inheritability of enslavement, it obscures the involvement of free (white) actors and social institutions in reproducing both slaves and the system of slavery. Social death comes to seem an attribute of the slave – that "original, indelible defect" – rather than a function of her enslavement. Increasingly, then, zombies at once figure the evacuation of agency we fear for ourselves and an excessive, aggressive agentiality that threatens to strip us of our agency, impelling us to acquiesce in efforts to consolidate the other's evacuated agency, through xenophobic legislation, for example.

Transformed into the communicable disease of Rage, rage is similarly decontextualized, re-rendered as pure savagery. This is intimated in the opening video montage, which equates anger and violence and invites us to assimilate all violent acts to one another. The necklacing becomes a hanging. The policemen beating civilians in Korea become the civilians harassing policemen in the Philippines. How does this refusal of differentiation matter? Necklacing, in which tires are placed around victims' necks and set alight, is of course a horrific act of violence. But the history of its use as a method of summary execution is complex: in apartheid South Africa, for example, necklacing often capped intra-community judicial proceedings against individuals thought to be collaborating with the white regime. *28 Days Later* decontextualizes and so departicularizes (this act of) necklacing, which instead of registering the ramifying effects of colonial state violence, comes to function as a spectacle of incomprehensible black-on-black violence. In *The Aftermath*, Clive picks up an Animal Freedom Front flyer that reads, "ANIMALS ARE OUR FRIENDS! DOES THE WAY THEY'RE TREATED MAKE YOU RAGE?!? GET INVOLVED!" (19). Not only do these rage-driven animal libbers resemble the enRaged, not only do they, enraged, release the chimpanzees that harbour Rage, but their anger is Rage, is, in other words, an agent of social dissolution. If anger leads inevitably to violence, and one act of violence, one violent actor, is much like any other, anger, mobilized in the service of even the most progressive of causes, must appear indefensible.

In *The Promise of Happiness*, Sara Ahmed observes that some embodied subjects – feminists, women of colour, queers – are more likely to be read as not only constitutionally unhappy, but the cause of other people's unhappiness. My anger about "how racism and sexism diminish life choices for women of color" is construed as "unattributed, as if you are against x because you are angry rather than being angry because you are against x."[43] My anger is read as the problem, not whatever it is that is making me angry. In a similar way, the "outbreak narrative … promotes … an understanding of communicable disease as a cause rather than an expression of social formations throughout history."[44] Garland and Boyle's critique of rage, elaborated through its decontextualization as the contagion of Rage, might be extended to encompass, for example, white rage, as the Major West plot (discussed below) indicates. But *28 Days Later* also risks dismissing social justice movements, to the extent that these are fuelled by anger, as the product of nothing but anger. Selena's outbreak narrative recalls, I've argued, the invasion narrative that concludes "Rivers of Blood": it started as rioting on TV; it ends as infection, coming in through your window from the street. Importantly, the catalyst for "Rivers of Blood" was the Race Relations Act (1968), a piece of legislation that Powell claimed would encourage immigrant communities to "consolidate their members, to agitate and campaign against their fellow citizens, and to overawe and dominate the rest with the legal weapons which the ignorant and the ill-informed have provided." In his speech, he states that the new legislation empowers "the stranger, the disgruntled, and the agent-provocateur." The noise and confusion that so trouble Powell's pensioner thus bespeak not the mere presence of immigrants but – as Powell's conflation of provocation, disgruntlement, and strangerhood suggests – their rage. For Powell, the black body is defined by an unjustified ragefulness. In a similar way, what the great Marxist theorist of riots E.P. Thompson might term *28 Days Later*'s "spasmodic" view of the enRaged, expressed in the jerky camera-work with which Boyle captures their motion, promotes a view of rage as an attribute of the enraged, framing these riotous others as embodiments of incomprehensible, uncomprehending, and unrelenting rage while failing (or refusing) to illuminate the many entangled factors that have contributed to their enragement.[45]

"The end of the world is extremely fucking nigh"[46]

Boyle and Garland's re-presentation of rage as Rage suggests that what is most horrifying about rage is its communicability, that is, its contagiousness. Just as Hillary Rodham Clinton, for example, once indicted video game violence for giving rise to "an epidemic of violence," so *28 Days Later* depicts the consequences of failing to maintain a proper boundary between reality and simulations of reality by itself collapsing the gap between the figural (an "epidemic" of violence) and the (ostensibly) literal (an epidemic of violence).[47] The film's making visible, material, of the transmissibility of an affect like rage may strike viewers with the force of revelation. In fact, however, the concept of contagion has long been used to describe "the circulation of ideas and attitudes," including cultural norms and feelings of belonging.[48] "The medical usage of the term" arrived late, Priscilla Wald claims, and "was no more and no less metaphorical than its ideational counterpart."[49] Of course, that the term contagion, from the

Latin for "with" or "together" (*con-*) and "touch" (*tangere*), so readily lends itself to medical usage, as denoting "the communication of disease from body to body" (*OED*), suggests that it must always have been reserved for forms of communication, sociability, and reproduction considered malign and unnatural, in a word, queer. As Wald concedes, "folly and immorality were more often labelled contagious than were wisdom or virtue."[50]

The way in which HIV/AIDS, another blood-borne disease, has been discursively rendered exemplifies this entwining of the medical and ideational meanings of contagion. Construed as the "gay" disease, AIDS early on seemed to panicked homophobes to make legible, literal, the spreading contamination of homosexuality. When, in June 1983, Moral Majority co-founder Greg Dixon warned, "If homosexuals are not stopped, they will in time infect the entire nation, and America will be destroyed," it was tellingly unclear whether Dixon feared AIDS or the "plague" of homosexuality, the communication of queerness to every household in the land.[51] As Kathryn Bond Stockton notes, "State propositions against 'promoting gay lifestyles'" convey "worry over queer propagations, even if they take, especially if they take, the form of ideas – as if queer children could now be copied from the idea of them."[52] The contagiousness of HIV does not then only figure (or materialize) the contagiousness of queerness. The contagiousness of HIV, the queerness of its methods of reproduction, also suggests the queerness of the ways in which queerness is propagated (through the circulation of ideas, for example), the queerness, that is, of the contagion of queerness. For the vertical chain of genetic transmission, the reproduction of life, HIV/AIDS substitutes the horizontal chain of infection, the reproduction of death. Mary Jacobus points out that "the exponential calculations brought to bear on forecasting the global spread of AIDS replicate Malthusian panic in the face of unlimited population growth."[53] So potent is this deathly proliferation that it not only mirrors but begins to infect, if you will, normative biological reproduction. Thus, as Stockton observes, "media reports on early death in black American communities now routinely yoke together AIDS, teen homicide, and infant mortality – even as they slide into a dirge on pregnant teens, as if reproduction is being seen in the guise of transmission, the replication of early death."[54] Rage too strips those it infects of the capacity to reproduce not just normally but normality itself; lacking futurity, the Infected promise futurelessness for the (non-zombified) body politic.[55] As one of the characters in *28 Days Later* remarks, the Infected will "never bake bread, plant crops, raise livestock." And yet, the enRaged are also extraordinarily prolific, circulating the death of enRagement throughout the British body politic.

The nature of HIV/AIDS, and, for that matter, homosexuality is such that, to quote Eve Sedgwick, "the trajectory toward gay genocide was never clearly distinguishable from an apocalyptic trajectory toward something approaching omnicide."[56] Getting rid of all queers, "however potent and sustained as a project or fantasy of modern Western culture, is not possible short of the eradication of the whole human species."[57] The ease with which, in *28 Days Later*, Rage moves from body to body, as if already there to begin with, likewise threatens the Manichean distinction between inside and outside that structures Christopher Priest's project, for example, in *Fugue for a Darkening Island*. Unlike Priest's refugees, Rage emerges within the borders of the nation, and so cannot be contained through the prophylaxis of national quarantine. This is not to say that the film deprecates, or counsels abandoning, all such attempts at containment, which it depicts, rather, as necessary but inevitably incomplete, at perpetual risk of coming undone. Thus, (what look like) the exigencies of survival require that the unInfected distance themselves from the Infected, over and over again: Rage, as she tells Jim, has readied Selena to kill her brother or sister or oldest friend "in a heartbeat," lest they infect her. That violence is necessary to mark the enRaged as outsiders to the body politic indicates, conversely, the effort that is required to produce the body politic as an autonomous collective with clearly defined boundaries, in relation to which non-normative subjects can be positioned as outsiders. Powell's pensioner may really feel threatened by her neighbours' children. This doesn't mean that her sense of threat is an effect produced by the children's threatening actions. Rather, as Sara Ahmed puts it, her words, Powell's, and the film's, generate effects, creating "impressions of others as those who have invaded the space of the nation, threatening its existence."[58] Narrating others as threatening, as invasive, creates impressions of others, impressing others in turn. But in delineating what or who is not inside the nation, these impressions also determine what or who is.

To this extent, as Elana Gomel suggests, apocalyptic fictions like *28 Days Later* disclose a utopian impulse. The suffering they proliferate clears the ground for new ways of life that might just as well surpass as fall short of the old, transforming, through purifying, the body politic. Structured according to the principle of enclosure, this promised "New Jerusalem" conjures, Gomel says, "an image of purity so absolute it denies the organic messiness of life."[59] Through the story of Henry West, it is true, *28 Days Later* critiques the ethos of containment that drives the "island solutions" I discussed in chapter 1. Ensconced behind his high perimeter wall, Major West means to "rebuild. Start again." But if "the first step to civilization" is "a wood-fired boiler providing [the unit] with hot water," the second, as becomes clear to Jim and Selena, requires women: following a scene in which his soldiers harass Selena, West explains to Jim, "I promised them women. Eight days ago, I found Jones with his gun in his mouth. He said he was going to kill himself because there was no future. What could I say to him? We fight off the infected or we wait until they starve to death, and then what? What do nine men do except wait to die themselves? I moved us from the blockade, I set the radio broadcasting, and I promised them women … 'cause women mean a future." Or as Garland's screenplay puts it, "women mean children. And children mean a future" (85). Thus, West's radio broadcasts net "the answer to infection" they themselves promise: Selena and the teenager Hannah (Megan Burns). In response to an epidemic of futurelessness, West dangles the carrot of a future secured by rape and forced breeding, turning to the containment of quarantine to ensure that his men will reproduce true. That West will rape women and incarcerate men (including the infected black soldier Mailer) in pursuit of this goal not only aligns Rage with other threats to the integrity of the body politic (women, people of colour), but makes visible the violence that the fantasy of violation, of having been violated, ends by justifying. Horrified, Jim refuses to acquiesce in West's plans: he helps Selena and Hannah escape, destroying the compound in the process. But although the film makes plain the costs and weaknesses of the fortified (national) body that is West's ideal, it nonetheless fantasizes about the promise of (a different kind of) containment, mobilizing inside-ness and insider-ness in response to the alterity of Rage.

The film imagines, first, that Rage can be contained, and not only conceptually or rhetorically, through being figured as invasive. Ultimately, the Infected, who cannot take in nourishment, starve to death. In this respect, Rage trumps other suppressive projects, functioning as a conveniently auto-genocidal solution to a problem it itself incarnates and (for a time) proliferates.[60] In addition, however, *28 Days Later* opposes the virulence or fertility of Rage to ideals of containment and interiority. In containing the threat of Rage by equating outbreak with invasion, the film also produces a vulnerable "inside" that it identifies with and as Englishness. Following the trio's escape from Major West's fortified compound, the film skips forward twenty-eight days to reveal Hannah, Selena, and Jim healing in a cottage in the Lake District. Their rescue is implied. Both elements of the coda – not only, that is, the domestic coziness of Jim, Selena, and Hannah's post-apocalyptic life, but also the film's pastoral turn – speak to the film's investment in "inside-ness."

Here, it is useful to compare *28 Days Later* with John Wyndham's 1951 novel *The Day of the Triffids*, which also concludes with its protagonists reconstituting familial units in a more or less pastoral landscape. The coda thus completes Garland's homage to *Day of the Triffids* and to the sub-genre that *Day of the Triffids* exemplifies, the "cosy catastrophe." According to the great British science-fiction writer Brian Aldiss, the "essence of the cosy catastrophe is that the hero should have a pretty good time (a girl, free suites at the Savoy, automobiles for the taking) while everyone else is dying off."[61] Wyndham's "cosy" reputation notwithstanding, *The Day of the Triffids* departs in significant ways from the pattern laid down by Aldiss. Bill acquires "a girl," Josella, and an opulent flat, but the pair, by choice, spend only a night there, "saying goodbye" to the "life and ways that were now finished."[62] Bill and the novel's other male characters mean to rebuild civilization, but not in flats "with a rent of some £2,000 a year" (92). Instead, its inhabitants transform Shirning from a site of middle-class leisure (the country-house) into a working farm, and in the process are themselves transformed, de-urbanized and ruralized. Necessitated by catastrophe, this conversion turns out, however, to have been also a dream of its middle-class owners: faced with yards and sheds in a state of distressing "suburban … tidiness," the Brents had wished to "restore the place one day to work on a limited scale" (243). What the entrenched middle class desires – an end to the horror show of creeping surburbanization – apocalypse delivers: "only so few years ago," Josella wryly remarks, "people were wailing about the way those bungalows were destroying the countryside. Now look at them" (269). The Shirning community evinces, moreover, a clear commitment to middle-class ideals of domesticity and intimacy: at its core, the community consists of two procreative couples, the Brents and the Masens. Early in the novel, Josella and Bill encounter a sociologist named Vorless who argues that sexual morality must be rethought if humanity is to survive. Addressing a gathering of sighted survivors, Vorless insists that "in the time now ahead of us a great many of these prejudices [against theft, for instance] will have to go, or be radically altered. We can accept and retain only one primary prejudice, and that is that *the race is worth preserving*" (132; emphasis in original). He concludes that those among the audience who "decide to join our community … will all have our parts to play. The men must work – the women must have babies … In our new world, … babies become very much more important than husbands" (132–3). Although Bill will not join Miss Durant in lambasting Vorless's plan on religious grounds, he is clearly unnerved by the suggestion that the exigencies of post-apocalyptic survival might free women to have sex beyond the bounds of marriage. Wyndham apparently concurs: if the "race" is to be preserved and babies had, it will not, *pace* Vorless, be at the cost of the companionate marriage.

28 Days Later may discredit Major West's methods of securing futurity, but not, I think, futurity itself, or the equation West makes between women, children, and futurity. Parsing the film's multiple endings and the different futures they envision illuminates Boyle and Garland's complex riff on reproductive futurism. Boyle and Garland developed four endings for *28 Days Later*, three of which were filmed. In what Boyle and Garland refer to as "the proper ending," Selena and Hannah transport Jim to a hospital where they struggle but finally fail to save his life.[63] Another variant reveals Hannah and Selena living in the Lake District, sans Jim. Commenting on their decision not to use "the proper ending," Boyle and Garland explain that although they themselves saw Selena and Hannah as "survivors" who are "going to keep going in the way that they've kept going up to this point in the film," "people seemed to feel that they were walking off to their doom."[64] Jim's death may indeed have seemed one death too many in what Boyle suggests is "a hard journey" of a film.[65] But it's tempting to ascribe the bleakness of this ending to the way it disrupts the film's romantic narrative, which the theatrical ending in contrast nicely fulfils. The Jim-Selena coupling reads more hopefully than the Selena-Hannah pairing, not only because its potential fertility represents a recovered futurity, but because this potentiality is underwritten by intimacy. Late-twentieth-century advances in reproductive technology mean that pregnancy is not precluded for a Jim-bereft Selena (or Hannah, for that matter) in the way that it is for the homosocial community headed by Major West. This the second variant ending jokingly concedes when Selena informs a chicken, "We're gonna have to fertilize you. We need offspring. Or in the long term, this isn't gonna work." Against varieties of forced and assisted reproduction, the theatrical coda pitches heterosexual intimacy as a natural solution to the catastrophe of proliferating futurelessness and (political) rage. The contingent and even transgressive nature of this new familial unit – its mixed racial and national composition, and the fact that no kin relationship bonds Hannah to the adults who care for her – only proves the power of intimacy, of love, to (re)constitute the social order in the atomizing aftermath of apocalypse. Extracting its characters from the thick social worlds through which they once daily moved and propelling them towards the isolation of intimacy, the film in a sense reproduces, restages, a Habermasian narrative of the development of the humanist subject: for Habermas, writes Elizabeth Povinelli, "intimate recognition … uniquely transformed socially thick people into purely human subjects … The relay of intimate recognition stripped the social attributes from a person even as it locked this socially deracinated self into a higher-order couplet and, vis-à-vis such couplets, into still higher orders of abstract collectivity such as the democratic state."[66] In both *28 Days Later* and *The Day of the Triffids*, the characters' departure from a realm given over to intimacy doesn't imply its abandonment or failure but rather its mobilization in the service of a more abstract collectivity.

Apocalyptic circumstances force pastoral coziness upon Jim, Selena, and Hannah, upon Bill, Josella, and the Brents. In both works, their high population density renders the cities uninhabitable; "clear[ing] out" into the countryside seems the logical thing to do (*The Day of the Triffids*, 102). Meanwhile, although Selena has learned to kill "your brother or your sister or your oldest friend" "in a heartbeat," at the manor, confronted by a Jim who is, as the screenplay suggests, "the vision of the Infected," Selena hesitates, recognizing Jim in and despite the signs of infection (96). They then kiss. This moment of intimate recognition follows Selena's realization that survival is not enough: earlier, watching Hannah interact with her father Frank (Brendan Gleeson), she had admitted, "I was wrong when I told you [Jim] that staying alive is as good as it gets." The evolving demands of post-apocalyptic survival educate Selena into intimacy. Meanwhile, Jim, as Boyle and Garland suggest on the commentary track, discovers in himself the masculine authority, tempered by an openness to intimacy, he once looked to Frank and Henry West to supply. In a sense, however, apocalyptic circumstances also make pastoral coziness *possible*, enabling a renewed investment in domesticity and interiority anchored in heterosexual intimacy. This is more or less explicit in *The Day of the Triffids* which, like other Wyndham science fictions, registers unease about the moral disorder it suggests has accompanied post-war shifts in gender norms.[67] Said by Bill to possess a strength that "had most likely not been applied to anything more important than hitting balls, dancing, and, probably, restraining horses," Josella enters *The Day of the Triffids* as a thoroughly "modern young woman" (72; 77). Author of a notorious volume entitled *Sex Is My Adventure*, Josella lacks basic domestic skills like cooking. As late as their reunion at Shirning, she tells Bill, "I wasn't meant for this kind of life" (253). However, when, six years later, a visitor recalls her days as "Josella Playton, author of –," she informs him that he's "quite wrong … I'm Josella Masen, author of 'David Masen' [her son with Bill]" (281). Cynical and self-aware, Josella isn't domesticated exactly, but her willed transformation from girl-about-town to "farmer's wife" upends "modern" ideas about what it means to be a woman (253). Bill, on the other hand, awakens to the perils attendant upon the modern cult of specialization. "Looking back at the shape of things" pre-comet, Bill

> finds the amount we did not know and did not care to know about our daily lives … not only astonishing, but somehow a bit shocking. I knew practically nothing, for instance, of such ordinary things as how my food reached me, where the fresh water came from, how the clothes I wore were woven and made, how the drainage of cities kept them healthy. Our life had become a complexity of specialists all attending to their own jobs with more or less efficiency, and expecting others to do the same. (17)

In the post-apocalyptic world that Bill now inhabits, such partiality of view endangers lives. Compelled to attend to the complex totality of human needs, Bill is also "happier inside me than I ever was before": "no longer a cog," he emerges "my own master" (272; 66).

Critical to Bill Masen's contentment is his renewed proximity to – and growing mastery over – the natural world. Having witnessed the death throes of urban civilization, he is cheered by the resilience of nature: "under a blue sky where a few clouds sailed like celestial icebergs the cities," "sterile, stopped for ever," "became a less oppressive memory, and the sense of living freshened us again like a clean wind" (181). For Bill, the countryside is "a place one could work and tend, and still find a future" (181). *28 Days Later* likewise heralds the countryside as a site of renewal, but not on the basis of its agricultural potential. Unlike other apocalyptic and post-apocalyptic films, which draw viewers' horrified attention to the human as well as material debris that an epidemic like Rage will necessarily have left in its wake, the landscapes of *28 Days Later* are remarkably people-free, adhering to a Romantic aesthetic of ruination. Boyle and Garland have stressed the fantastic emptiness of the early scenes, in which London appears devoid of living, dead, and infected bodies, and even of vehicles. It is only when Jim enters a church that he realizes the city is still (in a sense) inhabited. More significant still, I think, is the film's depiction of rural England. In one critical scene, Jim, Selena, Hannah, and Hannah's doomed father Frank catch sight of a "family" of galloping horses while picnicking amidst some venerable ruins. When Hannah asks whether the horses are infected, Frank responds, "They're doing just fine." The scene is a poignant one. The glorious spectacle of "natural" family feeling anchors Selena's realization that "all the death, all the shit – it doesn't really mean anything to Frank and Hannah – because, well she's got a dad, and he's got his daughter." At the same time, juxtaposing picturesque ruins, the non-perishable goods of a very perishable civilization, and animal vitality, the scene conveys a sense of loss, impending change, and the bankruptcy of narratives of progress. Whereas Bill Masen sees in the countryside possibilities for rebuilding a culture through cultivation, in *28 Days Later*, horses run free, "doing just fine" without us. Perhaps in the twenty-first century, with BSE and foot-and-mouth conditioning global perceptions of Britain as a "diseased island," it is no longer possible to see in agriculture the redemption Bill Masen could find there in 1951.[68] The film does not necessarily decry this development. Later shots of nearly empty motorways cutting across a depopulated countryside and presided over by beating windmills, remind us that nobody remains to work and tend the land. And yet, decommissioned, these landscapes of utility function as aesthetic objects; they are sheerly beautiful. Contrasting Boyle's post-agricultural rural landscape with the hellish rural landscape of Alfonso Cuarón's 2006 post-apocalyptic film *Children of Men*, for example, in which the only horseflesh we see is dead, presumptively diseased, and heaped for ease of immolation, we note the irony of a world made beautiful by apocalypse.

The film's pastoral aesthetic might be seen as marking a departure from, or alternative to, the domestic idyll of the coda. In fact, however, they complement one another, and not only insofar as the English pastoral tradition encompasses representations of the sort of rustic life to which apocalypse reduces Jim, Selena, and Hannah. The Lake District is, after all, an iconically English landscape, so that the trio's retreat constitutes a return to England-as-home as well as to the home-as-institution. In this respect, *28 Days Later* mobilizes the kind of organicist national imaginary that (re)surfaced, David Matless has shown, around the middle of the twentieth century, linking Englishness with the soil, and inspiring "back to the land" movements that identified men and women's proper tasks as farming and housekeeping respectively.[69] We could say then that *28 Days Later* proposes countering the savagery of Rage through reinvesting in organic England, the countryside "freshening" a jaded urban populace like "a clean[sing] wind." But recall that Selena's account of Rage's origins has the disease originating in small villages and market towns. It's not clear that rural Britain (still? yet?) exists as a resource to be drawn on. Rather, the outbreak of Rage reinvigorates an organicist national imaginary precisely to the extent that it devastates British civilization, producing, in effect, an empty space in which to start again. If the demographic catastrophe of Rage requires Jim and the other survivors to exit, cast off, the habits, people, and spaces in which homeliness once inhered, it ends by restoring "Jerusalem" to them, an England reclaimed from "satanic mills" and invasive bodies to become, as Blake desired, a "green & pleasant land" once more.[70] Patrick Sharp claims that American post-apocalyptic fiction responds to the globalization of space by returning us to "the local space [and values] of the American frontier."[71] In a similar way, *28 Days Later* revives the colonial dream of starting again, discarding the tropical space of the (post)colony for an emphatically English neopastoral landscape that, rid of the threat of savagery, proves magnificently conducive to pioneerism.

According to this reading, the apocalypticism of a film like *28 Days Later* manifests as utopian to the extent that it identifies in the catastrophe it mourns possibilities for regeneration, promising renewal not just for the apocalyptic world it describes, but for our own. Building on arguments made in chapter 4, however, I want to suggest that the "apocalyptic desire that finds satisfaction in elaborating fictions of the End" registers as utopian in another way as well, insofar as the threat of invasion defines the nation as an "inside" that must be protected from a threatening "outside," operating, in fact, as an "island solution."[72] Identifying otherness as something external to the nation, narratives of invasion suggest that the nation can only be existentially threatened from without, ignoring the possibility that, as Derrida observes, the community may be threatened by the impulse to protect itself, the "auto-immunitary [that] haunts the community and its system of immunitary survival like the hyperbole of its own possibility."[73] Positioning the good white citizen as he who is "hated, and who is threatened and victimized by the law and polity," the British white supremacist websites Ahmed reads in *The Cultural Politics of Emotion* cover over by reframing the hatred the white supremacist is supposed to feel for a variety of embodied others (interracial couples, child molesters, aliens) as love.[74] Aryans do not hate others, these websites insist, but love whiteness, or rather, love whiteness in hating others, a hate that then "sticks" (to use Ahmed's language) the nation and its white subjects together.[75] Hatred is, moreover, displaced onto the other, whose property it becomes, so that it is the other who is understood to commit (as it were) hate crimes against the self, rather than the other way around. In *28 Days Later*, Rage circulates through the violent acts of the Infected, who bite, scratch, vomit on, and tear at their victims. However, it also circulates, tellingly, through the violent acts of the unInfected, whose frenzied attempts to fend off the Infected result in copious bloodletting. On the DVD commentary track, Boyle and Garland marvel at the abandon with which Selena dismembers Mark, whom she believes to have been infected. How evenly, to paraphrase Eve Sedgwick, the phobia about Rage-positive blood keeps pace with the "rage for keeping that dangerous blood in broad, continuous circulation."[76] A tension emerges here, between an *anxiety* over the penetrability of the nation, a concern that, to cite Ahmed once again, the nation is "taken in" whenever it "take[s] in," and an *insistence* on the penetrability of the nation, which justifies its orientation as a "body that stands apart or keeps its distance from others."[77] What else can you do, with the barbarians on their way? As Ghassan Hage writes about late-twentieth-century Australian discourses of whiteness, paranoid national subjects invest in "images of disintegration to weave the story of a desperate rearguard action by a disintegrating nationalist trying at all cost to save a disintegrating national order."[78] On the one hand, then, allegories of trespass make manifest, configure, select threats to the national body. On the other hand, however, they authorize the state to undertake certain actions – instituting restrictive immigration policies, for example – in the name of national defence. "The white subjects claim the place of hosts ('our shores') at the same time as they claim the position of victim."[79] To be a victim is to be a host.

Apocalyptic dramas of invasion and overwhelmment do not, to be sure, appeal uniquely to Britons; the currency of such rhetorics across a range of historical and geopolitical contexts may explain why, although her examples are drawn largely from twenty-first-century British political discourse, Sara Ahmed does not attend to the particular significance of their articulation of hatred, victimhood, and whiteness vis-à-vis post-war conceptions of British identity. Still, the neopastoralism of *28 Days Later* invites us to think about the role that allegories of trespass have played in metropolitan debates about the proper nature and scope of Britain's relationship with its overseas territories and citizens, that is, about what is "inside," what "outside," Britain and Britishness, from at least the Second World War on. My argument here owes much to Jed Esty's *A Shrinking Island*, which charts an "inward turn" in twentieth-century British cultural production, as Britain's disarticulation from the spaces and machinery of empire forced – freed – her writers to (re)discover a truly national culture at home. In this context, it is productive to consider Danny Boyle and Alex Garland's own ongoing collaboration, which commenced when Boyle adapted Garland's first novel, *The Beach* (1997), for the screen. *The Beach* features a protagonist gripped by a desire for self-mastery and heroic agency, which he nostalgically imagines to have been available to past generations of (British) men, but no longer. A child of the 1970s, Richard describes himself as having been "born twenty years too late," "too late," that is, to serve in the Vietnam War: enraptured by Hollywood's 'Nam, Richard "always wanted to" "escape off the embassy roof," but must instead derive excitement from travel and video games (52). Played as an American by Leonardo DiCaprio in Boyle's film of *The Beach* (2000), in the novel Richard is importantly British. His sense of belatedness, expressed in the fetish he makes of the Vietnam War, reflects Britain's diminished status in a world it once dominated, and its supersession as an imperial power by the United States. If, like Odd Arne Westad, we see the Cold War as "a continuation of European colonial interventions and of European attempts at controlling Third World Peoples," Britain's decision not to commit troops to Vietnam reads like a decision to forfeit a game in which it was once a (perhaps the) major player.[80] What Richard mourns, arguably, is the loss of empire, and with it the loss of arenas in which to discover and demonstrate one's masculinity and national character. Home to "the beach," a utopian community of Western travellers, the remote Thai island to which Richard is guided by a fellow traveller at once fulfils the travellers' exoticist dream of escaping the contaminations of modernity, and serves Richard – the paradox is a familiar one – as a set for the colonial war games he's experienced cinematically and now stages in virtual reality (5). In the end, of course, Richard's island community is, like others I've examined, rent by violence. The travellers' Eden proves incompatible with Thai plans for the island: the natives' black market take on postcolonial economic development – they run part of the island as a marijuana plantation – triumphs, realizing Richard's violent fantasies and – thus – destroying the beach. Like *Heart of Darkness*, then, to which it inevitably refers (via *Apocalypse Now*), *The Beach* reveals the iconic locales of adventure fiction to be contested spaces in which the white male body and psyche are, as Jen Hill puts it, dramatically endangered rather than empowered.[81] With *28 Days Later*, Boyle and

Garland move from periphery to metropole, an "inward turn" that concedes the vulnerability of white masculinity even at home, only to present, via the apocalypse of Rage, a more lasting solution to the catastrophe of evacuated (masculine) agency, anchored in a re-pastoralized English landscape.[82]

But situating *28 Days Later* thus, as part of an "inward turn" in Boyle and Garland's work, and in British cultural production more generally, risks obscuring the extent to which texts like *28 Days Later* work to produce the metropole as an inside to which Britons may not only turn, but *re*turn. In *A Shrinking Island*, Esty tends to assume that the location of national culture is known in advance, even if its content must be elaborated: Englishness is *inward*; it is *that inwardness to which one turns.* As Alissa Karl helpfully puts it,

> Esty's astute tracking of the move to insular Englishness in the late modernist period ... presumes, consciously or not, the preexistence of a national unit that becomes the object of contemplation, identification, or analysis in the face of imperial retrenchment. It is as if the national or imperial "center" was somehow already there, however much it may be differently asserted in the wake of historical and geopolitical change and however much it may be subject to "reverse colonization."[83]

In the aftermath of empire, where Britishness is located, what is inside Britain and Britishness and what is outside, whether Britain was or must be conceived as the inside to its erstwhile imperial outside, are objects of contestation, not consensus, and never more so than during the immigration controversies of the 1950s, 1960s, and 1970s.

Even describing these controversies as "about immigration" concedes too much. If some Britons sincerely feel that immigrants pose a threat to British livelihoods and, indeed, the British way of life, it would be a mistake nevertheless to see such feelings as (only) a natural response to the disturbing fact of uncontrolled immigration. During the 1950s and 1960s, even as immigration developed into a national controversy, Britain actively encouraged immigration from Eire and continental Europe, while pursuing the large-scale emigration schemes that sent thousands of Britain-born Britons to Australia and New Zealand. It should also be noted that which subjects are accounted immigrants changes over time. Like the term "invader," the term "immigrant," which interpellates individuals as outsiders wishing to enter *into* a country, works to distinguish the nation's "insides" from its "outsides." In the 1960s, as Kathleen Paul has convincingly demonstrated, politicians and bureaucrats "deftly manipulate[ed] language in internal reports, parliamentary and press statements, and official documents" in order to effect "a tiered process of reconstruction, transforming migrants of color from British subjects into Commonwealth immigrants while racializing the term 'Commonwealth immigrant' to refer only to migrants of colour."[84] The Colonial Office's attempt to depict "the [*Windrush*] migrants as alien invaders who were somehow trying to circumvent imperial rules by independently migrating to Britain" represents an early instance of this sort of rhetorical sleight-of-hand.[85]

The transformation of British subjects into immigrants was achieved legislatively as well as rhetorically, through limiting access to the privileges of British citizenship, namely, the right of abode. Recall that until 1962, all inhabitants of the British empire shared a common nationality: British subject status was accorded all persons born or naturalized in any of Britain's sovereign territories. In 1962, however, the government introduced a voucher system for would-be migrant British subjects, hoping thereby to reduce the number of unskilled labourers admitted to Britain. The "great merit" of the 1962 Commonwealth Immigrants Act was its discretion: ostensibly colour-blind, the act's "restrictive effect" could yet be made to "operate on coloured people almost exclusively."[86] With the Commonwealth Immigrants Act of 1968, the government began to make explicit the discriminatory edge of British immigration policy, reserving the right of abode for United Kingdom and Colonies citizens who had been born, naturalized, or adopted in the United Kingdom; whose parents or grandparents had been born, naturalized, or adopted in the United Kingdom; or who were registered as such in Canada, Australia, New Zealand, the Union of South Africa, Newfoundland, India, Pakistan, Southern Rhodesia, or Ceylon.[87] The 1971 Immigration Act tightened the criteria for patriality still further, enlarging the pool of alienated British subjects who were required to submit to immigration controls. By the time the Conservatives passed a new Nationality Act in 1981, where one was born mattered less than to whom, as the right of abode was withheld from even British-born individuals unless they could prove that their parents or grandparents had been British citizens. The 1971 Immigration Act has been called a whitewash, a triumph for conceptions of Britishness as "an inheritance of race."[88] This is true, so far as it goes. As Paul points out, the act "legally differentiated between the familial community of Britishness composed of the truly British – those descended from white colonizers – and the political community of Britishness composed of individuals who had become British through conquest or domination."[89] While the former were mostly white, the latter were mostly not. But if the 1971 Immigration Act rearticulates British citizenship as a function of race, and specifically as a function of whiteness, it does so, I want to suggest, by articulating a new geography of Britishness. After all, British common law has always recognized the citizenship rights of individuals born to citizen-fathers beyond the territorial borders of the British empire. What happened in 1971, we could say, was a kind of territorial in-drawing, whereby much of what was once imagined as British territory was made over as alien. This territorial in-drawing permitted the remaking of (some) British citizens as immigrants, forced to petition for entry to a community to which they thought they already belonged.

Foregrounding those nativist projects that strove to realize cultural decolonization and democratization, Jed Esty acknowledges that "English particularism has [also] been the basis for a rearguard politics of ethnic identity in contemporary Britain."[90] My readings of fantasies of overwhelmment and demographic collapse, from "Rivers of Blood" to *28 Days Later* and beyond, suggest the reverse, drawing attention to the way in which "a rearguard politics of ethnic identity" has given rise to a particularizing project that sutures British identity to the singular space of the British Isles, what I termed in chapter 1 an island solution.[91] For a recent example, we need only look to the rhetoric of the xenophobic and white supremacist British National Party (BNP). On 23 April 2010, the BNP, which advocates an end both to immigration and to British participation in the European Union, released its General Election Manifesto in Stoke-on-Trent. In the introduction, leader Nick Griffin asserts that "the BNP believes in genuine ethnic and cultural diversity and the right of all peoples to be free of colonization and rule by others – including the indigenous people of these islands."[92] This is not the only occasion on which BNP officials and affiliates have mobilized the language of indigeneity to formulate their program for Britain. In a 2009 address to the Wolverhampton BNP, James Whittall drew on the United Nations' 2007 Declaration on the Rights of Indigenous Peoples (UNDRIP) in demanding for "indigenous" Britons the right to resist "colonization," by which he meant immigration.[93] A headline on the BNP website reads, "Third World Benefit Fraud Rife in Britain as Colonisation Speeds Up." The website also promotes a booklet entitled *Four Flags: The Indigenous People of Great Britain*, which quotes from what it calls the United Nations Charter on Indigenous Peoples to show how the "indigenous" people of Britain are fully protected from "dispossession of their territory" through "mass [*sic*] population transfers" and from "forced integration and assimilation" and "destruction of their identity and culture."[94] As is clear from the way the BNP frames immigration in terms of colonization, it seeks to articulate British indigeneity with whiteness, which it reads as an indicator of ancestral connection to the land. To scholars of colonialism, that the BNP mobilizes the language of indigeneity in the service of an openly xenophobic and white supremacist agenda must seem noxious. Still, it can be difficult to see how to critique the BNP's claims without undermining the discourse and politics of indigeneity more broadly. After all, Britons *are* indigenous to the British Isles – aren't they? If indigeneity is taken to inhere in individuals who can claim a more or less unbroken, genealogically derived connection to a particular place, then perhaps, indeed, the BNP is correct to identify its constituents as indigenous.[95] As we've seen, however, birth (to a Briton born) in the British Isles has only recently become an essential component of statutory Britishness, the fruit of earlier panics about a "rising tide of colour." More politically productive definitions of indigeneity, moreover, centre the experience of colonization, not, as Alice Te Punga Somerville insists, because "it belongs at the centre of how specific Indigenous communities think about themselves," but because to "refuse to recognise this colonial context is to take the heat out of the politics of resistance and decolonisation in which [Indigenous] communities are involved" and which animates the UN Declaration on the Rights of Indigenous Peoples.[96] The BNP insists, to be sure, that native-born Britons, white Britons, are a colonized people, asserting a likeness between immigration and colonization we should vigorously reject. It is also important, however, to consider why the BNP should make use of the language of indigeneity in advancing its distinctly regressive demands for redress. In effect, the BNP makes colonization over into the project of individuals at least some of whom experienced (or are the descendants of people who experienced) colonization at the hands of the very nation state the BNP now frames as under threat – of colonization. This is not only perverse, but a form of national thinking that remembers – or rather, disremembers – the history of Britain's exploits as an empire by first negating the rights of former colonial subjects to the space of Britain, and going on to claim their experience as "victims."

I am not advocating a return to the Common Code, which, if it stressed the accessibility and mobility of Britishness, did so in the interests of imperial cohesion; it is not clear that, by the 1960s and 1970s, Jamaicans or Australians or Kenyans would have happily held on to Britishness, no matter how expansively it persisted in defining itself. Nevertheless, as fantasies of collapse and invasion circulate, fuelling ever more restrictive immigration and asylum policies, it seems important to disrupt the claims of particularism, integrity, and even indigeneity, upon which the myth of endangered Britain appears to rest but actually underwrites. In emphasizing the racializing effects of post-war British immigration and nationality legislation, accounts like Ian Baucom's can appear to suggest that twenty-first-century conceptions of British citizenship are problematic insofar as they are raced. It's not that this isn't true. Arguably, the contradictions of imperial Britishness only really became unbearable once the multiracial character of the polity they made possible was brought home to metropolitan Britons. At the same time, the BNP's indigenist formulation of the project of white supremacy forces us to attend to the specificity of the post-imperial situation that at once gave rise to and was effaced by the racial turn in British discourses of citizenship, the better to understand how not just Britain's imperial past, but the desire to bury this past, continues to organize debates about race, nationality, immigration, and the welfare state. There are multiple dimensions to this "afterlife." I have drawn on the work of Kathleen Paul and others to show how, as part of the process of decolonization, especially non-white British overseas subjects were strategically re-rendered as outsiders seeking belonging in a community to which, it was decided, they could articulate no prior claim. According to Paul Gilroy, it is precisely insofar as "incoming strangers" are felt to "not only *represent* the vanished empire but also refer consciousness to the unacknowledged pain of its loss and the unsettling shame of its bloody management," that they have had to be framed as invaders bent on victimizing their welcoming hosts.[97] Since, as Gilroy suggests, even immigrants originating in countries without a history of (British) colonization are now thus interpellated, contesting anti-immigrant and anti-immigration sentiment in Britain requires contesting post-imperial amnesia as well. Recalling the history that first granted and then denied millions of non-Britain-born subjects the right to lay claim to the property of Britain and Britishness should not only lead us to recognize the force of their demands for inclusion within the community of Britishness. In addition, I think, we are invited to revisit the assumptions about belonging and the limits of community that shape decisions about how social goods, including the right of abode from which so many other entitlements derive, should be distributed. If, as Michael Walzer writes, "the idea of distributive justice presupposes a bounded world within which distributions take place," then "the first and most important distributive question" must be, "how is that group constituted."[98] What the claims of British overseas subjects to the social goods of Britishness make visible is the dependence of those goods on the labour and other resources of people who are, or can be made out to be, external to the nation, *including but not limited to* former colonial subjects and their descendants. How might acknowledging their claims open up the scene of distributive justice to a more properly global (or planetary) terrain of action?

The Return of the Native

In attending to continuities between the spatial imaginaries of apocalyptic fictions like *28 Days Later* and the spatial stories on which the paranoid white nationalisms of Enoch Powell and the BNP depend, it is not my purpose to suggest that Boyle and Garland are purveyors of white supremacism. Rather, like Kathleen Paul, Stuart Hall, and others, I think that it is important to acknowledge the extent to which the "extreme" conception of British nationality elaborated by Powell in "Rivers of Blood," now "synonymous in popular lore with opposition to 'coloured immigration,'" falls "within the realm of established 'official' [or mainstream] conceptions of British nationality."[99] In 2007, Channel 4 aired *Face of Britain*, a three-part television series that purported to show Britons "'who we really are' by tracing [our genetic] links back to ancient Celts, Anglo-Saxons, Vikings and Normans."[100] As Anne-Marie Fortier argues in a recent essay, *Face of Britain* demonstrates how contemporary research in population genetics, in this case a study led by the Oxford scientist Walter Bodmer, can help to support conclusions like the BNP's, even when the geneticists involved take care to discredit BNP "science." According to Fortier, the understanding of British indigeneity proliferated by the study and documentary resonates with the definition of British indigeneity advanced by the BNP. Thus, for example, the rhetorical and visual tropes through which *Face of Britain* represents "average" Britishness work to articulate Britishness with whiteness and rurality. It is notable, too, that Bodmer's team declined to include immigrants and immigrant descendants in their "Genetic Domesday Book" on the grounds that the genetic history of such people "relates to their country of origin, not to the British Isles," a claim which, as Fortier points out, "whitewashes the colonial history of Britain, [denying] the relationship between the history of a large section of this immigrant population and the more general pattern of British history."[101] In a similar way, the account of British history that underpinned Danny Boyle's vision for the opening ceremony of the 2012 London Olympics occluded the centrality of empire to many of the events, movements, and institutions it highlighted as having shaped modern Britain. If the opening ceremony recalls the pageant that the unconventional Miss La Trobe stages in Virginia Woolf's 1941 novel *Between the Acts*, a text Jed Esty cites as evidence of the "inward reorientation (or deorientalizing) of English culture," it lacks that play's productive scepticism about its own eccentric method.[102] Boyle repatriated even *The Tempest*, long read as a reflection on New World histories of encounter and dispossession, by repurposing Caliban's encomium to the island which he loves and has lost for delivery by Kenneth Branagh's Isambard Kingdom Brunel, the Victorian engineer. Although some viewers, pointing to Boyle's manifest interest in the British protest traditions of labour and feminism, read the awkwardness of this fit as drawing attention, precisely, to a history of such appropriations, it is nonetheless striking that only the struggles of the suffragettes and working-class militants, and not those of abolitionists, for example, were represented on stage. There's something at once perverse and fitting about *New York Times* columnist Sarah Lyall's admiring description of the opening ceremony, a spectacle devoid of explicit references to Britain's imperial history, as the coming-out party for a nation finally "secure in its own post-empire identity."[103]

How Boyle might otherwise have treated this history, so integral to the making of modern Britain, is difficult to say. As Paul Gilroy observes, when "colonial history and memory" do manifest in twenty-first-century British public discourse, "they have usually been whitewashed in order to promote imperialist nostalgia or sanctified so that they endorse the novel forms of colonial rule currently being enforced by the economic and military means at the disposal of a unipolar global order."[104] Commemorative projects that recover anti-slavery and anti-colonial activism for a specifically British tradition of dissent do a different kind of whitewashing work to the extent that they imply that the slave trade, for example, did not play a critical role in the formation of modern Britain. It is doubtful whether a nuanced assessment of the nation, its failures, responsibilities, and obligations can be launched via the opening and closing ceremonies of the Olympic Games (although it is also dangerous to foreclose on such venues as possible sites of significant critical work). At the same time, what is important about the insularity of the story Boyle chose to tell on 27 July 2012 is the light it sheds on the place of empire in (some conceptions of) Britain's "post-empire identity." In this context, it is instructive to juxtapose Lyall's review of the 2012 opening ceremony with one British journalist's response to the show that opened the 2010 Winter Olympics in Vancouver. Tickled by what he saw as the lewd symbolism of the four glass totem poles that welcomed the Olympics to Vancouver, *The Guardian*'s Martin Kelner wondered if

> political correctness kept [viewers] quiet, as the poles were part of the welcome to Canada from the four host first nations. It has become the sine qua non of these shindigs that the Aboriginal folk who inhabited the land in the days before Starbucks and 24-hour news channels play a major part, which can feel a little patronizing, but given Canada's generally benign – although not untainted – race relations record, it felt more appropriate in Vancouver than it did in Sydney [in 2000], for instance.[105]

It's a little patronizing of Kelner to dismiss the use of Aboriginal protocols of welcome as mere "political correctness," as if their inclusion did not at least admit Indigenous territorial priority, a by no means insignificant concession. Still, he's right to suggest that events such as the Olympics mobilize Indigenous iconography and ceremonial protocols to primitivist nationalist ends. This is not even to mention the despoliation of Indigenous resources and communities from which large-scale state-funded events like the Olympics benefit and to which they contribute. At the same time, Kelner takes care not to implicate himself (and other Britons) in such projects by diagnosing their effects as a consequence of "tainted" race relations and the importation of American goods like Starbucks and 24-hour news channels. Nowhere does he concede Britain's involvement in the process by which the land was made available for capitalization. And yet, Vancouver is located in *British* Columbia, after all.

It is for Canadians – and Australians and New Zealanders – to confront their settlement on stolen land. But Britons too have profited from this history of dispossession; it is also their inheritance. According to Anne-Marie Fortier, the BNP first took up the language of indigeneity in 2009, when the House of Commons again declared that it would not ratify International Labour Organisation Convention 169 on Tribal and Indigenous Peoples (a forerunner to the Declaration on the Rights of Indigenous Peoples) on the grounds that "there are no indigenous peoples in the United Kingdom."[106] Of course, the BNP's response – that there are indeed indigenous peoples in the United Kingdom who require protection against the threat of further "colonization" – is disingenuous. The histories of dispossession, dislocation, forced assimilation, and despoliation, recognition of which is signalled by ratification of such documents as Convention 169, are manifestly British concerns not because Britain is home to indigenous peoples, but because (settler) colonial projects of de- and re-territorialization were at one time also British ones. "With its hilariously quirky Olympic opening ceremony," writes Lyall, "Britain presented itself to the world … as something it has often struggled to express even to itself: a nation secure in its own post-empire identity, whatever that actually is." In contrast, the BNP seeks to secure Britishness by invoking a paranoid national subject, insecure and entrapped. Both assume, nonetheless, the integrity of Britain's island story, electing island solutions at the expense of a thorough reckoning with the colonial past – and present.

Envoi

I opened *Better Britons* with a discussion of Miria George's *and what remains*, a play set in the international departures lounge at Wellington Airport. Concluding chapters like this one are likewise sites of departure, in which authors take leave of readers while leaving something behind, some insight that marks a departure, or at least offers hope for a departure, from tired habits of thought and the energy-sapping clutch of histories that just won't let go. Resurfacing periodically to highlight this or that threat to the body politic, demographic panics and dramas of invasion can seem themselves rather like zombies, atavistic in their attachment to ideals of order, purity, and uniformity, espousing tropes and ideas that should be dead but seem instead to keep on proliferating. If they limn crises, identifying hitches in the social and biological machinery of reproduction, they appear also, in the regularity with which they get trotted out, to do some of the work of buttressing the status quo, framing the unfamiliar (the unfamilial) in infuriatingly familiar terms. Here they are again, you say, rolling your eyes, grabbing hold of your weapons, wondering whether there isn't something different, something better, you could be doing with your time.

But departure is not without its own "histories of arrival."[1] This George emphasizes in the way that she riffs on (or has Anna riff on) the interrogative ritual fundamental to airport customs and immigration exit protocols. Upon exiting New Zealand, all travellers must fill out a departure card that asks for their name, nationality, occupation, and place of residence, as well as the destination, purpose, and length of their proposed trip; they must declare their intention to move substantial amounts of money out of the country. Although we do not witness the characters' encounter with New Zealand border protection officials, the cleaner Anna, who claims to be unable to leave New Zealand, pelts questions at Ila, Solomon, and Mary: she wants to know whether Solomon's "going home," and if he has dependants (11; 13); she asks Ila where she's headed and whether she can "afford to go," commenting, "You've got a lot of stuff" (10; 15; 6); she wonders why Mary "is leaving today," and whether her father took with him "many things" when he left (44). The economic drift of Anna's questioning frames the act of departure as a reckoning, in which travellers must declare what they are taking out of the nation, the things they carry, including, as Solomon observes, "the baggage you can't see" (11). This "baggage," bespeaking the unevenness with which power is distributed in colonial capitalist states like New Zealand, conditions each character's relationship with the nation state, making departure either possible or unthinkable: Ila and Solomon can afford to go; Anna cannot; Peter can afford not to go; Mary cannot afford not to. In *and what remains*, focusing on the scene of departure rather than the scene of arrival, around which settler projects of nation building so often revolve, reorients attention away from the baggage migrants bring to the nation to the baggage the nation bequeaths them, that is, the legacy of Indigenous dispossession. Midway through *and what remains*, all departures out of the airport are delayed, leading Solomon to inquire, "How long is delayed?" (29). Ila responds, "However long it takes" (29). By the time flights resume, everybody save Mary has chosen to remain in New Zealand: Ila and Solomon cancel their trips, while Anna declines the offer of Ila's ticket. Mary's departure, which is not voluntary, sounds an ominous note about the prospects for decolonization in Aotearoa New Zealand: Ila may be content to wait "however long it takes," but Māori are on the verge of losing Aotearoa *now*. Still, we might learn from the use George makes of the space-time of delayed departure to stage a conversation in which Solomon, Ila, and Anna come round to acknowledging truths about New Zealand's treatment of Māori – and their involvement therein – that they've previously denied knowing. In this way, *and what remains* suggests that the political charge of departure inheres in the opportunity it affords the departing to consider what it is they are departing from. This is a departure (from the amnesiac professions of ignorance with which the settler characters seek to defend themselves to Mary) that also turns away from the solution of departure.

It is just such a departure that I seek here, enjoining not (only) remembrance, but openness to "the futurity inherent in remembrance," "the eruptive force of remembering otherwise."[2] I am compelled by Roger Simon's exploration of "the past's claim on the interminable redemptive struggle toward a 'democracy still to come,'" in which he suggests taking up histories of violence and suffering as inheritances whose "disruptive risks and possibilities" may propel us to "the learning necessary for sustaining democratic communities."[3] Simon focuses on the work of witnessing, the "touch of the past" that comes by way of encounters with the harrowing stories of harrowed others, asking how "the presentation and engagement with documents of historical witness [might] initiate the work of inheritance through which one can experience a questioning of and transformation in one's own unfolding stories and the frames on which one might argue for a possible future."[4] Marianne Hirsch poses similar questions in her work on postmemory, drawing attention to the ethical exigencies (and pitfalls) of witnessing.[5] But what of those stories that communicate not the experiences of the *victims* of such historical traumas as the Holocaust or "breeding out the colour" but the experiences of their *perpetrators*, both narrowly and broadly conceived? Histories of systemic mass violence can seem to belong to the injured and their descendants rather than to the agents of injury and their successors. There are good reasons for privileging the authority of the former, their stories and needs, over the authority, stories, and needs of the latter. At the same time, it is worth asking how we might (re)inherit – be transformed by – our own "unfolding stories," to which the histories of others return us. How, in reflecting on the events that have culminated in the expulsion of Māori, are Ila, Solomon, Anna, and Peter awakened to an awareness of their complicity in the dispossession of Māori, which they did not, perhaps, actively further, but for which they nonetheless bear responsibility as non-Indigenous people, as settlers?

In moving remembrance "beyond the boundaries of a singular corporeal body," Simon and Hirsch help to explain how responsibility attaches to individuals not directly involved, by reason of temporal distance, in the depredations of a colonial order regularly construed as terminated.[6] Writing in August 1996, just before the release of *Bringing Them Home*, then governor general Sir William Deane suggested that although "individual Australians" must feel "national shame" at the "wrongfulness of the past dispossession, oppression and degradation of the Aboriginal peoples," they need not "feel or acknowledge personal guilt," having taken "no part in what was done in the past."[7] As Sara Ahmed points out in her reading of the shame Deane ascribes to the national body, "national shame" operates as "not only a mode of recognition of injustices committed against others, but also a form of nation building" that "restore[s] or reconcile[s] the nation to itself," helping to contain the decolonizing potential of the kind of memory work undertaken by the HREOC enquiry (see chapter 2).[8] Deane checks the "eruptive force of remembering otherwise" by displacing shame from individual bodies to the collective, which obscures how "such wrongdoing shapes lives in the present."[9] Invasion, as Patrick Wolfe has observed, is a structure not an event.[10] In the remainder of this concluding chapter, I want to return attention to the "singular corporeal body" as a site and agent of remembrance, asking not just how embodied individuals are involved in the passing on of historical memory, but what it means to think about remembrance as an embodied act. In the reading of *Voyage in the Dark* that anchors chapter 3, I suggested that Anna's treacherous body surfaces a history of sexual violence and racial mixing which Anna, like her fellow creoles, would rather forget. Here, I turn to *28 Weeks Later* (2007), the sequel to the film at the heart of chapter 5, *28 Days Later*, in order to flesh out the implications of corporealizing inheritance.

Taking as its premise the return of Rage, following ostensible containment, to Britain, *28 Weeks Later* is itself a revenant, a sequel that returns Rage to world cinemas. In a sense, however, *28 Weeks Later* is a film about Rage that only masquerades as a sequel, since although Danny Boyle and Alex Garland served as executive producers on the film and participated in its development and making, *28 Weeks Later* was directed by a Spaniard, Juan Carlos Fresnadillo, who collaborated on the screenplay with Spaniards Enrique López Lavigne and Jesús Olmo, and Briton Rowan Joffe. Like Mexican director Alfonso Cuarón's adaptation of *Children of Men*, *28 Weeks Later* is undeniably a film about Britain, but it is a British film made by Spaniards, hinting at the globalization, the circulation, of processes of reproduction. Not surprisingly, perhaps, *28 Weeks Later* does not repeat the containment narrative of the first film, turning this on its head by intimating that Rage cannot, in the end, be contained.

28 Weeks Later begins, in a sense, where the first film leaves off, focused on the routinized survival of three housebound couples. As husband and wife Don and Alice prepare a meal from cans of chickpeas and tomatoes in a darkened kitchen, they discuss their children, whom the couple sent on a school trip to Spain just before the outbreak of Rage. We then meet the other inhabitants of the house: Sally, Jacob, and homeowners Karen and Geoff. Sitting down to their meal, the survivors hear a child at the front door demanding to be let in. Alice (Catherine McCormack) complies: "It's a kid," she tells Don (Robert Carlyle). Panic sets in. Sally, concerned about a missing boyfriend, ventures over to the door, where she is attacked by an Infected. The enRaged swarm the house. Cornered in one of the upstairs rooms, Alice begs Don to help her and the child, but he turns away in an attempt to preserve himself. Arrived at a nearby river, he escapes – alone – by boat. Twenty-eight weeks later, American-led NATO forces have declared Britain free from infection and commenced the rebuilding process. Those Britons who managed to survive the infection or who happened to be abroad at the time of the outbreak are gathered and housed in District One, a secure compound on the Isle of Dogs (once an island, now separated from the Thames by forty metres of infilled land). Don is reunited with his children, Tammy (Imogen Poots) and Andy (Mackintosh Muggleton), to whom he delivers a sanitized account of Alice's death, neglecting to mention his own raging sense of guilt. Warned of the dangers London poses them, Tammy and Andy nevertheless slip out of the compound to visit their old family home. Here they discover Alice, alive and apparently uninfected. District One's chief medical officer, an American scientist named Scarlet (Rose Byrne), ascertains that Alice is in fact an asymptomatic carrier, infected with Rage but thus far unaffected by it. That Alice can nonetheless transmit the disease is confirmed when she and Don kiss. EnRaged, Don beats Alice to death. Everything now starts again. Unable to prevent the infection from spreading, the military approves the extermination of all persons on the ground, military and civilian alike. The remainder of the film follows Tammy and Andy on the run, with only Scarlet, the sniper Doyle (Jeremy Renner), and a helicopter pilot named Flynn (Harold Perrineau) to help them survive the military's containment efforts and elude the pursuing Infected. When Doyle asks Scarlet why she's involved herself with the children, she explains, "Their mother had very special blood, a natural kind of immunity to the virus. Not all genetic traits are passed on, you know. They can skip a generation or vanish altogether, but …" Doyle understands: "but they might have it," the agent, that is, that prevents Rage from taking hold. Convinced of the truth of Scarlet's insistence that the children's lives are "far more valuable than mine or yours," Doyle dies trying to protect them. So, later, does Scarlet. During a harrowing climactic confrontation in the Underground, Don bites Andy. Tammy then shoots and kills her father. With Andy displaying signs that he indeed possesses his mother's "very special blood," the children rendezvous with Flynn at Wembley Stadium, and are flown to the continent. A brief coda dated twenty-eight days later shows us Flynn's helicopter spattered with blood. In the final scene of the film, a group of Infected runs through a tunnel towards the Eiffel Tower. Rage has gone global.

In their commentary on the film, Fresnadillo and Lavigne say that they wanted to show how family matters ramify outwards to "affect the whole nation."[11] This holds true at the level of plot: a child longs for a photograph to remember his mother by, a husband longs for his wife's forgiveness, and so the virus is released. But what does it mean for a family to be at the heart of this story? After all, the first film presents pastoral cosiness as the "answer to infection." To quote Jacob in the overture to the second film, "It's just us in here, and them out there." Scarlet's qualms notwithstanding – "Nobody told me we're now admitting children" – the NATO rebuilding effort too promises, even as it is also premised upon, the resumption of normal family life. It therefore requires that Tammy and Andy reunite with their father. Whereas, in *28 Days Later* and *The Aftermath*, visual media proved dangerously contaminating, communicating epidemics of rage/Rage to a vulnerable public, in *28 Weeks Later*, the camera functions as an instrument of surveillance, anchoring military projects of control and containment. At night, Doyle, bored, trains his gunsights on the compound's apartment high-rises. Wondering "what's on the TV," he quickly locates a couple having sex, but appears entranced by his glimpse of Don, Tammy, and

Andy putting themselves to bed. Counterpointing the military's formal surveillance of entry points, access corridors, and site perimeters, ad hoc endeavours like Doyle's bring scenes of intimacy, domestic, sexual, and otherwise, into the purview of the surveilling eye. In these snapshots of family life resumed Doyle discerns what he will kill to protect, what he will lay down his life to defend. In this militarized context, Rage resurfaces to disrupt family life just as the latter is beginning to re-knit.

But there's another way to read the transition from tracking "them out there" to targeting, however playfully and affectionately, "us in here." With Rage well and truly sprung, the NATO commander played by Idris Elba instructs his men to shoot at will without pausing to differentiate between the Infected and the (as yet) unInfected. When Andy enters his target-view, Doyle baulks. Disregarding orders, he leaves his post and assists in Scarlet's plan to extract the children. Doyle's feels like the right choice. We might decide that Commander Stone's decision reflects the inhumanity of a military man unwilling to make the necessary saving distinction between "us in here" and "them out there" (now, of course, also "in here") and so resist Rage's imperative to not thus discriminate, to make no distinction between Infected and unInfected, "us" and "them," "in here" and "out there." *28 Weeks Later* also suggests, however, that Doyle's joking surveillance of private space complements his apparently more purposeful surveillance of the unsafe city outside: a break-out (outbreak), it will become clear, is as much a possibility as a break-in. In *28 Weeks Later*, Rage puts unbearable pressure on the institution of the family – children are repeatedly shown having to escape their mums and dads – but it also emerges as something organic to family life. Sally opens the door to Rage, but Rage, perhaps, has always already been lurking inside. This is most graphically represented in Don's brutal murders of Alice and later Scarlet, in which writers Fresnadillo and Lavigne encourage us to see the spectres of domestic and sexual violence. Don's Rage, they suggest, typifies the rage of "the abusive husband."[12] The entanglement of intimacy with violence is played for nervous laughs in the first film, when Hannah, stoned, attacks Jim because she can't tell whether he's kissing Selena or biting her (he's kissing her). From the beginning, in contrast, *28 Weeks Later* insists on reading the family as a site of violence, as perhaps underwritten by violence, and intimacy as a close companion and even accessory to violence.

Far from being a prophylactic, then, in *28 Weeks Later* the family emerges as the source of infection, thanks to the military's investment in family reunions and the survival of the intimate couple, as well as to the exigencies of descent, the communicative potential of the blood tie. The film's coda hints that responsibility for the destruction of Europe rests with the occupants of the helicopter:

Andy, perhaps, infects Tammy or Flynn, neither of whom knows what Andy's apparent immunity means and how it functions, and contagion blossoms from there. Intriguingly, then, it is Alice and Andy's immunity to the effects of the virus that permits the virus to survive and propagate. Rage contains the seeds of its own extirpation; its very virulence keeps it confined to mainland Britain. EnRaged, Alice, Tammy, and Andy would starve to death. Alice's immunity, however, and the force of maternal inheritance, guarantees not only her own and her children's survival but the survival of Rage as well. As in the other rebuilding efforts that I've examined in this book, the (quasi) insular geography and architecture of District One reflects its orientation towards the future and away from the past. Compare, for instance, the modern architecture of District One's Canary Wharf location – given its history, not perhaps the most auspicious site for such a critical project of urban revitalization – to the "old" London through which Jim wanders at the beginning of *28 Days Later*.[13] Insulated from a London as yet uncleansed of corpses and evacuation debris, the inhabitants of District One aim to leave the past behind, to forget, in particular, the hard calculus of survival. In contrast, like Montgomery in *The Island of Dr. Moreau*, Andy and Tammy insist on knowing "how [Don] came to be alone in that boat" (Wells 4). Anxious to refresh their memories of the mother they believe dead, the children brave the dangerous city to revisit their, as it turns out, far more dangerous old home. The genetic inheritance that Andy, at least, receives from his mother, figures both a particular moment of the past – Don's betrayal of Alice, marked in the small hemorrhage that makes visible both the taint of Rage and her immunity to its effects – and the irrepressibility of the past, its zombie-like refusal to die. This inheritance, transmitted via the mechanism of heterosexual biological reproduction, preserves the children (more or less) Rage-free and alive. And of course we want the children to live – don't we? Mining the discourse of reproductive futurism, the narrative of *28 Weeks Later* assumes and stokes the viewer's desire – which is also the desire of every adult character in the film – to see the children kept safe. Recall that Alice's predicament at the beginning of the film arises because she (twice) makes the choice to aid a child. Like Alice, Scarlet, Doyle, Flynn, even the Infected Don, we want the children to live because they hold out the promise of a cure; because children represent the future as against the futurelessness of Rage; because who, as Lee Edelman asks, would "stand *against* reproduction, *against* futurity, and so against *life*? Who *would* destroy the Child?"[14] Even Fresnadillo and Lavigne note the riskiness of Flynn's decision to take Tammy and Andy with him at film's end.

The film's conclusion advances an argument not, I think, for infanticide, for an auto-immunitary response that would, like AIDS, end by destroying the body (politic), but for the necessity of moving beyond a model of bodily and communal health premised on "perfect internal cleanliness, where the inside of the body [politic] is perfectly distinct from and untouched by what is outside," and utterly unaffected by any past or future "incursion[s]."[15] Is Andy "healthy" or "sick"? If Rage survives because we survive, if we survive because Rage survives, how to extract "us" from the virus? Whence our exemption, our immunity, from the community of Rage? In her reading of the two *28* films, Sarah Trimble situates Andy in relation to broader "paranoid formulations of youth as weakening a body politic perceived as fragile or, in Ahmed's terms, wounded," invoking a passage from *Plague on Us*, a 1941 tract by the American journalist Geddes Smith, in which Smith describes children as immigrants "into the human herd – immigrants whose susceptibility dilutes herd resistance and so helps to keep certain diseases in circulation."[16] The stress Smith lays on the essential foreignness of children illuminates the political promise of the film's suggestion that even the Infected Andy might, in the end, be one of "us." But if children are (like) immigrants, I want to consider how immigrants might, in their turn, be (like) children, allowing the familiarity – indeed, the familiality – of (our) children, assimilated to the foreignness of the immigrant, to infect in its turn the foreignness of the immigrant, who, in her very strangeness, her alienation from "us," may be recognized as finally familiar, finally familial. If strangeness is not to remain the property of the other, not only must family become strange, but the stranger be recognized as already in some sense family. This is not, as Derrida warns, "to domesticate him. To neutralize him through naturalization. To assimilate him so as to stop frightening oneself (making oneself fear) with him."[17] For me, to say that the stranger is family is to open to the possibility that the family is strange, the stranger, as in the classic horror scenario, already inside the house, there among us, there inside us.

This is also the hidden threat of the 1971 Immigration Act, which, in reserving full citizenship rights only for those of Britain's overseas subjects whose fathers or grandfathers had been born or naturalized in Britain, turned to the risky fiction of paternity to secure the reproduction of Britishness-as-whiteness. Ann Laura Stoler notes that in the Netherlands, where women's citizenship status similarly followed that of their husbands, "debates over the citizenship rights of European women in mixed-marriages in the Indies were less concerned with the civil status of women than with another consequence: the conferral of Dutch citizenship on their native husbands and mixed-blood sons. It was the clarity of racial membership, among other things, that jurists and policymakers had in mind."[18] This may have been true of British jurists and policymakers as well. But because non-British women acquired British citizenship upon marriage to British men, and because British men, unlike British women, could pass their citizenship onto their children, qualifying the citizenship rights accorded (white)

British women has never prevented native spouses and mixed-blood children from being admitted to the familial community of Britishness. Deriving citizenship from descent does not, then, guarantee the reproduction of Britishness as whiteness. Nobody knows this better than me, a person of mixed racial descent, who gained her British citizenship not from her mother, a Chinese woman born in British Hong Kong, but from her father, a white British man.

It would be possible to read Andy's survival, or the accessibility of British citizenship to mixed-race children, as errors that speak, alternately, to the difficulty of reproducing Britishness – how to craft nationality law in so airtight a way that whites alone will meet the criteria for admission? – and the ease with which the reproduction of Britishness – all reproduction – is liable to go awry. In the first instance, the disturbance is contained through being framed as, in Sara Ahmed's terms, an "end point," the "black sheep" "whose proximity threatens the family line" through appearing to embody "an alternative line of descent," yet is too much the exception to challenge the rule of (patri)lineality.[19] In the second instance, the error is reframed as a beginning, from which "a mixed and queer genealogy might … unfold."[20] If, as Ahmed writes, reproduction "depends on moments of deviation, where what deviates does not take us off line but creates instead 'small differences' that approximate the qualities that are assumed to pass along the line," the explosive difference of these bodies threatens – promises – to take the nation irrevocably "off line."[21] Not only do they give the lie to the guarantee of essentialism by being, as Françoise Vergès (quoting Édouard Glissant) puts it, "'proposition[s]' in which the glorification of a 'unique origin, race being its guardian,' is [rendered] inoperative"; they speak to the radical potential of reproduction itself to throw up new identities, alliances, and configurations of community.[22] But as much as they testify to the ease with which reproduction can (and hopefully will) swerve off line, Andy, like Anna Morgan, is the product of a particular history of intimacy and violence, which can be known. Rather than take Andy's monstrousness, or Anna's, as a manifestation of the inevitably mixed character of the British (or any other) body politic, it is critical that we recognize their hybridity as having a history. "Framed as newcomers, strangers and immigrants," Trimble writes, "youth are targeted by rites of incorporation and tactics of governance because they *arrive*. They bring with them biological, genetic, experiential, and familial histories that might reanimate within the body politic, rising up and recombining extant formations in unforeseen ways."[23] In other words, the difference they promise derives from the force with which they insist on the histories of their arrival, written, in Andy's case, on the surface of the body.

There are risks in turning to the body as an archive. To be sure, Foucault has taught us to view the body as a historical artefact. It is probably not controversial to say, with Elizabeth Grosz, that the body "is produced through and in history"; we know to attend to the ways in which the "relations of force, of power, produce the body through the use of distinct techniques (the feeding, training, supervision, and education of children in any given culture) and harness the energies and potential for supervision that power itself has constructed."[24] However, what does it mean to claim that history is "produced through and in" the body? In a striking passage in *Queer Phenomenology*, Sara Ahmed offers the following gloss on Marx's famous statement that "men make their own history, but … in a present given and inherited from the past": "If the conditions in which we live are inherited from the past, then they are 'passed down' not only in blood and genes, *but also through the work or labor of generations.* The 'passing' of history is a social as well as a material way of organizing the world that shapes the materials out of which life is made as well as the very 'matter' of bodies."[25] Writing about the inheritances we receive from our families, Ahmed draws attention to the labour that is involved in passing down even those inheritances we conceive as genetic (my father's colouring, my mother's nose). I want to highlight another implication of this passage, that not only physical characteristics but those "conditions in which we live" are passed down, shaping the "very 'matter' of bodies," implying that what we receive and inherit from the past can be gleaned from the way in which the body is "shaped." More simply: if, as Stacy Alaimo and Susan Hekman observe, "political decisions are scripted onto material bodies," can bodies be "read" for what they tell us about past political decisions?[26] Of course, what is legible as telling a story is itself part of the story. It is one thing to suggest that historical traumas, for example, may lodge themselves in the body, manifesting as nausea or paralysis, heightened blood pressure, a tremor. It may seem reasonable that we should see in a scar, lowered blood cell counts, or bleeding in the eye, the signs of a beating, radiation poisoning, or Rage.[27] But that the difference supposed to indicate a miscegenated ancestry is not always visible, or not to everyone, makes plain the extent to which our corporeal literacies are conditioned by those very histories of arrival which they purport to reveal. Some bodies – those identified as female, or black, or multiracial – present as more history-laden, more vulnerable to the "passing down" of history, than others (jiving with a familiar reading of the body as itself essentially "a medium, a carrier or bearer of information that comes from elsewhere").[28] Blackness was once taken as a marker of the "curse of Ham," after all. Not only, then, must we attend to the testimony of those bodies that appear unmarked, but our reading projects must themselves be historicized. In *Voyage in the Dark*, for example, it is not so much Anna Morgan's (possibly) miscegenated body as the interpretive interest it excites that attests to a history – it may be repressed – of cross-racial intimacy and sexual violence.

In the end, the bodies in *Voyage in the Dark* and *28 Weeks Later* activate, but also resignify, the kind of genealogical project Foucault describes in his 1977 essay "Nietzsche, Genealogy, History." Here, drawing on Nietzsche, Foucault opposes a critical genealogical project, anchored in a vision of the body as articulated with history, to a more conventional genealogical project that sees in genealogy a tool for the capture of purity and reproduction of sameness. "Guided by genealogy," he says, the purpose of history is "not to discover the roots of our identity, but to commit itself to its dissipation. It does not seek to define our unique threshold of emergence, the homeland to which metaphysicians promise a return; it seeks to make visible all those discontinuities that cross us."[29] Although Foucault clearly conceives of genealogy as more than a mode of familial investigation – elsewhere, he defines genealogy as a "coupling together of scholarly erudition and local memories, which allows us to constitute a historical knowledge of struggles and to make use of that knowledge in contemporary tactics" – the term nonetheless positions historical enquiry in uneasy proximity to the work of family history, and especially that brand of family history that specializes in tracing embodied descent lines, or *Herkunft*.[30] Certainly, in embracing genealogy as a figure for historical inquiry, Foucault redefines genealogy as well as history. As Alys Weinbaum notes, Foucault "adamantly insists that Nietzsche never uses the term [*Herkunft*] to indicate quantities that he believes to be organic, knowable, or 'pure'": according to Foucault, the genealogist isn't interested in resemblances, but pursues instead those "numberless beginnings, whose faint traces and hints of color are readily seen by a historical eye."[31] Foucault also emphasizes the body's total imprintation by history, coming near, perhaps, to Sara Ahmed's claim that the "very 'matter' of bodies" is shaped by the "passing down" of history.[32] Whether Foucaultian genealogy takes the form, primarily, of a history of bodies; whether it is aimed, primarily, at the dissipation of those narratives of purity that underwrite many communities of belonging, producing the nation as a clearly defined inside to a threatening outside, is, however, difficult to decide. Although "genealogy in its own right gives rise to questions concerning our native land, native language, or the laws that govern us," "its intention," Foucault insists, "is to reveal the heterogenous systems which, masked by the self, inhibit the formation of any form of identity."[33] Moving from "questions concerning our native land, native language, or the laws that govern us" to a concern with those "heterogenous systems which … inhibit the formation of any form of identity," "Nietzsche, Genealogy, History" invites critique along the lines Eric Santner pursues in appraising the work of Paul de Man. Struggling to read de Man's later deconstructionist writings in the light of the articles he wrote for collaborationist newspapers in occupied Europe during the Second World War, Santner suggests that de Man "sought to *displace* and *disperse* the particular, historical tasks of mourning which for him, as is now known, were substantial and complex, with what might be called structural mourning, that is, mourning for those 'catastrophes' that are inseparable from being-in-language."[34] As Santner goes on to ask, however, is attending to "the death that de Man has explicitly identified as a fundamentally 'linguistic predicament,' … an adequate mode of coming to terms with one's complicity, however indirect or ambivalent, in a movement responsible for the extermination of millions"?[35] Without suggesting that Foucault is engaged in a comparable exercise of displacement and dispersal, I want to take Santner's query as an invitation to reground genealogy in the history of bodies, as illuminating not just the impossibility of identity, the extent to which, as Stuart Hall puts it, "all identity is constructed across difference," but the particular histories of differentiation (and assimilation) which the official story of identity strives to overwrite.[36]

The work I have set out to accomplish in *Better Britons* is critically genealogical in Foucault's sense, disrupting the smooth narratives of settlement, repatriation, and homemaking that undergird post-imperial conceptions of British and settler identity. In doing so, however, it makes visible other (af)filiations, other genealogies, that indeed promise, for Indigenous people, say, a return to the homeland. Exposing the "discontinuities that cross us," when this "us" designates the beneficiaries of settler colonialism, for example, can have material consequences, I want to insist. If doing genealogical work "release[s]" settler subjects by "presenting [us] with other origins than those in which [we] prefer to see [ourselves]," we are not thereby released from having to account or offer redress for the effects of the latter, which persist in the present.[37] On the contrary: what these "other origins" disrupt, surely, is precisely that amnesia that our preferred origin stories, in circulating the fiction of our ab-originality, have made mandatory. This, ultimately, will be the real departure: an anamnesis that may come too late (as Miria George warns), but without which no future will arrive at all.

Notes

Introduction

1 Throughout *Better Britons*, I follow the Māori convention of using macrons to indicate long vowels in words like "Māori" and "Pākehā" (except where my sources do not). For similar reasons, I make use of the Hawaiian glottal stop the ʻokina (the word for which itself requires the use of a ʻokina, and which resembles a single opening quote mark), where appropriate. I have also chosen not to italicize Māori and other non-English words, including the many Latin and French phrases that have entered into (especially scholarly) English. There are, as Māori literary critic Alice Te Punga Somerville notes, "various schools of thought around whether Māori [and other indigenous languages] should be italicized in this kind of English text" (*Once Were Pacific: Māori Connections to Oceania* [Minneapolis: Minnesota UP, 2012], 217). On the one hand, "italicizing Māori prevents it from being incorporated into the English language as a set of loanwords rather than retaining its integrity as a quotation from a distinct language" (217). On the other hand, "leaving the Māori language in roman type" reframes Māori as "not a foreign (or to use the term of the *Chicago Manual of Style*, 'unfamiliar') language" (217–18). Te Punga Somerville's project of situating Māori and English "side by side as center languages" is appropriate for a book written from within the particular context of Aotearoa New Zealand, as *Better Britons* is not (218). And yet, as I mulled over whether and what to italicize, I found myself hesitating: although it seemed absurd to italicize all "foreign" words, including commonplaces like "vice versa," italicizing some "foreign" words but not others ("Māoritanga," for example, or "coup de grâce," but not "status quo") as more and less foreign came to seem objectionable. Where does one draw the line, and what does it signify?

2 Miria George, *and what remains* (Wellington: Tawata, 2007), 43. Hereafter references in the text.

3 John Smythe, “Inconceivable,” review of *and what remains*, by Miria George, directed by Hone Kouka, City Gallery, Wellington, in *Theatreview: The New Zealand Performing Arts Review and Directory*, 26 August 2006, http://theatreview.org.nz/.

4 Laurie Atkinson, “Implausible Leap of Faith Required,” review of *and what remains*, by Miria George, directed by Hone Kouka, City Gallery, Wellington, in *Dominion Post*, 30 August 2006.

5 Qtd. in Helen Smyth, *Rocking the Cradle: Contraception, Sex and Politics in New Zealand* (Wellington: Steele Roberts, 2000), 19.

6 Throughout *Better Britons*, I capitalize the term “Indigenous” when referring to a specific people (or set of peoples) and their land, culture, and intellectual and citizenship projects. I do not capitalize terms like “indigenous” and “indigeneity” when describing the kinds of relationships which settlers (for example) seek to establish with particular places, where, that is, discourses of indigeneity are being mobilized as a way of at once appropriating and effacing the sovereignty claims of Indigenous peoples.

7 See Angus McLaren, *Our Own Master Race: Eugenics in Canada, 1885–1945* (Toronto: McClelland & Stewart, 1990) for a fuller discussion of Canadian eugenicist discourse and policy.

8 Homi Bhabha, *The Location of Culture* (Abingdon: Routledge, 2004), 13.

9 Ernest Renan, “What Is a Nation,” trans. Martin Thom, in *Nation and Narration*, ed. Homi Bhabha (London: Routledge, 1990), 11.

10 Ibid., 11.

11 Thus, for example, doubling down on statements made in 2009, Pākehā columnist, broadcaster, and former Wanganui mayor Michael Laws contributed an opinion piece to the 3 June 2012 edition of the *Sunday Star-Times*, in which he urged that all Māori women be sterilized (“Pay them, sterilise them, but don’t let them have kids” reads the title of the article). In April 2013, Palmerston North city councillor Bruce Wilson suggested that if Māori women could not be trusted to give up smoking in front of their children, they should be sterilized.

12 Eric Hobsbawm, *The Age of Extremes: The Short Twentieth Century, 1914–1991* (London: Michael Joseph, 1994), 211.

13 Report of the Inter-Imperial Relations Committee of the Imperial Conference 1926, National Archives of Australia (NAA), A4640/32.

14 Scholars who have contributed to the “imperial turn” in British historical and literary studies include Simon Gikandi (*Maps of Englishness: Writing Identity in the Culture of Colonialism* [New York: Columbia UP, 1996]); Kathleen Paul (*Whitewashing Britain: Race and Citizenship in the Postwar Era* [Ithaca: Cornell UP, 1997]); Ian Baucom (*Out of Place: Englishness, Empire, and the Locations of Identity* [Princeton: Princeton UP, 1999]); Catherine Hall (*Civilising Subjects: Metropole and Colony in the English Imagination 1830–1867* [Chicago: U of

Chicago P, 2002]); Jane Garrity (*Step-Daughters of England: British Women Modernists and the National Imaginary* [Manchester: Manchester UP, 2003]); Jed Esty (*A Shrinking Island: Modernism and National Culture in England* [Princeton, NJ: Princeton UP, 2004]); James Buzard (*Disorienting Fiction: The Autoethnographic Work of Nineteenth-Century British Novels* [Princeton: Princeton UP, 2005]); and, in a contrarian mode, Bernard Porter (*The Absent-Minded Imperialists: Empire, Society, and Culture in Britain* [Oxford: Oxford UP, 2004]). Important recent work on settler colonialism includes Gillian Whitlock, *The Intimate Empire: Reading Women's Autobiography* (London: Cassell, 2000); Jennifer Henderson, *Settler Feminism and Race Making in Canada* (Toronto: U of Toronto P, 2003); Patrick Wolfe, *Settler Colonialism and the Transformation of Anthropology: The Politics and Poetics of an Ethnographic Event* (London: Cassell, 1999) and "*Corpus nullius*: The Exception of Indians and Other Aliens in US Constitutional Discourse," *Postcolonial Studies* 10, no. 2 (2007): 127–51; Daniel Coleman, *White Civility: The Literary Project of English Canada* (Toronto: U of Toronto P, 2008); Jodi A. Byrd, *The Transit of Empire: Indigenous Critiques of Colonialism* (Minneapolis: U of Minnesota P, 2011); Scott Lauria Morgensen, *Spaces between Us: Queer Settler Colonialism and Indigenous Decolonization* (Minneapolis: U of Minnesota P, 2011) and "The Biopolitics of Settler Colonialism: Right Here, Right Now," *Settler Colonial Studies* 1 (2011): 52–76; and Mark Rifkin, *When Did Indians Become Straight? Kinship, the History of Sexuality, and Native Sovereignty* (Oxford: Oxford UP, 2011). A journal devoted to the study of settler colonialism, *Settler Colonial Studies*, has also recently been established (2011). My debts to feminist, queer, and Indigenous studies are detailed elsewhere in this introduction.

15 Although the convergence of projects of sexual discipline, colonial governance, and post-imperial nation-formation has not received the attention it deserves from scholars who place empire and decolonization at the heart of twentieth-century conceptions of British and settler identity, this is not to neglect the work of scholars of eighteenth-and nineteenth-century imperialism, including Margaret D. Jacobs ("The Eastmans and the Luhans: Intermarriage between White Women and Native American Men, 1875–1935," *Frontiers* 23, no. 2 [2002] and *White Mother to a Dark Race: Settler Colonialism, Maternalism, and the Removal of Indigenous Children in the American West and Australia, 1880–1940* [Lincoln: U of Nebraska P, 2009]), Radhika Mohanram (*Black Body: Women, Colonialism, and Space* [Minneapolis: U of Minnesota P, 1999] and *Imperial White: Race, Diaspora, and the British Empire* [Minneapolis: U of Minnesota P, 2007]), and Ann Stoler (*Race and the Education of Desire: Foucault's* History of Sexuality *and the Colonial Order of Things* [Durham: Duke UP, 1995] and *Carnal Knowledge and Imperial Power: Race and the Intimate in Colonial Rule* [Berkeley: U of California P, 2002]), to whose discussions of colonial formations of gender, sexuality, and intimacy *Better Britons* is deeply indebted.

16 Ella Shohat, "Notes on the 'Post-Colonial,'" *Social Text* 31/32 (1992): 102. See also Anne McClintock, "The Angel of Progress: Pitfalls of the Term 'Post-Colonialism,'" *Social Text* 31/32 (1992): 88.

17 The phrase "the colonial present" is Derek Gregory's, from his genealogical account of the War on Terror, *The Colonial Present* (Malden: Blackwell, 2004).

18 Robert J.C. Young, *Postcolonialism: An Historical Introduction* (Oxford: Blackwell, 2001), 60.

19 Paul Gilroy, *Postcolonial Melancholia* (New York: Columbia UP, 2005), 90.

20 Ibid., 100. In a talk at Goldsmiths College on 11 May 2012, Ahmed described a genre of argumentation she calls "overing," which, through dismissing some forms of critique as "over," "creates the impression that we are over what is being critiqued" ("Introduction to Feminist Genealogies").

21 Stuart Hall, "The Problem of Ideology: Marxism without Guarantees," *Journal of Communication Inquiry* 10, no. 2 (June 1986): 41; italics in original.

22 Coleman, *White Civility*, 7–8. Here, Coleman quotes from the work of the Caribbean Canadian poet and essayist M. NourbeSe Philip, who argues that "multiculturalism, as we know it, has no answers for the problems of racism, or white supremacy – unless it is combined with a clearly articulated policy of anti-racism, directed at rooting out the effects of racist and white supremacist thinking ... And we cannot begin such an eradication by forgetting how [this] brutal aspect of Canadian culture was formed. It is for this reason that an understanding of the ideological lineage of this belief system is so important to any debate on racism and multiculturalism" (qtd. ibid. 7).

23 Gilroy, *Postcolonial Melancholia*, 14.

24 Jacques Derrida, *Specters of Marx: The State of the Debt, the Work of Mourning, and the New International*, trans. Peggy Kamuf (New York: Routledge, 2006), 120.

25 Avery Gordon, *Ghostly Matters: Haunting and the Sociological Imagination* (Minneapolis: U of Minnesota P, 2008), 19.

26 Leela Gandhi, *Postcolonial Theory: A Critical Introduction* (New York: Columbia UP, 1998), 4.

27 Stuart Hall and Bill Schwarz, "State and Society, 1880–1930," in *The Hard Road to Renewal: Thatcherism and the Crisis of the Left* (London: Verso, 1988), 95.

28 Ibid., 96.

29 See, for example, Simon Szreter, *Fertility, Class and Gender in Britain, 1860–1940* (Cambridge: Cambridge UP, 1996).

30 Alys Eve Weinbaum, *Wayward Reproductions: Genealogies of Race and Nation in Transatlantic Modern Thought* (Durham: Duke UP, 2004), 3. Patricia E. Chu, *Race, Nationalism and the State in British and American Modernism* (Cambridge: Cambridge UP, 2006).

31 See, among others, Michael Warner, ed., *Fear of a Queer Planet: Queer Politics and Social Theory* (Minneapolis: U of Minnesota P, 1993); Lauren Berlant, *The Queen of America Goes to Washington City* (Durham: Duke UP, 1997); Donna Haraway, *Modest_Witness@Second_Millennium.FemaleMan©_Meets_OncoMouse™: Feminism and Technoscience* (New York: Routledge, 1997); Judith Butler, *Antigone's Claim: Kinship between Life and Death* (New York: Columbia UP, 2000); Lee Edelman, *No Future: Queer Theory and the Death Drive* (Durham: Duke UP, 2004); and Jasbir Puar, *Terrorist Assemblages: Homonationalism in Queer Times* (Durham: Duke UP, 2007).

32 Alexandra Halkias, *The Empty Cradle of Democracy: Sex, Abortion, and Nationalism in Modern Greece* (Durham: Duke UP, 2004), 3.

33 Jacqueline Stevens, *Reproducing the State* (Princeton: Princeton UP, 1999), 10.

34 Defense of Marriage Act of 1996, Pub. L. 104–199 (1996); Stevens, *Reproducing the State*, 136.

35 Chu, *Race, Nationalism and the State*, 35.

36 M. Jacqui Alexander, "Not Just Any (Body) Can Be a Citizen: The Politics of Law, Sexuality and Postcoloniality in Trinidad and Tobago and the Bahamas," *Feminist Review* 48 (Autumn 1994): 5.

37 See Velma Demerson's *Incorrigible* (Waterloo: Wilfrid Laurier UP, 2004) for more about Demerson's life and experience as an "incorrigible."

38 In 1967, while defending his proposal to decriminalize "homosexual acts" performed in private between consenting adults, then minister of justice Pierre Trudeau famously told Canadian reporters, "There's no place for the state in the bedrooms of the nation." Although the phrase is often assumed to have originated with Trudeau, it was in fact coined by journalist Martin O'Malley.

39 Qtd. in Stevens, *Reproducing the State*, 63.

40 Edelman, *No Future*, 3.

41 Qtd. in Stevens, *Reproducing the State*, 14.

42 Michel Foucault, *The History of Sexuality: Volume I: An Introduction*, trans. Robert Hurley (New York: Vintage, 1978), 25.

43 Ibid., 25–6.

44 Ibid., 124.

45 Monographs that develop Foucault's insights in contexts beyond eighteenth- and nineteenth-century France include Lisa Forman Cody, *Birthing the Nation: Sex, Science, and the Conception of Eighteenth-Century Britons* (Oxford: Oxford UP, 2006); Doris Sommer, *Foundational Fictions: The National Romances of Latin America* (Berkeley: U of California P, 1991); Lauren Berlant, *The Queen of America Goes to Washington City*; Ann Laura Stoler, *Race and the Education of Desire* as well as *Carnal Knowledge and Imperial Power*; and Alexandra Halkias, *The Empty*

Cradle of Democracy. Recent histories of eugenics in Britain and elsewhere include Daniel Kevles, *In the Name of Eugenics: Genetics and the Uses of Human Heredity* (New York: Knopf, 1985); Richard Soloway, *Birth Control and the Population Question in England, 1877–1930* (Chapel Hill: U of North Carolina P, 1982) and *Demography and Degeneration: Eugenics and the Declining Birth Rate in Twentieth-Century Britain* (Chapel Hill: U of North Carolina P, 1990); Angus McLaren, *Our Own Master Race*; Nancy Stepan, *"The Hour of Eugenics": Race, Gender, and Nation in Latin America* (Ithaca: Cornell UP, 1991); Pauline Mazumdar, *Eugenics, Human Genetics and Human Failings: The Eugenics Society, Its Sources and Its Critics in Britain* (London: Routledge, 1992); Wendy Kline, *Building a Better Race: Gender, Sexuality, and Eugenics from the Turn of the Century to the Baby Boom* (Berkeley: U of California P, 2001); Dan Stone, *Breeding Superman: Nietzsche, Race and Eugenics in Edwardian and Interwar Britain* (Liverpool: Liverpool UP, 2002); Christina Cogdell, *Eugenic Design: Streamlining America in the 1930s* (Philadelphia: U of Pennsylvania P, 2004); Chloe Campbell, *Race and Empire: Eugenics in Colonial Kenya* (Manchester: Manchester UP, 2007); as well as *The Oxford Handbook of the History of Eugenics*, ed. Alison Bashford and Philippa Levine (Oxford: Oxford UP, 2010). Studies by literary critics include William Greenslade, *Degeneration, Culture and the Novel: 1880–1940* (Cambridge: Cambridge UP, 1994); Donald Childs, *Modernism and Eugenics: Woolf, Eliot, Yeats, and the Culture of Degeneration* (Cambridge: Cambridge UP, 2001); Daylanne English, *Unnatural Selections: Eugenics in American Modernism and the Harlem Renaissance* (Chapel Hill: U of North Carolina P, 2002); and Daniel Shea, "Going into Labor: Production and Reproduction in Fin de Siècle British Literature," PhD diss. (University of Oregon, 2006).

46 Karl Pearson, *Darwinism, Medical Progress and Eugenics: The Cavendish Lecture, 1912, an Address to the Medical Profession* (London: Dulau, 1912), 17, 26.

47 Ibid., 27.

48 Francis Galton, *Inquiry into the Human Faculty* (London: Macmillan, 1883), 25.

49 See Jane E. Lewis, *The Politics of Motherhood: Child and Maternal Welfare in England, 1900–1939* (London: Croom Helm, 1980) for more on maternalism. The New Zealander Frederick Truby King's influential manual *Feeding and Care of Baby* (London: Macmillan, 1913) is typical of the period's childcare literature. According to historian Keith Sinclair, King's Plunket system "stressed the importance of fresh air, good food and long walks for the expectant mother. If possible the birth should be without instrumental assistance. The baby was to be breast-fed, every four hours by day and ignored at night. It should not be fed merely because it cried. Toilet training must commence within the first six weeks. Babies should not be rocked, tickled or otherwise 'spoiled.' Everything was supposed to be organised by the clock. The emphasis was upon health, self-control, discipline. Great stress was laid upon cleanliness and hygiene. An army of Plunket nurses called at the parents' homes,

measuring and weighing the babies and recording their progress" (*A Destiny Apart: New Zealand's Search for National Identity* [Wellington: Allen & Unwin, 1986], 222). No longer committed to King's program of childrearing, the Plunket Society remains an important provider of bicultural child and family health services in New Zealand.

50 Greenslade, *Degeneration, Culture and the Novel*, 15.

51 *Degeneration: The Dark Side of Progress* (New York: Columbia UP, 1985), ed. Sander Gilman and Edward Chamberlin, remains a useful introduction to degeneration discourse. Other critical studies include Elaine Showalter, *Sexual Anarchy: Gender and Culture at the Fin de Siècle* (New York: Viking, 1990) and Greenslade, *Degeneration, Culture and the Novel*.

52 Francis Galton, *Hereditary Genius: An Inquiry into Its Law and Consequences* (1869; repr. Cleveland: World, 1962), 36. Hereafter references in the text.

53 Karl Pearson, *The Groundwork of Eugenics* (London: Dulau, 1912), 38. Hereafter references in the text.

54 Early Plunket Society slogan qtd. in Erik Olssen, "Truby King and the Plunket Society: An Analysis of a Prescriptive Ideology," *New Zealand Journal of History* 15, no. 1 (1981): 12.

55 "New Zealand's Unborn Citizens," *The Dominion*, 23 April 1937.

56 Stephen Garton, "Eugenics in Australia and New Zealand: Laboratories of Racial Science," in *The Oxford Handbook of the History of Eugenics*, 249.

57 See, among others, Laura Tabili, *"We Ask for British Justice": Workers and Racial Difference in Late Imperial Britain* (Ithaca: Cornell UP, 1994) and *Global Migrants, Local Culture: Natives and Newcomers in Provincial England, 1841–1939* (Houndmills: Palgrave Macmillan, 2011).

58 Galton, *Hereditary Genius*, 33. The Alien Acts passed between 1905 and 1920 targeted both communities.

59 M.E. Fletcher, *Report on the Investigation into the Colour Problem in Liverpool and Other Ports* (Liverpool: Liverpool Association for the Welfare of Half-Caste Children, 1930).

60 See Chloe Campbell, *Race and Empire*, especially the chapter "Metropolitan Responses," for more on metropolitan engagements with Kenyan eugenics.

61 Stoler, *Race and the Education of Desire*, 127.

62 See Sander Gilman, "The Hottentot and the Prostitute: Toward an Iconography of Female Sexuality," in *Difference and Pathology: Stereotypes of Sexuality, Race, and Madness* (Ithaca: Cornell UP, 1985).

63 This is Radhika Mohanram's argument in the second and third chapters of *Imperial White*.

64 Mohanram, *Imperial White*, 81.

65 See Nancy Leys Stepan, "Biological Degeneration: Races and Proper Places," in *Degeneration: The Dark Side of Progress*, 97–120; Warwick Anderson, "Geography, Race and Nation: Remapping 'Tropical' Australia, 1890–1930," *Historical Records*

of Australian Science 11, no. 4 (1997): 457–68; and Alison Bashford, "'Is White Australia Possible?' Race, Colonialism and Tropical Medicine," *Ethnic and Racial Studies* 23, no. 2 (2000): 248–71 for more on turn-of-the-century concerns about the debilitating effects of travel and migration upon, especially, northern Europeans.

66 Lewis, *The Politics of Motherhood*, 15.

67 Qtd. in Barbara Brookes, *Abortion in England 1900–1967* (London: Croom Helm, 1988), 30.

68 Lynette Finch, *The Classing Gaze: Sexuality, Class and Surveillance* (St Leonards: Allen & Unwin, 1993), 108.

69 Nancy Stepan makes this point in her history of Latin American eugenics, "*The Hour of Eugenics*."

70 Randall Hansen and Desmond King, "Eugenic Ideas, Political Interests, and Policy Variation: Immigration and Sterilization Policy in Britain and the U. S.," *World Politics* 53, no. 2 (2001): 251. According to Daniel Kevles, divisions within the eugenicist community in Britain also hampered efforts to get eugenics on the government's agenda.

71 Marilyn Lake, "White Man's Country: The Trans-National History of a Nation Project," *Australian Historical Studies* 34, no. 122 (2003): 349–50; italics in original.

72 James Belich, *Replenishing the Earth: The Settler Revolution and the Rise of the Anglo-World, 1783–1939* (Oxford: Oxford UP, 2009), 461. In *Whitewashing Britain*, Kathleen Paul notes that 80% of the emigrants who left Britain between 1946 and 1960 settled in the white dominions, namely, Australia, Canada, New Zealand, South Africa, and Rhodesia (25). Their passage was in many cases government-sponsored.

73 The term "repatriation" connotes a restoration: one is repatriated – returned – to one's homeland. In Canadian political discourse, however, "repatriation" is used to describe the final stage in Canada's accession to independent post-settler nationhood: the transfer of constitutional authority from Westminster to Ottawa in 1982. Of course, it doesn't make sense to speak of *re*patriating the constitution when there never was a Canadian constitution to start with. At the same time, the nonsense of repatriation exposes the constructed character of national space, suggesting how national identity may be produced as originary, aboriginal, through being "returned." It is with this (non)sense in mind that I mobilize the concept of repatriation throughout *Better Britons*.

74 James Belich, *Paradise Reforged: A History of the New Zealanders from the 1880s to the Year 2000* (Honolulu: U of Hawai'i P, 2001).

75 Stuart Murray, *Never a Soul at Home: New Zealand Literary Nationalism and the 1930s* (Wellington: Victoria UP, 1998), 15.

76 Michelle Elleray, "Unsettled Subject: The South Pacific and the Settler," PhD diss. (Cornell U, 2001), 113.

77 Elleray, "Unsettled Subject," 113.
78 Qtd. in Murray, *Never a Soul at Home*, 23.
79 Terry Goldie, *Fear and Temptation: The Image of the Indigene in Canadian, Australian, and New Zealand Literatures* (Kingston: McGill-Queen's UP, 1989), 12.
80 Goldie, *Fear and Temptation*, 13.
81 Elizabeth Povinelli, "The Governance of the Prior," *Interventions* 13, no. 1 (2011): 13–30.
82 Avtar Brah, *Cartographies of Diaspora: Contesting Identities* (Routledge, 1996), 188.
83 Robert J. C. Young, *The Idea of English Ethnicity* (Malden: Blackwell, 2008), 1–2.
84 Baucom, *Out of Place*, 3.
85 Because I do not see the question of how Britishness relates to Englishness as settled even today – the descriptor "British" is not consistently employed to refer *uniquely* to the empire (as opposed to the nation) or the United Kingdom (as opposed to that portion of the United Kingdom that is not either Scotland, Wales, or Northern Ireland) – I do not thus distinguish between them in *Better Britons*, except where my sources lead me to do so. In general, it is the flexibility of Britishness, the contingency of its referentiality, that interests me here.
86 Hobson, *Imperialism: A Study* (New York: Cosimi, 2006), 328. Hereafter references in the text.
87 Radhika Viyas Mongia, "Race, Nationality, Mobility: A History of the Passport," in *After the Imperial Turn: Thinking with and through the Nation*, ed. Antoinette Burton (Durham: Duke UP, 2003), 208. Throughout the first half of the twentieth century, as Laura Tabili documents in "*We Ask for British Justice*," the British Home Office too worked to prevent British overseas subjects of colour from settling in Britain, but stopped short of prohibiting their entry outright.
88 Baucom, *Out of Place*, 10; emphasis in original. The last fifty years have also seen the question of what purpose Britishness serves as against the particularisms of Englishness, Scottishness, Welshness, and Irishness posed with, in some cases, violent force.
89 See Sara Ahmed, *Queer Phenomenology: Orientations, Objects, Others* (Durham: Duke UP, 2006), esp. chapter 2, for more about "straightening devices" (92).
90 Cathy J. Cohen, "Punks, Bulldaggers, and Welfare Queens: The Radical Potential of Queer Politics?" *GLQ* 3, no. 4 (1997): 442. Mark Rifkin builds on Cohen's argument in *When Did Indians Become Straight?*
91 See, for example, the work of Scott Morgensen and Mark Rifkin, as well as the essays in *Sexuality, Nationality, Indigeneity*, ed. Daniel Heath Justice, Mark Rifkin, and Bethany Schneider, *GLQ* 16, nos. 1–2 (2010): 1–339; and *Queer Indigenous Studies: Critical Interventions in Theory, Politics, and Literature*, ed. Qwo-Li Driskill, Chris Finley, Brian Joseph Gilley, et al. (Tucson: U of Arizona P, 2011). In general, (settler) feminist and queer theoretical takes on the politics of reproduction have tended to occlude the extent to which reproductive futurism

buttresses, and is buttressed by, colonial projects both current and past. Even Jasbir Puar's *Terrorist Assemblages*, a book that traces the incorporation of queer subjects and political agendas into the imperial project of the American "war on terror," overlooks queer complicity with the ongoing project of settler colonialism. Puar's omissions may (inadvertently) confirm her point about the compromised nature of queer citizenship, but this does not really mitigate the failure to acknowledge that, as Scott Morgensen reminds us, American "homonationalism" is always already "settler homonationalism" ("Settler Homonationalism: Theorizing Settler Colonialism within Queer Modernities," *GLQ* 16, nos. 1–2 [2010]: 107).

92 Rifkin, *When Did Indians Become Straight?* 8.

93 J. Kēhaulani Kauanui, *Hawaiian Blood: Colonialism and the Politics of Sovereignty and Indigeneity* (Durham: Duke UP, 2008), 10. Ghassan Hage makes a similar intervention, emphasizing the spatial projects of racist acts, which he suggests are better conceived as "nationalist practices … even if racist modes of thinking are deployed within them" (*White Nation: Fantasies of White Supremacy in a Multicultural Nation* [New York: Routledge, 2000], 32).

94 This doesn't mean, as Ila points out, that the state will not thus target "brown girls" in the future, just that they're not currently a priority (George 36).

95 Patrick Wolfe, "Structure and Event: Settler Colonialism, Time, and the Question of Genocide," in *Empire, Colony, Genocide: Conquest, Occupation, and Subaltern Resistance in World History*, ed. A. Dirk Moses (New York: Bergahn, 2008), 112.

96 Povinelli, "The Governance of the Prior," 20; italics in original.

97 Wolfe, *Settler Colonialism and the Transformation of Anthropology*, 188.

98 Gilroy, *Postcolonial Melancholia*, 100–1.

99 Weinbaum, *Wayward Reproductions*, 5.

100 Examples of work in this vein are too numerous to particularize, but two co-authored essays by Mao and Walkowitz, the introduction to their collection *Bad Modernisms* (Durham: Duke UP, 2006), and "The New Modernist Studies," *PMLA* 123, no. 3 (2008), offer instructive surveys of recent developments in the field.

101 Douglas Mao and Rebecca Walkowitz, "The New Modernist Studies," 738.

102 Susan Stanford Friedman, "Planetarity: Musing Modernist Studies," *Modernism/Modernity* 17, no. 3 (2010): 474.

103 Chu, *Race, Nationalism and the State*, 16–17.

104 Kristin Bluemel, *George Orwell and the Radical Eccentrics: Intermodernism in Literary London* (New York: Palgrave Macmillan, 2004), 6.

105 See David Eng, Judith Halberstam, and José Esteban Muñoz, "Introduction: What's Queer about Queer Studies Now," *Social Text* 84/85, no. 3–4 (Winter 2005), for more about "subjectless critique," which has also recently been taken up as a useful model by Indigenous studies scholars (see, for example, the introduction to *Queer Indigenous Studies* and Andrea Smith, "Queer Theory and Native Studies: The Heteronormativity of Settler Colonialism," *GLQ* 16, nos. 1–2 [2010]: 44).

106 Stephen Ross, "Uncanny Modernism, or Analysis Interminable," in *Disciplining Modernism*, ed. Pamela L. Caughie (Houndmills: Palgrave Macmillan, 2009), 42–3; italics in original.

107 Ahmed, *Queer Phenomenology*, 56.

108 Alison Light's *Forever England* undertakes the kind of reorientation I have in mind, but has largely been neglected by scholars of British modernism, which suggests that it is not just analytical objects which our disciplinary orientations render more and less reachable, but scholarly interlocutors as well.

109 Ahmed, *Queer Phenomenology*, 122.

110 James C. Scott, *Seeing Like a State: How Certain Schemes to Improve the Human Condition Have Failed* (New Haven: Yale UP, 1998), 88.

111 James Holston, *The Modernist City: An Anthropological Critique of Brasília* (Chicago: U of Chicago P, 1989), 56.

112 The term "clean-sweep planning" is Alison Ravetz's, first discussed in her monograph *Remaking Cities: Contradictions of the Recent Urban Environment* (London: Croom Helm, 1980).

113 Scott, *Seeing Like a State*, 94.

114 Adam Parkes, *Modernism and the Theatre of Censorship* (Oxford: Oxford University P, 1996).

115 Childs, *Modernism and Eugenics*, 14; Christina Hauck, "Abortion and the Individual Talent," *ELH* 70, no. 1 (2003): 223–66. For further examples of work on sex and marriage in early-twentieth-century British cultural production, see Davida Pines, *The Marriage Paradox: Modernist Novels and the Cultural Imperative to Marry* (Gainesville: UP of Florida, 2006); and Barry McCrea, *In the Company of Strangers: Family and Narrative in Dickens, Conan Doyle, Joyce, and Proust* (New York: Columbia UP, 2011).

116 Kim Scott, *Benang: From the Heart* (Fremantle: Fremantle Arts Centre P, 1999), 10, 19. Hereafter references in the text.

117 Alice Te Punga Somerville, response to John Smythe's "Inconceivable," *Theatreview: The New Zealand Performing Arts Review and Directory*, 29 August 2007, http://theatreview.org.nz/.

118 Nicholas Thomas, *Colonialism's Culture: Anthropology, Travel, and Government* (Princeton: Princeton UP, 1994), 106.

119 Henderson, *Settler Feminism and Race Making in Canada*, 5.

120 Dominick LaCapra, *History, Politics, and the Novel* (Ithaca: Cornell UP, 1987), 4.

121 Friedrich Schlegel qtd. in Chris Bongie, *Exotic Memories: Literature, Colonialism, and the Fin de Siècle* (Stanford: Stanford UP, 1991), 14.

122 Marilyn Strathern, *Reproducing the Future: Essays on Anthropology, Kinship, and the New Reproductive Technologies* (New York: Routledge, 1992), 164.

123 James Kincaid, *Child-Loving: The Erotic Child and Victorian Culture* (New York: Routledge, 1992), 4.

124 Edelman, *No Future*, 11.

125 Marilyn Strathern makes a similar argument in *Reproducing the Future*.

126 Pember Reeves, *State Experiments in Australia and New Zealand*, vol. 1 (New York: Dutton, 1903), 68. For more on New Zealand's utopian tradition, see Lucy Sargisson and Lyman Tower Sargent, *Living in Utopia: New Zealand's Intentional Communities* (Aldershot: Ashgate, 2004) and Jonathan Lamb, "The Idea of Utopia in New Zealand," in *Quicksands: Foundational Histories in Australia and Aotearoa New Zealand*, ed. Klaus Neumann, Nicholas Thomas, and Hilary Ericksen (Sydney: U of New South Wales P, 1999), 78–97. The subtitle Stephen Garton gives his essay on Australian and New Zealand eugenicist thought, "Laboratories of Racial Science," is only one among many similar instances.

127 Eleanor Dark, "Prelude to Christopher, ca. 1934," Eleanor Dark Papers, State Library of New South Wales, MLMSS 4545/2.

128 Dane Kennedy, *Islands of White: Settler Society and Culture in Kenya and Southern Rhodesia, 1890–1939* (Durham: Duke UP, 1987), 2.

129 Lake, "White Man's Country," 350.

130 Jane Carey, "'Women's Objective – A Perfect Race': Whiteness, Eugenics, and the Articulation of Race," in *Re-Orienting Whiteness*, ed. Leigh Boucher, Jane Carey, and Katherine Ellinghaus (New York: Palgrave Macmillan, 2009), 183–98.

131 Cecil Cook, memorandum, 27 June 1933, NAA, A659 1940/1/408.

132 Gayatri Chakravorty Spivak, *A Critique of Postcolonial Reason: Toward a History of the Vanishing Present* (Cambridge: Harvard UP, 1999), 228.

133 Jean Rhys, *Voyage in the Dark* (1934; repr. New York: Norton, 1982), 188. Hereafter references in the text.

134 Interdepartmental Committee on Abortion, 1937, National Archives (UK; hereafter NAUK), MH 71/23.

135 T.S. Eliot, "East Coker," line 209, in *Four Quartets* (1944; repr. London: Faber & Faber, 1983), 27.

136 Gikandi, *Maps of Englishness*, ix.

137 Gilroy, *Postcolonial Melancholia*, 12.

138 Alison Bashford, "Epilogue: Where Did Eugenics Go?" in *The Oxford Handbook of the History of Eugenics*, 539.

139 Britain's pastoral past also figured prominently in the opening ceremony Boyle developed for the 2012 London Olympics, something I discuss in greater detail in chapter 5.

140 This astonishing claim appears in both official and unofficial BNP statements, including the BNP's 2010 General Election manifesto. See also Paul Oakley, "All Indigenous People Have Right to Avoid Colonisation, Wolverhampton BNP Told," *British National Party*, 7 October 2009, http://www.bnp.org.uk/.

141 Haraway, *Modest_Witness*, 265.
142 Kauanui, *Hawaiian Blood*, 3.
143 Andrea Smith, "Queer Theory and Native Studies," 47. See also Jennifer Denetdale, "Carving Navajo National Boundaries: Patriotism, Tradition, and the Dine Marriage Act of 2005," *American Quarterly* 60 (2008): 289–94, and Mark Rifkin, *When Did Indians Become Straight?*
144 Elizabeth Povinelli, *The Empire of Love: Toward a Theory of Intimacy, Genealogy, and Carnality* (Durham: Duke UP, 2006), 200.
145 Ahmed, *Queer Phenomenology*, 125.
146 Morgensen, *Spaces between Us*, 26.
147 Rifkin, *When Did Indians Become Straight?* 31; italics in original.

Chapter 1: An Island Solution

1 Government Policy with regard to Aboriginals in the Northern Territory, NAA, A1/15 1937/70.
2 Ibid.
3 Ibid.
4 Valerie Hartouni, "*Brave New World* in the Discourses of Reproductive and Genetic Technologies," in *In the Nature of Things: Language, Politics, and the Environment*, ed. Jane Bennett and William Chaloupka (Minneapolis: U of Minnesota P, 1993), 86.
5 Karl Pearson, *The Academic Aspect of the Science of National Eugenics* (London: Dulau, 1911), 3.
6 Karl Pearson, *The Problem of Practical Eugenics* (London: Dulau, 1912), 31.
7 Rod Edmond and Vanessa Smith, "Editors' Introduction," in *Islands in History and Representation*, ed. Rod Edmond and Vanessa Smith (London: Routledge, 2003), 1.
8 Paul Gilroy, *The Black Atlantic: Modernity and Double Consciousness* (Cambridge, MA: Harvard UP, 1993), 14.
9 Fátima Vieira, "The Concept of Utopia," in *The Cambridge Companion to Utopian Literature*, ed. Gregory Claeys (Cambridge: Cambridge UP, 2010), 5.
10 See, for example, Jill Dolan, *Utopia in Performance: Finding Hope at the Theater* (Ann Arbor: U of Michigan P, 2005), and José Esteban Muñoz, *Cruising Utopia: The Then and There of Queer Futurity* (New York: New York UP, 2009).
11 Ruth Levitas, "The Imaginary Reconstruction of Society: Utopia as Method," in *Utopia Method Vision: The Use Value of Social Dreaming*, ed. Tom Moylan and Raffaella Baccolini (Oxford: Peter Lang, 2009), 53.
12 Fredric Jameson, *Archaeologies of the Future: The Desire Called Utopia and Other Science Fictions* (London: Verso, 2005), 15. Hereafter references in the text.

13 Phillip Wegner, "Here or Nowhere: Utopia, Modernity, and Totality," in *Utopia Method Vision*, 121, emphasis in original; Jill Dolan, "Utopia in Performance," *Theatre Research International* 31, no. 2 (2006): 165. See also Bruce Mazlish, "A Tale of Two Enclosures: Self and Society as a Setting for Utopias," *Theory, Culture & Society* 20, no. 1 (2003): 43–60, which questions More's decision to enclose "the inhabitants of his utopian commonwealth in a more or less timeless and unchanging amber" in the light of his opposition to the land enclosure movement (45).
14 Antoine Hatzenberger, "Islands and Empire: Beyond the Shores of Utopia," *Angelaki* 8, no .1 (2003): 119.
15 Vieira, "The Concept of Utopia," 9.
16 Wegner, "Here or Nowhere," 125; emphasis in original.
17 Aldous Huxley, *Brave New World* (1932; repr. New York: HarperCollins, 1998), xvii. Hereafter references in the text.
18 Strathern, *Reproducing the Future*, 165.
19 Edelman, *No Future*, 11. It is worth noting that our conception of the child is not without a history, and may be provisionally dated (in Britain) to the Factory Act of 1802, when legislators enshrined conceptions of childhood as a "special state, as not just a period of training for adulthood but a stage of life of value in its own right" (Jackie Wullschläger, *Inventing Wonderland: The Lives and Fantasies of Lewis Carroll, Edward Lear, J.M. Barrie, Kenneth Grahame, and A.A. Milne* [New York: Free Press, 1995], 12).
20 Edelman, *No Future*, 23.
21 Jameson, *Archaeologies of the Future*, 206–7.
22 Eleanor Dark, *Prelude to Christopher* (1934; repr. Adelaide: Rigby, 1961), 26. Hereafter references in the text.
23 Unlike Jameson, who uses the capitalized "Utopia" to refer to the abstract concept, I capitalize "Utopia" and "Utopians" only when referring to the Brave New World and its citizens.
24 "A.F." means "After Ford": as Mond explains, "the introduction of Our Ford's [that is, Henry Ford's] first T-Model … [was] chosen as the opening date of the new era" (52).
25 Galton, *Hereditary Genius*, 428.
26 Kevles, *In the Name of Eugenics*, 86.
27 H.G. Wells, *The Island of Dr. Moreau* (1896; repr. New York: Dover, 1996), 61–2. Hereafter references in the text.
28 This is taken from the title of one of Bruno Latour's essays on the laboratory ("Give Me a Laboratory and I Will Raise the World," in *Science Observed: Perspectives on the Social Study of Science*, ed. Karin D. Knorr-Cetina and Michael Mulkay [London: Sage, 1983], 141–70).
29 See, for example, Bruno Latour, *Science in Action: How to Follow Scientists and Engineers through Society* (Cambridge: Harvard UP, 1987).

30 Latour, "Give Me a Laboratory and I Will Raise the World," 154; emphasis in original.

31 David Cahan, "The Geopolitics and Architectural Design of a Metrological Laboratory: The Physikalisch-Technische Reichsanstalt in Imperial Germany," in *The Development of the Laboratory: Essays on the Place of Experiment in Industrial Civilization*, ed. Frank A.J.L. James (London: Macmillan, 1989), 138.

32 Latour, "Give Me a Laboratory and I Will Raise the World," 147.

33 Jean-François Lyotard, *The Postmodern Condition: A Report on Knowledge*, trans. Geoff Bennington and Brian Massumi (Minneapolis: U of Minnesota P, 1979), 54–5.

34 David Gooding, Trevor Pinch, and Simon Schaffer, "Preface," in *The Uses of Experiment: Studies in the Natural Sciences*, ed. David Gooding, Trevor Pinch, and Simon Schaffer (Cambridge: Cambridge UP, 1989), xiv.

35 Frank Manuel, *Utopian Thought in the Western World* (Cambridge: Cambridge UP, 1966), 80.

36 Richard H. Grove, *Green Imperialism: Colonial Expansion, Tropical Island Edens and the Origins of Environmentalism, 1600–1860* (Cambridge: Cambridge UP, 1995), 5.

37 Cogdell, *Eugenic Design*, 157.

38 In 1910, Davenport wrote to Mary Harriman, "It is going to be a purifying *conflagration* some day" (qtd. in Kevles, *In the Name of Eugenics*, 56; emphasis in original). The sentiment and language of Davenport's letter are echoed in a chapter of D.H. Lawrence's 1920 novel *Women in Love* (repr. New York: Viking, 1960) entitled, appropriately enough, "Island." Here, Birkin asks Ursula whether she doesn't "find it a beautiful clean thought, a world empty of people, just uninterrupted grass, and a hare sitting up?" (119). "If only man was swept off the face of the earth," Birkin continues, "creation would go on so marvelously, with a new start, non-human. Man is one of the mistakes of creation – like the ichthyosauri. If only he were gone again, think what lovely things would come out of the liberated days; – things straight of the fire" (120). For Birkin, "dirty humanity" is mouldering in a perpetual chrysalis phase, and thus represents, "like monkeys and baboons," a developmental dead-end (120). Its vestigial presence in the world constitutes a contaminating mistake to be purged in preparation for a "new start, non-human" (120).

39 Cahan, "The Geopolitics and Architectural Design of a Metrological Laboratory," 138.

40 Greg Dening, *Readings/Writings* (Melbourne: Melbourne UP, 1998), 170.

41 Greg Dening, *Islands and Beaches: Discourse on a Silent Land – Marquesas, 1774–1880* (Honolulu: U of Hawai'i P, 1980), 158.

42 Ibid., 3.

43 Ibid.

44 See, among others, Epeli Hau'ofa, "Our Sea of Islands," in *Inside Out: Literature, Cultural Politics, and Identity in the New Pacific*, ed. Vilsoni Hereniko and Rob Wilson (Lanham, MD: Rowman & Littlefield, 1999), 27–38; and Elizabeth DeLoughrey, *Routes and Roots: Navigating Caribbean and Pacific Island Literatures* (Honolulu: U of Hawai'i P, 2007), for more on this transoceanic turn.

45 Thomas More, *Utopia*, trans. Clarence Miller (New Haven: Yale UP, 2001), 53.

46 Louis Marin, *On Representation*, trans. Catherine Porter (Stanford: Stanford UP, 2001), 100.

47 Diana Loxley calls the island "*the* theme of colonialism" (*Problematic Shores: The Literature of Islands* [New York: St Martin's P, 1990], xi).

48 DeLoughrey, *Routes and Roots*, 6–7.

49 Ironically, given what follows, I have not been able to trace an origin for this phrase, which is ubiquitous in Australian and New Zealand historiography and national self-imagining. Pamela Cheek has shown how the South Seas served eighteenth-century British and French writers as a screen on which to project utopian fantasies (*Sexual Antipodes: Enlightenment, Globalization and the Placing of Sex* [Stanford: Stanford UP, 2003], 14).

50 Qtd. in Rae McGregor, *The Story of a New Zealand Writer: Jane Mander* (Dunedin: Otago UP, 1998), 44; J.G.A. Pocock, *The Discovery of Islands: Essays in British History* (Cambridge: Cambridge UP, 2005), 187; James Belich, *Replenishing the Earth*, 5.

51 Michel-Rolph Trouillot, "Anthropology as Metaphor: The Savage's Legacy and the Postmodern World," *Review* 14, no. 1 (1991): 36.

52 Leslie A. Fiedler, *Love and Death in the American Novel* (New York: Stein & Day, 1966), 143.

53 Elaine Showalter, "The Apocalyptic Fables of H. G. Wells," in *Fin du Siècle/Fin du Globe: Fears and Fantasies of the Late Nineteenth Century*, ed. John Stokes (New York: St Martin's, 1992), 79.

54 See Cyndy Hendershot, "The Animal Without: Masculinity and Imperialism in *The Island of Dr. Moreau* and 'The Adventure of the Speckled Band,'" *Nineteenth Century Studies* 10 (1996): 1–32.

55 "Kanaka" has, however, been reclaimed recently by several Pacific Islander groups, including the Melanesian inhabitants of New Caledonia, who call themselves Kanaks.

56 Hau'ofa, "Our Sea of Islands," 31.

57 Edmond and Smith, "Editors' Introduction," 1.

58 William Shakespeare, *The Tempest* (1611; repr. New York: Random House, 2008), 2.1.147.

59 DeLoughrey, *Routes and Roots*, 7.

60 Phillip Wegner, *Imaginary Communities: Utopia, the Nation, and the Spatial Histories of Modernity* (Berkeley: U of California P, 2002), xvi.
61 Zygmunt Bauman, "Utopia with No Topos," *History of the Human Sciences* 16, no. 1 (2003): 19.
62 Wegner, *Imaginary Communities*, 54.
63 James Buzard, "Mass-Observation, Modernism, and Auto-ethnography," *Modernism/Modernity* 4, no. 3 (1997): 105.
64 Kathleen Wilson, *The Island Race: Englishness, Empire and Gender in the Eighteenth Century* (London: Routledge, 2003), 55.
65 Ibid., 72.
66 For more on nineteenth-century exoticism, see Bongie, *Exotic Memories*.
67 Rod Edmond, *Representing the South Pacific: Colonial Discourse from Cook to Gauguin* (Cambridge: Cambridge UP, 1997), 6.
68 Trouillot, "Anthropology as Metaphor," 42.
69 See Peter Hulme, *Colonial Encounters: Europe and the Native Caribbean 1492–1797* (London: Routledge, 1986). According to Michael Parrish Lee, Wells's numerous representations of cannibalism draw similar parallels between a "'civilized' desire for knowledge" and the "cannibalistic hunger for flesh" ("Reading Meat in H.G. Wells," *Studies in the Novel* 42, no. 3 [2010]: 250).
70 Joseph Conrad, *Heart of Darkness* (1902; repr. New York: Norton, 2005), 36.
71 Carey Snyder, *British Fiction and Cross-Cultural Encounters: Ethnographic Modernism from Wells to Woolf* (New York: Palgrave Macmillan, 2008), 82.
72 Fredric Jameson, "Modernism and Imperialism," in *Nationalism, Colonialism, and Literature*, ed. Seamus Deane (Minneapolis: U of Minnesota P, 1990), 50–1.
73 Esty, *A Shrinking Island*, 8.
74 Light, *Forever England*.
75 Esty, *A Shrinking Island*, 2.
76 Buzard, *Disorienting Fiction*.
77 Baucom, *Out of Place*, 12.
78 See, inter alia, George Lamming, *The Pleasures of Exile* (Ann Arbor: U of Michigan P, 1992); Aimé Césaire, *A Tempest* (New York: TCG Productions, 2002); Paul Brown, "'This thing of darkness I acknowledge mine': *The Tempest* and the Colonial Encounter," in *Political Shakespeare: New Essays in Cultural Materialism*, ed. Jonathan Dollimore and Alan Sinfield (Manchester: Manchester UP, 1985), 48–71; and Hulme, *Colonial Encounters*.
79 Joseph B. Herring, *The Enduring Indians of Kansas: A Century and a Half of Acculturation* (Lawrence: UP of Kansas, 1990), 14.
80 Melissa L. Meyer, *The White Earth Tragedy: Ethnicity and Dispossession at a Minnesota Anishinaabe Reservation, 1889–1920* (Lincoln: U of Nebraska P, 1994), 1.

81 Thomas Biolsi, *Organizing the Lakota: The Political Economy of the New Deal on the Pine Ridge and Rosebud Reservations* (Tucson: U of Arizona P, 1992), 31.
82 John R. Gillis, "Taking History Offshore: Atlantic Islands in European Minds, 1400–1800," in *Islands in History and Representation*, 24.
83 Ireland was England's first island colony, while the former Ottoman possession of Cyprus became a British protectorate in 1878. Following annexation in 1914, relations between Greek Cypriots, Turkish Cypriots, and the British-led administration grew increasingly tense, as demonstrated by the anti-British riots and guerilla attacks of the 1930s and 1950s, respectively, and the intercommunal violence of the post-independence era.
84 For more on the American-ness of the Brave New World, see Peter Firchow, "Wells and Lawrence in Huxley's *Brave New World*," *Journal of Modern Literature* 5, no. 2 (1976): 260–78; Jerome Meckier, "Debunking Our Ford: *My Life and Work* and *Brave New World*," *South Atlantic Quarterly* 78 (Autumn 1979): 448–59 and "Aldous Huxley's Americanization of the Brave New World Typescript," *Twentieth Century Literature* 48, no. 4 (2002): 427–60.
85 See, for instance, Firchow, "Wells and Lawrence in Huxley's *Brave New World*," as well as Carey Snyder, "'When the Indian Was in Vogue': D. H. Lawrence, Aldous Huxley, and Ethnological Tourism in the Southwest," *Modern Fiction Studies* 53, no. 4 (2007): 662–96.
86 D.H. Lawrence, "America, Listen to Your Own," in *Phoenix: The Posthumous Papers of D. H. Lawrence*, ed. Edward McDonald (New York: Viking, 1978), 90.
87 See William Sanders's short story "The Undiscovered" (*The Year's Best Science Fiction: Fifteenth Annual Collection*, ed. Gardner Dorzois [New York: St Martin's, 1998], 224–44), in which Shakespeare is taken captive by the Cherokee nation, for whom he writes *Hamlet*.
88 Gilroy, *The Black Atlantic*, 14; Salman Rushdie, *The Satanic Verses* (London: Viking, 1988), 343.
89 Lyman Tower Sargent, "Colonial and Postcolonial Utopias," in *The Cambridge Companion to Utopian Literature*, 202, 209.
90 See John Kellett, "William Lane and 'New Australia': A Reassessment," *Labour History* 72 (May 1997): 1–18, and Bruce Scates, "'We are not … [A]boriginal … we are Australian': William Lane, Racism, and the Construction of Aboriginality," *Labour History* 72 (May 1997): 35–49, for more on William Lane and "New Australia."
91 Eleanor Dark, "Prelude to Christopher, ca. 1934," Eleanor Dark Papers.
92 Ibid.
93 Carey, "'Women's Objective – A Perfect Race,'" 183–4.
94 Elizabeth MacMahon, "Encapsulated Space: The Paradise-Prison of Australia's Island Imaginary," *Southerly* 65, no. 1 (2005): 35.

95 Rod Edmond, "Abject Bodies/Abject Sites: Leper Islands in the High Imperial Era," in *Islands in History and Representation*, 144.
96 See Edmond, "Abject Bodies/Abject Sites" and Elizabeth MacMahon, "The Gilded Cage: From Utopia to Monad in Australia's Island Imaginary," in *Islands in History and Representation*, 190–202, as well as MacMahon's later essay "Encapsulated Space" for more on Canberra's habit of lopping off islands "in order to preserve the health and integrity of the nation" (Edmond 144).
97 Qtd. in Kennedy, *Islands of White*, 2.

Chapter 2: Whiteness for Beginners

1 On the much-debated question of whether such technologies of settler colonial rule should be categorized as genocidal, see Wolfe, "Structure and Event," who suggests that a term like "structural genocide" may allow scholars to "retain the specificity of settler colonialism," which, in a sense, institutionalizes genocide as the founding condition of the state, "without downplaying its impact by resorting to a qualified genocide" (121).
2 Kline, *Building a Better Race*, esp. chap. 5.
3 Patrick Brantlinger, *Dark Vanishings: Discourse on the Extinction of Primitive Races, 1800–1930* (Ithaca: Cornell UP, 2003), 159–60.
4 Thomas Skidmore, *Black into White: Race and Nationality in Brazilian Thought* (Durham: Duke UP, 1993), 77. See *Black into White* and Stepan's *"The Hour of Eugenics"* for more on the Brazilian "whitening thesis."
5 Report of the Initial Conference of Commonwealth and State Aboriginal Authorities, 21–23 April 1937, NAA, A659 1942/1/8104.
6 The statistics for Western Australia are similar. My marriage statistics for the Territory are incomplete, due to the limited availability of the annual reports. (I had access only to reports for the years 1931–2, 1933–4, 1934–5, 1936–7, and the less detailed report of 1938–9. The administrative year ran from 30 June.) It is also true that, as contemporary officials and commentators continually lamented, cross-racial sexual and reproductive activity did not occur only, or even primarily, within the bounds of what Europeans considered marriage. Finally, the problematic nature of Australian population statistics from this period should be recognized. For instance, the section of the 1901 Australian constitution that excluded Aboriginals from being counted in the national census was struck down only in 1967. Northern Territory population figures recorded in official 1930s reports do not, accordingly, register the presence of Aboriginals, who in fact greatly outnumbered all other population groups in the region. In addition, just who counted as an Aboriginal or a half-caste was a contested legal determination with serious consequences for Indigenous people. In birth statistics provided by the Northern

Territory's chief medical officer (Dr Cook) for 1934–5, "European births include 11 (19 per cent.) from the mating of Europeans with Half-castes," while "Half-caste births include only 11 per cent. from the mating of Europeans with aboriginals – 70 per cent. from Half-caste with Half-caste" (Northern Territory, Annual Report, 1934–1935, NAA, A1/15 1935/6731). Whitening, then, is already occurring within the realm of statistics.

7 *Bringing Them Home: Report of the National Inquiry into the Separation of Aboriginal and Torres Strait Islander Children from Their Families* (Sydney: Human Rights and Equal Opportunity Commission, 1997), chap. 2 ("National Overview"), http://www.humanrights.gov.au/pdf/social_justice/bringing_them_home_report.pdf.

8 *Bringing Them Home*, chap. 2 ("National Overview").

9 Cecil Cook, memorandum, 27 June 1933, NAA, A659 1940/1/408; Russell McGregor, "'Breed out the Colour' or The Importance of Being White," *Australian Historical Studies* 33, no. 120: 286.

10 Keith Windschuttle, "Manne Avoids the Real Debate," *Quadrant Online* 54 (May 2010), http://www.quadrant.org.au/. Windschuttle is one of the chief "combatants" in the "history wars" that have raged in the last two decades over the shape and meaning of Australian history. Robert Manne is another: see *Whitewash: On Keith Windschuttle's* The Fabrication of Aboriginal History (Melbourne: Black, 2003), the collection of essays he edited in response to the publication of Windschuttle's book. For an (admittedly partisan) account of the history wars, see Stuart Macintyre and Anna Clark, *The History Wars* (Melbourne: Melbourne UP, 2003).

11 *Canberra Times*, letter from the National Council of Women of Australia, 21 June 1934, NAA, A452 1952/420.

12 A.O. Neville, *Australia's Coloured Minority: Its Place in the Community* (Sydney: Currawong, 1947), 68.

13 Ann McGrath, "The State as Father: 1910–1960," in Patricia Grimshaw et al., *Creating a Nation* (Grimwood: McPhee Gribble, 1994), 293. Several scholars have made the point being argued here, including Wolfe (see, inter alia, *Settler Colonialism and the Transformation of Anthropology*, esp. chap. 6, and "Structure and Event").

14 Ann Laura Stoler, *Along the Archival Grain: Epistemic Anxieties and Colonial Common Sense* (Princeton: Princeton UP, 2009), 20.

15 In the 1930s, Indigenous people living in the Australian Capital Territory (i.e., Canberra and its surrounds) came under the jurisdiction of New South Wales.

16 "Welcome to the National Archives," *National Archives of Australia*, 14 July 2010, http://www.naa.gov.au/.

17 Stoler, *Along the Archival Grain*, 8.

18 Ibid., 33.

19 Ibid., 9–10.

20 *Bringing Them Home*, Recommendations. Kim Scott's *Benang* traces one Aboriginal man's fraught engagement with the archive of "breeding out the colour." See my "Reading Closely: Writing (and) Family History in Kim Scott's *Benang*," *Postcolonial Text* 7, no. 3 (2012): n.p., for more on *Benang*'s anguished treatment of Aboriginal (archival) literacies.
21 Anna Haebich, *Broken Circles: Fragmenting Indigenous Families 1800–2000* (Fremantle: Fremantle Arts Centre, 2000), 217.
22 Ibid., 244.
23 *Brisbane Daily Herald*, 8 June 1933, NAA, A659 1940/1/408.
24 H.C. Brown, the Secretary of the Interior, to his minister, 3 November 1933, NAA, A659 1940/1/408.
25 Report of J.A. Carrodus, 20 November 1934, NAA, A659 1940/1/408.
26 Windschuttle, "Manne Avoids the Real Debate."
27 J.A. Carrodus to Frank Forde, the MP for Capricornia, 1 January 1935, NAA, A1/15 1935/10753.
28 Adam Ashforth, *The Politics of Official Discourse in Twentieth Century South Africa* (Oxford: Clarendon, 1990), 5.
29 Ibid., vii; italics in original.
30 *Northern Standard*, 30 June 1933, NAA, A659 1940/1/408.
31 Extract from *Hansard*, 28 June 1934, NAA, A659 1940/1/408.
32 See Jacques Derrida, *Archive Fever: A Freudian Impression*, trans. Eric Prenowitz (Chicago: U of Chicago P, 1996).
33 NAA, A659 1940/1/408.
34 Stoler, *Along the Archival Grain*, 1.
35 Haebich, *Broken Circles*, 222–3.
36 Scott, *Seeing Like a State*, 90.
37 All citations regarding the Odegaard case may be found in NAA, A1/15 1936/3096, unless otherwise stated.
38 Aboriginals working in Darwin were required to live in the Kahlin Compound, which included the area around Kahlin Beach. The Half-Caste Home was located next door, "sufficiently remote from the Compound to obviate [in theory] the mixing of Half-castes and Full-bloods" (letter from the Superintendent of the Kahlin Compound to the Government Resident, 4 July 1927, NAA, A659 1939/1/15580).
39 E.T. Asche to the Northern Territory Administrator, 28 April 1933, NAA, A1/15 1933/3589.
40 Government Policy with regard to Aboriginals in the Northern Territory, NAA, A1/15 1937/70.
41 Tony Austin, *I Can Picture the Old Home So Clearly: The Commonwealth and "Half-caste" Youth in the Northern Territory 1911–1939* (Canberra: Aboriginal Studies P, 1993), 67.

42 Report of the Initial Conference of Commonwealth and State Aboriginal Authorities, 21–23 April 1937, NAA, A659 1942/1/8104.

43 Duguid Papers, material from Mrs. Bennett, National Library of Australia (hereafter NLA), MS 5068 Series 11, Box 10 (Folder 11/2). I have focused here on the contradictory meanings of the paternalism that informed the state's treatment of Aboriginals. But as Margaret Jacobs has shown in her comparative account of child removal practices in Australia and the United States, maternalism too played an important role in legitimating such policies, with white women reformers "cast[ing] themselves as important political players who would solve the Indian and Aboriginal 'problem' by metaphorically and literally mothering indigenous people and their children" (*White Mother to a Dark Race*, 88).

44 Cecil Cook, memorandum, 23 July 1932, NAA, A1/15 1933/479.

45 Bessie Rischbieth Papers, NLA, MS 2004 Series 12 304–519.

46 Cecil Cook to the Government Resident at Alice Springs, 21 January 1930, NAA, A1/15 1933/479.

47 Report of the Initial Conference of Commonwealth and State Aboriginal Authorities, 21–23 April 1937, NAA, A659 1942/1/8104.

48 Qtd. in Myra Willard, *History of the White Australia Policy to 1920* (Melbourne: Melbourne UP, 1923), 119. Hereafter references in the text.

49 Parkes qtd. in McGregor, "'Breed out the colour,'" 295; Jack Lang, *I Remember* (Sydney: Invincible, 1956), 32, 36.

50 Australia was not alone in enacting such restrictive immigration legislation. Its language tests, for instance, were modelled on South African entrance requirements, while the poll tax, or head tax, was a notorious feature of Canadian and New Zealand anti-Chinese immigration legislation.

51 Blackbirding is usually described as a form of coerced labour or even kidnapping. Nicholas Thomas argues, however, that "while the larger inequalities of these relationships [between labourers and white traders] are quite inescapable," kidnappings cannot have been characteristic of "a system which entailed thousands of recruits and which lasted for decades" (*Colonialism's Culture*, 139). Pointing out the missionary origins of narratives of Indigenous victimization, Thomas seeks to leave scope for "active and collaborative … indigenous engagement in exploitation relationships" (139).

52 The Immigration Restriction Act was repealed only in 1958, and elements of the policy remained in force until the 1970s. Coupled with the recent introduction of generous baby bonuses, a chill in Commonwealth policy regarding Indigenous land rights, discrimination, immigration, and refugees, particularly since the 11 September 2001 attacks on US targets, has led some commentators to warn of a revival of the White Australia ideal. Perhaps as a result, whiteness has begun to receive a fair amount of critical attention from Australian scholars.

53 See, for instance, P.F. Donovan, *A Land of Possibilities: A History of South Australia's Northern Territory* (St Lucia: Queensland UP, 1981).

54 See Anderson, "Geography, Race and Nation" and Bashford, "'Is White Australia Possible?'" for more. Anxieties about (especially northern) Europeans' capacity to adapt to tropical conditions were by no means confined to Anglo-Australians, but informed British, German, and American racial theory.

55 In *The Invention of Terra Nullius: Historical and Legal Fictions on the Founding of Australia* (Paddington: Macleay, 2005), Michael Connor lambastes the eminent historian Henry Reynolds (among others) for "inventing" the concept and misrepresenting its importance to the legal and ideological frameworks used to justify settlement. In his classic *The Law of the Land*, Reynolds himself questions – to very different ends – whether imperial officials were ever so convinced of Australia's status as terra nullius as "the traditional legal view" has held (see the chapter "Land Rights, Then and Now" in *The Law of the Land* [Ringwood: Penguin, 1992] for more). As Reynolds but not Connor recognizes, however, whether or not the principle of terra nullius was ever formulated as such, the courts long behaved as though native title had been extinguished, with appalling consequences for Indigenous people. The Australian courts did not overturn terra nullius until 1992, when the Australian High Court recognized a form of native title in its landmark *Mabo* decision.

56 The Treaty of Waitangi/Te Tiriti o Waitangi can be read in English and Māori at http://www.nzhistory.net.nz/.

57 Brantlinger, *Dark Vanishings*, 4.

58 George Gawler, qtd. in Henry Reynolds, "The Law of the Land," *Aboriginal Law Bulletin* 57 (1987): n.p.

59 See, for example, the 1819 finding of New South Wales Attorney General Samuel Shepherd and Solicitor General Robert Gifford that "the part of New South Wales possessed by His Majesty" could not be taxed directly by the crown because he had not acquired the land "by conquest or cession," but had rather taken possession of it "as desert and uninhabited" (qtd. in Stuart Banner, *Possessing the Pacific: Land, Settlers, and Indigenous People from Australia to Alaska* [Cambridge: Harvard UP, 2007], 27).

60 Report of the Initial Conference of Commonwealth and State Aboriginal Authorities, 21–23 April 1937, NAA, A659 1942/1/8104.

61 Ibid.

62 All material cited from the Spencer report can be found in NAA, A1/14 1930/1542.

63 *Sydney Morning Herald*, 8 April 1937, NAA, A659 1942/1/8104.

64 Nancy Leys Stepan, *Picturing Tropical Nature* (Ithaca: Cornell UP, 2001), 95. See also Deborah Poole, *Race, Vision, and Modernity: A Visual Economy of the Andean Image World* (Princeton: Princeton UP, 1997) and James R. Ryan, *Picturing Empire:*

Photography and the Visualization of the British Empire (London: Reaktion, 1997), as well as Jane Lydon, *Eye Contact: Photographing Indigenous Australians* (Durham: Duke UP, 2005), for more on the complex role of photography in colonial knowledge projects as both an instrument of dominance and site of resistance.

65 Stepan, *Picturing Tropical Nature*, 95.

66 Stoler, *Race and the Education of Desire*, 45.

67 Stepan, *Tropical Nature*, 93.

68 Ibid., 106.

69 *Photography's Other Histories* (Durham: Duke UP, 2003), edited by Christopher Pinney and Nicolas Peterson, focuses on these efforts as they are launched from different locations vis-à-vis the archive. See also the work of Aboriginal artists like Brenda Croft, discussed in the conclusion to Lydon's *Eye Contact*, and Tracey Moffatt.

70 At the same time, Spencer's other photographs of Indigenous individuals do not inevitably conform to the requirements of typing, even when produced for more strictly ethnographic purposes (as in the 1899 volume *Native Tribes of Central Australia* [London: Macmillan, 1899], co-authored with Frank J. Gillen). See *The Aboriginal Photographs of Baldwin Spencer*, ed. Geoffrey Walker (Ringwood: Viking O'Neill, 1987) for a selection of Spencer's photographic work.

71 Cecil Cook to the Association for the Protection of Native Races, 28 April 1931, NAA, A1/15 1936/6595; Russell McGregor, *Imagined Destinies: Aboriginal Australians and the Doomed Race Theory, 1880–1939* (Carlton South: Melbourne UP, 1998), 112.

72 Letter from William Cooper, the secretary of the Aborigines' Advancement League, to the Department of the Interior, NAA, A659 1942/1/8104. For more on Cooper, see Bain Attwood and Andrew Markus, *Thinking Black: William Cooper and the Australian Aborigines' League* (Canberra: Aboriginal Studies, 2004), a collection of Cooper's letters prefaced by a short biography.

73 *Adelaide Register*, 19 March 1929, NAA, A1/15 1928/10743. The photographs, taken by a Dr W.D. Walker, can be found in the same NAA file. Walker's photographs are primarily of individuals obviously afflicted with disease. They are difficult to look at, both for the reasons the *Register* adduces and because of their dispassionate disregard for individual persons and their rights to privacy. Indeed, some of the photographs have been withdrawn from public circulation within the archive.

74 Pinney, "Introduction: How the Other Half …," in *Photography's Other Histories*, 1.

75 Elizabeth Edwards, *Raw Histories: Photographs, Anthropology and Museums* (Oxford: Berg, 2002), 20.

76 Roland Barthes, *Camera Lucida: Reflections on Photography*, trans. Richard Howard (New York: Hill & Wang, 1981), 96.

77 Eduardo Cadava, *Words of Light: Theses on the Photography of History* (Princeton: Princeton UP, 1997).

78 Brantlinger, *Dark Vanishings*, 38.

79 Qtd. in Skidmore, *Black into White*, 77.

80 Mary Louise Pratt, *Imperial Eyes: Travel Writing and Transculturation* (London: Routledge, 1992) and Robert J.C. Young, *Colonial Desire: Hybridity in Theory, Culture and Race* (London: Routledge, 1995) reproduce examples of these extraordinarily comprehensive compendia.

81 The photograph of the Rosses is labelled "1," while that of Norman Bray is labelled "7."

82 *West Australian*, 17 September 1931, NLA, MS 2004 Series 12 1–303.

83 *Canberra Times*, 21 June 1934, NAA, A452 1952/420.

84 *Melbourne Herald*, 27 July 1934, NAA, A452 1952/420.

85 *Sydney Morning Herald*, 21 June 1934, NAA, A452 1952/420; *Canberra Times*, 21 June 1934, NAA, A452 1952/420. Photographs of the potential adoptees accompanied the articles. In responding to the ministry's call for adoptive parents, one woman enclosed a clipping, on which she had circled the lightest child pictured, and written, in pen, "I would like this one."

86 Report of the Royal Commissioner Appointed to Investigate, Report, and Advise upon Matters in Relation to the Condition and Treatment of Aborigines, NLA, MS 2004 Series 12 304–519.

87 *Melbourne Herald*, 27 July 1934, NAA, A452 1952/420.

88 The effort to read (dream) the future into the present characterizes other half-caste legislation in this period as well. In 1930, for instance, Cook proposed legislation designed to "ensure that half-caste youths shall be trained, especially in the pastoral industry," by forcing employers of Aboriginals to apprentice half-caste boys. Cook pointed to the Northern Territory's "insensate policy" of dragging a half-caste up "in [the] alien invironment [*sic*]" of an "Aboriginal Camp" only to "vest him [at the age of 21] with the rights and privileges we cherish as citizens" (Wages of Aboriginals and Half-Castes, Northern Territory, NAA, A1/15 1938/329). Legislation was necessary, he told a sceptical gathering of pastoral lessees, union representatives, and mission workers, "in order that the halfcaste who is to be a white man after the age of 21 shall be a white boy up to the age of 21" (NAA, A1/15 1938/329). For Cook, however, half-caste labour issues were never just about (male) workers. Cook further justified the need for compulsory apprenticeships by citing the threat a growing "coloured" population posed white workers: the best strategy, he said, was to "treat the Half-Caste as a white, educating him to compete on equal terms with the white citizen"(NAA, A1/15 1933/479). But, he pointed out, boys "competent to take work on the same basis as white men" would have sisters "elevated to white standard" and married to white settlers, a fantastic scenario

capped by a "very appreciably diminish[ed]" "coloured birth-rate" (NAA, A1/15 1933/479). If the way to eliminate competition from non-white workers was to transform those workers into whites, then Cook's scheme wasn't about equality, but about *identity*, about forcing an end to difference rather than an end to treatment based on difference. Eventually, full citizenship would only confirm what education and, more important, right reproduction, had already accomplished: the whitening of the Northern Territory half-caste. What is striking about the rationale Cook provides for the Apprentices Regulations is that government action – the provision of training and perhaps, ultimately, equal wages – is predicated on a future status the government is already bound to deliver. Education secures, even authenticates, the half-caste's future citizenship, but it is his future citizenship that justifies educating the half-caste in the first place.

89 The association of futurity with whiteness is a not uncommon feature of miscegenation discourse. In Brazil, for instance, adherents of the whitening thesis cast miscegenation as an evolutionary battleground that the "stronger" "white genes" and "influence of sexual selection" (for lighter partners) would eventually claim for whiteness (João Batista de Lacerda, qtd. in Skidmore 66).

90 Cecil Cook to the Northern Territory Administrator, 7 February 1933, NAA, A659 1940/1/408.

91 J. Kēhaulani Kauanui, "'A blood mixture which experience has shown furnishes the very highest grade of citizen-material': Selective Assimilation in a Polynesian Case of Naturalization to U. S. Citizenship," *American Studies* 45, no. 3 (2004): 13; emphasis in original.

92 In differentiating between race as type and race as lineage, I draw on the work of Michael Banton, especially *Racial Theories* (Cambridge: Cambridge UP, 1998). *Racial Theories* is organized chronologically, the implication being, I think, that Euro-American racial theory moves – progresses – from conceptualizing race in terms of designation, to conceptualizing race in terms of lineage, and so on through to the current (if fragile) orthodoxy of social construction. As Banton's own work suggests, however, there is at least considerable overlap between these various modes of racialist understanding; if the scholarship on racial theory is any indication, race appears to be defined by, if nothing else, contradiction and confusion.

93 Ibid., 46.

94 Mother All White quotes taken from NAA, A659 1940/1/408 (*Northern Standard*, 20 June 1933).

95 See Mickey Dewar, *In Search of the "Never-Never": Looking for Australia in Northern Territory Writing* (Darwin: Northern Territory UP, 1997) for occurrences of the term in Territory writing. Interestingly enough, the term "white elephant," which

English-speakers use to describe something in which much has been invested (usually money) with little or no return, has itself a colonial history. The *Oxford English Dictionary* glosses "white elephant" in two ways: as "a. A rare albino variety of elephant which is highly venerated in some Asian countries. b. *fig.* A burdensome or costly possession (from the story that the kings of Siam were accustomed to make a present of one of these animals to courtiers who had rendered themselves obnoxious, in order to ruin the recipient by the cost of its maintenance). Also, an object, scheme, etc., considered to be without use or value." As Sarah Amato points out, "taken together, the literal and figurative definitions contradict and refute each other in a racist and malicious way, implying somehow that the religious significance of the elephant is a scheme without use or value" and perpetuating Anglo-American stereotypes of the East as decadent and superstitious ("The White Elephant in London: An Episode of Trickery, Racism and Advertising," *Journal of Social History* 43, no. 1 [2009]: 35).

96 See Amato, "The White Elephant in London" for more on the controversy and its meanings.

97 W.H. Flower, "The White Elephant," *The Times*, 21 January 1884.

98 This would not have been the first time Barnum arranged for an obvious fraud to be exhibited alongside, though apparently in competition with, his own more artful humbug. In 1842, James W. Cook explains, Barnum "hired a competitor, Henry Bennett, to exhibit a poor imitation of [Barnum's own] Feejee Mermaid" near to where Barnum's spectacle was currently under contract (*The Arts of Deception: Playing with Fraud in the Age of Barnum* [Cambridge, MA: Harvard UP, 2001], 101). In a dizzying display of promotional chutzpah conducted under cover of anonymous puffs and exposés, and with the cooperation of gullible and sales-hungry newspaper editors, Barnum managed simultaneously to question and uphold the authenticity of his two mermaids, no doubt attracting larger audiences for both. As Cook argues, "Barnum and his fellow practitioners of artful deception were able to … refashion potentially upsetting and immoral acts of fraud into more manageable and acceptable [and highly profitable] forms of amusement" (23).

99 "An Interesting Experiment," *New York Times*, 21 April 1884.

100 Ibid.

101 Ibid.

102 Anne McClintock reproduces the ad in *Imperial Leather: Race, Gender, and Sexuality in the Colonial Conquest* (New York: Routledge, 1995), 213.

103 She was not alone in this. Women's advocacy groups, including Bessie Rischbieth's Australian Federation of Women Voters, repeatedly urged the Commonwealth to install (white) women protectors in the Northern Territory to protect Aboriginal women from predatory men, white and non-white alike.

104 Norman B. Tindale, "Survey of the Half-Caste Problem in South Australia," *Proceedings of the Royal Geographical Society of Australasia, Vol. XLII, Session 1940–41* (Adelaide: Royal Geographical Society of Australasia, 1941), 67.

105 Cecil Cook, memorandum, 27 June 1933, NAA, A659 1940/1/408.

106 Emily Curtis, secretary of the Metropolitan Branch Women's Section of the United Country Party, to the Minister of the Interior, 19 August 1934, NAA, A452 1952/420.

107 W.H. Stanner, *Sunday Sun*, 11 June 1933, NAA, A659 1940/1/408; emphasis in original.

108 Ibid.

109 Ibid.

110 Ibid.

111 Ibid.

112 McGregor, "'Breed out the colour,'" 299.

113 Cecil Cook, memorandum, 27 June 1933, NAA, A659 1940/1/408.

114 All material regarding the Nannups is from NLA, MS 5068 Series 11, Box 10 (Folder 11/2).

115 Tindale, "Survey of the Half-Caste Problem in South Australia," 131.

116 *Kanak v. National Native Title Tribunal*, qtd. in *Bringing Them Home*, chap. 11 ("The Effects").

117 Confidential evidence qtd. in *Bring Them Home*, chap. 11.

118 Rev. Bernie Clarke, qtd. ibid.

119 Kay Torney, "Blackbirds and Lost Babies: Narratives of Child-Stealing in Australia and the Pacific Islands," *Journal of the South Pacific Association for Commonwealth Literature and Language Studies* 37 (1993): n.p. Accessible through the website of the Murdoch University School of Media, Communication and Culture.

120 NAA, A1/15 1936/6595.

121 McGregor, "'Breed out the colour,'" 294.

122 NAA, A1/15 1936/6595. See *Lost in the Whitewash: Aboriginal-Asian Encounters in Australia, 1901–2001* (Canberra: Australian National UP, 2003), a collection of essays edited by Penny Edwards and Shen Yuenfang, for more on Aboriginal–Asian relations in the Northern Territory during the twentieth century, and how attending to such interactions promises to unsettle national and nationalist historiographies. In his essay "Anti-Minorities History: Perspectives on Aboriginal–Asian Relations," for example, Minoru Hokari suggests that rather than make of Asian–Aboriginal interactions an alternative national history, we conceive of the ostensible nation as "*a place of conjunction or a site of convergence* between different places, cultures, and nations" (94; emphasis in original). Focused on the conquest paradigm of white settlement, I am myself guilty, of course, of relegating Asian-Aboriginal families and relations to a footnote.

123 Resolutions passed by the Metropolitan Branch Women's Section, United Country Party, 2 August 1934, NAA, A452 1952/420.

124 Only once did Cook note "the definite qualities of value" – "intelligence, stamina, resource, high resistance to the influences of tropical environment and the character of pigmentation which even in high dilution will serve to reduce the at present high incidence of Skin Cancer in the blonde European" – the half-caste's "aboriginal inheritance brings to the hybrid," and that in the memo claiming "breeding out" as the "only instrument of realizing … an All White Australia" (Cecil Cook, memorandum, 27 June 1933, NAA, A659 1940/1/408).

125 Xavier Herbert, correspondence, NLA, MS 758 Series 3. The degree of Herbert's involvement in the establishment of the important Euraustralian League is contested. Frances de Groen, Herbert's biographer, believes Herbert to be grossly exaggerating his role in the league's formation (*Xavier Herbert: A Biography* [St Lucia: U of Queensland P, 1998]). However, Aboriginal activist Joe McGinness, whose brother Val worked with Herbert both at the Compound and, in circumstances of increasing tension, on the McGinness mining claim, acknowledges Herbert's aid in setting up what would become the Australian Half-Caste Progressive Association (Joe McGinness, *Son of Alyandabu: My Fight for Aboriginal Rights* [St Lucia: U of Queensland P, 1991], 23–4). Herbert's claims bespeak sympathy for half-castes and their aims, a commendable gesture weakened by its extravagance and arrogance, and the fact that Herbert was not above using his work with Aboriginals to score points with and against the government. See Joe McGinness, *Son of Alyandabu*, and Sue Stanton, "The Australian Half-Caste Progressive Association: The Fight for Freedom and Rights in the Northern Territory," *Journal of Northern Territory History* 4 (1993): 37–46, for brief histories of the organization.

126 Xavier Herbert, *Capricornia* (1938; repr. North Ryde: Angus & Robertson, 1985), 314. Hereafter references in the text.

127 Mohanram, *Black Body*, xii.

128 Arjun Appadurai, "Putting Hierarchy in Its Place," *Cultural Anthropology* 3, no. 1 (1988): 37.

129 Mohanram, *Black Body*, 15.

130 Elizabeth DeLoughrey, "'The litany of islands, the rosary of archipelagoes': Caribbean and Pacific Archipelagraphy," *Ariel* 32, no. 1 (2001): 28.

131 Rajagopalan Radhakrishnan, "Nationalism, Gender and the Narrative of Identity," in *Nationalisms and Sexualities*, ed. Andrew Parker et al. (New York: Routledge, 1992), 84.

132 Mohanram, *Black Body*, 83.

133 D.H. Lawrence and Mollie Skinner, *The Boy in the Bush* (1924; repr. Cambridge: Cambridge UP, 1990), 22–3; emphasis in original.

134 Spivak, *A Critique of Postcolonial Reason*, 228.
135 Report of the Initial Conference of Commonwealth and State Aboriginal Authorities, NAA, A659 1942/1/8104.
136 See Daisy Bates, *The Passing of the Aborigines: A Lifetime Spent among the Natives of Australia* (1938; repr. London: John Murray, 1944).
137 *Melbourne Herald*, 27 July 1934, NAA, A452 1952/420.
138 Jonathan Culler, *On Deconstruction: Theory and Criticism after Structuralism* (Ithaca: Cornell UP, 1982), 189.
139 "Breeding out" didn't cost any money to administer, unless you count the housing incentives for mixed couples. This was definitely a point in its favour: throughout the 1930s, the Commonwealth repeatedly denied requests from Cook for money to repair the roof of the Darwin Half-Caste Home, while effectively starving the Home's inhabitants.
140 Poole, *Race, Vision, and Modernity*, 209.
141 Derrida, qtd. in Barbara Johnson, "The Frame of Reference: Poe, Lacan, Derrida," in *The Purloined Poe: Lacan, Derrida, and Psychoanalytic Reading*, ed. John P. Muller and William J. Richardson (Baltimore: Johns Hopkins UP, 1988), 231.
142 Pinney, "Introduction," 3.
143 Ibid., 4.

Chapter 3: "I kept on dreaming about the sea"

1 Wally Seccombe, "Starting to Stop: Working Class Fertility Decline in Britain," *Past and Present* 126, no. 1 (February 1990): 151. There are as yet few accounts of what is sometimes called the demographic transition specific to Australia or New Zealand. Although I have consulted Smyth's *Rocking the Cradle* as well as the relevant archives, the narrative I develop here draws primarily from the work of British historians.
2 Szreter, *Fertility, Class and Gender in Britain, 1860–1940*, 1.
3 Seccombe, "Starting to Stop," 156.
4 See Seccombe, "Starting to Stop," and Soloway, *Birth Control and the Population Question in England*, for examples of arguments that stress the role of contraception in the fertility decline; the work of Angus McLaren, including *Birth Control in Nineteenth-Century England* (London: Holmes & Meier, 1978), for more on abortion's role especially in working-class tactics of fertility regulation; and Szreter's *Fertility, Class and Gender* for the argument that (attempted) abstinence was the chief means of fertility control until contraceptive devices such as the condom became at once more pleasurable and more respectable. The Bradlaugh-

Besant trial of 1877 disseminated information about contraception to the public in an especially spectacular way; doctors' increasing tendency to intervene in working-class reproductive life also worked to alert men and women that limitation was both possible and desirable, even if they generally stopped short of informing patients how not to have children (for more on the trial, see Sripati Chandrasekhar, *"A dirty, filthy book": The Writings of Charles Knowlton and Annie Besant on Reproductive Physiology and Birth Control and an Account of the Bradlaugh-Besant Trial* [Berkeley: U of California P, 1981]). Similar lessons were learned from other social élites, whose small(er) families provided notable examples of limitation in action. But information did not only trickle down from above, since techniques, remedies, and caveats also circulated through informal peer and community networks and through institutions such as the penny press. By the 1930s, the appeals of activists like Marie Stopes and eminences such as Lord Dawson, the king's personal physician and a prominent churchman, had helped to make birth control a respectable topic of public discussion, laying the groundwork for Memorandum 153 (1931), a Ministry of Health document that "authorized the provision of limited information about contraception to married women whose lives would clearly be jeopardized by pregnancy" (Hauck, "Abortion and the Individual Talent," 228). It is not clear, meanwhile, that individual men and women routinely differentiated between abortion and contraception. Although a series of nineteenth-century acts criminalized abortion at all stages of pregnancy, rendering abortion the only illegal surgical operation, many women continued, far into the twentieth century, to understand abortion according to an older ethical (non-medical) framework that sanctioned abortion prior to "quickening." In marketing their wares, the makers of remedies for "female complaints" rarely distinguished abortifacients from contraceptives. If such confusion appears strategic, a refusal to inhabit the zone of illegality established by the law, it also reflects the tendency of women to situate abortion as part of a continuum of practices of birth control, and not only as a measure of last resort. Tania McIntosh points out that abortion may well have been "a positive choice" for women: unlike the rhythm method, coitus interruptus, or abstinence, abortion did not require the cooperation of the woman's lover or husband. It was cheaper than contraceptive devices, which were, moreover, tarnished through their association with prostitution and the campaigns against venereal disease ("'An Abortionist City': Maternal Mortality, Abortion, and Birth Control in Sheffield, 1920–1940," *Medical History* 44 (2000): 93–4, 89). At the same time, as Seccombe notes, although "the rate of induced abortion seems to have risen substantially" during the period in question, this alone cannot account for the scope and rate of the fertility decline, which leads Szreter to posit an increased emphasis on abstinence as compatible with, and even integral to, conceptions of normative marital sexuality (Seccombe, "Starting to Stop," 154; Szreter, *Fertility, Class and Gender*, esp. chaps. 8 and 9).

5 Septic Abortion, Committee of Inquiry: Report, National Archives of New Zealand/Te Rua Mahara o te Kāwanatanga (NANZ), H1 131/139/14; emphasis in original.

6 See the first chapter of Szreter's *Fertility, Class and Gender* for an overview of the historiography of the fertility decline that stresses the importance of attending to "local and cultural variation" as well as "the political and ideological aspects of historical change" in accounting for this critical demographic phenomenon (66).

7 Resolution [by the clergy and ministers of Christchurch] on the "The McMillan Report" upon the Problem of Abortion in New Zealand, NANZ, ABQU 632 Accession W4452 Box 18 5/12/3.

8 William Beveridge, *Social Insurance and Allied Services* (London: HMSO, 1942), 154.

9 Statement of the representative of His Grace Archbishop O'Shea, NANZ, H1 131/139/15.

10 Pearson, *The Groundwork of Eugenics*, 38.

11 Abortion – Recommendations arising out of the committee's report 1937–1945, NANZ, H1 131/139/16.

12 Susan Grayzel, *Women's Identities at War: Gender, Motherhood, and Politics in Britain and France during the First World War* (Chapel Hill: U of North Carolina P, 1999), 101.

13 Barbara Brookes, *Abortion in England*, 114.

14 Septic Abortion, Committee of Inquiry: Report, NANZ, H1 131/139/14.

15 Kate Fisher says that historians have, perhaps as a consequence, replicated this focus to too great an extent. See her "'She was quite satisfied with the arrangements I made': Gender and Birth Control in Britain 1920–1950," *Past and Present* 169, no. 1 (2000): 161–93 for an account, grounded in oral history, of the role British working-class men played in circulating knowledge about contraception.

16 "Law and Ethics of Abortion," *British Medical Journal*, no. 3722 (7 May 1932): 844; Anthony Ludovici, "The Case against Legalised Artificial Abortion," *Abortion* (London: Allen & Unwin, 1935), 104.

17 Septic Abortion, Committee of Inquiry: Report, NANZ, H1 131/139/14.

18 Anthony Ludovici, *Lysistrata, or Women's Future and Future Woman* (London: Kegan Paul, Trench, Trubner & Co., 1924), 107.

19 Anna Davin, "Imperialism and Motherhood," *History Workshop Journal* 5, no. 1 (1978): 27.

20 Brookes, *Abortion in England*, 70.

21 See Davin, "Imperialism and Motherhood," Lewis, *The Politics of Motherhood*, and the essays collected in *Mothers of a New World: Maternalist Politics and the Origins of Welfare States*, ed. Seth Koven and Sonya Michel (New York: Routledge, 1993),

for more on the intersections between the ideology of maternalism and the development of welfare-state bureaucracies in the twentieth century.

22 Mary Lou Emery, *Jean Rhys at "World's End": Novels of Colonial and Sexual Exile* (Austin: U of Texas P, 1990), 79.

23 F. Tennyson Jesse, *A Pin to See the Peepshow* (1934; repr. London: Virago, 1982), 290; Rosamund Lehmann, *The Weather in the Streets* (1936; repr. Garden City: Dial, 1983), 284; ellipses in original. Hereafter all references in the text.

24 Meg Gillette, "Manners in Dorothy Parker's 'Lady with a Lamp' and Kay Boyle's *My Next Bride*," *Studies in American Fiction* 35, no. 2 (2007): 161; Nicole Moore, "The Politics of Cliché: Sex, Class and Abortion in Australian Realism," *Modern Fiction Studies* 47, no. 1 (2001): 74.

25 Patricia Mann, *Micro-Politics: Agency in a Post-Feminist Era* (Minneapolis: U of Minnesota P, 1994), 91; Judith Wilt, *Abortion, Choice, and Contemporary Fiction: The Armageddon of the Maternal Instinct* (Chicago: U of Chicago P, 1990), 20. Wilt is referring to the stories collected in *Women Exploited*, a 1985 publication issued by an organization called WEBA (Women Exploited by Abortion) that strives to harness the regret (some) women experience in the wake of abortion to an anti-choice political stance.

26 Drucilla Cornell, *The Imaginary Domain: Abortion, Pornography & Sexual Harassment* (New York: Routledge, 1995), 34, 33.

27 Sally Minogue and Andrew Palmer, "Confronting the Abject: Women and Dead Babies in Modern English Fiction," *Journal of Modern Literature* 29, no. 3 (2006): 106.

28 Edelman, *No Future*, 2, 16.

29 Ibid., 11. Numerous scholars have made the latter point, including José Muñoz in *Cruising Utopia*, 95.

30 *British Medical Journal*, qtd. in Brookes, *Abortion in England*, 2; Hauck, "Abortion and the Individual Talent," 233.

31 Patricia Hill Collins, "Shifting the Center: Race, Class, and Feminist Theorizing About Motherhood," in *Mothering: Ideology, Experience, and Agency*, ed. Evelyn Nakano Glenn et al. (New York: Routledge, 1994), 53.

32 Deborah Kelly Kloepfer, *The Unspeakable Mother: Forbidden Discourse in Jean Rhys and H. D.* (Ithaca: Cornell UP, 1989), 64. Other treatments of mother-daughter alienation in Rhys include Kloepfer, "'Voyage in the Dark': Jean Rhys' Masquerade for the Mother," *Contemporary Literature* 26, no. 4 (1985): 443–59; Teresa F. O'Connor, *Jean Rhys: The West Indian Novels* (New York: New York UP, 1986); and the essays by Laura Niesen de Abruna and Elaine Savory Fido in *Motherlands: Black Women's Writing from Africa, the Caribbean and South Asia*, ed. Susheila Nasta (New Brunswick, NJ: Rutgers UP, 1992).

33 See the introduction to Judith Butler's *Frames of War: When Is Life Grievable?* (London: Verso, 2009).

34 I draw here on the work of Gayatri Spivak, who, as Ian Baucom neatly summarizes it, "borrows the notion of foreclosure from Lacan but grafts onto his conception of foreclosure as the psychic expulsion or abjection 'of an incompatible idea together with [its] affect' Abraham and Torok's notion of encrypting. Foreclosure, thus understood, names a double and contradictory process of expelling from and secreting within" (*Specters of the Atlantic: Finance Capital, Slavery, and the Philosophy of History* [Durham: Duke UP, 2005], 155; insertion in original).

35 *Praeteritio* describes those moments when, as Barbara Johnson puts it, "a text elaborates itself by detailing at length what it says it will *not* speak about" ("Teaching Deconstructively," in *Writing and Reading Differently: Deconstruction and the Teaching of Composition and Literature*, ed. G. Douglas Atkins and Michael L. Johnson [Lawrence: UP of Kansas, 1985], 142).

36 During the interwar years, Britons continued to use the term "abortion" to describe both induced and spontaneous abortions. I follow the late-twentieth- and twenty-first-century practice of reserving the term "abortion" for the former and calling the latter miscarriages.

37 Brookes, *Abortion in England*, 22; Finch, *The Classing Gaze*, 111.

38 Women who carried out their own abortions do not seem to have been covered by the act.

39 Brookes, *Abortion in England*, 37.

40 Ibid., 36. Having helped to bring abortion within the compass of the law, doctors have since played a central role in facilitating (some would say managing) women's access to abortion, not only before but following passage of the 1967 Abortion Act. In modifying (but not replacing) the 1861 Offences Against the Person Act, the Abortion Act allows for medical termination of pregnancy "if two registered medical practitioners are of the opinion, formed in good faith, (a) That the continuance of the pregnancy would involve risk to the life of the pregnant woman, or of injury to the physical or mental health of the pregnant woman or any existing children of her family, greater than if the pregnancy were terminated; or (b) That there is a substantial risk that if the child were born it would suffer from such physical or mental abnormalities as to be seriously handicapped." Note that although we often speak as though Britain legalized abortion in 1967, in fact, as Penelope Deutscher observes, the Abortion Act only carves out a medically sanctioned space of exception for abortions conducted given certain conditions ("The Inversion of Exceptionality: Foucault, Agamben, and 'Reproductive Rights,'" *South Atlantic Quarterly* 107, no. 1 [2008]: 60). (Canada is among the only nations in the world in which access to abortion is not restricted by law.) That the act of abortion is now in most instances unprosecutable does not wholly mitigate the continued illegality of the procedure.

41 In doing so, it was following in the footsteps of New Zealand, which had convened a similar inquiry in 1936.

42 Davin, "Imperialism and Motherhood," 11.
43 Stephen Brooke, "'A New World for Women'?: Abortion Law Reform in Britain during the 1930s," *American Historical Review* 106, no. 2 (2001): 435.
44 McIntosh, "'An Abortionist City,'" 76.
45 Brookes, *Abortion in England*, 62.
46 Ludovici, "The Case against Legalised Artificial Abortion," 96.
47 Charlotte Haldane, *Motherhood and Its Enemies* (Garden City: Doubleday, Doran & Co., 1928), 212.
48 Brookes, *Abortion in England*, 114.
49 Ibid., 110.
50 J.W. Ballantyne, "An Address on the Nature of Pregnancy and Its Practical Bearings," *British Medical Journal* no. 2772 (14 February 1914): 349–55.
51 "Law and Ethics of Abortion," 844.
52 Geoffrey Theobald, "Some Effects of Emancipation on the Health of Women," *Journal of State Medicine* 44, no. 3 (1936): 366.
53 *Report on an Investigation into Maternal Mortality* (London: HMSO, 1937), 117.
54 Brooke, "'A New World for Women,'" 436.
55 Haldane, *Motherhood and Its Enemies*, 95.
56 Ludovici, "The Case against Legalised Artificial Abortion," 63; *Lysistrata*, 12.
57 Ludovici, *Lysistrata*, 41.
58 Arthur Power, *Conversations with James Joyce*, ed. Clive Hart (New York: Harper & Row, 1974), 63.
59 All references to the trial of Edith Thompson and Frederick Bywaters sourced from NAUK, HO 144/2685 unless otherwise noted. Read alongside Justice Shearman's, the judge's summation in *Strong Poison*, Dorothy Sayers's 1930 novel about another professional woman accused of murder, appears positively charitable: he acknowledges that the jury members "may perhaps think that one step into the path of wrongdoing makes the next one easier," but cautions them against "giv[ing] too much weight to that consideration" (5).
60 Qtd. in René Weis, *Criminal Justice: The True Story of Edith Thompson* (London: Hamish Hamilton, 1988), 247.
61 Power, *Conversations with James Joyce*, 64. On the first point, see, for example, the "Man on the Street" feature conducted by the *Daily Sketch* on the day Edith and Freddie were executed. This survey became the basis for a portion of *Finnegans Wake* (see Vincent Deane, "Bywaters and the Original Crime," in *Finnegans Wake: "teems of times,"* ed. Andrew Treip [Amsterdam: Rodopi, 1994], 165–83).
62 Weis, *Criminal Justice*, 70.
63 Before the nineteenth century, at least, the conditions under which a condemned woman might "plead the belly" were also the conditions under which an abortion ceased to be legal: just as abortion was legal only up until the moment when a

woman felt the foetus move, or quicken, so only women whose pregnancies had "quickened" could argue for a stay of execution.

64 Nicholas de Genova, "The Legal Production of Mexican/Migrant 'Illegality,'" *Latino Studies* 2, no. 2 (2004): 166.

65 See also Deborah Boehm, *Intimate Migrations: Gender, Family, and Illegality among Transnational Mexicans* (New York: New York UP, 2012).

66 Nicholas de Genova, "'Illegality' and Deportability in Everyday Life," *Annual Review of Anthropology* 31 (2002): 427.

67 Nicholas de Genova, *Working the Boundaries: Race, Space, and "Illegality" in Mexican Chicago* (Durham: Duke UP, 2005), 237.

68 See NAUK, MH 71/26 for the written and verbal evidence the Eugenics Society submitted to the Inter-Departmental Committee on Abortion. Even activists otherwise sympathetic to the plight of overworked and exhausted working-class women were sceptical of their intellectual capacity to employ mechanical and chemical forms of birth control.

69 Qtd. in Hermione Lee, *Virginia Woolf* (New York: Alfred A. Knopf, 1997), 330.

70 The comparison is further complicated by the fact that both novels are set many years before the time of publication.

71 Brooke, "'A New World for Women,'" 441.

72 Lee's *Virginia Woolf* teases out the autobiographical implications of this passage; Childs's *Modernism and Eugenics* offers a detailed discussion of Woolf's eugenicism.

73 Molly Hite, *The Other Side of the Story: Structures and Strategies of Contemporary Feminist Narratives* (Ithaca: Cornell UP, 1989), 28.

74 Childs, *Modernism and Eugenics*, 102. Thus, for instance, a belief in the inheritability of "moral insanity" may have contributed to Vivien and T.S. Eliot's decision not to have children.

75 Dionne Brand, *A Map to the Door of No Return* (Toronto: Doubleday Canada, 2001), 13.

76 Qtd. in Angela Woollacott, *To Try Her Fortune in London: Australian Women, Colonialism, and Modernity* (New York: Oxford UP, 2001), 5.

77 See Appadurai, "Putting Hierarchy in Its Place" and Gillian Beer, "Can the Native Return?" in *Open Fields: Science in Cultural Encounter* (Oxford: Clarendon, 1996), 31–54, for more on the term "native."

78 Stepan, *Picturing Tropical Nature*, 164.

79 Vanessa Smith, *Literary Culture and the Pacific: Nineteenth-Century Textual Encounters* (Cambridge: Cambridge UP, 1998), 54.

80 Jean Rhys, *Wide Sargasso Sea* (1967; repr. New York: Norton, 1982), 67.

81 See, among others, Gilman's *Difference and Pathology* for more on the Khosian woman known to Europeans as the "Hottentot Venus."

82 Peter Hulme, "The Locked Heart: The Creole Family Romance of *Wide Sargasso Sea* – An Historical and Biographical Analysis," *Jean Rhys Review* 6, no. 1 (1995): 22.

83 Ibid.

84 Woollacott, *To Try Her Fortune in London*, 14.

85 Many of the relevant critical accounts are cited elsewhere in the chapter, but see also Elizabeth Nunez-Harrell, "The Paradoxes of Belonging: The White West Indian Woman in Fiction," *Modern Fiction Studies* 31, no. 2 (1985): 281–93 and Sue Thomas, *The Worlding of Jean Rhys* (Westport: Greenwood P, 1999).

86 De Abruna, "Family Connections," 258.

87 O'Connor, *Jean Rhys*, 10.

88 Laura E. Ciolkowski, "Navigating the Wide Sargasso Sea: Colonial History, English Fiction, and British Empire," *Twentieth Century Literature* 43, no. 3 (1997): 343, 347.

89 Butler, *Antigone's Claim*, 79.

90 Aldous Huxley, *Eyeless in Gaza* (1936; repr. London: Chatto & Windus, 1955), 446.

91 There's a sense in which Anna may just as well have died. Indeed, Rhys originally planned for Anna to die. On 10 June 1934, Rhys wrote to Evelyn Scott that editor Michael Sadleir "likes it [*Voyage*] ... but he also wants it cut. Not of course his own taste he explains but to please prospective readers ... My dear it is so mad – really it is not a disgusting book – or even a very grey book. And I *know* the ending is the only possible ending" (*The Letters of Jean Rhys*, ed. Francis Wyndham and Diana Melly [New York: Viking Penguin, 1984], 25). Sadleir, it appeared, objected to Anna's death following the abortion. Forty years later, Rhys recorded her conversation with Sadleir:

> "Why do you end it like that?"
> "Because that's the way it must end."
> "You mean the girl dies?"
> "Of course; there is no other end."
> "Oh, I don't know; so gloomy; people won't like it. Why can't she recover and meet a rich man?"
> "But how horrible," I said. "How *all wrong*."
> "Well, then, a poor, good-natured man," he said impatiently. (*Smile Please: An Unfinished Autobiography* [New York: Harper & Row, 1979], 127; emphasis in original)

Rhys capitulated, cutting approximately 2500 words, restoring Anna to life if not to romantic joy, and hence missing Sadleir's point altogether (just as he had missed hers).

92 Baucom, *Specters of the Atlantic*, 155.

93 Sue Thomas, "'Tearing me in two so slowly so slowly': Jean Rhys's Representations of Abortion," *Jean Rhys Review* 12, no. 1 (2002): 8.

94 Derek Walcott, *Ti-Jean and His Brothers*, in *Plays for Today*, ed. Errol Hill (1958; repr. Harlow, UK: Longman, 1985), 32. Hereafter references in the text.

95 According to Meillassoux, "the captive always appears therefore as marked by an original, indelible defect which weighs heavily upon his destiny. This is, in Izard's words, a kind of "social death." He can never be brought to life again as such since, in spite of some specious examples (themselves most instructive), of fictive rebirth, the slave will remain forever an unborn being (non-né)" (qtd. in Orlando Patterson, *Slavery and Social Death: A Comparative Study* [Cambridge, MA: Harvard UP, 1982], 38). Meillassoux's discussion of social death informs Orlando Patterson's influential *Slavery and Social Death*.

96 Dionne Brand, *At the Full and Change of the Moon* (Toronto: Alfred A. Knopf, 1999), 8. Hereafter references in the text.

97 Toni Morrison, *Beloved* (1987; repr. New York: Vintage, 2004), 74. Hereafter references in the text.

98 Caroline Rody, *The Daughter's Return: African-American and Caribbean Women's Fictions of History* (New York: Oxford UP, 2001), 7.

99 Jamaica Kincaid, *The Autobiography of My Mother* (New York: Farrar, Straus & Giroux, 1996), 225–6.

100 Gilroy, *The Black Atlantic*, 68.

101 Hortense Spillers, "Mama's Baby, Papa's Maybe: An American Grammar Book," *Diacritics* 17, no. 2 (1987): 79–80; emphasis in original.

102 Peter Hulme, *Remnants of Conquest: The Island Caribs and Their Visitors, 1877–1998* (Oxford: Oxford UP, 2000), 232.

103 In this scene, Anna appears, as Leah Reade Rosenberg writes of Rhys, to be "identify[ing] with an Afro-Caribbean" mulatta, a choice that "may appear self-destructive or masochistic," yet "embodies a criticism of English constructions of Creole womanhood" insofar as it signals acceptance of the "black" sexuality against which Creolity defines itself as white ("Creolizing Womanhood: Gender and Domesticity in Early Anglophone Caribbean National Literatures," PhD diss. [Cornell U, 2000], 273. However, Anna's identification with the house servant is uncomfortable. Repeating Maillotte's name and age (eighteen), she insists, "*But I like it like this. I don't want it any way but this*" (56; italics in original). Her "but" bespeaks an elided objection: "but I'm not like Maillotte Boyd because I like it like this." In her moment of identification with Maillotte Boyd, Anna realizes slavery's intersection with (other) systems of sexual exploitation and subordination, an intersection that then has to be disavowed because the distance between the mulatta slave-concubine and the creole prostitute is both too great and too close for comfort.

104 See Sara Ahmed, *The Cultural Politics of Emotions* (New York: Routledge, 2004) for more about how emotions are not something "I" or "we" have, but work to constitute "I" and "we" as (for example) subjects who feel rage.

105 Urmila Seshagiri, "Modernist Ashes, Postcolonial Phoenix: Jean Rhys and the Evolution of the English Novel in the Twentieth Century," *Modernism/Modernity* 13, no. 3 (2006): 493–4.

106 Sara Ahmed, *Strange Encounters: Embodied Others in Post-Coloniality* (London: Routledge, 2000), 8.

107 Mary Lou Emery, "The Poetics of Labor in Jean Rhys's Global Modernism," *Philological Quarterly* 90, nos. 2–3 (2011): 172.

108 Ahmed, *Strange Encounters*, 132; italics in original.

109 Nathan Stormer, "*Why Not?* Memory and Counter-Memory in 19th Century Abortion Rhetoric," *Women's Studies in Communication* 24, no. 1 (2001): 19.

110 Alissa G. Karl, "Rhys, Keynes, and the Modern(ist) Economic Nation," *Novel* 43, no. 2 (2010): 438. Karl shows how "*Voyage*'s numerous refusals of formal closure both test and contest the economic idea that the boundaries of the self-enclosed nation are determined by its balanced components within," an elegant argument whose focus on economistic theories of nation-ness complements mine on reproductive discourses of the same (426).

111 Baucom, *Out of Place*, 40.

112 Veronica Marie Gregg, *Jean Rhys' Historical Imagination: Reading and Writing the Creole* (Chapel Hill: U of North Carolina P, 1995), 135. See also Mary Lou Emery's reading of *Voyage in the Dark* in the fourth chapter of *Jean Rhys at "World's End"* and Mary Hanna, "White Women's Sins or Patterns of Choice and Consequence in the Two Endings of 'Voyage in the Dark,'" *Journal of West Indian Literature* 15, nos. 1–2 (2006): 132–63.

113 Andrew Thacker, *Moving through Modernity: Space and Geography in Modernism* (Manchester: Manchester UP, 2003), 192.

114 Ahmed, *Strange Encounters*, 78.

115 Baucom, *Specters of the Atlantic*, 309.

116 Thomas, "'Tearing me in two so slowly so slowly,'" 15.

117 Seshagiri, "Modernist Ashes, Postcolonial Phoenix," 497. See also the discussion of Rhys's theming of impasse in the fourth chapter of Christopher GoGwilt's *The Passage of Literature: Genealogies of Modernism in Conrad, Rhys, and Pramoedya* (Oxford: Oxford UP, 2011).

118 Baucom, *Specters of the Atlantic*, 326, 315.

119 Derek Walcott, "The Sea Is History," qtd. in Baucom, *Specters of the Atlantic*, 310.

120 Brookes, *Abortion in England*; Brooke, "'A New World for Women'"; Johanna Schoen, *Choice and Coercion: Birth Control, Sterilization, and Abortion in Public Health and Welfare* (Chapel Hill: U of North Carolina P, 2005).

121 Stella Browne, testimony before the Inter-Departmental Committee on Abortion, NAUK, MH 71/21. As Stephen Brooke argues, few interwar abortion activists saw their work as necessitated by "a new or modern category of femininity, in which freedom from reproduction and physical and political autonomy were central elements of women's subjectivity" ("'A New World for Women,'" 447–8).

122 Stella Browne, testimony before the Inter-Departmental Committee on Abortion, NAUK, MH 71/21.

Chapter 4: Apprehending Loss

A version of this chapter was published in *Lighted Windows: Critical Essays on Robin Hyde*, ed. Mary Edmond-Paul (Dunedin: U of Otago P, 2008).

1 Virginia Woolf, *Three Guineas*, in *A Room of One's Own and Three Guineas* (1938; repr. London: Penguin, 1993), 117. Hereafter references in the text.

2 Grayzel, *Women's Identities at War*, 3.

3 Septic Abortion, Committee of Inquiry: Evidence, NANZ, H1 131/139/15; statement of Mrs H.D. Baker, 18 December 1936, ibid.

4 Interdepartmental Committee on Abortion, NAUK, MH 71/22.

5 See James Thomas and A. Susan Williams, "Women and Abortion in 1930s Britain: A Survey and Its Data," *Social History of Medicine* 11, no. 2 (1998): 283–309, for more on what the Joint Council of Midwifery Survey reveals about interwar practices of birth control and discourses of sexuality.

6 As Barbara Brookes writes, "Debates about abortion have often obscured the realities of life for women to whom abortion was not a matter of philosophical nicety or medical expertise, but a necessary survival strategy" (*Abortion in England*, n.p.). To a limited (compromised) degree, however, interwar debates about abortion and other aspects of sexual and reproductive life did bring into view, or encourage speech about, aspects of intimate personal experience that would in earlier eras have remained obscured. Roy Porter and Lesley A. Hall claim that sex became an increasingly visible, even respectable, object of scientific and literary investigation during the interwar decades (*The Facts of Life: The Creation of Sexual Knowledge in Britain 1650–1950* [New Haven: Yale UP, 1995], 291). I discussed the proliferation of literary representations of abortion in chapter 3. Direct testimony about Edwardian and Georgian sexual and reproductive life exists as well, in the form of the thousands of heart-rending letters written by working-class women in support of the 1913 Maternity Insurance Benefit, and by working- and middle-class men and women seeking advice from birth control activist Marie Stopes on matters of family limitation. Stopes published a portion of this correspondence in 1929 as *Mother England: A Contemporary History Self-Written by Those Who Have Had No Historian* (repr. London: John Bale,

Sons, & Danielsson, 1930). Along with the Joint Council of Midwifery Survey, Ernest Lewis-Faning's *Report on an Enquiry into Family Limitation and Its Influence on Human Fertility during the Past Fifty Years* (London: HMSO, 1949) furnishes additional data about pre- and interwar practices of contraception and abortion. These sources have not been as deeply plumbed as they might. Although the archives of professional and activist bodies such as the Joint Council of Midwifery constitute rich sources of information about the lives of working-class and middle-class women, they have tended to be read quantitatively rather than qualitatively, for the statistics they provide (of contraceptive use, for example) rather than as richly textured non-fiction accounts of working- and middle-class life.

7 Jacques Derrida, qtd. in Gayatri Chakravorty Spivak, "Speculation on Reading Marx: After Reading Derrida," in *Post-Structuralism and the Question of History*, ed. Derek Attridge, Geoff Bennington, and Robert Young (Cambridge: Cambridge UP, 1987), 43; emphasis in original.

8 Sarah Trimble, "Undead Ends: Contested Re-Beginnings in Apocalyptic Film and Television," PhD diss. (McMaster U, 2012), 192.

9 Interdepartmental Committee on Abortion, NAUK, MH 71/23.

10 Kathleen Marks, *Toni Morrison's* Beloved *and the Apotropaic Imagination* (Columbia: U of Missouri P, 2002), 10.

11 Brantlinger, *Dark Vanishings*, 4.

12 Robin Hyde, *Wednesday's Children* (1937; repr. Auckland: New Women's, 1989), 130. Hereafter references in the text.

13 All biographical information drawn from *The Book of Iris: A Life of Robin Hyde* (Auckland: Auckland UP, 2002), by Wilkinson's son Derek Challis and friend Gloria Rawlinson.

14 It is likely that she committed suicide. She had recently arrived in London, looking, like so many of her white settler peers, to establish herself with metropolitan and hence colonial audiences as a writer to be reckoned with. See Rachel Barrowman's *A Popular Vision: The Arts and the Left in New Zealand 1930–1950* (Wellington: Victoria UP, 1991); Murray, *Never a Soul at Home*; Mary Edmond-Paul, *Her Side of the Story: Readings of Mansfield, Mander & Hyde* (Dunedin: U of Otago P, 1999); Elleray, "Unsettled Subject"; and Lawrence Jones, *Picking up the Traces: The Making of a New Zealand Literary Culture 1932–1945* (Wellington: Victoria UP, 2003) for more on Robin Hyde's place in the literary culture of her day, and on New Zealand cultural production between the wars more generally; and Woollacott, *To Try Her Fortune in London* for more on settler women's experiences of the metropole.

15 Letter to John Schroder, 25 April 1937, qtd. in Challis and Rawlinson, 418.

16 Robin Hyde, *The Book of Nadath* (Auckland: Auckland UP, 1999), 3. Hereafter references in the text. See Michele Leggott's introduction for an account of the poem's complicated manuscript history.

17 Hyde told John Schroder, tongue-half-in-cheek, that "The Book of Nadath" was "written in verses like the Scripture, but I thought, much better" (letter to John Schroder, 25 April 1937, qtd. in Challis and Rawlinson, 418).

18 Virginia Woolf, "Thoughts on Peace during an Air-Raid," *Selected Essays* (1940; repr. Oxford: Oxford University Press, 2008), 217.

19 Lenore Davidoff et al., *The Family Story: Blood, Contract and Intimacy 1830–1960* (London: Longman, 1999), 222. See also Sue Thomas's discussion of the "amateur," and Alissa Karl's of the superfluous woman, in their work on *Voyage in the Dark*. Introduced in Dorothy Sayers's seventh Peter Wimsey novel *Strong Poison* (1930), Katharine Climpson's investigative bureau, which fronts as a typing agency and employs only women "of the class unkindly known as 'superfluous'" – widows, spinsters, women deserted by their husbands, divorced women, retired school-teachers, actresses, failed entrepreneurs, and "even a few Bright Young Things" – is very much of its time (49).

20 Ludovici, *Lysistrata*, 107.

21 M.H. Holcroft, "The Waiting Hills," in *Discovered Isles: A Trilogy* (1943; repr. Christchurch: Caxton, 1950), 132.

22 Sylvia Townsend Warner, *Lolly Willowes, Or the Loving Huntsman* (New York: Viking, 1926), 60. Hereafter references in the text.

23 In *Step-Daughters of England*, Jane Garrity convincingly argues that Lolly's witchy career reclaims "the community of the nation for the English lesbian" by queering nationalist discourses of place (162).

24 Edmond-Paul, *Her Side of the Story*, 172.

25 Ibid., 171.

26 Ibid., 173.

27 Robin Hyde, *A Home in This World* (Auckland: Longman, 1984), 10.

28 Elleray, "Unsettled Subject," 228.

29 Fleur Adcock, "Vigorous Designs," *Times Literary Supplement*, 2–8 February 1990, 123.

30 Susan Ash, "Critical Afterword," in *Wednesday's Children*, 295.

31 Daphne Patai, "Imagining Reality: The Utopian Fiction of Katherine Burdekin," in *Rediscovering Forgotten Radicals: British Women Writers, 1889–1939*, ed. Daphne Patai and Angela Ingram (Chapel Hill: U of North Carolina P, 1993), 227; emphasis in original.

32 David Harvey, *Spaces of Hope* (Berkeley: U of California P, 2000), 17.

33 Jacqueline Rose, *States of Fantasy* (Oxford: Clarendon, 1996), 5.

34 Benedict Anderson, *Imagined Communities: Reflections on the Origin and Spread of Nationalism* (London: Verso, 1991), 6.

35 Benedict Anderson, *The Spectre of Comparisons: Nationalism, Southeast Asia, and the World* (London: Verso, 1998), 334.

36 Anderson, *Imagined Communities*, 36.
37 Jonathan Culler, "Anderson and the Novel," *Diacritics* 29, no. 4 (1999): 37.
38 Ibid.
39 See I.H. Kawharu, "Mana and the Crown: A Marae at Orakei," in *Waitangi: Māori and Pākehā Perspectives of the Treaty of Waitangi*, ed. I.H. Kawharu (Auckland: Oxford UP, 1989), 211–33, for a more detailed account of Ngāti Whātua's struggle to retain and then regain tangata whenua status at Ōrākei.
40 Lee qtd. in Challis and Rawlinson 439; letter to Lee, 18 August 1937, qtd. in Challis and Rawlinson 439.
41 Letter to Lee, 18 August 1937, qtd. in Challis and Rawlinson, 439.
42 Letter to Lee, 18 August 1937, qtd. in Challis and Rawlinson, 440. In 1840, the Treaty of Waitangi/te Tiriti o Waitangi was signed by Lieutenant Governor William Hobson (on behalf of Queen Victoria) and over 500 Māori rangatira (chiefs). Among the many critical accounts of the Treaty/te Tiriti and its significance for Māori, Pākehā, and Māori-Pākehā relations, both historically and in the present, see Claudia Orange, *The Treaty of Waitangi* (North Sydney: Allen & Unwin, 1987) and *Waitangi*, the collection of essays edited by Kawharu.
43 Butler, *Frames of War*, 22.
44 Marks, *Toni Morrison's* Beloved, 2.
45 Brantlinger, *Dark Vanishings*, 4. See *Dark Vanishings* and Russell McGregor, *Imagined Destinies* for more on different articulations of the "doomed race" or "fatal impact" theory.
46 James Belich, *Making Peoples: A History of the New Zealanders from Polynesian Settlement to the End of the Nineteenth Century* (Honolulu: U of Hawai'i P, 2002), 174.
47 Robin Hyde, "Prayer for a New People," in *Young Knowledge: The Poems of Robin Hyde*, ed. Michele Leggott (Auckland: Auckland UP, 2003), 265.
48 We might contrast the settler's necrophilic conception of indigeneity with the rather different conception suggested by the multifaceted Māori word whenua, which means "placenta" and "land." Following the birth of a child, the placenta is traditionally buried in the land of which she and her family are tangata whenua.
49 Dana Luciano, *Arranging Grief: Sacred Time and the Body in Nineteenth-Century America* (New York: New York UP, 2007), 72; Brantlinger, *Dark Vanishings*, 62.
50 Marks, *Toni Morrison's* Beloved, 2.
51 Nicholas Thomas, *Possessions: Indigenous Art/Colonial Culture* (London: Thames and Hudson, 1999), 12.
52 Jane Stafford and Mark Williams, *Maoriland: New Zealand Literature 1872–1914* (Wellington: Victoria UP, 2006), 11.
53 Jessie Mackay, *The Spirit of the Rangatira and Other Ballads* (Melbourne: George Robertson, 1889), n.p.

54 Robin Kearns and Lawrence Berg, "Proclaiming Place: Towards a Geography of Place Name Pronunciation," *Social & Cultural Geography* 3, no. 3 (2002): 285.
55 Paraphrased in Sinclair, *A Destiny Apart*, 208.
56 Elsdon Best, *Tuhoe: Children of the Mist* (1925; repr. Wellington: Reed, 1972). See Te Miringa Hohaia, ed., *Parihaka: The Art of Resistance* (Wellington: City Gallery Wellington/Victoria UP, 2001); Dick Scott, *Ask That Mountain: The Story of Parihaka* (Auckland: Raupo, 2008); and Hazel Riseborough, *Days of Darkness: Taranaki, 1878–1884* (Wellington: Allen & Unwin, 1989) for more on the atrocities at Parihaka.
57 Māoritanga is among the words Māori use to describe themselves as a people. The online Māori Dictionary (http://www.maoridictionary.co.nz/) defines Māoritanga as "Māori culture, practices and beliefs."
58 Letter to Downie Stewart, March 1937, qtd. in Challis and Rawlinson, 403. Indeed, the struggle she joined briefly and self-consciously in 1937 would bear fruit decades later when, following the high-profile occupation of Bastion Point in Auckland, the New Zealand government recognized Ngāti Whātua authority at Ōrākei.
59 Brantlinger, *Dark Vanishings*, 4; Jacques Derrida, *Specters of Marx*, 120.

Chapter 5: Shrunk in the (White)wash

1 Schoen, *Choice and Coercion*, 143.
2 Cogdell, *Eugenic Design*, xiv.
3 Haraway, *Modest Witness*, 313.
4 Nikolas Rose, *The Politics of Life Itself: Biomedicine, Power, and Subjectivity in the Twenty-First Century* (Princeton: Princeton UP, 2007), 133.
5 Martin Amis, qtd. in Ginny Dougary, "The Voice of Experience," *The Times*, 9 September 2006.
6 Matt Carr, "You are now entering Eurabia," *Race & Class* 48, no. 1 (2006): 2–3. The neologism "Eurabia," Carr explains, was coined by Gisele Litmann, an Egyptian-born Briton who now lives in Switzerland, where she writes under the pseudonym Bat Ye'or, or "Daughter of the Nile." Litmann's "Eurabia is a consciously designed political project, whose seeds were sown in the European Community's establishment, at the height of the 1973 oil crisis, of the Euro-Arab Dialogue (EAD), a long-term program initially conceived by France and intended to forge closer political, cultural, and economic links between Europe and the Arab world"; commentators have since adopted the term to "describe the Islamicized culture that is supposedly emerging from the ruins of 'post-Christian' Europe" (Carr 6).
7 Niall Ferguson, "The Origins of the Great War of 2007 – and How It Could Have Been Prevented," *Daily Telegraph*, 15 January 2007.

8 Ibid.

9 Enoch Powell, speech, Conservative Association Meeting, Birmingham, 20 April 1968, repr. at http://www.telegraph.co.uk/comment/3643823/Enoch-Powells-Rivers-of-Blood-speech.html. All subsequent references to this speech cite this reprint.

10 Paul, *Whitewashing Britain*, 178. See also Stuart Hall et al., *Policing the Crisis: Mugging, the State, and Law and Order* (New York: Holmes & Meier, 1978), 245ff.

11 See, for example, David Starkey's 12 August 2011 appearance on BBC Two's current affairs program Newsnight to discuss the London riots, during which he described Enoch Powell's "prophesy" as "absolutely right in one sense. The Tiber did not foam with blood but flames lambent, they wrapped around Tottenham and wrapped around Clapham" (Ben Quinn, "David Starkey Claims 'the Whites Have Become Black,'" *The Guardian*, 13 August 2011). See also Denys Blakeway's film *Rivers of Blood*, made for BBC Two's 2008 "White Season."

12 Carr, "You Are Now Entering Eurabia," 15.

13 Ibid., 2.

14 Ferguson, "The Origins of the Great War of 2007."

15 Kathryn Joyce, "Review: Demographic Winter: The Decline of the Human Family," *Harvard Divinity Bulletin*, Spring 2008 (article accessed through the author's website, http://www.kathrynjoyce.wordpress.com/).

16 In light of such returns, I am currently working on an essay that investigates the reproducibility of discourse, the circulation, or transmission, of tropes trans-historically. What does it mean that interwar and twenty-first-century jeremiads about the need to defend the body politic against a variety of "enemies at the gate" so closely resemble one another as to be in some cases interchangeable? What are the mechanisms by which such repetitions are achieved?

17 Baucom, *Out of Place*, 12; emphasis in original.

18 Edward Shils qtd. in Spencer R. Weart, *Nuclear Fear: A History of Images* (Cambridge: Harvard UP, 1988), 106.

19 Odd Arne Westad, *The Global Cold War: Third World Interventions and the Making of Our Times* (Cambridge: Cambridge UP, 2005), 3.

20 Ibid., 3.

21 Michael Graham Fry, "Britain, France, and the Cold War," in *The End of Empire: The Transformation of the USSR in Comparative Perspective*, ed. Karen Dawisha and Bruce Parrott (Armonk: M.E. Sharpe, 1997), 123.

22 Westad, *The Global Cold War*, 5.

23 Christopher Priest, *Fugue for a Darkening Island* (London: Faber & Faber, 1972), 49. Hereafter references in the text.

24 Alex Garland, *28 Days Later: Screenplay* (London: Faber & Faber, 2002), vii. Hereafter references in the text.

25 William Golding's *Lord of the Flies* (1954), in which nuclear catastrophe turns a group of British boys into a pack of murderous castaways, and the post-nuclear disaster novels *Ape and Essence* (Aldous Huxley, 1948), *The Chrysalids* (John Wyndham, 1955), and *On the Beach*, in which only the Antipodes persist to shelter (for a time) Euro-American civilization, offer further evidence of this apocalyptic turn in the island adventure narrative.

26 Kirsten Ostherr employs the term "contagion-cam" to describe the "disembodied point-of-view shot[s]" to track in extreme close-up "specks of contagion" as these move from host to host (*Cinematic Prophylaxis: Globalization and Contagion in the Discourse of World Health* [Durham: Duke UP, 2005], 187–8). See, for instance, the movie-theatre contagion sequence in *Outbreak* (1995).

27 Ostherr, *Cinematic Prophylaxis*, 180.

28 Richard Preston, "Crisis in the Hot Zone," *New Yorker*, 26 October 1992, 68.

29 Priscilla Wald, *Contagious: Cultures, Carriers, and the Outbreak Narrative* (Durham: Duke UP, 2008), 45.

30 *28 Days Later*, dir. Danny Boyle, screenplay by Alex Garland (2002; Twentieth Century Fox, 2007), DVD. All citations from the film, unless otherwise noted.

31 Hereafter I refer to the comic book as *The Aftermath*.

32 Rather than chapters, *The Aftermath* is divided into "stages" ("Development," "Outbreak," "Decimation," "Quarantine"), suggesting once again a queasy likeness between communicative media (here a comic book) and communicable disease.

33 Baucom, *Out of Place*, 23.

34 Qtd. in Paul, *Whitewashing Britain*, 131.

35 Thatcher, qtd. in Anthony M. Messina, *Race and Party Competition in Britain* (Oxford: Clarendon, 1989), 122.

36 Ahmed, *The Cultural Politics of Emotions*, 46.

37 Trimble, "Undead Ends," 95.

38 Alex Garland, *28 Days Later* (London: Faber & Faber, 2002), vii. Hereafter all references in the text. Since 2002, the canon of Dead films has grown significantly, with Romero contributing new entries entitled *Land of the Dead* (2005), *Diary of the Dead* (2008), and *Survival of the Dead* (2009), and other directors remaking *Dawn of the Dead* (2004) and *Day of the Dead* (2008).

39 Trimble, "Undead Ends," 102.

40 Meillassoux, qtd. in Patterson, *Slavery and Social Death*, 38.

41 See Patricia Chu's reading of *White Zombie* in her *Race, Nationalism and the State*, as well as Carole Pateman's classic book *The Sexual Contract* (Stanford: Stanford UP, 1988) for more on the relationship between the sexual and social contracts.

42 Jean Comaroff and John Comaroff, "Alien-Nation: Zombies, Immigrants, and Millennial Capitalism," *South Atlantic Quarterly* 101, no. 4 (2002): 789, 793.

43 Sara Ahmed, *The Promise of Happiness* (Durham: Duke UP, 2010), 68.

44 Wald, *Contagious*, 47.
45 E.P. Thompson, "The Moral Economy of the English Crowd in the Eighteenth Century," *Past and Present* 50, no. 1 (February 1971): 76.
46 This pronouncement is daubed on the wall of the church into which Jim, seeking information and solace, stumbles early in *28 Days Later*.
47 Qtd. in Adam Nagourney, "Hillary Clinton Seeks Uniform Sex and Violence Rating for a Range of Media," *New York Times*, 22 December 1999.
48 Wald, *Contagious*, 12.
49 Ibid.
50 Ibid.
51 Qtd. in Randy Shilts, *And the Band Played On* (New York: Penguin, 1987), 322.
52 Kathryn Bond Stockton, "Prophylactics and Brains: *Beloved* in the Cybernetic Age of AIDS," *Studies in the Novel* 28, no. 3 (1996): 435.
53 Mary Jacobus, *First Things: The Maternal Imaginary in Literature, Art, and Psychoanalysis* (New York: Routledge, 1995), 105.
54 Stockton, "Prophylactics and Brains, 435.
55 Recently, in *Survival of the Dead* especially, Romero seems to have begun to play with the idea that zombies might in fact not only achieve, but deserve, survivance qua zombies. This is a point to which I will return in my discussion of *28 Weeks Later*, the sequel to *28 Days Later*, in the Coda.
56 Eve Kosofsky Sedgwick, *Epistemology of the Closet* (Berkeley: U California P, 1990), 128.
57 Ibid., 130.
58 Ahmed, *The Cultural Politics of Emotions*, 46.
59 Elana Gomel, "The Plague of Utopias: Pestilence and the Apocalyptic Body," *Twentieth Century Literature* 46, no. 4 (Winter 2000): 405.
60 Powell, in contrast, proposes deportation as a solution to the problem of an over-fertile, illegitimately disgruntled, threatening "immigrant" population, not unaware that this must be a "difficult" and "unpopular" course of action for the government to undertake. Even the most committed Eurabianists have felt it necessary to distance themselves from the actions of Anders Behring Breivik, the Norwegian who, on 22 July 2011, murdered seventy-seven people in protest against what he perceived as the ongoing Islamification and feminization of Europe.
61 Brian Aldiss, *The Billion Year Spree: The True History of Science Fiction* (Garden City: Doubleday, 1973), 294.
62 John Wyndham, *The Day of the Triffids* (London: Michael Joseph, 1951), 96. Hereafter references in the text.
63 Danny Boyle and Alex Garland, "Alternate Theatrical Ending," commentary on *28 Days Later* DVD.
64 Ibid.

65 Ibid.
66 Povinelli, *The Empire of Love*, 189–90.
67 See, for example, *The Midwich Cuckoos* (1957; repr. London: Michael Joseph, 1986).
68 Danny Boyle and Alex Garland, *28 Days Later*, commentary.
69 See the chapters on "Organic England" in David Matless, *Landscape and Britishness* (London: Reaktion, 2001), as well as Raymond Williams, *The City and the Country* (New York: Oxford UP, 1975).
70 William Blake, "Jerusalem," from the preface to *Milton a Poem*, http://www.blakearchive.org.
71 Patrick Sharp, "Space, Future War, and the Frontier in American Nuclear Apocalypse Narrative," in Gary Westfahl, ed., *Space and Beyond: The Frontier Theme in Science Fiction* (Westport: Greenwood P, 2000), 151.
72 Gomel, "The Plague of Utopias," 405.
73 Jacques Derrida, "Faith and Knowledge: The Two Sources of 'Religion' at the Limits of Reason Alone," in *Acts of Religion*, trans. Gil Anidjar (Stanford: Stanford UP, 1998), 82.
74 Ahmed, *The Cultural Politics of Emotions*, 42–3.
75 Indeed, "Love Britain" is one of the BNP's current slogans.
76 Sedgwick, *Epistemology of the Closet*, 129.
77 Ahmed, *The Cultural Politics of Emotions*, 2; 4.
78 Hage, *White Nation*, 225–6.
79 Ahmed, *The Cultural Politics of Emotions*, 43.
80 Westad, *The Global Cold War*, 5.
81 Jen Hill, *White Horizon: The Arctic in the Nineteenth-Century Imagination* (Albany: SUNY P, 2007), 29.
82 Boyle and Garland's third film, *Sunshine* (2007), takes place on a spaceship whose crew has been tasked with reigniting the sun. Although the crew is wiped out through a series of accidents, suicides, and murders orchestrated by the maddened captain of another ship, they succeed in carrying out their mission, saving the Earth from permanent solar winter. Intriguingly, Boyle has compared *Sunshine* to *Apocalypse Now*, as a journey to "the heart of lightness" that is nonetheless rather like Coppola's "journey to the heart of darkness," suggesting that the film (which also stars Cillian Murphy, as *28 Days Later* was to have starred Leonardo DiCaprio) offers yet another turn on the themes running through *The Beach* and *28 Days Later* (Boyle, qtd. in Kilian Melloy, "The Light and the Darkness: Danny Boyle on 'Sunshine,'" *Edge*, 21 July 2007, http://www.edgeptown.com).
83 Karl, "Rhys, Keynes, and the Modern(ist) Economic Nation," 440.
84 Paul, *Whitewashing Britain*, 134.
85 Ibid., 116.

86 Qtd. ibid., 166. The 1925 Special Restriction (Coloured Alien Seamen) Order similarly worked to link colour with alien-ness, even if non-white British subjects were officially excluded from its remit.

87 Commonwealth Immigrants Act 1968, Elizabeth II Ch. 9, Section 1.

88 Baucom, *Out of Place*, 8. See also Paul, *Whitewashing Britain*.

89 Paul, *Whitewashing Britain*, 181.

90 Esty, *A Shrinking Island*, 5.

91 Given that the "shrinking" of Britain has been undertaken concurrently with the emergence of popular nationalist-devolutionist movements in Scotland and Wales, as well as Northern Ireland's problematization as a site of "trouble," one might well ask which regions of the Atlantic archipelago the project of particularization ultimately encompasses. Although I am not in a position to offer a definitive answer here, my suspicion is that it depends, sometimes taking shape as a commitment to Englishness specifically, sometimes encoding a transregional, even transnational conception of Britishness that incorporates some or all of the constituent parts of what is still called the United Kingdom of Great Britain and Northern Ireland. Like Selena's blackness, Jim's Irishness, largely a consequence of his portrayal by the Irish actor Cillian Murphy (how, one wonders, would Boyle have directed Leonard DiCaprio to play Jim if he had been able to secure the actor for the part as he desired?), complicates my reading of *28 Days Later* as invested in logics of insularity and English particularism. Linking Jim and Selena's survival with that of the white English child Hannah (her father Frank is played by the Irish actor Brendan Gleeson, who does not, however, use his Irish accent in the role), the film develops a vision of Englishness that can accommodate, even must accommodate, (ostensibly) non-English bodies so long as they manifest those domestic values the film codes as essentially English, so long, that is, as they participate in its "inward turn." However, in other post-war speculative and post-apocalyptic fictions, including films like *The Wicker Man* (1973) and *Doomsday* (2008), the "Celtic fringe" is a site of horror to precisely the extent that it harbours primitive survivals.

92 Nick Griffin, "Introduction," in *Democracy, Freedom, Culture and Identity: British National Party General Elections Manifesto 2010* (Welshpool: British National Party, 2010), 12. The manifesto is available online, through the BNP's official website (www.bnp.org.uk).

93 Oakley, "All Indigenous People Have Right to Avoid Colonisation, Wolverhampton BNP Told."

94 Blurbs for the book (see, for example, an article by Alan Robertson on the official BNP website entitled "Britain: A Nation of Immigrants?") incorporate passages from the UN Declaration on the Rights of Indigenous Peoples (http://www.un.org/esa/socdev/unpfii/documents/DRIPS_en.pdf), very slightly altered.

95 In a recent article, Anne-Marie Fortier shows just how much work is involved in articulating British indigeneity with whiteness (and rurality) through an analysis of the 2007 Channel 4 series *Face of Britain*, which I discuss in more detail in the conclusion to this chapter. See her "Genetic Indigenisation in 'The People of the British Isles,'" *Science as Culture* 21, no. 2 (2012), for more on the documentary.
96 Alice Te Punga Somerville, "The Lingering War Captain: Maori Texts, Indigenous Contexts," *Journal of New Zealand Literature* 24, no. 2 (2007), 24.
97 Gilroy, *Postcolonial Melancholia*, 101; emphasis in original.
98 Michael Walzer, *Spheres of Justice: A Defense of Pluralism and Equality* (New York: Basic Books, 1983), 31.
99 Paul, *Whitewashing Britain*, 178.
100 Fortier, "Genetic Indigenisation," 157–8.
101 Bodmer, qtd. in Fortier, "Genetic Indigenisation," 160; ibid., 160–1. The promotional material that accompanies the DVD of *Face of Britain* (WAG TV, 2008) heralds the program as a "Genetic Domesday Book."
102 Esty, *A Shrinking Island*, 39.
103 Sarah Lyall, "A Five-Ring Opening Circus, Weirdly and Unabashedly British," *New York Times*, 27 July 2012.
104 Gilroy, *Postcolonial Melancholia*, 3.
105 Martin Kelner, "Thrusting Young Nation Goes Ice Todger Mad as Vancouver Olympics Open," *The Guardian*, 15 February 2010.
106 Qtd. in Fortier, "Genetic Indigenisation," 154. However, the BNP is neither the only nor even the first white supremacist organization to make use of the language of indigeneity to package its demands. I have begun to explore this genealogy elsewhere.

Envoi

1 Ahmed, *Queer Phenomenology*, 41.
2 Roger I. Simon, *The Touch of the Past: Remembrance, Learning, and Ethics* (New York: Palgrave Macmillan, 2005), 4.
3 Ibid., 8.
4 Ibid., 9.
5 Marianne Hirsch, "The Generation of Postmemory," *Poetics Today* 29, no. 1 (Spring 2008): 104.
6 Roger I. Simon, "The Paradoxical Practice of *Zakhor*: Memories of 'What Has Never Been My Fault or Deed,'" in *Between Hope and Despair: Pedagogy and the Remembrance of Historical Trauma*, ed. Roger I. Simon, Sharon Rosenberg, and Claudia Eppert (Lanham: Rowman & Littlefield, 2000), 9.
7 Deane, qtd. in *Bringing Them Home*, chapter 1 ("The Inquiry").

8 Ahmed, *The Cultural Politics of Emotions*, 102.
9 Ibid., 102.
10 See, among others, his *Settler Colonialism and the Transformation of Anthropology*, 2.
11 Juan Carlos Fresnadillo and Enrique López Lavigne, *28 Weeks Later* (Twentieth Century Fox, 2007), DVD, commentary.
12 Ibid.
13 Intriguingly, Daniel Trilling opens his 2012 history of the rise of the far right in Britain, *Bloody Nasty People* (London: Verso, 2012), with a discussion of the notorious 1993 campaign that resulted in the election of BNP candidate Derek Beackon to represent the Isle of Dogs area of Millwall on the Tower Hamlets London Borough Council. Drawing attention to the Isle of Dogs' history as a "crossroads of empire," Trilling links the BNP's appeal to the devastating economic effects of the slowdown in shipping that eventually closed the West India Docks in 1980, after 178 years of service, combined with the Thatcher government's decision to redevelop the Isle of Dogs as "a world financial centre, focused on Canary Wharf" (13; 15).
14 Edelman, *No Future*, 16; emphasis in original.
15 Catherine Waldby, *AIDS and the Body Politic: Biomedicine and Sexual Difference* (London: Routledge, 1996), 70–1.
16 Trimble, "Undead Ends," 132; Geddes Smith, *Plague on Us* (New York: Commonwealth Fund, 1941), 141.
17 Derrida, *Specters of Marx*, 219.
18 Stoler, *Race and the Education of Desire*, 133.
19 Ahmed, *Queer Phenomenology*, 127.
20 Ibid., 127.
21 Ibid., 123.
22 Françoise Vergès, *Monsters and Revolutionaries: Colonial Family Romance and Métissage* (Durham: Duke UP, 1999), 9.
23 Trimble, "Undead Ends," 133; italics in original.
24 Elizabeth Grosz, *Volatile Bodies: Toward a Corporeal Feminism* (Bloomington: Indiana UP, 1994), 148–9.
25 Karl Marx, "The Eighteenth Brumaire of Louis Bonaparte," in *Later Political Writings* (Cambridge: Cambridge UP, 1996), 32; Ahmed, *Queer Phenomenology*, 125; emphasis in original.
26 Stacy Alaimo and Susan Hekman, "Introduction: Emerging Models of Materiality in Feminist Theory," in *Material Feminisms*, ed. Stacy Alaimo and Susan Hekman (Bloomington: Indiana UP, 2008), 8.
27 But see Adriana Petryna's *Life Exposed: Biological Citizens after Chernobyl* (Princeton: Princeton UP, 2002) for an account of the way in which, in a Ukraine devastated by the 1986 nuclear disaster at the Chernobyl nuclear reactor, diagnoses

of Acute Radiation Syndrome (ARS) have become counters in struggles over access to the material and emotional or psychological resources of (full) citizenship. Not only can diagnoses of ARS be purchased, but ARS has (at different times and according to different measures) been alternately under- and over-diagnosed.

28 Grosz, *Volatile Bodies*, 9.

29 Michel Foucault, "Nietzsche, Genealogy, History," in *Language, Counter-Memory, Practice: Selected Essays and Interviews*, ed. D.F. Bouchard (Ithaca: Cornell UP, 1977), 162.

30 Michel Foucault, *"Society Must Be Defended," Lectures at the Collège de France, 1975–76*, trans. David Macey (New York: Picador, 2003), 8.

31 Weinbaum, *Wayward Reproductions*, 45; Foucault, "Nieztsche, Genealogy, History," 145.

32 Foucault, "Nietzsche, Genealogy, History," 147.

33 Ibid., 162.

34 Eric Santner, *Stranded Objects: Mourning, Memory, and Film in Postwar Germany* (Ithaca: Cornell UP, 1990), 29; italics in original.

35 Ibid., 19.

36 Stuart Hall, "Minimal Selves," in *Black British Cultural Studies: A Reader*, ed. Houston Baker et al. (Chicago: U of Chicago P, 1996), 115.

37 Foucault, "Nietzsche, Genealogy, History," 164.

Bibliography

Archival Material

Aotearoa New Zealand

TE RUA MAHARA O TE KĀWANATANGA / ARCHIVES NEW ZEALAND

ABQU 632 Accession W4452, Box 18 5/12/3: Abortion Back Papers Pre-1940

H1 131/139/14: Septic Abortion: Committee of Inquiry: Report

H1 131/139/15: Septic Abortion: Committee of Inquiry: Evidence

H1 131/139/16: Abortion – Recommendations Arising out of the Committee's Report, 1937–1945

Australia

NATIONAL ARCHIVES OF AUSTRALIA

A1/14 1930/1542: Northern Territory – "Visit of Sir Baldwin Spencer to Northern Territory re Natives at Alice Springs" [Stuart and Hermannsburg mission station]

A1/15 1928/10743: Dr W.D. Walker, Report on Aborigines, Northern Australia

A1/15 1932/4262: Proposed Model Aboriginal State

A1/15 1932/10562: Northern Territory, Annual Report, 1931–1932

A1/15 1933/479: Apprentices (Half-Castes) Regulations Nth Aus/a and Centl Aus/a

A1/15 1933/3589: Sterilization of Mental Defectives, N.T.

A1/15 1934/8957: Northern Territory, Annual Report, 1933–1934

A1/15 1935/6731: Northern Territory, Annual Report, 1934–1935

A1/15 1935/10753: T.T. Willis re Marriage to Halfcaste

A1/15 1936/3096: (Mrs) C. Odegaard. (1) Classification as an Aboriginal. (2) Proposed Retention of Daughter in Aboriginal Compound

A1/15 1936/6595: Association for Protection of Native Races

A1/15 1937/70: Government Policy with regard to Aboriginals in the Northern Territory
A1/15 1937/13715: Northern Territory, Annual Report, 1936–1937
A1/15 1938/329: Wages of Aboriginals and Half-Castes, Northern Territory
A431 1946/3026: Dr Cook, Suggested Aboriginal Protection Policy, NT
A452 1952/420: Northern Territory, Transfer of Quadroon and Octoroon Children to Institutions in Southern States
A452 1952/543: NT – Reports of Director of Native Affairs on Policy for Aboriginals and Half-Castes
A461/7 D300/1: Aborigines and Half-Castes, North and Central Australia. Report by J.W. Bleakley
A659 42/1/173: Mrs Daisy M. Bates, Aboriginal Manuscripts
A659 1939/1/15580: Half Caste home, Darwin
A659 1940/1/408: Marriage of White Men to Half-Caste Women
A659 1940/1/1781: NT Annual Report, 1938–1939
A659 1942/1/8104: Conference of Commonwealth and State Aboriginal Authorities, Canberra, April 1937
A4640/32: Report of the Inter-Imperial Relations Committee of the Imperial Conference, 1926

NATIONAL LIBRARY OF AUSTRALIA

MS 758 Series 3: Xavier Herbert, Correspondence
MS 2004 Series 7 203–230: Bessie Rischbieth Papers
MS 2004 Series 12 1–303: Bessie Rischbieth Papers
MS 2004 Series 12 304–519: Bessie Rischbieth Papers
MS 5068 Series 11, Box 10 (Folder 11/2): Duguid Papers, Material from Mrs Bennett

STATE LIBRARY OF NEW SOUTH WALES

Mitchell Library MSS 4545/2: Eleanor Dark Papers

United Kingdom

NATIONAL ARCHIVES

FCO 50/431: Policy concerning control of immigration from Commonwealth into UK under Commonwealth Immigration Act of 1971
HO 144/2685: BYWATERS, Frederick and THOMPSON, Edith Convicted at Central Criminal Court (CCC) on 11 December 1922 for murder and sentenced to death
MH 71/21–27: Interdepartmental Committee on Abortion

WELLCOME LIBRARY FOR THE HISTORY AND UNDERSTANDING OF MEDICINE

PP/MCS A322: Marie Stopes Papers, Correspondence in Response to *John Bull* Articles

Print Sources

Adcock, Fleur. "Vigorous Designs." *Times Literary Supplement*, 2–8 February 1990: 2–8. Print.

Ahmed, Sara. "Introduction to Feminist Genealogies." Feminist Genealogies Workshop. Goldsmiths College, London, 11 May 2012.

Ahmed, Sara. *The Cultural Politics of Emotion*. New York: Routledge, 2004. Print.

Ahmed, Sara. *The Promise of Happiness*. Durham: Duke UP, 2010. Print.

Ahmed, Sara. *Queer Phenomenology: Orientations, Objects, Others*. Durham: Duke UP, 2006. Print.

Ahmed, Sara. *Strange Encounters: Embodied Others in Post-Coloniality*. London: Routledge, 2000. Print.

Alaimo, Stacy, and Susan Hekman. "Introduction: Emerging Models of Materiality in Feminist Theory." *Material Feminisms*. Ed. Stacy Alaimo and Susan Hekman. Bloomington: Indiana UP, 2008. 1–19. Print.

Aldiss, Brian. *The Billion Year Spree: The True History of Science Fiction*. Garden City: Doubleday, 1973. Print.

Alexander, M. Jacqui. "Not Just Any (Body) Can Be a Citizen: The Politics of Law, Sexuality and Postcoloniality in Trinidad and Tobago and the Bahamas." *Feminist Review* 48 (1994): 5–23. http://dx.doi.org/10.1057/fr.1994.39.

Alexie, Sherman. "The Farm." *The Raven Chronicles*, March 1997. http://www.ravenchronicles.org/raven/rvback/issues/0397/Alexie.htm.

Alexie, Sherman. "The Sin Eaters." *The Toughest Indian in the World*. New York: Atlantic Monthly P, 2000. 76–120. Print.

Amato, Sarah. "The White Elephant in London: An Episode of Trickery, Racism and Advertising." *Journal of Social History* 43, no. 1 (2009): 31–66. http://dx.doi.org/10.1353/jsh.0.0234.

Anderson, Benedict. *Imagined Communities: Reflections on the Origin and Spread of Nationalism*. London: Verso, 1991. Print.

Anderson, Benedict. *The Spectre of Comparisons: Nationalism, Southeast Asia, and the World*. London: Verso, 1998. Print.

Anderson, Warwick. *The Cultivation of Whiteness: Science, Health and Racial Destiny in Australia*. Carlton: Melbourne UP, 2003. Print.

Anderson, Warwick. "Geography, Race and Nation: Remapping 'Tropical' Australia, 1890–1930." *Historical Records of Australian Science* 11, no. 4 (1997): 457–68. http://dx.doi.org/10.1071/HR9971140457.

Angier, Carole. *Jean Rhys: Life and Work*. Boston: Little, Brown and Company, 1990. Print.

Appadurai, Arjun. "Putting Hierarchy in Its Place." *Cultural Anthropology* 3, no. 1 (1988): 36–49. http://dx.doi.org/10.1525/can.1988.3.1.02a00040.

Ariès, Phillipe. *Centuries of Childhood: A Social History of Family Life*. Trans. Robert Baldick. New York: Knopf, 1962. Print.

Ash, Susan. "Critical Afterword." *Wednesday's Children*. By Robin Hyde. 1937. Auckland: New Women's, 1989. 289–95. Print.

Ashforth, Adam. *The Politics of Official Discourse in Twentieth Century South Africa*. Oxford: Clarendon, 1990. Print.

Atkinson, Laurie. "Implausible Leap of Faith Required." Review of *and what remains*, by Miria George. City Gallery, Wellington. *Dominion Post*, 30 August 2006. Print.

Attewell, Nadine. "Reading Closely: Writing (and) Family History in Kim Scott's Benang." *Postcolonial Text* 7, no. 3 (2012): n.p. Web.

Attewell, Nadine. "No Alternative? Robin Hyde and the Politics of Loss." *Lighted Windows: Critical Essays on Robin Hyde*. Ed. Mary Edmond-Paul. Dunedin: U of Otago P, 2008. 53–66. Print.

Attwood, Bain, ed. *In the Age of Mabo: History, Aborigines and Australia*. St Leonards: Allen & Unwin, 1996. Print.

Attwood, Bain, and Andrew Markus. *Thinking Black: William Cooper and the Australian Aborigines' League*. Canberra: Aboriginal Studies P, 2004. Print.

Austin, Tony. *I Can Picture the Old Home So Clearly: The Commonwealth and "Half-caste" Youth in the Northern Territory 1911–1939*. Canberra: Aboriginal Studies P, 1993. Print.

Baird, Barbara, and Damien Riggs, eds. *The Racial Politics of Bodies, Nations and Knowledges*. Newcastle upon Tyne: Cambridge Scholars Publishing, 2009. Print.

Ballantyne, J.W. "An Address on the Nature of Pregnancy and Its Practical Bearings." *British Medical Journal* no. 2772 (14 February 1914): 349–55. Print.

Banner, Stuart. *Possessing the Pacific: Land, Settlers, and Indigenous People from Australia to Alaska*. Cambridge: Harvard UP, 2007. Print.

Banton, Michael. *Racial Theories*. Cambridge: Cambridge UP, 1998. http://dx.doi.org/10.1017/CBO9780511583407.

Barkan, Elazar. *The Retreat of Scientific Racism: Changing Concepts of Race in Britain and the United States between the World Wars*. Cambridge: Cambridge UP, 1992. Print.

Barrowman, Rachel. *A Popular Vision: The Arts and the Left in New Zealand 1930–1950*. Wellington: Victoria UP, 1991. Print.

Barthes, Roland. *Camera Lucida: Reflections on Photography*. Trans. Richard Howard. New York: Hill & Wang, 1981. Print.

Bashford, Alison. "Epilogue: Where Did Eugenics Go?" Bashford and Levine 539–558.

Bashford, Alison. "'Is White Australia Possible?' Race, Colonialism and Tropical Medicine." *Ethnic and Racial Studies* 23, no. 2 (2000): 248–71. http://dx.doi.org/10.1080/014198700329042.

Bashford, Alison, and Philippa Levine, eds. *The Oxford Handbook of the History of Eugenics*. Oxford: Oxford UP, 2010. http://dx.doi.org/10.1093/oxfordhb/9780195373141.001.0001.

Bates, Daisy. *The Passing of the Aborigines: A Lifetime Spent among the Natives of Australia*. 1938. London: John Murray, 1944. Print.

Baucom, Ian. *Out of Place: Englishness, Empire, and the Locations of Identity*. Princeton: Princeton UP, 1999. Print.

Baucom, Ian. *Specters of the Atlantic: Finance Capital, Slavery, and the Philosophy of History*. Durham: Duke UP, 2005. Print.

Bauman, Zygmunt. "Utopia with No Topos." *History of the Human Sciences* 16, no. 1 (2003): 11–25. http://dx.doi.org/10.1177/0952695103016001003.

Beer, Gillian. "Can the Native Return?" *Open Fields: Science in Cultural Encounter*. Oxford: Clarendon, 1996. 31–54. Print.

Beer, Gillian. "The Island and the Aeroplane: The Case of Virginia Woolf." *Virginia Woolf: The Common Ground*. Ann Arbor: U of Michigan P, 1996. 149–78. Print.

Beer, Gillian. "Island Bounds." Edmond and Smith 32–42. Print.

Beer, Gillian. "Writing Darwin's Islands: England and the Insular Condition." *Inscribing Science: Scientific Texts and the Materiality of Communication*. Ed. Timothy Lenoir. Stanford: Stanford UP, 1998. Print.

Behar, Michael. "Wish You Weren't Here." *The Observer*, 15 May 2005.

Belich, James. *Making Peoples: A History of the New Zealanders from Polynesian Settlement to the End of the Nineteenth Century*. Honolulu: U of Hawai'i P, 2002. Print.

Belich, James. *Paradise Reforged: A History of the New Zealanders from the 1880s to the Year 2000*. Honolulu: U of Hawai'i P, 2001. Print.

Belich, James. *Replenishing the Earth: The Settler Revolution and the Rise of the Anglo-World, 1783–1939*. Oxford: Oxford UP, 2009. Print.

Benítez-Rojo, Antonio. *The Repeating Island: The Caribbean and the Postmodern Perspective*. Trans. James E. Maraniss. Durham: Duke UP, 1992. Print.

Berlant, Lauren. *The Queen of America Goes to Washington City*. Durham: Duke UP, 1997. Print.

Best, Elsdon. *Tuhoe: The Children of the Mist*. 1925. Wellington: Reed, 1972. Print.

Beveridge, William. *Social Insurance and Allied Services*. London: HMSO, 1942. Print.

Bhabha, Homi. *The Location of Culture*. Abingdon: Routledge, 2004. Print.

Bhabha, Homi, ed. *Nation and Narration*. London: Routledge, 1990. Print.

Biolsi, Thomas. *Organizing the Lakota: The Political Economy of the New Deal on the Pine Ridge and Rosebud Reservations*. Tucson: U of Arizona P, 1992. Print.

Blakeway, Denys. "Rivers of Blood." BBC 2, 12 March 2008.

Boehm, Deborah. *Intimate Migrations: Gender, Family, and Illegality among Transnational Mexicans*. New York: New York UP, 2012. Print.

Boehmer, Elleke. *Empire, the National and the Postcolonial, 1890–1920: Resistance in Interaction*. Oxford: Oxford UP, 2003. Print.

Bongie, Chris. *Exotic Memories: Literature, Colonialism, and the Fin de Siècle*. Stanford: Stanford UP, 1991. Print.

Boucher, Leigh. "'Whiteness,' Geopolitical Reconfiguration, and the Settler Empire in Nineteenth-Century Victorian Politics." Boucher, Carey, and Ellinghaus 45–61. Print.

Boucher, Leigh, Jane Carey, and Katherine Ellinghaus, eds. *Re-Orienting Whiteness*. New York: Palgrave Macmillan, 2009. Print.

Boyle, Danny, dir. *The Beach*. 2000. Twentieth Century Fox, 2005. DVD.

Boyle, Danny, dir. *Sunshine*. 2007. Twentieth Century Fox, 2008. DVD.

Boyle, Danny, dir. *28 Days Later*. 2002. Twentieth Century Fox, 2007. DVD.

Brah, Avtar. *Cartographies of Diaspora: Contesting Identities*. New York: Routledge, 1996. Print.

Brand, Dionne. *At the Full and Change of the Moon*. Toronto: Alfred A. Knopf, 1999. Print.

Brand, Dionne. *In Another Place, Not Here*. New York: Grove, 1997. Print.

Brand, Dionne. *A Map to the Door of No Return*. Toronto: Doubleday Canada, 2001. Print.

Brantlinger, Patrick. *Dark Vanishings: Discourse on the Extinction of Primitive Races, 1800–1930*. Ithaca: Cornell UP, 2003. Print.

Brooke, Stephen. "'A New World for Women'?: Abortion Law Reform in Britain during the 1930s." *American Historical Review* 106, no. 2 (2001): 431–59. http://dx.doi.org/10.2307/2651613.

Brooke, Stephen. "Working-Class Women's Bodies: Bodies, Sexuality, and the 'Modernization' of the British Working Classes, 1920s to 1960s." *International Labor and Working Class History* 69 (2006): 104–22. Print.

Brookes, Barbara. *Abortion in England 1900–1967*. London: Croom Helm, 1988. Print.

Brookes, Martin. *Extreme Measures: The Dark Visions and Bright Ideas of Francis Galton*. New York: Bloomsbury, 2004. Print.

Brooks, Barbara, with Judith Clark. *Eleanor Dark: A Writer's Life*. Sydney: Macmillan, 1998. Print.

Brown, Paul. "'This thing of darkness I acknowledge mine': The Tempest and the Colonial Encounter." *Political Shakespeare: New Essays in Cultural Materialism*. Ed. Jonathan Dollimore and Alan Sinfield. Manchester: Manchester UP, 1985. 48–71. Print.

Burton, Antoinette. "Introduction: On the Inadequacy and Indispensability of the Nation." Burton 1–23.

Burton, Antoinette, ed. *After the Imperial Turn: Thinking with and through the Nation*. Durham: Duke UP, 2003. Print.

Butler, Judith. *Antigone's Claim: Kinship between Life and Death*. New York: Columbia UP, 2000. Print.

Butler, Judith. *Frames of War: When Is Life Grievable?* London: Verso, 2009. Print.

Butler, Judith. *Undoing Gender*. New York: Routledge, 2004. Print.

Buzard, James. *Disorienting Fiction: The Autoethnographic Work of Nineteenth-Century British Novels*. Princeton: Princeton UP, 2005. Print.

Buzard, James. "Mass-Observation, Modernism, and Auto-ethnography." *Modernism/Modernity* 4, no. 3 (1997): 93–122. http://dx.doi.org/10.1353/mod.1997.0042.

Byrd, Jodi A. *The Transit of Empire: Indigenous Critiques of Colonialism*. Minneapolis: U of Minnesota P, 2011. Print.

Cadava, Eduardo. *Words of Light: Theses on the Photography of History*. Princeton: Princeton UP, 1997. Print.

Cahan, David. "The Geopolitics and Architectural Design of a Metrological Laboratory: The Physikalisch-Technische Reichsanstalt in Imperial Germany." James 137–54.

Camiscioli, Elisa. *Reproducing the French Race: Immigration, Intimacy, and Embodiment in the Early Twentieth Century*. Durham: Duke UP, 2009. Print.

Campbell, Chloe. *Race and Empire: Eugenics in Colonial Kenya*. Manchester: Manchester UP, 2007. Print.

Carey, Jane. "'Women's Objective – A Perfect Race': Whiteness, Eugenics, and the Articulation of Race." Boucher, Carey, and Ellinghaus 183–98.

Carey, Jane, and Claire McLiskey, eds. *Creating White Australia*. Sydney: Sydney UP, 2009. Print.

Carpenter, Kevin. *Desert Isles and Pirate Islands: The Island Theme in Nineteenth-Century English Juvenile Fiction*. Frankfurt: Peter Lang, 1984. Print.

Carr, Matt. "You Are Now Entering Eurabia." *Race & Class* 48, no. 1 (2006): 1–22. http://dx.doi.org/10.1177/0306396806066636.

Césaire, Aimé. *A Tempest*. New York: TCG Productions, 2002. Print.

Challis, Derek, and Gloria Rawlinson. *The Book of Iris: A Life of Robin Hyde*. Auckland: Auckland UP, 2002. Print.

Chandrasekhar, Sripati. *"A dirty, filthy book": The Writings of Charles Knowlton and Annie Besant on Reproductive Physiology and Birth Control and an Account of the Bradlaugh-Besant Trial*. Berkeley: U of California P, 1981. Print.

Chartres, Annie Vivanti. *The Outrage*. New York: Knopf, 1918. Print.

Cheek, Pamela. *Sexual Antipodes: Enlightenment, Globalization and the Placing of Sex*. Stanford: Stanford UP, 2003. Print.

Chesterton, G.K. *Eugenics and Other Evils*. London: Cassel, 1922. Print.

Childs, Donald. *Modernism and Eugenics: Woolf, Eliot, Yeats, and the Culture of Degeneration*. Cambridge: Cambridge UP, 2001. http://dx.doi.org/10.1017/CBO9780511485022.

Chu, Patricia. *Race, Nationalism and the State in British and American Modernism.* Cambridge: Cambridge UP, 2006. http://dx.doi.org/10.1017/CBO9780511485039.

Ciolkowski, Laura E. "Navigating the Wide Sargasso Sea: Colonial History, English Fiction, and British Empire." *Twentieth Century Literature* 43, no. 3 (1997): 339–59. http://dx.doi.org/10.2307/441916.

Claeys, Gregory, ed. *The Cambridge Companion to Utopian Literature.* Cambridge: Cambridge UP, 2010. http://dx.doi.org/10.1017/CCOL9780521886659.

Clay, Diskin, and Andrea Purvis. "Introduction: Islands in the History of Greek Utopian Writing." *Four Island Utopias.* Ed. Diskin Clay and Andrea Purvis. Newburyport: Focus, 1999. Print.

Clayton, Daniel. *Islands of Truth: The Imperial Fashioning of Vancouver Island.* Vancouver: UBC P, 2000. Print.

Cody, Lisa Forman. *Birthing the Nation: Sex, Science, and the Conception of Eighteenth-Century Britons.* Oxford: Oxford UP, 2006. Print.

Cogdell, Christina. *Eugenic Design: Streamlining America in the 1930s.* Philadelphia: U of Pennsylvania P, 2004. Print.

Cohen, Cathy J. "Punks, Bulldaggers, and Welfare Queens: The Radical Potential of Queer Politics?" *GLQ* 3, no. 4 (1997): 437–65. Web.

Coleman, Daniel. *White Civility: The Literary Project of English Canada.* Toronto: U of Toronto P, 2008. Print.

Collins, Patricia Hill. "Shifting the Center: Race, Class, and Feminist Theorizing about Motherhood." *Mothering: Ideology, Experience, and Agency.* Ed. Evelyn Nakano Glenn et al. New York: Routledge, 1994. 45–65. Print.

Comaroff, Jean, and John Comaroff. "Alien-Nation: Zombies, Immigrants, and Millennial Capitalism." *South Atlantic Quarterly* 101, no. 4 (2002): 779–805. http://dx.doi.org/10.1215/00382876-101-4-779.

Connor, Michael. *The Invention of Terra Nullius: Historical and Legal Fictions on the Founding of Australia.* Paddington: Macleay, 2005. Print.

Conrad, Joseph. *Heart of Darkness.* 1902. New York: Norton, 2005. Print.

Cook, James W. *The Arts of Deception: Playing with Fraud in the Age of Barnum.* Cambridge: Harvard UP, 2001. Print.

Cooter, Roger. "Introduction." Cooter 1–18. Print.

Cooter, Roger, ed. *In the Name of the Child: Health and Welfare, 1880–1940.* London: Routledge, 1992. http://dx.doi.org/10.4324/9780203412237.

Cornell, Drucilla. *The Imaginary Domain: Abortion, Pornography & Sexual Harassment.* New York: Routledge, 1995. Print.

Cuarón, Alfonso, dir. *Children of Men.* 2006. Universal Studios, 2007. DVD.

Culler, Jonathan. "Anderson and the Novel." *Diacritics* 29, no. 4 (1999): 20–39. http://dx.doi.org/10.1353/dia.1999.0028.

Culler, Jonathan. *On Deconstruction: Theory and Criticism after Structuralism*. Ithaca: Cornell UP, 1982. Print.

Dark, Eleanor. *Prelude to Christopher*. 1934. Adelaide: Rigby, 1961. Print.

Davidoff, Leonore, Megan Doolittle, Janet Fink, et al., eds. *The Family Story: Blood, Contract and Intimacy 1830–1960*. London: Longman, 1999. Print.

Davies, Margaret Llewellyn, ed. *Maternity: Letters from Working Women*. London: Bell, 1915. Print.

Davin, Anna. "Imperialism and Motherhood." *History Workshop Journal* 5, no. 1 (1978): 9–66. http://dx.doi.org/10.1093/hwj/5.1.9.

Dawes, James. "Narrating Disease: AIDS, Consent, and the Ethics of Representation." *Social Text* 43 (1995): 27–44. http://dx.doi.org/10.2307/466625.

Dawson, Ashley. *Mongrel Nation: Diasporic Culture and the Making of Postcolonial Britain*. Ann Arbor: U of Michigan P, 2007. Print.

de Abruna, Laura Niesen. "Family Connections: Mother and Mother Country in the Fiction of Jean Rhys and Jamaica Kincaid." Nasta 257–89.

Deane, Vincent. "Bywaters and the Original Crime." *Finnegans Wake: "teems of times."* Ed. Andrew Treip. Amsterdam: Rodopi, 1994. 165–83. Print.

De Genova, Nicholas. "'Illegality' and Deportability in Everyday Life." *Annual Review of Anthropology* 31, no. 1 (2002): 419–47. http://dx.doi.org/10.1146/annurev.anthro.31.040402.085432.

De Genova, Nicholas. "The Legal Production of Mexican/Migrant 'Illegality.'" *Latino Studies* 2, no. 2 (2004): 160–85. http://dx.doi.org/10.1057/palgrave.lst.8600085.

De Genova, Nicholas. *Working the Boundaries: Race, Space, and "Illegality" in Mexican Chicago*. Durham: Duke UP, 2005. Print.

de Groen, Frances. *Xavier Herbert: A Biography*. St Lucia: U of Queensland P, 1998. Print.

DeLoughrey, Elizabeth. "'The litany of islands, the rosary of archipelagoes': Caribbean and Pacific Archipelagraphy." *Ariel* 32, no. 1 (2001): 21–51. Print.

DeLoughrey, Elizabeth. *Routes and Roots: Navigating Caribbean and Pacific Island Literatures*. Honolulu: U of Hawai'i P, 2007. Print.

Demerson, Velma. *Incorrigible*. Waterloo: Wilfrid Laurier UP, 2004. Print.

Denetdale, Jennifer. "Carving Navajo National Boundaries: Patriotism, Tradition, and the Dine Marriage Act of 2005." *American Quarterly* 60, no. 2 (2008): 289–94. http://dx.doi.org/10.1353/aq.0.0007.

Dening, Greg. *Islands and Beaches: Discourse on a Silent Land – Marquesas, 1774–1880*. Honolulu: U of Hawai'i P, 1980. Print.

Dening, Greg. *Performances*. Chicago: U of Chicago P, 1996. Print.

Dening, Greg. *Readings/Writings*. Melbourne: Melbourne UP, 1998. Print.

Derrida, Jacques. *Archive Fever: A Freudian Impression*. Trans. Eric Prenowitz. Chicago: U of Chicago P, 1996. Print.

Derrida, Jacques. "Faith and Knowledge: The Two Sources of 'Religion' at the Limits of Reason Alone." *Acts of Religion*. Ed. and trans. Gil Anidjar. Stanford: Stanford UP, 1998. Print.

Derrida, Jacques. *Specters of Marx: The State of the Debt, the Work of Mourning, and the New International*. Trans. Peggy Kamuf. New York: Routledge, 2006. Print.

Deutscher, Penelope. "The Inversion of Exceptionality: Foucault, Agamben, and 'Reproductive Rights.'" *South Atlantic Quarterly* 107, no. 1 (2008): 55–70. http://dx.doi.org/10.1215/00382876-2007-055.

Dewar, Mickey. *In Search of the "Never-Never": Looking for Australia in Northern Territory Writing*. Darwin: Northern Territory UP, 1997. Print.

Dolan, Jill. *Utopia in Performance: Finding Hope at the Theater*. Ann Arbor: U of Michigan P, 2005. Print.

Dolan, Jill. "Utopia in Performance." *Theatre Research International* 31, no. 2 (2006): 163–73. http://dx.doi.org/10.1017/S0307883306002100.

Donovan, P.F. *A Land of Possibilities: A History of South Australia's Northern Territory*. St Lucia: Queensland UP, 1981. Print.

Dougary, Ginny. "The Voice of Experience." *The Times*, 9 September 2006. Print.

Doyle, Jennifer. "Blind Spots and Failed Performance: Abortion, Feminism, and Queer Theory." *Qui Parle* 18, no. 1 (2009): 25–52. http://dx.doi.org/10.1353/qui.0.0007.

Driskill, Qwo-Li, Chris Finley, Brian Joseph Gilley, et al., eds. *Queer Indigenous Studies: Critical Interventions in Theory, Politics, and Literature*. Tucson: U of Arizona P, 2011. Print.

Durie, Mason. "The Treaty of Waitangi: Perspectives for Social Policy." Kawharu 280–99.

Dwork, Deborah. *War Is Good for Babies and Other Young Children: A History of the Infant and Child Welfare Movement in England, 1898–1918*. London: Tavistock, 1987. Print.

Edelman, Lee. *No Future: Queer Theory and the Death Drive*. Durham: Duke UP, 2004. Print.

Edelman, Lee. "The Plague of Discourse: Politics, Literary Theory, and 'AIDS.'" *Homographesis: Essays in Gay Literary and Cultural Theory*. New York: Routledge, 1994. 79–92. Print.

Edmond, Rod. "Abject Bodies/Abject Sites: Leper Islands in the High Imperial Era." Edmond and Smith 133–45.

Edmond, Rod. *Representing the South Pacific: Colonial Discourse from Cook to Gauguin*. Cambridge: Cambridge UP, 1997. http://dx.doi.org/10.1017/CBO9780511581854.

Edmond, Rod, and Vanessa Smith. "Editors' Introduction." Edmond and Smith 1–18.

Edmond, Rod, and Vanessa Smith. *Islands in History and Representation*. London: Routledge, 2003. Print.

Edmond-Paul, Mary. *Her Side of the Story: Readings of Mander, Mansfield & Hyde*. Dunedin: U of Otago P, 1999. Print.

Edwards, Elizabeth. *Raw Histories: Photographs, Anthropology and Museums*. Oxford: Berg, 2002. Print.

Edwards, Penny, and Shen Yuenfang. *Lost in the Whitewash: Aboriginal-Asian Encounters in Australia, 1901–2001*. Canberra: Australian National UP, 2003. Print.

Elleray, Michelle. "Unsettled Subject: The South Pacific and the Settler." Diss. Cornell U, 2001. Print.

Ellis, Markman. "'The cane-land isles': Commerce and Empire in Late Eighteenth-Century Georgic and Pastoral Poetry." Edmond and Smith 43–62.

Eliot, T.S. *Four Quartets*. 1944. London: Faber & Faber, 1983. Print.

Eliot, T.S. *The Waste Land*. 1922. San Diego: Harcourt, Brace, & Co, 1971.

Emery, Mary Lou. *Jean Rhys at "World's End": Novels of Colonial and Sexual Exile*. Austin: U of Texas P, 1990. Print.

Emery, Mary Lou. "The Poetics of Labor in Jean Rhys's Global Modernism." *Philological Quarterly* 90, nos. 2–3 (2011): 167–97. Web.

Eng, David L. *The Feeling of Kinship: Queer Liberalism and the Racialization of Intimacy*. Durham: Duke UP, 2010. Print.

Eng, David L., Judith Halberstam, and José Esteban Muñoz. "Introduction: What's Queer about Queer Studies Now." *Social Text* 84/85, nos. 3–4 (Winter 2005): 1–17. Print.

English, Daylanne. *Unnatural Selections: Eugenics in American Modernism and the Harlem Renaissance*. Chapel Hill: U of North Carolina P, 2002. Print.

Esty, Jed. *A Shrinking Island: Modernism and National Culture in England*. Princeton: Princeton UP, 2004. Print.

Face of Britain. Channel 4. 2007. WAG TV, 2008. DVD.

Faris, James. "Navajo and Photography." Pinney and Peterson 85–99.

Ferguson, Niall. "The Origins of the Great War of 2007 – and How It Could Have Been Prevented." *Daily Telegraph*, 15 January 2007.

Fiedler, Leslie A. *Love and Death in the American Novel*. New York: Stein & Day, 1966. Print.

Finch, Lynette. *The Classing Gaze: Sexuality, Class and Surveillance*. St Leonards: Allen & Unwin, 1993. Print.

Firchow, Peter. "Wells and Lawrence in Huxley's *Brave New World*." *Journal of Modern Literature* 5.2 (1976): 260–78. Print.

Fisher, Kate. "'She was quite satisfied with the arrangements I made': Gender and Birth Control in Britain 1920–1950." *Past & Present* 169, no. 1 (2000): 161–93. http://dx.doi.org/10.1093/past/169.1.161.

Fletcher, M.E. *Report on the Investigation into the Colour Problem in Liverpool and Other Ports*. Liverpool: Liverpool Association for the Welfare of Half-Caste Children, 1930. Print.

Fortier, Anne-Marie. "Genetic Indigenisation in 'The People of the British Isles.'" *Science as Culture* 21, no. 2 (2012): 153–75. http://dx.doi.org/10.1080/09505431.2011.586418.

Foucault, Michel. "Governmentality." *The Foucault Effect: Studies in Governmentality*. Ed. Graham Burchell, Colin Gordon, and Peter Miller. London: Havester Wheatsheaf, 1991. 87–104. Print.

Foucault, Michel. *The History of Sexuality. Volume I: An Introduction*. Trans. Robert Hurley. New York: Vintage, 1978.

Foucault, Michel. "Nietzsche, Genealogy, History." *Language, Counter-Memory, Practice: Selected Essays and Interviews*. Ed. D.F. Bouchard. Ithaca: Cornell UP, 1977. 139–64. Print.

Foucault, Michel. *"Society Must Be Defended": Lectures at the Collège de France, 1975–76*. Trans. David Macey. New York: Picador, 2003. Print.

Fresnadillo, Juan Carlos, dir. *28 Weeks Later*. 2007. Twentieth Century Fox, 2007. DVD.

Friedman, Susan Stanford. "Planetarity: Musing Modernist Studies." *Modernism/Modernity* 17, no. 3 (2010): 474–99. Print.

Frow, John. "A Politics of Stolen Time." *Meanjin* 57, no. 2 (1998): 351–67. Print.

Fry, Michael Graham. "Britain, France, and the Cold War." *The End of Empire: The Transformation of the USSR in Comparative Perspective*. Ed. Karen Dawisha and Bruce Parrott. Armonk: M.E. Sharpe, 1997. 121–54. Print.

Gandhi, Leela. *Postcolonial Theory: A Critical Introduction*. New York: Columbia UP, 1998. Print.

Galton, Francis. *Hereditary Genius: An Inquiry into Its Laws and Consequences*. 1869. Cleveland: World, 1962. Print.

Galton, Francis. *Inquiry into the Human Faculty*. London: Macmillan, 1883. Print.

Garland, Alex. *The Beach*. New York: Riverhead, 1997. Print.

Garland, Alex. *28 Days Later: Screenplay*. London: Faber & Faber, 2002. Print.

Garrity, Jane. *Step-Daughters of England: British Women Modernists and the National Imaginary*. Manchester: Manchester UP, 2003. Print.

Garton, Stephen. "Eugenics in Australia and New Zealand: Laboratories of Racial Science." Bashford and Levine 242–57. Print.

George, Miria. *and what remains*. Wellington: Tawata, 2007. Print.

Gikandi, Simon. *Maps of Englishness: Writing Identity in the Culture of Colonialism*. New York: Columbia UP, 1996. Print.

Gillen, Frank J., and Baldwin Spencer. *Native Tribes of Central Australia*. London: Macmillan, 1899. Print.

Gillette, Meg. "Making Modern Parents in Ernest Hemingway's "Hills Like White Elephants" and Viña Delmar's *Bad Girl*." *Modern Fiction Studies* 53, no. 1 (2007): 50–69. http://dx.doi.org/10.1353/mfs.2007.0023.

Gillette, Meg. "Manners in Dorothy Parker's 'Lady with a Lamp' and Kay Boyle's *My Next Bride*." *Studies in American Fiction* 35, no. 2 (2007): 159–79. Print.

Gillis, John R. "Taking History Offshore: Atlantic Islands in European Minds, 1400–1800." Edmond and Smith 19–31.

Gilman, Sander. *Difference and Pathology: Stereotypes of Sexuality, Race, and Madness*. Ithaca: Cornell UP, 1985. Print.

Gilman, Sander, and J. Edward Chamberlin, eds. *Degeneration: The Dark Side of Progress*. New York: Columbia UP, 1985. Print.

Gilroy, Paul. *The Black Atlantic: Modernity and Double Consciousness*. Cambridge: Harvard UP, 1993. Print.

Gilroy, Paul. *Postcolonial Melancholia*. New York: Columbia UP, 2005. Print.

GoGwilt, Christopher. *The Passage of Literature: Genealogies of Modernism in Conrad, Rhys, and Pramoedya*. Oxford: Oxford UP, 2011. Print.

Gold, Barri J. "Reproducing Empire: *Moreau* and Others." *Nineteenth Century Studies* 14 (2000): 173–98. Print.

Goldie, Terry. *Fear and Temptation: The Image of the Indigene in Canadian, Australian, and New Zealand Literatures*. Kingston: McGill-Queen's UP, 1989. Print.

Gomel, Elana. "From Dr. Moreau to Dr. Mengele: The Biological Sublime." *Poetics Today* 21, no. 2 (2000): 393–421. http://dx.doi.org/10.1215/03335372-21-2-393.

Gomel, Elana. "The Plague of Utopias: Pestilence and the Apocalyptic Body." *Twentieth Century Literature* 46, no. 4 (2000): 405–33. http://dx.doi.org/10.2307/827840.

Goode, John. "Writing Beyond the End." Stokes 14–36.

Gooding, David, Trevor Pinch, and Simon Schaffer. "Preface." Gooding, Pinch, and Schaffer. xiii–xvii.

Gooding, David, Trevor Pinch, and Simon Schaffer. *The Uses of Experiment: Studies in the Natural Sciences*. Cambridge: Cambridge UP, 1989. Print.

Gordon, Avery. *Ghostly Matters: Haunting and the Sociological Imagination*. Minneapolis: U of Minnesota P, 2008. Print.

Grayzel, Susan. *Women's Identities at War: Gender, Motherhood, and Politics in Britain and France during the First World War*. Chapel Hill: U of North Carolina P, 1999. Print.

Great Britain. Ministry of Health. *Report on an Investigation into Maternal Mortality*. London: HMSO, 1937. Print.

Greene, Roland. "Island Logic." Hulme and Sherman 138–45.

Greenslade, William. *Degeneration, Culture and the Novel: 1880–1940*. Cambridge: Cambridge UP, 1994. Print.

Gregg, Veronica Marie. *Jean Rhys' Historical Imagination: Reading and Writing the Creole*. Chapel Hill: U of North Carolina P, 1995. Print.

Gregory, Derek. *The Colonial Present*. Malden: Blackwell, 2004. Print.

Griffin, Nick. "Introduction." *Democracy, Freedom, Culture and Identity: British National Party General Elections Manifesto 2010*. Welshpool: British National Party, 2010. Print.

Grosz, Elizabeth. *The Nick of Time: Politics, Evolution, and the Untimely*. Durham: Duke UP, 2004. Print.

Grosz, Elizabeth. *Space, Time, and Perversion: Essays on the Politics of Bodies*. New York: Routledge, 1995. Print.

Grosz, Elizabeth. *Volatile Bodies: Toward a Corporeal Feminism*. Bloomington: Indiana UP, 1994. Print.

Grove, Richard H. *Green Imperialism: Colonial Expansion, Tropical Island Edens and the Origins of Environmentalism, 1600–1860*. Cambridge: Cambridge UP, 1995. Print.

Haebich, Anna. *Broken Circles: Fragmenting Indigenous Families 1800–2000*. Fremantle: Fremantle Arts Centre, 2000. Print.

Hage, Ghassan. *White Nation: Fantasies of White Supremacy in a Multicultural Nation*. New York: Routledge, 2000. Print.

Haldane, Charlotte. *Motherhood and Its Enemies*. Garden City: Doubleday, Doran & Co, 1928. Print.

Haldane, Charlotte. *Youth Is a Crime*. London: Faber & Faber, 1934. Print.

Haldane, J.B.S. *Heredity and Politics*. New York: Norton, 1938. Print.

Halkias, Alexandra. *The Empty Cradle of Democracy: Sex, Abortion, and Nationalism in Modern Greece*. Durham: Duke UP, 2004. Print.

Hall, Catherine. *Civilising Subjects: Metropole and Colony in the English Imagination*. Chicago: U of Chicago P, 2002.

Hall, Stuart. "Minimal Selves." *Black British Cultural Studies: A Reader*. Ed. Houston Baker, Manthia Diawara, and Ruth H. Lindeborg. Chicago: U of Chicago P, 1996. 114–19. Print.

Hall, Stuart. "The Problem of Ideology: Marxism without Guarantees." *Journal of Communication Inquiry* 10, no. 2 (June 1986): 28–44. Print.

Hall, Stuart, Chas Critcher, Tony Jefferson, John N. Clarke, and Brian Roberts. *Policing the Crisis: Mugging, the State, and Law and Order*. New York: Holmes & Meier, 1978. Print.

Hall, Stuart, and Bill Schwarz. "State and Society, 1880–1930." *The Hard Road to Renewal: Thatcherism and the Crisis of the Left*. By Stuart Hall. London: Verso, 1988. 95–121. Print.

Hanlon, David, and Geoffrey M. White, eds. *Voyaging through the Contemporary Pacific*. Lanham: Rowman & Littlefield, 2000. Print.

Hanna, Mary. "White Women's Sins or Patterns of Choice and Consequence in the Two Endings of 'Voyage in the Dark.'" *Journal of West Indian Literature* 15, nos. 1–2 (2006): 132–63. Web.

Hansen, Randall, and Desmond King. "Eugenic Ideas, Political Interests, and Policy Variation: Immigration and Sterilization Policy in Britain and the U. S." *World Politics* 53, no. 2 (2001): 237–63. http://dx.doi.org/10.1353/wp.2001.0003.

Haraway, Donna. *Modest_Witness@Second_Millenium.FemaleMan©_Meets_OncoMouse™: Feminism and Technoscience*. New York: Routledge, 1997. Print.

Harris, Neil. *Humbug: The Art of P. T. Barnum*. Boston: Little, 1973. Print.

Harris, Wilson. *The Womb of Space: The Cross-Cultural Imagination*. Westport: Greenwood P, 1983.

Hartouni, Valerie. "Brave New World in the Discourses of Reproductive and Genetic Technologies." *In the Nature of Things: Language, Politics, and the Environment*. Ed. Jane Bennett and William Chaloupka. Minneapolis: U of Minnesota P, 1993. 85–110. Print.

Harvey, David. *Spaces of Hope*. Berkeley: U of California P, 2000. Print.

Hatzenberger, Antoine. "Islands and Empire: Beyond the Shores of Utopia." *Angelaki* 8, no. 1 (2003): 119–28. Web.

Hauck, Christina. "Abortion and the Individual Talent." *ELH* 70, no. 1 (2003): 223–66. http://dx.doi.org/10.1353/elh.2003.0003.

Hau'ofa, Epeli. "Our Sea of Islands." *Inside Out: Literature, Cultural Politics, and Identity in the New Pacific*. Ed. Vilsoni Hereniko and Rob Wilson. Lanham: Rowman & Littlefield, 1999. 27–38. Print.

Henderson, Jennifer. *Settler Feminism and Race Making in Canada*. Toronto: U of Toronto P, 2003. Print.

Hendershot, Cyndy. "The Animal Without: Masculinity and Imperialism in *The Island of Dr. Moreau* and 'The Adventure of the Speckled Band.'" *Nineteenth Century Studies* 10 (1996): 1–32. Print.

Herbert, Xavier. *Capricornia*. 1938. North Ryde: Angus & Robertson, 1985. Print.

Herring, Joseph B. *The Enduring Indians of Kansas: A Century and a Half of Acculturation*. Lawrence: UP of Kansas, 1990. Print.

Hill, Jen. *White Horizon: The Arctic in the Nineteenth-Century Imagination*. Albany: SUNY P, 2007. Print.

Hirsch, Marianne. "The Generation of Postmemory." *Poetics Today* 29, no. 1 (Spring 2008): 103–28. Print.

Hite, Molly. *The Other Side of the Story: Structures and Strategies of Contemporary Feminist Narratives*. Ithaca: Cornell UP, 1989. Print.

Hobsbawm, Eric. *The Age of Extremes: The Short Twentieth Century, 1914–1991*. London: Michael Joseph, 1994. Print.

Hobson, J.A. *Imperialism: A Study*. 1902. New York: Cosimi, 2006. Print.

Hodge, Bob, and Vijay Mishra. *Dark Side of the Dream: Australian Literature and the Postcolonial Mind*. Sydney: Allen & Unwin, 1991. Print.

Hohaia, Te Miringa, ed. *Parihaka: The Art of Passive Resistance*. Wellington: City Gallery Wellington/Victoria UP, 2001. Print.

Hokari, Minoru. "Anti-Minorities History: Perspectives on Aboriginal-Asian Relations." Edwards and Yuenfang 85–101. Print.

Holcroft, M.H. *The Deepening Stream*. 1940. *Discovered Isles: A Trilogy*. Christchurch: Caxton, 1950. Print.

Holcroft, M.H. *The Waiting Hills*. 1943. *Discovered Isles: A Trilogy*. Christchurch: Caxton, 1950. Print.

Holston, James. *The Modernist City: An Anthropological Critique of Brasília*. Chicago: U of Chicago P, 1989. Print.

Honychurch, Lennox. *The Dominica Story: A History of the Island*. London: Macmillan, 1995. Print.

Hopkinson, Nalo. *Brown Girl in the Ring*. New York: Warner, 1998. Print.

Houlbrook, Matt. "'A Pin to See the Peepshow': Culture, Fiction and Selfhood in Edith Thompson's Letters, 1921–1922." *Past & Present* 207, no. 1 (2010): 215–49. http://dx.doi.org/10.1093/pastj/gtp049.

Hulme, Peter. *Colonial Encounters: Europe and the Native Caribbean 1492–1797*. London: Routledge, 1986. Print.

Hulme, Peter. "Islands and Roads: Hesketh Bell, Jean Rhys, and Dominica's Imperial Road." *Jean Rhys Review* 11, no. 2 (2001): 23–51. Print.

Hulme, Peter. "The Locked Heart: The Creole Family Romance of *Wide Sargasso Sea* – An Historical and Biographical Analysis." *Jean Rhys Review* 6, no. 1 (1995): 20–37. Print.

Hulme, Peter. *Remnants of Conquest: The Island Caribs and Their Visitors, 1877–1998*. Oxford: Oxford UP, 2000. Print.

Hulme, Peter, and William H. Sherman, eds. *"The Tempest" and Its Travels*. Philadelphia: U of Pennsylvania P, 2000. Print.

Human Rights and Equal Opportunity Commission of Australia. *Bringing Them Home*. Report of the National Inquiry into the Separation of Aboriginal and Torres Strait Islander Children from Their Families. 2 August 1995. http://www.humanrights.gov.au/pdf/social_justice/bringing_them_home_report.pdf.

Humble, Nicola. *The Feminine Middlebrow Novel 1920s to 1950s: Class, Domesticity, and Bohemianism*. Oxford: Oxford UP, 2001. Print.

Huxley, Aldous. *Brave New World*. 1932. New York: HarperCollins, 1998. Print.

Huxley, Aldous. *Eyeless in Gaza*. 1936. London: Chatto & Windus, 1955. Print.

Hyde, Robin. "Autobiography [193–?]." NZ MSS 412. Auckland City Library (Central Branch), Auckland.

Hyde, Robin. *The Book of Nadath*. Auckland: Auckland UP, 1999. Print.

Hyde, Robin. *Disputed Ground: Robin Hyde, Journalist*. Wellington: Victoria UP, 1991. Print.

Hyde, Robin. *The Godwits Fly*. 1938. Auckland: Auckland UP, 1979.

Hyde, Robin. *A Home in This World*. Auckland: Longman, 1984. Print.

Hyde, Robin. *Nor the Years Condemn*. 1938. Dunedin: U of Otago P, 1995.

Hyde, Robin. *Wednesday's Children*. 1937. Auckland: New Women's, 1989. Print.

Hyde, Robin. *Young Knowledge: The Poems of Robin Hyde*. Ed. Michele Leggott. Auckland: Auckland UP, 2003. Print.

Isherwood, Christopher. *Goodbye to Berlin*. New York: Random, 1939. Print.

Jacobs, Margaret D. *White Mother to a Dark Race: Settler Colonialism, Maternalism, and the Removal of Indigenous Children in the American West and Australia, 1880–1940*. Lincoln: U of Nebraska P, 2009. Print.

Jacobus, Mary. *First Things: The Maternal Imaginary in Literature, Art, and Psychoanalysis*. New York: Routledge, 1995. Print.

Jaimes, M. Annette. "Federal Indian Identification Policy: A Usurpation of Indigenous Sovereignty in North America." *The State of Native America: Genocide, Colonization, and Resistance*. Ed. M. Annette Jaimes. Boston: South End P, 1992. 124–38. Print.

James, Frank A.J.L., ed. *The Development of the Laboratory: Essays on the Place of Experiment in Industrial Civilization*. London: Macmillan, 1989. Print.

James, P.D. *The Children of Men*. New York: Borzoi, 1992. Print.

Jameson, Fredric. *Archaeologies of the Future: The Desire Called Utopia and Other Science Fictions*. London: Verso, 2005. Print.

Jameson, Fredric. "Modernism and Imperialism." *Nationalism, Colonialism, and Literature*. Ed. Seamus Deane. Minneapolis: U of Minnesota P, 1990. 43–66. Print.

Jesse, F. Tennyson. *A Pin to See the Peepshow*. 1934. London: Virago, 1982. Print.

Johnson, Barbara. "The Frame of Reference: Poe, Lacan, Derrida." *The Purloined Poe: Lacan, Derrida, and Psychoanalytic Reading*. Ed. John P. Muller and William J. Richardson. Baltimore: Johns Hopkins UP, 1988. 213–51. Print.

Johnson, Barbara. "Teaching Deconstructively." *Writing and Reading Differently: Deconstruction and the Teaching of Composition and Literature*. Ed. G. Douglas Atkins and Michael L. Johnson. Lawrence: UP of Kansas, 1985. 140–8. Print.

Jones, Lawrence. *Picking up the Traces: The Making of a New Zealand Literary Culture 1932–1945*. Wellington: Victoria UP, 2003. Print.

Joseph, Miranda. *Against the Romance of Community*. Minneapolis: U of Minnesota P, 2002. Print.

Joyce, Kathryn. "Review: *Demographic Winter: The Decline of the Human Family*." *Harvard Divinity Bulletin*, Spring 2008. Web.

Justice, Daniel Heath, Mark Rifkin, and Bethany Schneider, eds. *Sexuality, Nationality, Indigeneity*. Spec. issue of *GLQ* 16, nos. 1–2 (2010): 1–339. Print.

Karatani, Rieko. *Defining British Citizenship: Empire, Commonwealth, and Modern Britain*. London: Frank Cass, 2003. Print.

Karl, Alissa G. "Rhys, Keynes, and the Modern(ist) Economic Nation." *Novel* 43, no. 3 (2010): 424–42. http://dx.doi.org/10.1215/00295132-2010-023.

Kauanui, J. Kēhaulani. "'A blood mixture which experience has shown furnishes the very highest grade of citizen-material': Selective Assimilation in a Polynesian Case of Naturalization to U. S. Citizenship." *American Studies* 45, no. 3 (2004): 5–29. Print.

Kauanui, J. Kēhaulani. *Hawaiian Blood: Colonialism and the Politics of Sovereignty and Indigeneity*. Durham: Duke UP, 2008. Print.

Kawharu, I.H. "Mana and the Crown: A Marae at Orakei." Kawharu 211–33.

Kawharu, I.H., ed. *Waitangi: Māori and Pākehā Perspectives of the Treaty of Waitangi*. Auckland: Oxford UP, 1989. Print.

Kearns, Robin, and Lawrence Berg. "Proclaiming Place: Towards a Geography of Place Name Pronunciation." *Social & Cultural Geography* 3, no. 3 (2002): 283–302. http://dx.doi.org/10.1080/1464936022000003532.

Kellett, John. "William Lane and 'New Australia': A Reassessment." *Labour History* 72 (1997): 1–18. http://dx.doi.org/10.2307/27516462.

Kelner, Martin. "Thrusting Young Nation Goes Ice Todger Mad as Vancouver Olympics Open." *The Guardian*, 15 February 2010. Print.

Kennedy, Dane. *Islands of White: Settler Society and Culture in Kenya and Southern Rhodesia, 1890–1939*. Durham: Duke UP, 1987. Print.

Kevles, Daniel. *In the Name of Eugenics: Genetics and the Uses of Human Heredity*. New York: Knopf, 1985. Print.

Kincaid, Jamaica. *The Autobiography of My Mother*. New York: Farrar, Straus & Giroux, 1996. Print.

Kincaid, Jamaica. *A Small Place*. New York: Farrar, Straus & Giroux, 1988. Print.

Kincaid, James. *Child-Loving: The Erotic Child and Victorian Culture*. New York: Routledge, 1992. Print.

King, Frederick Truby. *Feeding and Care of Baby*. London: Macmillan, 1913. Print.

King, Michael. *The Penguin History of New Zealand*. Auckland: Penguin, 2003. Print.

Kirby, David A. "Are We Not Men? The Horror of Eugenics in *The Island of Dr. Moreau*." *Paradoxa* 17, no. 2 (2002): 93–108. Web.

Kline, Wendy. *Building a Better Race: Gender, Sexuality, and Eugenics from the Turn of the Century to the Baby Boom*. Berkeley: U of California P, 2001. Print.

Kloepfer, Deborah Kelly. *The Unspeakable Mother: Forbidden Discourse in Jean Rhys and H. D.* Ithaca: Cornell UP, 1989. Print.

Kloepfer, Deborah Kelly. "'Voyage in the Dark': Jean Rhys' Masquerade for the Mother," *Contemporary Literature* 26, no. 4 (1985): 443–59. Web.

Knapp, Jeffrey. *An Empire Nowhere: England, America, and Literature from Utopia to The Tempest*. Berkeley: U of California P, 1991. Print.

Koshy, Susan. *Sexual Naturalization: Asian Americans and Miscegenation*. Stanford: Stanford UP, 2004. Print.

Koven, Seth, and Sonya Michel, eds. *Mothers of a New World: Maternalist Politics and the Origins of Welfare States*. New York: Routledge, 1993. Print.

LaCapra, Dominick. *History, Politics, and the Novel*. Ithaca: Cornell UP, 1987. Print.

Lake, Marilyn. "White Man's Country: The Trans-National History of a Nation Project." *Australian Historical Studies* 34, no. 122 (2003): 346–63. http://dx.doi.org/10.1080/10314610308596259.

Lamb, Jonathan. "The Idea of Utopia in New Zealand." Neumann, Thomas, and Ericksen 78–97.

Lamming, George. *The Pleasures of Exile*. Ann Arbor: U of Michigan P, 1992. Print.

Lang, Jack. *I Remember*. Sydney: Invincible, 1956. Print.

Latour, Bruno. "Give Me a Laboratory and I Will Raise the World." *Science Observed: Perspectives on the Social Study of Science*. Ed. Karin D. Knorr-Cetina and Michael Mulkay. London: Sage, 1983. 141–70. Print.

Latour, Bruno. *Science in Action: How to Follow Scientists and Engineers Through Society*. Cambridge: Harvard UP, 1987. Print.

Lavin, Mary. *The House in Clewe Street*. Boston: Little, Brown & Co, 1945.

"Law and Ethics of Abortion." *British Medical Journal* no. 3722 (7 May 1932): 844. Print.

Lawrence, D.H. "America, Listen to Your Own." *Phoenix: The Posthumous Papers of D.H. Lawrence*. Ed. Edward McDonald. New York: Viking, 1978. 87–91. Print.

Lawrence, D.H. *Women in Love*. 1920. New York: Viking, 1960. Print.

Lawrence, D.H., and Mollie Skinner. *The Boy in the Bush*. 1924. Cambridge: Cambridge UP, 1990. Print.

Lawson, Alan. "Postcolonial Theory and the Settler State." Sugars 151–64. Print.

Lee, Hermione. *Virginia Woolf*. New York: Knopf, 1997. Print.

Lee, Michael Parrish. "Reading Meat in H.G. Wells." *Studies in the Novel* 42, no. 3 (2010): 249–68. Web.

Leggott, Michele. "Introduction." *The Book of Nadath*. By Robin Hyde. Auckland: Auckland UP, 1999. Print.

Lehmann, Beatrix. *Rumour of Heaven*. 1934. New York: Penguin, 1987. Print.

Lehmann, Rosamond. *The Weather in the Streets*. 1936. Garden City: Dial, 1983. Print.

Leigh, Mike, writ. and dir. *Vera Drake*. 2004. New Line, 2005. DVD.

Levitas, Ruth. "The Imaginary Reconstruction of Society: Utopia as Method." Moylan and Baccolini 47–68. Print.

Lewis-Faning, Ernest. *Report on an Enquiry into Family Limitation and Its Influence on Human Fertility during the Past Fifty Years*. Papers of the Royal Commission on Population, vol. 1. London: HMSO, 1949. Print.

Lewis, Jane E. *The Politics of Motherhood: Child and Maternal Welfare in England, 1900–1939*. London: Croom Helm, 1980. Print.

Lewis, Wyndham. *The Revenge for Love*. London: Cassell, 1937. Print.

Light, Alison. *Forever England: Femininity, Literature and Conservatism between the Wars*. London: Routledge, 1991. Print.

Loxley, Diana. *Problematic Shores: The Literature of Islands*. New York: St Martin's P, 1990. Print.

Luciano, Dana. *Arranging Grief: Sacred Time and the Body in Nineteenth-Century America*. New York: New York UP, 2007. Print.

Ludovici, Anthony. "The Case against Legalized Artificial Abortion." *Abortion*. By Stella Browne, Anthony Ludovici, and Harry Roberts. London: Allen & Unwin, 1935. 51–108. Print.

Ludovici, Anthony. *Lysistrata, or Women's Future and Future Woman*. London: Kegan Paul, Trench, Trubner & Co, 1924. Print.

Lyall, Sarah. "A Five-Ring Opening Circus, Weirdly and Unabashedly British." *New York Times*, 27 July 2012. Print.

Lydon, Jane. *Eye Contact: Photographing Indigenous Australians*. Durham: Duke UP, 2005. Print.

Lyotard, Jean-François. *The Postmodern Condition: A Report on Knowledge*. Trans. Geoff Bennington and Brian Massumi. Minneapolis: U of Minnesota P, 1979. Print.

MacDonald, Rowena, ed. *Between Two Worlds: The Commonwealth Government and the Removal of Aboriginal Children of Part-Descent in the Northern Territory*. Alice Springs: IAD P, 1996. Print.

Macintyre, Stuart, and Anna Clark. *The History Wars*. Melbourne: Melbourne UP, 2003. Print.

Mackay, Jessie. *The Spirit of the Rangatira and Other Ballads*. Melbourne: George Robertson, 1889. Print.

MacMahon, Elizabeth. "Encapsulated Space: The Paradise-Prison of Australia's Island Imaginary." *Southerly* 65, no. 1 (2005): 20–9. Web.

MacMahon, Elizabeth. "The Gilded Cage: From Utopia to Monad in Australia's Island Imaginary." Edmond and Smith 190–202.

Malinowski, Bronislaw. *Argonauts of the Western Pacific*. 1922. New York: Dutton, 1950. Print.

Mann, Patricia. *Micro-Politics: Agency in a Post-Feminist Era*. Minneapolis: U of Minnesota P, 1994. Print.

Manne, Robert, ed. *Whitewash: On Keith Windschuttle's* The Fabrication of Aboriginal History. Melbourne: Black, 2003. Print.

Mansfield, Katherine. *The Urewera Notebook*. Oxford: Oxford UP, 1978. Print.

Manuel, Frank. *Utopian Thought in the Western World*. Cambridge: Cambridge UP, 1966. Print.

Mao, Douglas, and Rebecca Walkowitz. "Introduction: Modernisms Bad and New." *Bad Modernisms.* Ed. Douglas Mao and Rebecca Walkowitz. Durham: Duke UP, 2006. 1–17. Print.

Mao, Douglas, and Rebecca Walkowitz. "The New Modernist Studies." *PMLA* 123, no. 3 (2008): 737–48. Print.

Marin, Louis. *On Representation.* Trans. Catherine Porter. Stanford: Stanford UP, 2001. Print.

Marks, Kathleen. *Toni Morrison's* Beloved *and the Apotropaic Imagination.* Columbia: U of Missouri P, 2002. Print.

Marx, Karl. "The Eighteenth Brumaire of Louis Bonaparte." *Later Political Writings.* Ed. Terrell Carver. Cambridge: Cambridge UP, 1996. 31–127. http://dx.doi.org /10.1017/CBO9780511810695.007

Matless, David. *Landscape and Britishness.* London: Reaktion, 2001. Print.

Mazlish, Bruce. "A Tale of Two Enclosures: Self and Society as a Setting for Utopias." *Theory, Culture & Society* 20, no. 1 (2003): 43–60. http://dx.doi.org/10.1177/ 0263276403020001920.

Mazumdar, Pauline. *Eugenics, Human Genetics and Human Failings: The Eugenics Society, Its Sources and Its Critics in Britain.* London: Routledge, 1992. Print.

McClintock, Anne. "The Angel of Progress: Pitfalls of the Term 'Post-Colonialism.'" *Social Text* 31/32 (1992): 84–98. Print.

McClintock, Anne. *Imperial Leather: Race, Gender, and Sexuality in the Colonial Conquest.* New York: Routledge, 1995. Print.

McCormick, Eric. *New Zealand Literature: A Survey.* London: Oxford UP, 1959. Print.

McCrea, Barry. *In the Company of Strangers: Family and Narrative in Dickens, Conan Doyle, Joyce, and Proust.* New York: Columbia UP, 2011. Print.

McGinness, Joe. *Son of Alyandabu: My Fight for Aboriginal Rights.* St Lucia: U of Queensland P, 1991. Print.

McGinness, Val. "Breakfast Was One Slice of Bread: A 'Half-caste' Boy in the Kahlin Compound." Told to Kathy Mills and Tony Austin. *Northern Perspective* 11 (Dry Season 1989): 1–10. Print.

McGrath, Ann. "'Black Velvet': Aboriginal Women and Their Relations with White Men in the Northern Territory, 1910–40." *So Much Hard Work: Women and Prostitution in Australian History.* Ed. Kay Daniels. Sydney: Fontana, 1984. 233–97. Print.

McGrath, Ann. "The State as Father: 1910–1960." Patricia Grimshaw et al. *Creating a Nation.* Grimwood: McPhee Gribble, 1994. 279–96. Print.

McGregor, Rae. *The Story of a New Zealand Writer: Jane Mander.* Dunedin: Otago UP, 1998. Print.

McGregor, Russell. "'Breed out the Colour' or The Importance of Being White." *Australian Historical Studies* 33, no. 120 (2002): 286–302. http://dx.doi.org/10.1080 /10314610208596220.

McGregor, Russell. *Imagined Destinies: Aboriginal Australians and the Doomed Race Theory, 1880–1939*. Carlton South: Melbourne UP, 1998. Print.

McIntosh, Tania. "'An Abortionist City': Maternal Mortality, Abortion, and Birth Control in Sheffield, 1920–1940." *Medical History* 44 (2000): 75–96. Print.

McLaren, Angus. *Birth Control in Nineteenth-Century England*. London: Holmes & Meier, 1978. Print.

McLaren, Angus. *Our Own Master Race: Eugenics in Canada, 1885–1945*. Toronto: McClelland & Stewart, 1990. Print.

Mead, Margaret. *Coming of Age in Samoa: A Psychological Study of Primitive Youth for Western Civilisation*. 1928. Morrow Quill, 1973. Print.

Meckier, Jerome. "Aldous Huxley's Americanization of the Brave New World Typescript." *Twentieth Century Literature* 48, no. 4 (2002): 427–60. http://dx.doi.org/10.2307/3176042.

Meckier, Jerome. "Debunking Our Ford: *My Life and Work* and *Brave New World*." *South Atlantic Quarterly* 78 (1979): 448–59. Print.

Melloy, Kilian. "The Light and the Darkness: Danny Boyle on 'Sunshine.'" *Edge*, 21 July 2007. http://www.edgeptown.com.

Messina, Anthony M. *Race and Party Competition in Britain*. Oxford: Clarendon, 1989. Print.

Meyer, Melissa L. *The White Earth Tragedy: Ethnicity and Dispossession at a Minnesota Anishinaabe Reservation, 1889–1920*. Lincoln: U of Nebraska P, 1994. Print.

Minogue, Sally, and Andrew Palmer. "Confronting the Abject: Women and Dead Babies in Modern English Fiction." *Journal of Modern Literature* 29, no. 3 (2006): 103–25. Web.

Mohanram, Radhika. *Black Body: Women, Colonialism, and Space*. Minneapolis: U of Minnesota P, 1999. Print.

Mohanram, Radhika. *Imperial White: Race, Diaspora, and the British Empire*. Minneapolis: U of Minnesota P, 2007. Print.

Mongia, Radhika Viyas. "Race, Nationality, Mobility: A History of the Passport." Burton 196–214.

Moore, Nicole. "The Politics of Cliché: Sex, Class and Abortion in Australian Realism." *Modern Fiction Studies* 47, no. 1 (2001): 69–91. http://dx.doi.org/10.1353/mfs.2001.0006.

More, Thomas. *Utopia*. Trans. Clarence Miller. New Haven: Yale UP, 2001. Print.

Morgensen, Scott Lauria. "The Biopolitics of Settler Colonialism: Right Here, Right Now." *Settler Colonial Studies* 1 (2011): 52–76. Web.

Morgensen, Scott Lauria. "Settler Homonationalism: Theorizing Settler Colonialism within Queer Modernities." *GLQ* 16, nos. 1–2 (2010): 105–31. Print.

Morgensen, Scott Lauria. *Spaces between Us: Queer Settler Colonialism and Indigenous Decolonization*. Minneapolis: U of Minnesota P, 2011. Print.

Moreton-Robinson, Aileen, ed. *Whitening Race: Essays in Social and Cultural Criticism.* Canberra: Aboriginal Studies P, 2004. Print.

Morrison, Toni. *Beloved.* 1987. New York: Vintage, 2004. Print.

Morton, John. "Aboriginality, Mabo and the Republic: Indigenising Australia." Attwood 117–35.

Moylan, Tom and Raffaella Baccolini, eds. *Utopia Method Vision: The Use Value of Social Dreaming.* Oxford: Peter Lang, 2009. Print.

Muñoz, José Esteban. *Cruising Utopia: The Then and There of Queer Futurity.* New York: New York UP, 2009. Print.

Murray, Stuart. *Never a Soul at Home: New Zealand Literary Nationalism and the 1930s.* Wellington: Victoria UP, 1998. Print.

Nagourney, Adam. "Hillary Clinton Seeks Uniform Sex and Violence Rating for a Range of Media." *New York Times,* 22 December 1999. Print.

Nairn, Tom. *The Break-Up of Britain.* Altona: Common Ground, 2003. Print.

Nasta, Susheila, ed. *Motherlands: Black Women's Writing from Africa, the Caribbean and South Asia.* New Brunswick: Rutgers UP, 1992. Print.

National Archives of Australia. "Welcome to the National Archives." 2010. http://www.naa.gov.au.

Neville, A.O. *Australia's Coloured Minority: Its Place in the Community.* Sydney: Currawong, 1947. Print.

Neumann, Klaus, Nicholas Thomas, and Hilary Ericksen, eds. *Quicksands: Foundational Histories in Australia and Aotearoa New Zealand.* Sydney: U of New South Wales P, 1999. Print.

Niles, Steve, with Dennis Calero, Nat Jones, and Diego Olmos. *28 Days Later: The Aftermath.* New York: Fox Atomic Comics, 2007. Print.

"New Zealand's Unborn Citizens." *The Dominion,* 23 April 1937. Print.

Nunez-Harrell, Elizabeth. "The Paradoxes of Belonging: The White West Indian Woman in Fiction." *Modern Fiction Studies* 31, no. 2 (1985): 281–93. http://dx.doi.org/10.1353/mfs.0.0150.

Oakley, Paul. "All Indigenous People Have Right to Avoid Colonisation, Wolverhampton BNP Told." *British National Party,* 7 October 2009. Web. http://www.bnp.org.uk.

O'Connor, Teresa F. *Jean Rhys: The West Indian Novels.* New York: New York UP, 1986. Print.

Olssen, Erik. "Truby King and the Plunket Society: An Analysis of a Prescriptive Ideology." *New Zealand Journal of History* 15, no. 1 (1981): 3–23. Print.

Orange, Claudia. *The Treaty of Waitangi.* North Sydney: Allen & Unwin, 1987. Print.

Ostherr, Kirsten. *Cinematic Prophylaxis: Globalization and Contagion in the Discourse of World Health.* Durham: Duke UP, 2005. Print.

O'Sullivan, Carol. "The Choice of an Ending: DVD and the Future(s) of Post-Apocalyptic Narratives." *Refractory: A Journal of Entertainment Media* 9 (4 July

2006). http://refractory.unimelb.edu.au/2006/07/04/the-choice-of-an-ending-dvd-and-the-futures-of-post-apocalyptic-narrative-carol-osullivan/.

Parkes, Adam. *Modernism and the Theatre of Censorship*. Oxford: Oxford UP, 1996. Print.

Parry, Clive. *British Nationality*. London: Stevens & Sons, 1951. Print.

Patai, Daphne. "Imagining Reality: The Utopian Fiction of Katherine Burdekin." Patai and Ingram 226–43.

Patai, Daphne, and Angela Ingram, eds. *Rediscovering Forgotten Radicals: British Women Writers, 1889–1939*. Chapel Hill: U of North Carolina P, 1993. Print.

Pateman, Carole. *The Sexual Contract*. Stanford: Stanford UP, 1988. Print.

Patterson, Orlando. *Slavery and Social Death: A Comparative Study*. Cambridge: Harvard UP, 1982. Print.

Paul, Kathleen. *Whitewashing Britain: Race and Citizenship in the Postwar Era*. Ithaca: Cornell UP, 1997. Print.

Pearson, Karl. *The Academic Aspect of the Science of National Eugenics*. London: Dulau, 1911. Print.

Pearson, Karl. *Darwinism, Medical Progress and Eugenics: The Cavendish Lecture, 1912, an Address to the Medical Profession*. London: Dulau, 1912. Print.

Pearson, Karl. *The Groundwork of Eugenics*. London: Dulau, 1912. Print.

Pearson, Karl. *National Life from the Standpoint of Science*. London: Cambridge UP, 1900. Print.

Pearson, Karl. *The Problem of Practical Eugenics*. London: Dulau, 1912. Print.

Pedersen, Susan. *Family, Dependence, and the Origins of the Welfare State: Britain and France, 1914–1945*. Cambridge: Cambridge UP, 1993. Print.

Petryna, Adriana. *Life Exposed: Biological Citizens after Chernobyl*. Princeton: Princeton UP, 2002. Print.

Pines, Davida. *The Marriage Paradox: Modernist Novels and the Cultural Imperative to Marry*. Gainesville: UP of Florida, 2006. Print.

Pinney, Christopher. "Introduction: How the Other Half …" Pinney and Peterson 1–14.

Pinney, Christopher, and Nicolas Peterson, eds. *Photography's Other Histories*. Durham: Duke UP, 2003. Print.

Pocock, J.G.A. *The Discovery of Islands: Essays in British History*. Cambridge: Cambridge UP, 2005. http://dx.doi.org/10.1017/CBO9780511614873.

Poole, Deborah. *Race, Vision, and Modernity: A Visual Economy of the Andean Image World*. Princeton: Princeton UP, 1997. Print.

Porter, Bernard. *The Absent-Minded Imperialists: Empire, Society, and Culture in Britain*. Oxford: Oxford UP, 2004. Print.

Porter, Roy, and Lesley A. Hall. *The Facts of Life: The Creation of Sexual Knowledge in Britain 1650–1950*. New Haven: Yale UP, 1995. Print.

Powell, Enoch. Speech. Conservative Association Meeting. Birmingham, 20 April 1968. http://www.telegraph.co.uk/comment/3643823/Enoch-Powells-Rivers-of-Blood-speech.html.

Povinelli, Elizabeth. *The Cunning of Recognition: Indigenous Alterities and the Making of Australian Multiculturalism*. Durham: Duke UP, 2002. Print.

Povinelli, Elizabeth. *The Empire of Love: Toward a Theory of Intimacy, Genealogy, and Carnality*. Durham: Duke UP, 2006. Print.

Povinelli, Elizabeth. "The Governance of the Prior." *Interventions* 13, no. 1 (2011): 13–30.

Power, Arthur. *Conversations with James Joyce*. Ed. Clive Hart. New York: Harper & Row, 1974. Print.

Pratt, Mary Louise. *Imperial Eyes: Travel Writing and Transculturation*. London: Routledge, 1992. Print.

Preston, Richard. "Crisis in the Hot Zone." *New Yorker*, 26 October 1992: 58–62. Print.

Price, Chris. "The Childish Empire and the Empire of Children: Colonial and Alternative Dominions in Robin Hyde's *Check to Your King* and *Wednesday's Children*." *Opening the Book: New Essays on New Zealand Writing*. Ed. Mark Williams and Michelle Leggott. Auckland: Auckland UP, 1995. 49–67. Print.

Priest, Christopher. *Fugue for a Darkening Island*. London: Faber & Faber, 1972. Print.

Puar, Jasbir. *Terrorist Assemblages: Homonationalism in Queer Times*. Durham: Duke UP, 2007. Print.

Quinn, Ben, "David Starkey Claims 'The Whites Have Become Black.'" *The Guardian*, 13 August 2011. Print.

Radhakrishnan, Rajagopalan. "Nationalism, Gender and the Narrative of Identity." *Nationalisms and Sexualities*. Ed. Andrew Parker, Mary Russo, Doris Sommer, and Patricia Yeager. New York: Routledge, 1992. 77–95. Print.

Ravetz, Alison. *Remaking Cities: Contradictions of the Recent Urban Environment*. London: Croom Helm, 1980. Print.

Reeves, Pember. *State Experiments in Australia and New Zealand*. Vol. 1. New York: Dutton, 1903. Print.

Reiss, Benjamin. *The Showman and the Slave: Race, Death and Memory in Barnum's America*. Cambridge: Harvard UP, 2001. Print.

Renan, Ernest. "What Is a Nation?" Trans. Martin Thom. *Nation and Narration*. Ed. Homi Bhabha. London: Routledge, 1990. 8–22. Print.

Reynolds, Henry. *Aboriginal Sovereignty: Reflections on Race, State and Nation*. St Leonards: Allen & Unwin, 1996. Print.

Reynolds, Henry. *The Law of the Land*. Ringwood: Penguin, 1992. Print.

Reynolds, Henry. "The Law of the Land." *Aboriginal Law Bulletin* 57 (1987): n.p. Web.

Rhys, Jean. "The Imperial Road." *Jean Rhys Review* 11, no. 2 (2001): 17–22. Print.

Rhys, Jean. *The Letters of Jean Rhys*. Ed. Francis Wyndham and Diana Melly. New York: Viking Penguin, 1984. Print.

Rhys, Jean. *Smile Please: An Unfinished Autobiography*. New York: Harper & Row, 1979. Print.

Rhys, Jean. *Voyage in the Dark*. 1934. New York: Norton, 1982. Print.

Rhys, Jean. *Wide Sargasso Sea*. 1967. New York: Norton, 1982. Print.
Rifkin, Mark. *When Did Indians Become Straight?: Kinship, the History of Sexuality, and Native Sovereignty*. Oxford: Oxford UP, 2011. Print.
Riseborough, Hazel. *Days of Darkness: Taranaki, 1878–1884*. Wellington: Allen & Unwin, 1989. Print.
Riseborough, Hazel. "Te Pāhuatanga o Parihaka." Hohaia 19–41.
Roberts, Dorothy E. *Killing the Black Body: Race, Reproduction, and the Meaning of Liberty*. New York: Pantheon, 1997. Print.
Robertson, Alan. "Britain: A Nation of Immigrants?" *British National Party*. N.d. http://www.bnp.org.uk.
Robins, Elizabeth. *The Convert*. 1907. London: The Women's P, 1980. Print.
Rody, Caroline. *The Daughter's Return: African-American and Caribbean Women's Fictions of History*. New York: Oxford UP, 2001. Print.
Roediger, David. *Wages of Whiteness: Race and the Making of the American Working Class*. London: Verso, 1999. Print.
Rose, Deborah Bird. "Histories and Rituals: Land Claims in the Territory." Attwood 35–54.
Rose, Jacqueline. *The Case of Peter Pan or The Impossibility of Children's Fiction*. Philadelphia: U of Pennsylvania P, 1992. Print.
Rose, Jacqueline. *States of Fantasy*. Oxford: Clarendon, 1996. Print.
Rose, Nikolas. *The Politics of Life Itself: Biomedicine, Power, and Subjectivity in the Twenty-First Century*. Princeton: Princeton UP, 2007. Print.
Rosenberg, Leah Reade. "Creolizing Womanhood: Gender and Domesticity in Early Anglophone Caribbean National Literatures." Diss. Cornell U, 2000. Print.
Ross, Stephen. "Uncanny Modernism, or Analysis Interminable." *Disciplining Modernism*. Ed. Pamela L. Caughie. Houndmills: Palgrave Macmillan, 2009. 33–52. Print.
Rushdie, Salman. *The Satanic Verses*. London: Viking, 1988. Print.
Ryan, James R. *Picturing Empire: Photography and the Visualization of the British Empire*. London: Reaktion, 1997. Print.
Said, Edward. *Culture and Imperialism*. New York: Knopf, 1994. Print.
Said, Edward. *Orientalism*. New York: Vintage, 1994. Print.
Sanders, William. "The Undiscovered." *The Year's Best Science Fiction: Fifteenth Annual Collection*. Ed. Gardner Dorzois. New York: St Martin's, 1998. 224–44. Print.
Santner, Eric. *Stranded Objects: Mourning, Memory, and Film in Postwar Germany*. Ithaca: Cornell UP, 1990. Print.
Sargent, Lyman Tower. "Colonial and Postcolonial Utopias." Claeys 200–22.
Sargisson, Lucy, and Lyman Tower Sargent. *Living in Utopia: New Zealand's Intentional Communities*. Aldershot: Ashgate, 2004. Print.
Savory Fido, Elaine. "Mother/lands: Self and Separation in the Work of Buchi Emecheta, Bessie Head, and Jean Rhys." Nasta 330–49. Print.

Sayers, Dorothy. *Strong Poison*. 1930. New York: HarperCollins, 1995. Print.
Scates, Bruce. "'We are not … [A]boriginal … we are Australian': William Lane, Racism, and the Construction of Aboriginality." *Labour History* 72 (1997): 35–49. http://dx.doi.org/10.2307/27516464.
Schmerl, Rudolph. "The Two Future Worlds of Aldous Huxley." *PMLA* 77, no. 3 (June 1962): 328–34. http://dx.doi.org/10.2307/460493.
Schoen, Johanna. *Choice and Coercion: Birth Control, Sterilization, and Abortion in Public Health and Welfare*. Chapel Hill: U of North Carolina P, 2005. Print.
Scott, Dick. *Ask That Mountain: The Story of Parihaka*. Auckland: Raupo, 2008. Print.
Scott, James. *Seeing Like a State: How Certain Schemes to Improve the Human Condition Have Failed*. New Haven: Yale UP, 1998. Print.
Scott, Kim. *Benang: From the Heart*. Fremantle: Fremantle Arts Centre, 1999. Print.
Seccombe, Wally. "Starting to Stop: Working Class Fertility Decline in Britain." *Past & Present* 126, no. 1 (1990): 151–88. http://dx.doi.org/10.1093/past/126.1.151.
Sedgwick, Eve Kosofsky. *Epistemology of the Closet*. Berkeley: U of California P, 1990. Print.
Seshagiri, Urmila. "Modernist Ashes, Postcolonial Phoenix: Jean Rhys and the Evolution of the English Novel in the Twentieth Century." *Modernism/Modernity* 13, no. 3 (2006): 487–505. http://dx.doi.org/10.1353/mod.2006.0074.
Shakespeare, William. *The Tempest*. 1611. New York: Random House, 2008. Print.
Sharp, Patrick B. "Space, Future War, and the Frontier in American Nuclear Apocalypse Narrative." *Space and Beyond: The Frontier Theme in Science Fiction*. Ed. Gary Westfahl. Westport: Greenwood P, 2000. 151–6. Print.
Shea, Daniel. "Going into Labor: Production and Reproduction in Fin de Siècle British Literature." Diss. U of Oregon, 2006. Print.
Shilts, Randy. *And the Band Played On*. New York: Penguin, 1987. Print.
Shiva, Vandana. *Biopiracy: The Plunder of Nature and Knowledge*. Boston: South End P, 1997. Print.
Shohat, Ella. "Notes on the 'Post-Colonial.'" *Social Text* 31/32 (1992): 99–113. Print.
Showalter, Elaine. "The Apocalyptic Fables of H. G. Wells." Stokes 69–84. Print.
Showalter, Elaine. *Sexual Anarchy: Gender and Culture at the Fin de Siècle*. New York: Viking, 1990. Print.
Simon, Roger I. "The Paradoxical Practice of *Zakhor*: Memories of 'What Has Never Been My Fault or Deed.'" *Between Hope and Despair: Pedagogy and the Remembrance of Historical Trauma*. Ed. Roger I. Simon, Sharon Rosenberg, and Claudia Eppert. Lanham: Rowman & Littlefield, 2000. 9–25.
Simon, Roger I. *The Touch of the Past: Remembrance, Learning, and Ethics*. New York: Palgrave Macmillan, 2005. Print.
Sinclair, Keith. *A Destiny Apart: New Zealand's Search for National Identity*. Wellington: Allen & Unwin, 1986. Print.

Skidmore, Thomas. *Black into White: Race and Nationality in Brazilian Thought.* Durham: Duke UP, 1993. Print.

Slemon, Stephen. "Unsettling the Empire: Resistance for the Second World." Sugars 139–50. Print.

Smith, Andrea. "Queer Theory and Native Studies: The Heteronormativity of Settler Colonialism." *GLQ* 16, no. 1–2 (2010): 41–68. http://dx.doi.org/10.1215/10642684-2009-012.

Smith, Geddes. *Plague on Us.* New York: Commonwealth Fund, 1941. Print.

Smith, Vanessa. *Literary Culture and the Pacific: Nineteenth-Century Textual Encounters.* Cambridge: Cambridge UP, 1998. Print.

Smith, Vanessa. "Pitcairn's 'Guilty stock': The Island as Breeding Ground." Edmond and Smith 116–32. Print.

Smyth, Helen. *Rocking the Cradle: Contraception, Sex and Politics in New Zealand.* Wellington: Steele Roberts, 2000. Print.

Smythe, John. "Inconceivable." Rev. of *and what remains*, by Miria George. City Gallery, Wellington. *Theatreview: The New Zealand Performing Arts Review and Directory*, 26 August 2006. Web.

Snader, Joe. *Caught between Worlds: British Captivity Narratives in Fact and Fiction.* Lexington: U of Kentucky P, 2000. Print.

Snyder, Carey. *British Fiction and Cross-Cultural Encounters: Ethnographic Modernism from Wells to Woolf.* New York: Palgrave Macmillan, 2008. Print.

Snyder, Carey. "'When the Indian Was in Vogue': D.H. Lawrence, Aldous Huxley, and Ethnological Tourism in the Southwest." *Modern Fiction Studies* 53, no. 4 (2007): 662–96. http://dx.doi.org/10.1353/mfs.2008.0005.

Sollors, Werner. *Neither Black Nor White Yet Both: Thematic Explorations of Interracial Literature.* New York: Oxford UP, 1997. http://dx.doi.org/10.1093/acprof:oso/9780195052824.001.0001.

Soloway, Richard. *Birth Control and the Population Question in England, 1877–1930.* Chapel Hill: U of North Carolina P, 1982. Print.

Soloway, Richard. *Demography and Degeneration: Eugenics and the Declining Birth Rate in Twentieth-Century Britain.* Chapel Hill: U of North Carolina P, 1990. Print.

Sommer, Doris. *Foundational Fictions: The National Romances of Latin America.* Berkeley: U of California P, 1991. Print.

Sontag, Susan. *AIDS and Its Metaphors.* New York: Farrar, Straus & Giroux, 1989. Print.

Sorrenson, Keith. "Towards a Radical Reinterpretation of New Zealand History: The Role of the Waitangi Tribunal." Kawharu 158–78.

Spillers, Hortense. "Mama's Baby, Papa's Maybe: An American Grammar Book." *Diacritics* 17, no. 2 (1987): 64–81. http://dx.doi.org/10.2307/464747.

Spivak, Gayatri Chakravorty. *A Critique of Postcolonial Reason: Toward a History of the Vanishing Present.* Cambridge: Harvard UP, 1999. Print.

Spivak, Gayatri Chakravorty. "Speculation on Reading Marx: After Reading Derrida." *Post-Structuralism and the Question of History*. Ed. Derek Attridge, Geoff Bennington, and Robert Young. Cambridge: Cambridge UP, 1987. 30–62. Print.

Stafford, Jane, and Mark Williams. "Fashioned Intimacies: Maoriland and Colonial Modernity." *Journal of Commonwealth Literature* 37, no. 1 (2002): 31–48. Print.

Stafford, Jane, and Mark Williams. *Maoriland: New Zealand Literature 1872–1914*. Wellington: Victoria UP, 2006. Print.

Stanton, Sue. "The Australian Half-Caste Progressive Association: The Fight for Freedom and Rights in the Northern Territory." *Journal of Northern Territory History* 4 (1993): 37–46. Print.

Stepan, Nancy Leys. "Biological Degeneration: Races and Proper Places." Gilman and Chamberlin 97–120.

Stepan, Nancy Leys. *"The Hour of Eugenics": Race, Gender, and Nation in Latin America*. Ithaca: Cornell UP, 1991. Print.

Stepan, Nancy Leys. *Picturing Tropical Nature*. Ithaca: Cornell UP, 2001. Print.

Stevens, Jacqueline. *Reproducing the State*. Princeton: Princeton UP, 1999. Print.

Stockton, Kathryn Bond. "Prophylactics and Brains: *Beloved* in the Cybernetic Age of AIDS." *Studies in the Novel* 28, no. 3 (1996): 434–66. Print.

Stokes, John, ed. *Fin du Siècle/Fin du Globe: Fears and Fantasies of the Late Nineteenth Century*. New York: St Martin's, 1992. Print.

Stoler, Ann Laura. *Along the Archival Grain: Epistemic Anxieties and Colonial Common Sense*. Princeton: Princeton UP, 2009. Print.

Stoler, Ann Laura. *Carnal Knowledge and Imperial Power: Race and the Intimate in Colonial Rule*. Berkeley: U of California P, 2002. Print.

Stoler, Ann Laura. *Race and the Education of Desire: Foucault's* History of Sexuality *and the Colonial Order of Things*. Durham: Duke UP, 1995. Print.

Stone, Dan. *Breeding Superman: Nietzsche, Race and Eugenics in Edwardian and Interwar Britain*. Liverpool: Liverpool UP, 2002. Print.

Stone, Lawrence. *The Family, Sex and Marriage in England 1500–1800*. Abridged. New York: Harper, 1979. Print.

Stopes, Marie. *Married Love: A New Contribution to the Solution of Sex Difficulties*. Toronto: McClelland & Stewart, 1931. Print.

Stopes, Marie, ed. *Mother England: A Contemporary History Self-Written by Those Who Have Had No Historian*. 1929. London: John Bale, Sons & Danielsson, 1930. Print.

Stormer, Nathan. "*Why Not?* Memory and Counter-Memory in 19th Century Abortion Rhetoric." *Women's Studies in Communication* 24, no. 1 (2001): 1–29. http://dx.doi.org/10.1080/07491409.2001.10162425.

Strathern, Marilyn. *Reproducing the Future: Essays on Anthropology, Kinship, and the New Reproductive Technologies*. New York: Routledge, 1992. Print.

Sugars, Cynthia, ed. *Unhomely States: Theorizing English-Canadian Postcolonialism*. Peterborough: Broadview, 2004. Print.

Szreter, Simon. *Fertility, Class and Gender in Britain, 1860–1940*. Cambridge: Cambridge UP, 1996. http://dx.doi.org/10.1017/CBO9780511582240.

Tabili, Laura. *Global Migrants, Local Culture: Natives and Newcomers in Provincial England, 1841–1939*. Houndmills: Palgrave Macmillan, 2011. Print.

Tabili, Laura. *"We Ask for British Justice": Workers and Racial Difference in Late Imperial Britain*. Ithaca: Cornell UP, 1994. Print.

Te Punga Somerville, Alice. "The Lingering War Captain: Maori Texts, Indigenous Contexts." *Journal of New Zealand Literature* 24, no. 2 (2007): 20–43. Print.

Te Punga Somerville, Alice. *Once Were Pacific: Māori Connections to Oceania*. Minneapolis: U of Minnesota P, 2012. Print.

Te Punga Somerville, Alice. Response to John Smythe's "Inconceivable." *Theatreview: The New Zealand Performing Arts Review and Directory*, 29 August 2007, n.p. Web.

Thacker, Andrew. *Moving through Modernity: Space and Geography in Modernism*. Manchester: Manchester UP, 2003. Print.

Theobald, Geoffrey. "Some Effects of Emancipation on the Health of Women." *Journal of State Medicine* 44, no. 3 (1936): 366. Print.

Thomas, James, and A. Susan Williams. "Women and Abortion in 1930s Britain: A Survey and Its Data." *Social History of Medicine* 11, no. 2 (1998): 283–309. http://dx.doi.org/10.1093/shm/11.2.283.

Thomas, Kate. "Post Sex: On Being Too Slow, Too Stupid, Too Soon." *South Atlantic Quarterly* 106, no. 3 (2007): 615–24. http://dx.doi.org/10.1215/00382876-2007-019.

Thomas, Nicholas. *Colonialism's Culture: Anthropology, Travel, and Government*. Princeton: Princeton UP, 1994. Print.

Thomas, Nicholas. *Possessions: Indigenous Art/Colonial Culture*. London: Thames and Hudson, 1999. Print.

Thomas, Sue. "'Tearing me in two so slowly so slowly': Jean Rhys's Representations of Abortion." *Jean Rhys Review* 12, no. 1 (2002): 7–27. Print.

Thomas, Sue. *The Worlding of Jean Rhys*. Westport: Greenwood P, 1999. Print.

Thompson, E.P. "The Moral Economy of the English Crowd in the Eighteenth Century." *Past & Present* 50, no. 1 (1971): 76–136. http://dx.doi.org/10.1093/past/50.1.76.

Tindale, Norman B. "Survey of the Half-Caste Problem in South Australia." *Proceedings of the Royal Geographical Society of Australasia* 42, Session 1940–41. Adelaide: Royal Geographical Society of Australasia, 1941. Print.

Torney, Kay. "Blackbirds and Lost Babies: Narratives of Child-Stealing in Australia and the Pacific Islands." *Journal of the South Pacific Association for Commonwealth Literature and Language Studies* 37 (1993): n.p. Web.

Trilling, Daniel. *Bloody Nasty People: The Rise of Britain's Far Right*. London: Verso, 2012. Print.

Trimble, Sarah. "Undead Ends: Contested Re-Beginnings in Apocalyptic Film and Television." Diss. McMaster U, 2012. Print.

Trouillot, Michel-Rolph. "Anthropology as Metaphor: The Savage's Legacy and the Postmodern World." *Review* 14, no. 1 (1991): 29–54. Web.

Turner, Stephen. "Settlement as Forgetting." Neumann, Thomas, and Ericksen 20–38.

Urwin, Cathy, and Elaine Sharland. "From Bodies to Minds in Childcare Literature: Advice to Parents in Inter-War Britain." Cooter 174–99.

Vergès, Françoise. *Monsters and Revolutionaries: Colonial Family Romance and Métissage*. Durham: Duke UP, 1999. Print.

Vieira, Fátima. "The Concept of Utopia." Claeys 3–27.

Walcott, Derek. *Ti-Jean and His Brothers*. In *Plays for Today*. Ed. Errol Hill. Harlow, UK: Longman, 1985. 21–71. Print.

Wald, Priscilla. *Contagious: Cultures, Carriers, and the Outbreak Narrative*. Durham: Duke UP, 2008. Print.

Waldby, Catherine. *AIDS and the Body Politic: Biomedicine and Sexual Difference*. London: Routledge, 1996. Print.

Walker, Geoffrey, ed. *The Aboriginal Photographs of Baldwin Spencer*. Ringwood: Viking O'Neill, 1987. Print.

Walker, Ranginui. *Ka Whawhai Tonu Matou/Struggle without End*. Auckland: Penguin, 1990. Print.

Walzer, Michael. *Spheres of Justice: A Defense of Pluralism and Equality*. New York: Basic Books, 1983. Print.

Ware, Vron. *Beyond the Pale: White Women, Racism and History*. London: Verso, 1991. Print.

Warner, Michael, ed. *Fear of a Queer Planet: Queer Politics and Social Theory*. Minneapolis: U of Minnesota P, 1993. Print.

Warner, Sylvia Townsend. *Lolly Willowes, Or the Loving Huntsman*. New York: Viking, 1926. Print.

Waugh, Evelyn. *Vile Bodies*. 1930. Harmondsworth: Penguin, 1981. Print.

Weart, Spencer R. *Nuclear Fear: A History of Images*. Cambridge: Harvard UP, 1988. Print.

Wegner, Phillip. "Here or Nowhere: Utopia, Modernity, and Totality." Moylan and Baccolini 113–29.

Wegner, Phillip. *Imaginary Communities: Utopia, the Nation, and the Spatial Histories of Modernity*. Berkeley: U of California P, 2002. Print.

Weinbaum, Alys Eve. *Wayward Reproductions: Genealogies of Race and Nation in Transatlantic Modern Thought*. Durham: Duke UP, 2004. Print.

Weis, René. *Criminal Justice: The True Story of Edith Thompson*. London: Hamish Hamilton, 1988. Print.

Wells, H.G. *The Island of Dr. Moreau*. 1896. New York: Dover, 1996. Print.

Westad, Odd Arne. *The Global Cold War: Third World Interventions and the Making of Our Times*. Cambridge: Cambridge UP, 2005. http://dx.doi.org/10.1017/CBO9780511817991.

Whitlock, Gillian. *The Intimate Empire: Reading Women's Autobiography*. London: Cassell, 2000. Print.

Willard, Myra. *History of the White Australia Policy to 1920*. Melbourne: Melbourne UP, 1923. Print.

Williams, Raymond. *The City and the Country*. New York: Oxford UP, 1975. Print.

Wilson, Kathleen. *The Island Race: Englishness, Empire and Gender in the Eighteenth Century*. London: Routledge, 2003. Print.

Wilt, Judith. *Abortion, Choice, and Contemporary Fiction: The Armageddon of the Maternal Instinct*. Chicago: U of Chicago P, 1990. Print.

Windschuttle, Keith. *The Fabrication of Aboriginal History*. Vol. 1. Paddington: Macleay, 2002. Print.

Windschuttle, Keith. "Manne Avoids the Real Debate." *Quadrant Online* 54 (2010). Web.

Wolfe, Patrick. "Corpus nullius: The Exception of Indians and Other Aliens in US Constitutional Discourse." *Postcolonial Studies* 10, no. 2 (2007): 127–51. http://dx.doi.org/10.1080/13688790701348540.

Wolfe, Patrick. "Race and the Trace of History (For Henry Reynolds)." *Studies in Settler Colonialism: Politics, Identity and Culture*. Ed. Fiona Bateman and Lionel Pilkington. Houndmills: Palgrave Macmillan, 2011. 272–96. Print.

Wolfe, Patrick. *Settler Colonialism and the Transformation of Anthropology: The Politics and Poetics of an Ethnographic Event*. London: Cassell, 1999. Print.

Wolfe, Patrick. "Structure and Event: Settler Colonialism, Time, and the Question of Genocide." *Empire, Colony, Genocide: Conquest, Occupation, and Subaltern Resistance in World History*. Ed. A. Dirk Moses. New York: Bergahn, 2008. 102–32. Print.

Woolf, Virginia. *Three Guineas*. 1938. *A Room of One's Own and Three Guineas*. London: Penguin, 1993. Print.

Woolf, Virginia. "Thoughts on Peace during an Air-Raid." 1940. *Selected Essays*. Oxford: Oxford UP, 2008. 216–19. Print.

Woolf, Virginia. *The Years*. 1937. Oxford: Oxford UP, 1992.

Woollacott, Angela. *To Try Her Fortune in London: Australian Women, Colonialism, and Modernity*. New York: Oxford UP, 2001. Print.

Wullschläger, Jackie. *Inventing Wonderland: The Lives and Fantasies of Lewis Carroll, Edward Lear, J.M. Barrie, Kenneth Grahame, and A.A. Milne*. New York: Free P, 1995. Print.

Wyndham, John. *The Day of the Triffids*. London: Michael Joseph, 1951. Print.

Wyndham, John. *The Midwich Cuckoos*. 1957. London: Michael Joseph, 1986. Print.

Young, Robert J.C. *Colonial Desire: Hybridity in Theory, Culture and Race*. London: Routledge, 1995. Print.

Young, Robert J.C. *The Idea of English Ethnicity*. Malden: Blackwell, 2008. Print.

Young, Robert J.C. *Postcolonialism: An Historical Introduction*. Oxford: Blackwell, 2001. Print.

Zelizer, Viviana. *Pricing the Priceless Child: The Changing Social Value of Children*. New York: Basic, 1985. Print.

Zweiniger-Bargielowska, Ina. "'Raising a Nation of Good Animals': The New Health Society and Health Education Campaigns in Interwar Britain." *Social History of Medicine* 20, no. 1 (2007): 73–89. http://dx.doi.org/10.1093/shm/hkm032.

Index

www.ingramcontent.com/pod-product-compliance
Lightning Source LLC
Chambersburg PA
CBHW030537310726
48979CB00010B/1946/J
* 9 7 8 1 4 4 2 6 4 7 0 2 2 *